The Irish Clans is an epic story immersed in the tumultuous Irish revolutionary period of 1915 through 1923, while the world is embroiled in the Great War and its aftermath. The once mighty McCarthy and O'Donnell Clans, overthrown in ancient times, are not extinct. They are linked on two continents by a medieval pact entwining military history and religious mythology. Divine intervention plays a pivotal role in unearthing the secrets of the Clans' treasure and heroic exploits. The patriotism and passion of Celtic heritage lies at the heart of this intriguing story.

Other novels in the series:

A tragedy at sea sets in motion the search for life's true treasures, both in 1915 Ireland, when the funeral of Fenian Rossa fans the flames of revolution, and in America, where the clans begin a journey toward their destiny in **Searchers**, *the first book of the series.*
Published March 2016

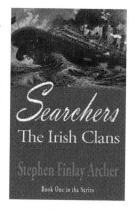

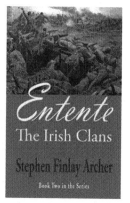

The mysteries of an ancient Clans Pact deepen beneath the horrors of WWI as Irish Rebels march toward revolution in **Entente**, *the second book in the series.*
Published May 2017

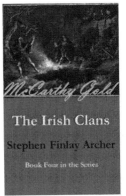

In the aftermath of the Easter Rising, the Clans Adventurers seek the McCarthy Gold while Collin seeks his sister and the villain Boyle seeks their treasures and their deaths in **McCarthy Gold**, the fourth book in the series.

The fortunes of the O'Donnell Clan are explored in **Revolution**, the fifth book in the series, set in the midst of the Irish Revolution's upheaval, leading to the Anglo-Irish Treaty of 1921.

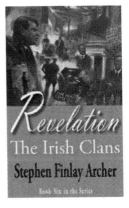

The Clans, while supporting the Irish Civil War in 1922-1923, seek to unravel and unearth an ancient religious mystery that has confounded civilization for centuries in **Revelation**, the sixth book in the series.

TESTIMONIALS

Newspaper Reviews by Scott Thomas Anderson

Sierra Lodestar, September 13, 2017

. . . *One of the most meticulous writers of historic fiction on the Emerald Isle isn't based in Dublin, but rather in the California Gold Country . . . Given that 39 million people in the U.S. have Irish roots, Archer's clan series offers a welcome doorway for anyone to start imagining that chaotic and tragic Irish past so unbreakably tied to the American experience.*

Sacramento News and Review, September 14, 2017

. . . *In studying the Rising, Archer saw a moment in time he thinks also encapsulates the best of American character: bravery in the face of oppression; blood-soaked sacrifice for high principles; the power of persuasive writing when it's aimed at finding justice. "I thought if I wrote about those ideals and added an interesting story, maybe it would get some readers thinking about our own society, and where it's headed today," Archer said.*

Amazon Five Star Reviews ★ ★ ★ ★ ★

Entente: I love the historical feel of the book
from *A.Bibliophiles.Book.Blog*

I'm not sure what it is, but something about these books just draws me in and entertains me immensely! I love the historical feel of the book, mixed with the fiction of the story; it's such a blurred line of reality and fiction that is so intriguing. This book has been researched and written so well, the story ties together flawlessly and it's so easy to read. The story continues to be action packed with danger, love, war and the whole mystery with the family clans, and the epic cliffhanger leaves you with so many questions that you NEED answered!—Will everything work out in the end? Will she remember who she is? Will they live through their ordeal? Will he find his sister? So many questions!—I need to read the next book ASAP because I need to know what happens to these characters. They're all amazing and you can't help but feel so invested in their lives. I would highly recommend this series. It's amazing.

Entente did not disappoint, with just as much excitement and intrigue as *Searchers*

I was so excited when Entente arrived at my house. I couldn't wait to continue the story of Morgan and Tadgh. Entente did not disappoint, just as much excitement and intrigue as Searchers. The storyline continues to delight and educate at the same time. I am thoroughly enjoying the series and am excited to find out what happens in the next book. Keep Writing.

Searchers: Irish Background or Not, This Book Is Absolutely Worth Reading!

Fabulous read! A lot of research went into this book. The history is incredibly interesting, and the storyline was captivating. This book is very well written. It holds your interest from beginning to end, and leaves you anxiously awaiting the next series in this saga. Mr. Archer combines just the right amount of history, intrigue, mystery, romance and violence to [pique] your interest page after page. This book is worth reading for anyone, Irish or otherwise.

Rising

The Irish Clans

Book Three in the Series

Stephen Finlay Archer

To Steffanie
Enjoy
Stephen Finlay Archer

Manzanita Writers Press
Angels Camp, California

Rising: The Irish Clans
Book Three in the Series

ISBN: 978-0-9986910-0-8
Library of Congress Control Number: 2018965369
Publisher: Manzanita Writers Press
    manzapress.com

Cover design: Stephen Archer
Book Layout design: Joyce Dedini
Rising Cover credits:
Front cover: *Montage of the Irish Easter Rising 1916*, painting by Norman Teeling
Back cover: *The General Post Office in Flames*, painting by Norman Teeling
Image of Folio 48R, *an Cathach,* courtesy of the Royal Irish Academy

Searchers Book One front cover:
    The Sinking of the Lusitania, courtesy of the Everett Collection
Entente Book Two front cover:
    Canadians at Ypres, The Belgian Front 1915, painting by William Barnes Wollen, courtesy of the Princess Patricia's Canadian Light Infantry Museum
McCarthy Gold Book Four front cover:
    The Money Diggers, painting by John Quidor, courtesy of the Brooklyn Museum
Revolution: Book Five front cover:
    The Burning of the Customs House, painting by Norman Teeling
Revelation: Book Six front cover:
    Montage of the Irish Civil War, painting by Norman Teeling

This is a work of fiction. Any resemblance of my fictional characters to real persons, living or dead, is purely coincidental. The depictions of historical persons in these novels are not coincidental, and to the best of my knowledge, are historically sound. Some historical aspects have been augmented or adjusted for dramatic purposes.

In 490 BCE, the Greeks repulsed a menacing Persian invasion at the Battle of Marathon. Ten years later, Xerxes I amassed a huge army and navy to once again attack, and this time, conquer all of Greece. A modern estimate of the strength of his land forces is 150,000 warriors. King Leonidas of Sparta formulated a battle plan with the Athenian politician and general Themistocles. The Spartan king led the Greek land forces north to block the pass at Thermopylae *, while Themistocles commanded the Greek naval forces to block the Straits of Artemisium.

The combined strength of the Greek army was 7,000 men. Outnumbered over twenty to one, they held off the Persian on-slaught for seven days before the rear guard was annihilated in one of history's most famous last stands. After the second day, a Greek traitor showed the Persians a path that could be used to outflank his countrymen. Leonidas realized his predicament and dismissed the bulk of the army to fight another day, leaving only 300 Spartans, 700 Thespians, and 400 Thebans to guard his army's retreat. I'm sure he knew that his reduced troops would be martyred for the cause of freedom. They were outnumbered approximately ninety to one, yet they held out five more days, fighting to their death.

This stalling action gave Themistocles the time to regroup and attack the Persian navy at Salamis where he won a decisive victory.

After capturing Athens, but fearing being trapped in Greece without his navy, Xerxes I withdrew much of his army to Asia by land, losing most to starvation and disease. The next year the Greek army decisively defeated the remaining Persian force at the battle of Plataea, thereby ending the Persian threat.

This is considered one of the most dramatic ancient examples of the potential of an overpowered patriotic army defending its na-tive soil.

In the modern era, there are a few equivalent valiant military stands and wars. One of the most courageous was the Irish War of Independence against the oppressor, Britain, in the early twentieth century. The Irish Rising during Easter week 1916 can be compared to the Battle at Thermopylae, in which the Irish rebels were out-numbered 20,000 to 1,400, or 15 to 1. The battle was even more one-sided, favoring the British. Their troops were well-armed and used machine guns and artillery to smoke out the rebels, destroying key parts of Dublin's infrastructure in the process. The Irish rebels had rifles, at best, and far too few of them at that.

The rebel leaders of the Irish Revolutionary Brotherhood (IRB), like Leonidis, knew they would be martyrs from the outset of the Rising. In fact, that was their strategy after the British intercept-ed the German arms shipment intended for the Irish Volunteers a few days earlier. The leaders' intent was to start the revolution, hold out as long as possible, and have the British treat the rebels harshly, thereby inciting the Irish citizens to subsequently rise and overthrow their enemy.

Like Leonidis, Padraig Pearse, the Commander-in-Chief of the rebels, chose to allow the bulk of his troops to retreat and fight an-other day, while he stayed to fight and die. Pearse ordered a stop to the fighting after six days so that Dublin's citizens and most of his fighting force would be spared. He knew full well that he and his rebel leaders would likely be summarily executed.

In both cases this tactic worked. Motivated by their heroics at Thermopylae, the Greeks eventually defeated the Persians when their citizens rose up and drove their enemy from Athens. Similarly motivated by Greek heroics, the Irish rebels of the Easter Rising set in motion the revolution that eventually drove the British out of Dublin and their country. But I am getting ahead of the storyline.

Most of the leaders of the Easter Rising were Gaelic academics, not military men. It is entirely possible that Padraig Pearse, a stu-dent of ancient history, modeled his battle plan after the Greeks at Thermopylae. As he often told his troops, "Blood sacrifice is neces-sary to cleanse the heart of the country."

Much has been written about this famous Easter Rising. When

I went to Dublin for the book launching of my first novel, *Searchers*, and for the centennial celebrations of the 1916 Rising in March 2016. I found that approximately five hundred books had been written during the two previous years in Europe about the Easter Rising, most of them nonfiction. How is that for competition?

One particularly poignant example is *The Children of the Rising*, by Joe Duffy, a well-known RTO broadcast personality. He documented the story of the forty children who died during the insurrection.

The General Post Office in Dublin, site of the headquarters of the rebels during the Rising, opened a marvelous museum about the Rising just in time for the centennial in 2016. For more historical information about this Irish Thermopylae, I can recommend visiting a national treasure called GPO Witness History, located at the General Post Office site itself, or online at *www.gpowitnesshistory.ie*. There you will find a stone garden commemorating the lost children of the Rising, so that their sacrifice won't be forgotten.

I was mindful of the hallowed ground I had tread when I wrote *Rising*, the third novel of *The Irish Clans* series. I stand in awe of the courageous moral high ground of the IRB leaders and their Irish Volunteers. I hope that you will enjoy my treatment of this important struggle for freedom as our rebel characters Tadgh and Morgan, along with their historical partner Peader O'Donnell fight for freedom and search out the mysteries of the Clans Pact.

* References: *Wikipedia* Sources and
https://www.ancient.eu/thermopylae

INSPIRATION

Ireland's Vow [6.1]

Come! Liberty, come! we are ripe for thy coming—
Come freshen the hearts where thy rival has trod—
Come, richest and rarest!—come purest and fairest!
Come, daughter of Science! Come, gift of the God!

Long, long have we sighed for thee, coyest of maidens—
Long, long have we worshipped thee, queen of the brave!
Steadily sought for thee, readily fought for thee,
Purpled the scaffold and glutted the grave!

On went the fight through the cycle of ages,
Never our battle-cry ceasing the while;
Forward ye valiant ones! Onward battalioned ones!
Strike for your Erin, your own darling Isle!

Still in the ranks are we, struggling with eagerness,
Still in the battle for freedom are we!
Words may avail in it—swords if they fail in it,
What matters the weapon, if only we're free? . . .

by Denis Florence MacCarthy (1817 -1882)

DEDICATION

Montage of the Irish Easter Rising, 1916
Painting by Norman Teeling (B & W rendition)

The Battle has Begun
- Fighting at the General Post Office, Connolly Wounded
Painting by Norman Teeling (B & W rendition)

This novel is dedicated to the Irish men and women who fought on the side of liberty and justice in the Easter Rising of 1916. They were the flame that lit the torch of freedom in Ireland. Without their sacrifice, all of Ireland might still be under oppressive British rule with their Irish Gaelic heritage essentially obliterated. (see Historical Background)

Patriots of the Irish Easter Rising, 1916
by Stephen Finlay Archer

Brave Padraig, sage Thomas, stout John and the rest,
Stood up to the Brits and were up to the test,
These patriot warriors, outnumbered were they,
Proclaimed the Republic, on God's ascent day.

The Limeys brought cannon, machine guns and more,
They pounded old Dublin in out and out war,
The rebels' few rifles were nary enough,
Yet their courage is legend, heroic stuff.

Like the brave Greeks' last stand at Thermopylae,
To a man and a woman, from death did not shy,
Their moral commitment to country and kin,
To liberate Ireland from Britain's great sin.

Their statement was made, they held out for a week,
The fate of this battle becoming quite bleak.
With patriots, citizens, shot and in peril,
Pearse laid down their arms, both bullet and barrel.

The British were ruthless; the martyrs were shot,
They went to their deaths with one brave single thought,
They'd given their all for their true Gaelic cause,
With no accolades, and no need for applause.

They'd all lit the flame that would always burn bright,
Their countrymen, surely, would take up this fight.
It was a grand start, not the end of the tale,
Their hot torch of freedom would someday prevail.

ACKNOWLEDGEMENTS

Once again, the author is indebted to Manzanita Writers Press of Angels Camp, California, for its tireless support in editing, producing, and marketing of these novels. Of particular note are its founding director and creative editor Monika Rose, and editor Suzanne Murphy, as well as book designer Joyce Dedini and eBook designer Jennifer Hoffman, who took me under their wing to wrestle my manuscripts into shape. Thank you, ladies!

There are a number of readers who have given me constructive feedback for *Rising*, including Bob Kolakowski, Kathy Archer, Joy Roberts, Amber Herron, and Victoria Bors. Thank you all.

Most of all, I wish to express my undying love and appreciation to the woman who, for more than thirty years, has been the wind beneath my wings, my darling wife Kathy. She has wholeheartedly supported this new journey in our lives, even though it wasn't in our plans when we retired from the aerospace business more than a decade ago. It is she who wisely recommended that I finish writing the entire Irish Clans series of novels rather than focus on marketing. My readers, who have been requesting the release of Book Three *Rising,* can thank Kathy for her gentle nudging.

I dedicate this third book of the Irish Clans saga to the men and women of high moral standards who rose up against the powerful British oppressor in the Irish Easter Rising of 1916, knowing full well that they would only win this battle through their martyrdom. They had a firm belief that the citizens of Ireland would eventually free their country after they witnessed excessive British brutality towards the Irish people during the Rising.

This dedication was again a tough decision since my beloved Kathy is my muse, and to her I owe everything. I hope that she will continue to be the wind beneath my wings. She is my love. Grandly and forever.

In March 2016, after holding the book launch for Book One *Searchers* at the Temple Bar pub in Dublin, my wife and I witnessed the more than 500,000 people assembled during the Centennial events to honor these men and women of the Easter Rising. The celebratory throngs included British and Irish officials, marching bands, and military parades. This was a far cry from the derision initially shown by the citizens of Dublin in 1916 when the rebels surrendered. They were not looking for accolades at that pivotal moment in history, just action from the oppressed citizenry. We honor them still.

The front and back cover art, as well as additional paintings about the Easter Rising on the dedication page and in the historical background section, are provided by the gifted Irish artist Norman Teeling. With his inspirational paintings of the Rising and the War of Independence, among other notable works of art, Norman keeps the magnificent fight for Irish freedom in the forefront of our thoughts. These striking images of strong moral courage are particularly pertinent in the social and political climate of today. Thank you, my friend.

An Cathach, one of the oldest and most precious relics of the Celtic civilization, purportedly written 1,457 years ago by St. Columba, is carefully preserved in the Royal Irish Academy in Dublin. In 2014, I visited this establishment, just as Tadgh and Peader had done during the Easter Rising in 1916. Although I was not allowed to see this relic, I did read some of the proceedings of the RIA regarding Reverend Lawlor's paper about *an Cathach of St. Columba*. I wish to thank the RIA for the use of the image of folio 48R, which is displayed on the back cover.

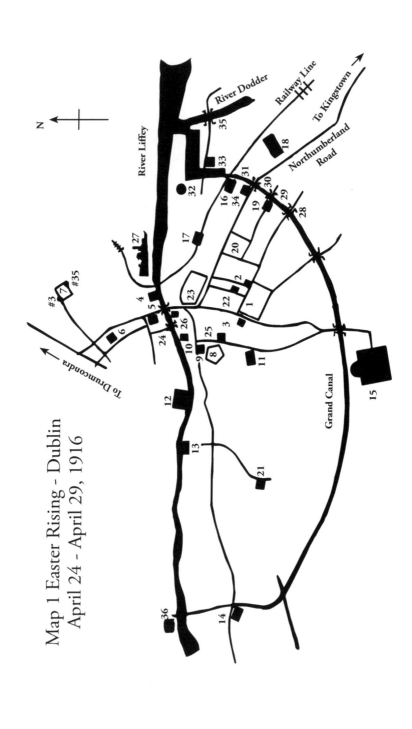

Map 1 Easter Rising - Dublin
April 24 - April 29, 1916

Table 1 Easter Rising Locations Map 1 Legend

1	St. Stephens Green	13	Mendicity Institution	25	South City Market (Arcade)
2	Shelbourne Hotel	14	Kilmainham Gaol	26	Wicklow Hotel
3	College of Surgeons	15	Portobello Barracks	27	HMV Helga Gunship
4	Liberty Hall	16	Boland's Bakery	28	Macartney Bridge
5	General Post Office	17	Westland Row Station	29	Huband Bridge
6	Rotunda Hospital	18	Beggar's Bush Barracks	30	McKenney's Bridge
7	Mountjoy Square	19	St. Stephens Church	31	Macquay's Bridge
8	The Castle	20	Merrion Square	32	Gas Works
9	City Hall	21	Marrowbone Lane Distillery	33	Boland's Mill
10	Temple Bar Pub	22	Royal Irish Academy	34	Clanwilliam House
11	Jacob's Factory	23	Trinity College	35	Ringsend Bridge
12	Four Courts	24	Ha'Penny Foot Bridge	36	Phoenix Park Magazine Fort

CONTENTS

Contents

Chapter One
Easter Rising

Day One - St. Stephens
Easter Monday, April 24, 1916
Liberty Hall, Dublin, Ireland

*I*n the Christian calendar, Easter Monday is a day of celebration, the day that the Lord Jesus was resurrected before ascending into Heaven following his brutal sacrifice for mankind on the Roman cross of Calvary. This is the fervent belief of both the Catholic and Protestant churches across the world, including those of Ireland. Yet on this glorious day, three hundred and fourteen years after the Protestant British defeated the remaining Catholic Irish Clans and Spaniards at the Battle of Kinsale, these warring factions were destined to once more take up arms against each other. Just as in the Gaelic past, the Irish revolutionaries were still fighting to restore their religion, their birthright, their Gaelic heritage, and their autonomous rights to their verdant country. Religion was symbolic of the greater prize.

Approximately fourteen hundred Irish Volunteers and their supporters turned out in Dublin for the Easter Rising. About four hundred and twenty of these, including the swarthy Irish Republican Brotherhood member Tadgh McCarthy and his sleek partner, Morgan, set out from Liberty Hall, the headquarters of John Connolly's Irish Citizen's Army, located on the north side of the River Liffey, just east of what they called O'Connell Street.

Tadgh was dressed in his olive drab outfit, hardly a soldier's uniform. He had worn it since they'd left home at Creagh to meet up with the gun-running patriot Roger Casement and the German arms shipment bound for Tralee the previous Thursday.

That seemed like a lifetime ago. The fact that his clothes needed laundering was the least of his problems.

What a debacle. The German *Aud-Norge* supply ship and the 20,000 rifles and ammunition destined for the rebels now lay scuttled at the mouth of Queenstown Harbour, useless to the cause. The bloody Royal Irish Constabulatory had taken a bedraggled Roger Casement into custody despite Tadgh and Morgan's best efforts. Now Padraig Pearse and the entire Irish Republican Brotherhood leadership were hell-bent on starting the revolution without proper weapons against the well-equipped British army. Martyrdom.

But in Tadgh's mind, all that didn't matter. The glorious revolution against the British oppressor was beginning at long last. At a strapping six-foot-one with his bushy moustache and all, Tadgh surely fit the part. Even the Luger from Kapitan Schwieger, an unlikely brother-in-arms who had ironically been the marauder that torpedoed his lover's ship, seemed an especially fitting weapon for a revolution against Britain.

He worried about Morgan, though. His lithe, five-foot-seven partner and lover had proven her mettle on several occasions when he was being attacked, here in Ireland, and on the Continent at the tragic Western Front. She fought fiercely when it came to his well-being. Now she was expected to fight the vermin British for the cause of Ireland.

He could see that Morgan had no stomach for it. Whatever had been her mysterious background that remained hidden behind her black ringleted hair and sultry green eyes in the wake of the *Lusitania* sinking beneath her feet—before the beneficial amnesia hit her, she had obviously been a saver of lives. It had been almost a year since that fateful day in May when a German torpedo had caused almost thirteen hundred deaths just eight miles off the south coast of Ireland, since Tadgh had found and pulled his love out of the frigid sea, almost dead herself. How he had agonized over her condition and his feeble attempts to bring her back to life at his home in Creagh. It seemed like an eternity ago now, back before their capture by the Germans and their harrowing escape from the Belgian trenches. But she had survived and now was the jewel in his life, almost as important as his fight for Irish freedom. A damned fine nurse she had proved to be since then, even though she didn't remember her name or origin. They had been fighting over her view of this essentially unarmed revolution's insanity, spurred on by Tadgh's passive mentor, the playwright Sean O'Casey. Padraig Pearse had questioned her loyalty to the cause, but Tadgh knew in his heart that she would fight by his side, if only to protect him.

As they were marching west toward O'Connell Bridge, Tadgh scrutinized the unhappy entourage. "The lucky ones are carrying the antiquated 'Howth' single shot rifles."

"The rest have pitchforks, clubs, or nothing but their own fists," Morgan lamented, adjusting the plain black trousers that Padraig's mother had given her, then falling in step with Tadgh.

"Clearly, our weak-kneed Volunteers leader MacNeill's countermand in the newspapers against the Rising yesterday has reduced the force considerably, Morgan. I think that we've only got about a fifth of the muster that was expected. Here, take Boyle's Webley for defense. I've got my Luger."

"You don't really expect me to use this, do you?" Morgan accepted the revolver and held it gingerly. "Will it go off?"

"Not unless you release the safety and pull the trigger. Here, let me show you."

After being instructed, Morgan tucked the weapon out of sight into her waistband under her shirtwaist. "Very few men and women are wearing uniforms, Tadgh. When the fighting starts, how are the English going to distinguish between rebels and the general population?"

The question had no answer. "They will probably fire indiscriminately," Tadgh surmised, while internally acknowledging once again the perceptiveness of his mate. He simply didn't know.

They saw the Headquarters battalion of about three hundred peel off, heading up O'Connell, making for the General Post Office. This group included five of the Military Council leaders[1] —Pearse, the President and Commander-in-Chief of the self-proclaimed 'Provisional Irish Republic'; James Connolly, the Commandant of Dublin; Tom Clarke, the senior statesman-turned warrior; Sean MacDermott; and Joseph Mary Plunkett. Due to his ill health, Plunkett was accompanied by his young aide-de-camp and Tadgh's old school chum, Michael Collins, who was smartly dressed in a starched uniform.

"It's a fine day for a Rising, Mick," Tadgh shouted to Collins as the GPO contingent turned north.

"It's a start, to be sure, Tadgh. You watch your back. I'll need you later."

"Same to you."

"Do you know who that is with Mr. Connolly, that woman carrying the interesting green flag with stars?"

"Yes, Morgan. That's Dr. Kathleen Lynn, one of the first woman doctors to graduate from the College of Surgeons here in Dublin. She's a socialist like Peader and a member of the Irish Citizens Army with James."

"Is she now. I'd like to meet her after the revolution if we're still alive. I wonder how she became a doctor in a man's profession. And the banner?"

"That's the flag of the ICA. They call it the Starry Plough. It's a symbol of the worker's party militancy. You see the sword as part of the plough? And the seven silver stars on the plough are the celestial Big Bear constellation, so named as the plough of the universe."

They overheard Connolly say to his ICA compatriot, "Bill, we're going out to be slaughtered."

Tadgh saw The O'Rahilly drive up, recognizing the man from a prior occasion. He was a fine lawyer by trade who had become the Director of Arms for the Volunteers. Overnight, he had been an emissary for MacNeil, carrying the countermand to rebel forces throughout south-eastern Ireland. Seeing that the Rising was going ahead despite his leader's objections, he joined the Headquarters battalion, saying, "Well, I've helped to wind up the clock, I guess I might as well hear it strike. Help me, boys. We'll load up this motorcar of mine with bombs and some of the old rifles."

MacNeill himself, of course, failed to show up.

"It's a sorry ragtag group we've got here, Tadgh," Morgan said, nervously adjusting the Webley that was pinching her midriff.

"But what a glorious cause, lass, and that's the God's honest truth," Tadgh retorted, trying to encourage his reluctant partner. "At least it isn't raining. Don't worry about the Webley. I left it in the safe condition."

Commandant Mike Mallin's ICA battalion, a hundred strong, set out south across the River Liffey to commandeer St. Stephens Green on the south side of Trinity College. There were no shouts and cheers, just grim determination on all the faces. They all knew the score.

"Tadgh, where are the English soldiers?" Morgan asked, as they arrived at a strategic location on the northwest corner of the park under Fusilier's Arch.

"I don't know. They must have believed that MacNeill's countermanding notice in the paper would have stopped any plans for a Rising."

Citizens at first took a curious attitude that turned to belligerence when the Volunteers started to dig trenches at the entrances and put up barricades around the perimeter of the Park, especially around the arch. But they offered no immediate resistance.

"Halt." Michael Mallin fired a warning shot past the front window of Dublin Tram Company's No. 308 as it started to turn clockwise around the arch. Passengers fled like rats leaving a sinking ship as the tram ground to its unplanned stop.

"Hands up," Mallin ordered, and the tram conductor cautiously raised his hands above his head. "Now back this up ten feet, then get out."

The conductor obliged and then skedaddled west on the now-vacant South King Street.

"Help me, boys," Mallin cried, as he moved to push the tram over. Forty men heaved to and rocked the tram until it fell over on its side, partially blocking St. Stephen's Street North from the arch towards Grafton Street. That completed the barricade of the park's northwest corner.

"Tadgh, why is there a fence around the entire park?" Morgan asked, hoisting a shovel with the rest of the men.

"I lived close to the park during my playwriting days, so I know the history here." Tadgh hefted another shovelful of loam from the flower bed and stopped to catch his breath. "As you can see, Morgan, St. Stephen's Park is normally a twenty-two-acre haven of tranquility in the middle of this bustling city. In the early eighteen hundreds, the elites who lived around its periphery built this fence to keep out the riff-raff, as they put it."

Morgan wiped his brow with her neckerchief. "So that's why it's six feet high with spear-shaped finials that face outward."

"Precisely, *aroon.*"

"But now it seems that everyone can use it." Morgan watched outraged Monday walkers, disturbed from their Easter stroll through the tranquil gardens, scurry out through the exits to safety. "Except, of course, today, since we're barricading it."

Tadgh continued, "In the late eighteen hundreds, Sir Arthur Guinness, Lord Ardilaun, convinced the City fathers, both financially and politically, to modernize the park and to open it to artisans and the general population. They inserted eleven entrance gates in the fence, including at the four corners. Between the corners you can see the three equally spaced pedestrian gates along the thousand feet of the park's north side, which normally provide Dublin citizens access."

"I think that it is very beautiful with its central lake and such," Morgan mused, noticing the bluebirds and starlings that were still flitting in the magnificent oak trees as the sunlight sifted through their branches. "Even if we are chewing up the flower beds."

Morgan had dropped her shovel and was about to set off into the Park's interior to determine the best location for a first aid station when she noticed a powerful, dominating woman arrive on foot and then stop to consult with Commandant Mallin. The leader was a splendid-looking young man with a black moustache almost as thick as Tadgh's.

"This is Countess Constance Markiewicz herself, Commandant Mallin's deputy," Tadgh said, by way of introduction to Morgan when the imposing countess stopped in front of them. "She's one of Connolly's staunch ICA members."

Morgan surveyed the tall, high cheek-boned, still-beautiful woman of about forty-five years. Despite the implications of her title, her life had not likely been an easy one. With her black hair in a bun, mostly swept under the wide-brimmed feathered hat worn at a jaunty angle, she bore a resemblance to Queen Nurse Elizabeth of Belgium. Her determined steely-eyed gaze seemed to penetrate Morgan's soul. Here was a woman who wouldn't hesitate to use the pistol held firmly in her right hand. A heavy woolen uniform with its confining leather straps and tightly wound putties over black battalion boots added to her severe authoritative bearing. *Don't mess with the countess.*

"Constance will be taking charge of the support services for our battalion, I expect," Tadgh rattled on, obviously in awe of this woman. "Won't ya now, ma'am."

"Yes. And who might this be, McCarthy?"

"Let me introduce you to Morgan, my partner, a fine nurse and a member of the IRB."

"Really, a woman in the IRB and not the women's Cumann na mBann?"

"Yes, dear lady. She has saved my life and will save yours if need be. Padraig approved her, don't ya know."

"Did he now? Well, I'm all for promoting women, Tadgh. You

should know," she winked. Morgan instinctively reached out to grab Tadgh's hand.

"I see there's more to it than the IRB, my boy." Constance was chuckling now. "Is Morgan the woman you were telling me about?"

Tadgh picked up on her reference. "Yes, that's right. She wore the clothes I borrowed from you after I rescued her from the sea. Her's were, how shall I say it, tattered, to say the least."

It dawned on Morgan. "Oh, thank you, Countess. You have no idea how wonderful it was to get such fine clothes to wear after my ordeal when the Lusitania sank. I'm very pleased to make your acquaintance." Morgan reached out her hand.

Constance grasped Morgan's hand firmly. "The least I could do." Her eyes surveyed Morgan and rested on her middle. "You have a fine figure. I hope they fit given Tadgh used nautical dimensions to describe your measurements." She tossed her head towards him.

"Perfectly." Morgan met the woman's eyes and paused, then continued. "I've been trying to identify a safe location for a first aid station here in the park."

Morgan watched the countess sweep her eyes around the interior of St. Stephens Green. She selected the glass hothouse in the middle of the park in the distance on the other side of the lake. Pointing southward, she announced, "That will be our triage station. That way we can cover the southern flank if need be." Upon her orders, some Volunteers within earshot immediately began moving supplies.

"Won't the potential of flying glass be a problem with that location, Countess?"

"At least it is in a centralized building and not close to the perimeter," Markiewicz suggested, eyeing Morgan suspiciously.

Morgan turned to Tadgh for guidance. "What is the strategic importance of this park, *mavourneen*? It seems a very vulnerable location."

Tadgh had to admit that they were quite exposed among the tulip beds. He didn't have an answer.

Commandant Mallin stared down into their deepening foxhole. "This park is on a major route from the south port of Kingstown into the heart of the city. By controlling St. Stephens Green and streets around it, we can stop the English from advancing up to our General Post Office headquarters from the south."

Tadgh cast his eyes around the periphery of the park. "Shouldn't we be taking control of all the major buildings overlooking our position?"

"We don't have enough men. We will retreat to the fortress-like Royal College of Surgeons over there on the west side of the park if it becomes necessary," Mallin stated, pointing at a formidable two-story edifice. "However, it is currently occupied by medical students whom we don't want to displace. It may become a problem."

Tadgh and Morgan looked at the imposing stone structure with its massive front columns and agreed that it would be a strong fortification.

"Surely we should use that building for triage," Morgan said, looking westward.

"As long as we are in control of the park, I want the triage station to be away from the streets close to the battlefield. The British could attack us from the College," the Countess remonstrated, looking vexed.

Morgan pointed eastward toward the tall building on the north side of the St. Stephen's Street at the corner of Kildare, overlooking the park. "Why aren't we capturing that building? It would provide a commanding view of the whole area."

Tadgh examined the imposing eight-story brick edifice, nodding concurrence with her tactical prowess.

Mallin answered immediately. "That's the Shelbourne Hotel. We can't take it over from the citizens who are staying there. That wouldn't be right."

"What if the English occupy it and use its strategic location to fire down on us?" Morgan persisted, pointing to its expansive flat roof above a dormered upper floor. "It's only about three hundred feet west of the northeast entrance to the park. We'd be like sitting ducks. So many would be killed."

"Well, now. I think you're right, aroon. That roof would be an excellent location to command the northern side of St. Stephen's Green." Tadgh smiled and gave his love a thumbs up sign. She was developing a perceptive military intuition.

"I don't think that they would do that," the commandant concluded. "Too many innocent civilians would be put at risk. And besides, with the poor turnout, we don't have the manpower to defend a hotel. Too many entrances."

Tadgh came to his lover's aid. "I think that they would just evacuate the building before occupying it."

Their attention was abruptly diverted by a minor explosion in a direction northwest of the park.

"Good God, what was that?" Morgan asked, noticing a wisp of smoke far in the distance.

"Twelve twenty-five. Right on schedule," Mike Mallin confirmed, checking his watch. "That was our boys blowing up the magazine at Phoenix Park—the first action of the revolution."

"Doesn't sound loud enough for the munitions to have exploded," Tadgh observed, returning to the task of digging his foxhole.

Close to one-thirty, a courier showed up from the headquarters battalion carrying a copy of the "Proclamation of the Easter Rising,"[1] which he said Padraig Pearse had read aloud to the few cynical onlookers outside the GPO. Morgan read it, beginning from its heading, 'The Provisional Government of the Irish Republic to the People of Ireland.' She ended, identifying the seven signatures of the Military Council members. The top signatory was Thomas Clarke. She read the words aloud, "'We declare the right of the people of Ireland to the ownership of Ireland, and to the unfettered control of Irish destinies, to be sovereign and indefensible.'" She looked up at Tadgh who had stopped digging and was staring at her with a gleam in his eye. The words resonated with them both. Tadgh took the paper from her outstretched hands and posted it on one of the barricades by the Fusiliers' Arch. They gazed at it for a moment, silent.

Then Tadgh and Morgan continued to dig their foxhole at the northwest corner of the park in the flower bed, just inside Fusilier's Arch. The barricades of the overturned tram, wagons, and debris gave them cover from that location toward Trinity to the north and the Castle to the northwest. They noticed that the Countess and several of the men were digging at the pedestrian entrance about halfway along the north side at the center gate, close to a statue that could provide some cover when needed.

"Make no mistake, even with a hundred rebels and the enclosing fence, this park is not defendable," Tadgh said, mid-afternoon, "I wonder what fortifications we've constructed on the southwest side where the British forces may try to advance from Kingstown?"

"Tadgh, I agree that this location for our trench gives us the best protection from potential snipers on the top of the Shelbourne Hotel. It's as close as we can get to the Royal College of Surgeons building."

Tadgh put down his shovel and stretched. "I'm going to check on our Kerry motorcycle, Morgan. I parked it down the alley in back of the College." He had positioned it there earlier that morning after he dropped Morgan off at Liberty Hall, realizing that the College would be the most defensible building on the square. "I brought a tarpaulin to hide it from prying eyes. If the worst happens, it may provide our only escape route." He would follow orders, yet he was mindful of Michael Collins' instruction. Clearly his friend had a longer view of the fight than this initial Rising.

That evening an hour before dark, as the damp cold settled into their foxhole, a second courier arrived with news. Morgan stood up painfully from her reclining position against Tadgh in their five-foot-square by three-foot-deep foxhole to greet him as he rounded the overturned tram and entered the park under the arch. Tadgh jumped up and almost shot him in the gloom before he could identify himself.

Still crouched in their own crude and moldy-smelling foxholes, which they had excavated at twenty-foot intervals along the northern boundary of the park, other Volunteers started poking their heads up to find out what was going on. There hadn't been time to connect the holes into a proper trench.

The courier's disheveled uniform was stained with blood, but his voice remained strong and steady.

Mallin, a quarter of the way, and Constance, halfway across the northern edge of the park, jumped out of their holes and ran west to meet the soldier at the arch.

The courier leaned wearily against the eastern side of Fusilier's Arch as he ticked off the deployment status of the Volunteers, pointing in the appropriate directions as he talked. Checking his notes and clearing his throat, he announced, "Most of the intended control points have been taken by us without force." This included the Four Courts to the northwest by Ned Daly leading Battalion Number One of two hundred and fifty with Sean Heuston's group of thirty occupying the Mendicity Institute opposite the Four Courts across the River Liffey. Their job is to stop the enemy advancing from the west out of the Royal and Marlborough Barracks.

"What happened at Phoenix Park west of Four Courts?" Tadgh asked the courier, voice cracking. "We heard a very minor explosion at noon."

"Unfortunately, our men were not able to blow up the entire magazine fort because the enemy had already removed all the high explosives for the war on the continent. But the Fianna boys did their job and set the fuses. We acquired a few rifles and some ammunition that Ned and Sean are now using."

"We could use some of them here," Tadgh said, jumping out of the foxhole and grabbing the courier by the collar to emphasize his request.

"They are all spoken for, I'm sorry to say."

He then went on to explain that Eamon Ceannt and his Battalion Number Four of one hundred had occupied the South Dublin Union Hospital in the southwest while Jacob's Biscuit Factory in the south was controlled by Thomas MacDonagh and his two hundred Volunteers of Battalion Number Two. Both were positioned to guard against the enemy approaching from the Curragh camp to the southwest in County Kildare.

"All's quiet on this front," Mallin said, scanning his eyes north up Grafton Street towards Trinity College.

The courier accepted a drink from a canteen of water that Morgan supplied from their foxhole and continued, "Boland's Flour Mill in the southeast is occupied by Eamon de Valera leading Battalion Number Three of one hundred and thirty to stop the British coming from the south. De Valera has sent Mike Malone and eleven good men to occupy houses that overlook Mount Street Bridge on the Northumberland Road. If the English land forces at Kingstown, they will likely come north through there on the way to the city, if they don't come a half-mile west up through St. Stephen's Green, that is."

"Well, we're ready for them if they come this way," Mallin said, brandishing his revolver patriotically.

Tadgh knew that this just wasn't so. Their ICA Battalion of only a hundred Volunteers was so spread out that a well-equipped British battalion could sweep through the park and cut them to pieces.

The courier wiped his salt-caked mouth. "There have been some skirmishes, especially near our headquarters at the GPO, as the British start to get organized. A troop of the 6th Reserve Cavalry Regiment, dispatched from Marlborough Barracks, proceeded down O'Connell Street. As it passed Nelson's Pillar, level with the GPO, our Volunteers opened fire, killing three cavalrymen and two horses. The cowardly Limeys retreated."

Mallin asked, "Do you know what happened at the Castle? We heard gunfire."

The courier massaged his temples with the fingers of his right hand and nodded. "Sean Connolly attacked Dublin Castle but failed to secure it. So, he took nearby City Hall instead. I'm sad to report that he is our first casualty, shot by an English sniper when he raised the tricolor flag on the roof of City Hall. Dr. Lynn and I were with him when he died."

"I knew him well," Tadgh reminisced. "A stout lad of strong Fenian stock. He had a role in my play at the Abbey Theatre, don't ye know. I read in the newspaper just yesterday that he was the lead actor in the play 'Under Which Flag' a few weeks ago. Ironic. The play was about an Irishman torn between serving in the Irish and British armies. It ended with Sean raising the green flag and uttering the immortal lines, 'Under this flag only will I serve; under this flag, if need be, only will I die'. We'll miss him, but oh, what a glorious death."

"He is the first of many, no doubt," Morgan mumbled, giving the soldier a piece of dried bread that had been saved for their dinner. She took a bite herself and nearly choked.

Tadgh patted Morgan on the back to help clear her windpipe, then looked to the courier, "Is that all?"

The soldier took a bite of the bread and concluded his report, "Given the meager turnout, Connolly feels that this was the best deployment of resources that our forces could muster. I've been to each of our strongholds now and I'm heading back to the GPO. Once the enemy mobilizes, our communications may get cut off."

Tadgh had been looking east at the towering Shelbourne Hotel seven hundred feet distant where the lights were just blinking on and turned to face the courier. "What's the word about the lack of English response?"

"They were caught flat-footed with many of their men out of the city at the Fairyhouse Races today, but they should have been more visible by now. It's baffling. They let us parade on St. Patrick's

Day, so maybe they still think it's a drill. We have no news from outside Dublin."

"So far, so good," Commandant Mallin commented loudly. "Tell Connolly that."

"I will. God bless you all here at the Green." With that they saw the courier scurry through the arch disappearing up Grafton Street in the gathering gloom.

Tadgh sensed that the lack of response was ominous, at best. "It's going to get cold tonight," he advised Morgan as they settled into their cramped space, with legs bent, backed up against stone and dirt. Each Volunteer had only a horse-hair blanket to fend off the elements as they tried to get some sleep in their uncomfortable positions.

Morgan pulled their two blankets around Tadgh and herself. "You told me once that you only knew the countess platonically, right?" She was a little afraid of the answer but needed to know.

"When Yeats was working with me on my play a couple of years ago at the Abbey Theatre, he was quite fond of the Countess's little suffragette sister, Eva. I met her and Constance through Yeats."

"How *well* did you know her, really?"

"Just in passing, my love." Tadgh looked away, over toward where Constance and her men were preparing their spot for the night, five hundred feet to the east. They had managed to connect their foxholes into a mini-trench to house all ten of them.

Morgan saw him wink and thought she knew what it meant. "She's a lot older than you."

"Just in passing, to be sure."

The story hadn't changed from when Tadgh first brought her the clothes, but Morgan wasn't convinced. "Leastways, we have each other. How awful for the women who have been left on their own at home, dreading what will happen to their men."

Tadgh looked back at his woman, stroked her forehead, and held her in his arms in that damp, cold hole. Morgan nestled into him with her back against his chest. She could see the anguish in the eyes of the men in the foxholes near them, their heads poking up above the flowerbeds. That would be awful for them, seeing Tadgh and Morgan cuddling, with their own worries about missing their families with the probability of never seeing them again. To blot out that sight, she turned her face toward Tadgh, shivering into his shoulder, knowing full well that he would protect her at all costs. It was her job to keep him alive no matter what happened to them both.

At ten that evening, Augustine Birrell, Chief Secretary for Ireland, scorched the phone line from his London home to Dublin Castle.

"What the hell is going on over there, Matthew?" he demanded of Nathan, his under-secretary at the Castle.

"We guessed wrong, sir," Matthew Nathan responded. "Lord Lieutenant Wimborne was right. We should have rounded them up yesterday."

"Do we know how many there are and whether this insurrection is contained in Dublin?"

"A pretty good idea, sir. General Lowe estimates approximately fourteen hundred in all, spread out at strategic locations west, southwest, south, and southeast. Their headquarters is the General Post Office, an easy target for us. Reports indicate that approximately one thousand Volunteers mustered on Sunday in Cork under Tomas Mac Curtain. But they disbanded because of MacNeill's countermand. There's a small group in Wexford, another in Galway, a third in Tyrone, and a fourth on Falls Road in Belfast, but they won't be a problem, sir."

"Is the Castle secure?"

"Yes, sir. I was there with the Postmaster General when the rebels tried to take over. They killed a guard, but we got the gates closed and locked. Then they just gave up and moved on to City Hall.

That was a major military mistake on their part because, at that point, we were basically defenseless. Now we have some reinforcements, so we have control and communications."

"What's your plan, Matthew?"

"We have arranged for sixteen thousand troops to arrive and be deployed by tomorrow night. General Lowe will surround the rebels, cutting off their supply lines. Then we will split their forces north and south by controlling the Liffey. This will disrupt communications among their city outposts."

"What about the general population? Is there any sign that they will join the fight?"

"Just the opposite, sir. They were curious at first, but now they are angry at the rebels because they know there will be damage to their city. There has been looting of nearby stores on Sackville Street."

"That they call O'Connell Street?"

"The same, sir."

Having been conciliatory in prior months to no avail, Birrell went on the offensive. "I want the country put under martial law immediately with curfews imposed. Anyone carrying weapons of any kind, and not wearing a British military or police uniform, shall be apprehended or shot," he ordered. "Furthermore, I want Liberty Hall destroyed and the GPO captured as soon as possible. Cut off the head of the snake—"

"—and the rest will die," Matthew completed the sentence.

"Precisely. Asquith wants this matter dealt with swiftly and powerfully."

"What about preserving the infrastructure of the city, sir?"

Birrell answered without hesitation. "Do whatever it takes to flush them out of their nests."

"So be it, sir. We have the HMY *Helga*, an armed auxiliary patrol yacht, standing by at Kingstown, equipped with a pair of twelve-pounders. If we bring her up the Liffey, with the artillery that we will have at Trinity, we can obliterate Liberty Hall in short order and commence shelling the GPO."

"Do it," Birrell ordered. "Keep me posted."

With that out of the way, Matthew asked the question that was searing his brain. "What's the climate like at Number Ten Downing, sir?"

"Our careers are finished, if that's what you're asking about," Birrell answered curtly. Then he hung up.

Chapter Two
Easter Rising

Day Two
Tuesday. April 25, 1916
Tadgh's Foxhole, St. Stephen's Green, Dublin, Ireland

*T*adgh got about two hours of semi-sleep and awoke at five-thirty, half an hour before dawn. He smelled rather than saw the cold mist that had settled in off the Liffey River, making him shiver. The blankets covering them were soaking, and the shoulder muscle that tore when the RIC bullet whistled through him during the attack in the B&C Brewery loading area, ached like hell, numbing his left hand.

Morgan stirred beside him and murmured, "You got the tea on, darling?"

Tadgh loved that about her.

"I'm going to see what is happening out there," he whispered, giving his love a light kiss on the cheek. "Don't show your head out of this foxhole until I get back."

Morgan nodded sleepily and reached beneath her. "There's a root that's been poking my back all night. I thought it was your knee until you got up. Come back to me, you hear?" she whispered, rubbing her lower back and then pulling the blanket close around.

"Won't be long."

Minutes later, after skirting back around the barricades, he dropped down into the foxhole. "Well, now. Just as we thought, British soldiers are entering the back of the Shelbourne Hotel and moving some of the residents out into the cold street."

Morgan welcomed him back under the blankets. "We'd better warn the others." She sat up and called out softly to the man in the

41

trench on her right and asked him to pass on the news. Tadgh did the same on his left.

Within minutes, as dawn broke, Commandant Mallin walked over to Tadgh's foxhole with two of the Volunteers.

"What's this about the King being in the Shelbourne Hotel, having his breakfast, and waiting for us Republicans to surrender to him?"

Morgan's message must have been completely garbled as it moved down the line.

"Get down!" Tadgh screamed, as shots rang out from the roof of the Shelbourne Hotel. One of the two Volunteers fell where he stood. Bullets thudded into the east side of the Fusiliers' Arch, and the Commandant dove into Tadgh's foxhole.

"That's what I was tryin' to tell everyone," Tadgh yelled, as machine gun fire erupted and raked the rebel positions on the north side of the park.

Morgan jumped out of the foxhole to check the condition of the fallen Volunteer. "Get back here!" Tadgh shouted, grabbing her legs and pulling her down as bullets rained on them. One whizzed past their heads. If he had not yanked her, she would have been a headshot casualty.

The foxholes were not that deep, and Tadgh could see that the Volunteers were pinned down by the machine guns from above. The guns stopped momentarily, likely rearming.

"We've got to retreat to the west side, now," he demanded, and Mallin agreed. The commandant dove for his foxhole to warn the countess and her men.

He yelled across the north side of the park at Constance that she should sound the retreat. Almost immediately, most of the Volunteers jumped out of their trenches and ran for the Royal College of Surgeons. The machine guns started up again, raining bullets down on the Volunteers, and several men were cut down in their tracks. Tadgh dashed for the west side of the arch, pulling Morgan with him to keep her from jumping back up in the killing field to save the fallen. Bullets thudded against the stone beside him. From his vantage point, and with a firm grasp on Morgan, he attempted to take a sniper shot at the roof of the Shelbourne, but his Luger wasn't accurate enough at that range.

Then Tadgh spied a Howth 1871 Mauser single shot rifle lying beside a fallen Volunteer in the open ten feet east of the arch. "Stay here, Morgan, behind the arch." He dove for the inert Volunteer and his rifle as bullets kicked up dust around him. He checked the man who wasn't breathing. Several soldiers darted past him to the safety of the arch and its barricade, one holding his limp, bloodied arm. Picking up the rifle and using the soldier's body as a shield, Tadgh dragged him back behind the arch.

Morgan announced, "He's dead," having checked for a pulse. She closed the man's eyelids reverently.

"Do not go back for the wounded, lass," Tadgh shouted, stripping the unfortunate man of his bullet bandolier. "Stay here and tend to any wounded that make it to the arch." He checked the breech of the old bolt action Mauser. *Loaded.*

Circling northward around the west side of the barricade in the street, Tadgh found a hidden vantage point behind the overturned tram. Volunteers writhed in pain just in front of him near the barricade, yelling. A wounded orderly crawled to them for assistance. Bullets spattered into the tram, pinging off the exposed wheels and penetrating the undercarriage, while Mallin shouted down the line to conserve ammunition. The acrid smell of gunpowder singed Tadgh's nostrils as he peered past the corner of the tram at the roof of the Shelbourne. The machine gun sharpshooter was most likely focused on the field between himself and the arch. Tadgh guessed the distance at seven hundred feet. If he remembered his target practice with this weapon at Rathfarnham, that should mean a trajectory drop of about five feet. Tadgh heard his first shot clank off metal, likely the tripod below the machine gun. He could see the startled gunner at the roof edge momentarily jump back. Then the deadly rat-a-tat started again. Tadgh adjusted his height. With the second shot, the machine gun fell silent, and Tadgh could see British soldiers dragging their comrade away.

"Run now," Mallin yelled from his foxhole at the Volunteers who started to take advantage of this respite to scramble to the arch and barricade. Mallin stayed behind, in his position halfway between the arch and the enemy, firing at the Shelbourne while his men scampered to safety. Then he made a dash to the arch.

After a pause, the machine gun bullets started whizzing again. The British had erected a barricade of their own on the roof of the Shelbourne, so it would be much harder to silence the infernal machine. Tadgh could not get another direct shot.

Fortunately, the Volunteers nearest the arch had escaped their foxholes, although Tadgh counted four brave rebels lying prone in the road. One was crawling toward the arch when a bullet struck him in the back and stopped him cold.

Constance, almost opposite the British soldiers in the hotel, had stayed with her men in their mini-trench within the northern boundary of the park in an attempt to keep the Tommies contained in the Shelbourne. She was pinned down but had some tree cover.

"We'll be back to get you," Mallin yelled to Constance, "as soon as we can get these men to the College." Constance waved a reply as another volley of machine gun bullets sliced through the trees near her.

"We'll stop any British approaching from the Shelbourne," she hollered back, aiming her C96 "Broomhandle" Mauser pistol-carbine and returning fire.

"Fall back to the college," Mallin shouted, as he ushered the Volunteers across York Street on the west side of the park.

Using the arch as a barrier, Tadgh and Morgan assisted the retreating rebels to the safety of the college. They found a south side entrance where they were met by students who quickly surrendered the building.

The doctoral students and Morgan fell to work treating the wounded.

"Where are your first aid supplies?" Morgan demanded.

"We don't have any. This is an education center. We go to the hospital for practice," one of the students blurted out.

One of Constance's triage nurses burst through the door. Morgan grabbed her by the arm. "Supplies, girl?"

"Still in the Glass House in the park. We didn't expect to have to retreat so soon."

Morgan watched as the Volunteers streamed in through the side entrance. Several more were wounded, the more serious helped by their compatriots. The scene took on the look of the Belgian front to her, but at least here, limbs were not blown off yet.

"We've got to go and get those supplies," Morgan urged Tadgh, who was organizing defenses inside the main hall, as Mallin continued to shepherd his troops outside to safety.

Tadgh could see from the condition of the Volunteers that she was right.

"All right. We'd better do this now while we still have some control of the park." He motioned to nearby able-bodied men, "You three, come with me. Morgan, you stay here."

"Not on your life," she replied, stepping up to face him. "I know where the supplies are, and besides, I have to be with you in case you get wounded and need me to patch you up again. Where you go, I go, mavourneen."

Tadgh could see the defiance and love in her eyes. "It's *your* life I'm worried about," he shot back, adding, "so stay close to me." He bolted out the door, Morgan and the others following.

"Hold up here," he ordered, when they reached the southeast corner of the college. "I'll scout out the situation." Machine gun and carbine rifle fire was incessant, and they could hear the screams of the wounded.

Returning along the retreat path, Tadgh darted across the tram tracks on St. Stephen's Green West Street and disappeared behind the barricade that they had made the day before.

When he returned, out of breath, he reported, "Our men are

holding their own, so far. The British fire is only coming from the Shelbourne, targeting the Countess' trench. There's no telling if they are occupying other buildings around the perimeter of the Park. Our Volunteers appear to have abandoned the trenches on all sides except the north, and I can see five wounded men on the ground near Fusilier's Arch."

"What's to be done, Tadgh?" Morgan whispered.

"You'll stay here with me." He told the others, "You three tend to the wounded and get them to safety. Now lass, show me where those supplies are in the glass house. Everyone, keep your heads down!"

With that said, the three Volunteers headed northeast back into the park, while Tadgh and Morgan headed southeast towards the paned structure. Once inside the park, the two encountered the monument of a seated Lord Ardilaun, former head of the Guinness Brewery Company. Tadgh pointed, "This is a statue of the man I told you about. It seems appropriate that we are making a stand in the People's Park, don't ya think?"

"Over this way!" Morgan shouted, as they passed by the waterfall at the western end of the lake.

They were about to emerge from the shelter of the western trees. Tadgh judged that they had to cross an open expanse of about two hundred feet to reach their destination in the treed area ahead. To the distant left, he could see the Shelbourne in plain sight over the lake. So far, they had not been spotted.

"We've got to run like the wind now, Morgan. Don't stop until you're in those trees, no matter what. I'll go first. Then you follow."

With that, he sprinted across the clearing. Seconds later, he was in the trees and he motioned for her to make her dash. Tadgh watched Morgan run across the open area with powerful strides. Then machine gun fire stitched the ground behind her. She dove forward into Tadgh's arms, and he pulled her to safety behind a stout sycamore tree.

"That was a close call, lass." He held her, feeling the pounding of her heart against him, her limbs trembling. They ducked under dense foliage around the tree. Morgan kissed him hard on the mouth, while bullets zinged above them.

Tadgh peered around the sycamore and saw the greenhouse ahead in the trees, with sparse cover for them until they reached it. Unfortunately, he could see that the machine gunner on the Shelbourne had a direct view of the building.

"Okay, darlin'. Here's what we have to do now. I'm thinkin' they'll get tired of waiting for us to move and will redirect their fire on the foxholes shortly. When that happens, we need to run from tree to tree until we get to the greenhouse. Once there, we are exposed again, so we will then crawl the last few feet. When we get inside, we need to stay low to the ground. Agreed?"

Morgan put her hand to Tadgh's lips. "Understood, dear. You take such good care of me, my love."

"Well, now. I'm just protecting the mother of my future children," he shot back with a twinkle in his eye. "Would you like to be buried with my people?"

"Is that a backhanded proposal?" Morgan blurted, looking up into his amber eyes.

"Yes. It's a traditional Gaelic expression. Take it however you want, lass." Tadgh laughed, and took off darting from tree to tree when the bullets ceased flying. She followed him across the open area, and they reached the glass house without incident. When they crashed through the doorway, Morgan and Tadgh fell to the ground, out of breath.

Tadgh was first to get up. "All right, where are the supplies?"

Morgan crawled among the plants and located the first aid kits they had risked their lives to find. "Here they are, in three knapsacks."

They had barely gotten two of the packs strapped to their backs, when sunlight glinted from the glossy white Red Cross metal box protruding from Morgan's backpack and lit up a portion of the glass house. This must have caught the eye of the sniper high up on the roof of the Shelbourne, as he opened fire, with bullets pinging all around them.

"Let's get out of here!" Tadgh shouted, as bullets exploded glass into a shower around them. "Head south and keep this structure between you and the Shelbourne," he ordered, as he grabbed the third knapsack.

They heard the bullets thudding into the ground behind them as they ran. By the time they crossed "The Ride," a circular track around the inside of the park, they were back in the trees still headed south, away from the Shelbourne and the college. Fifty feet farther on, they approached the head gardener's vine-covered cottage in the southwest corner of the park. The sniper's bullets had stopped flying in their direction.

Tadgh held out his hand to lead Morgan. "We need to circle back to the college, staying west of the park."

Morgan hesitated for moment. "Yes, and hopefully not soon."

"What?"

"I'd love to marry you, mavourneen, but I don't want to be buried with your people just yet."

"Where is a preacher when you need one?" Tadgh pulled on her arm.

Morgan gasped, her hand shooting up to her right shoulder.

"What is it, lass?" Tadgh glanced at Morgan's back. "My God. Stop moving. Which knapsack has the gauze and tape in it?"

"The one in your hand. Why?"

"A piece of glass is lodged in your right shoulder. Do you not feel the pain?"

"I did just then." Morgan turned to look at the back of her shoulder. "What is it?"

Tadgh gingerly eased her knapsack from her left shoulder, then peeled the coat off her back.

When the glass came out with the coat, Morgan flinched at needles of pain and the sight of blood cascading down her arm. Tadgh eased her to the ground and hurriedly retrieved antiseptic and bandaging. He described the condition of the wound that she could not see, telling her that he didn't see any glass remaining in her shoulder. Morgan determined there was no need for stitches, and Tadgh made a quick job of cleaning and covering the wound. She kept a tight hold on Tadgh's knee as he bent to his work. "Now you're the one saving me when I'm injured. There's a switch. You make a fine nurse, my love."

"Not my calling, I'm afraid, but it'll have to do for now."

When he finished, he gently pressed his lips against the bandage. "My proposal must have so distracted you that you could have lost a foot as well and not noticed it. I must mind the effect I have on you, aroon."

"I see where Mr. Guinness used to live," Morgan said, halting to read from a plaque in the yard identifying the cottage as Arlibaun Lodge. "This is the kind of home where I imagine our sons and daughters might grow up."

"I thought that you wanted to live in a cottage by Queenstown Harbour," Tadgh replied. "So, you've been thinking about this for some time, have you, my love?"

"A girl has to have something to look forward to, doesn't she?"

The silence surrounding the pair was broken by a thin reedy voice, and they looked into the cottage yard to see an old man approaching them, dressed in country garb and lugging a fustian bag under his arm. He muttered repeatedly that he was late and took no apparent notice of the bedraggled couple as he hurried by. It was peculiar that this wizened old-timer seemed not at all curious about strangers out in the park, but perhaps the man was a little blind.

"Hold on there, sir," Tadgh called after him as the figure headed northward in the park.

Startled, the man stopped and jerked around to face them. "Who are you?"

"I wouldn't go out there just now, sir. You're liable to get shot, don't ya know."

"Are they trying to shoot my ducks again? I'll put a stop to that foolishness, so I will."

When the old man turned to go, Morgan grabbed him by the arm and pointed to the wound in her shoulder. "It's very dangerous in the park right now, sir. Why don't you tell us who you are and what you're late for."

The man responded to Morgan's touch and tone of voice. "I'm Henderson, Head Gardener for this park. Each morning at seven o'clock, I go out and feed my ducks on the lake, rain or shine, lass."

"It's a different kind of rain out there today, sir. There are some very bad men shooting at us from up high in the Shelbourne Hotel. They're not after your ducks."

"Oh, good. That's a relief." The man's forehead wrinkled, and then his toothless mouth opened in silent mirth. "Then they won't mind if I get on with feeding my pretties, will they."

He turned and shuffled off north in the direction of the lake before they could stop him.

"Wait here, lass. I mean it. I'll be right back." Tadgh took off after the old man.

Morgan was feeling woozy from their recent adventure. "Right you are, lover. Hurry back," she said, as she slumped down on a nearby park bench.

Tadgh reached the edge of the trees just as the man started throwing seed from his bag to the ducks gathering at the base of the waterfall. Completely exposed to the snipers, Tadgh expected that any moment the enemy would redirect their fire at him. To his amazement, the snipers stopped firing altogether. A lull fell over the scene as the old man flung the seeds out in a kind of ritual, and Tadgh was silent witness to its sanctity. His bag emptied, the head gardener turned and walked back to where a dumbfounded Tadgh stood at the tree line.

"My ducks are all right," he commented, as he passed. "It's a fine day and the tulips are starting to bloom." As he disappeared into the trees, the shooting recommenced with vigor.

Tadgh caught up with Morgan just as the old man walked into the cottage and closed the door. Seeing the look of incredulity in his eyes, Morgan said, "They stopped to let the gardener feed his ducks, didn't they. At least there is still a shred of sanity and respect for tradition in the People's Park."

Tadgh waited until after a police lorry cruised past before leading Morgan safely through the back streets to the college's side entrance. There they met the triage nurse, who clasped her hands when she saw them. "Look, they've got the first aid supplies."

Morgan and the other nurses tended the wounded. It was reported that the three Volunteers had reached the downed men near the arch and two of them had each carried a man to the temporary safety of the college. The third Volunteer had died while attempting the same rescue, falling beside the comrade he was to have retrieved.

Meanwhile, Tadgh ventured out to the barricades. He could see that the Volunteers still in the north foxholes were wearing down. They were pinned, and sporadic gunfire led him to think they must be running low on ammunition. Since enemy fire came from one source, he reasoned that the British forces were still very limited in the area. But that wouldn't last much longer. He thought of Constance and her troops being overrun by the enemy.

Tadgh reported to Commandant Mallin. "I entreat you to make an effort to withdraw all Volunteers to the college, while we still have some firepower."

Mallin nodded. "A small force should take this message to Constance and provide cover fire for the withdrawal," he stated, looking around the college's main room for volunteers. "We'll have to extract any injured and dead Volunteers caught in the process."

"I volunteer to lead this party," Tadgh offered, coming forward.

Mallin's eyes locked on the younger man who had bravely stepped up. "These are my men, and I'll lead them, but I would appreciate your support, Tadgh."

Morgan overheard them planning the mission and decided she would go, too. They would need a nurse for the fallen, she reasoned. This time she did not vocalize her intentions.

A courier arrived from the GPO with news.

"In addition to your battle here at St. Stephen's, the British are getting organized. There have been some skirmishes at the Four Courts. I must report, however, that we have not captured either Dublin Castle or Trinity College just north of you. I barely made it through to you here, so I am not sure how long we can keep our lines of communication open."

"Damn." Tadgh knew that they had better hurry to consolidate their entire force in the college before British reinforcements arrived.

Eight Volunteers, rifles slung on their backs, headed out to the barricade with four stretcher bearers bringing up the rear. From there they could see eastward along the northern side of the park to Constance's location and beyond. Nine brave Volunteers led by Constance Markiewicz still held the line against superior firepower from the Shelbourne. They had managed to dig their small trench deeper, using the excavated earth to build a low wall that gave them some meager protection.

"It looks like they are about five hundred feet east of Fusiliers' Arch and about two hundred feet west of the Shelbourne, give or take," Tadgh said. Mallin confirmed Tadgh's estimate with a nod.

Morgan followed to the southeast corner of the College, where she could see them positioning themselves for the rescue. The countess's Volunteers were focused on the Shelbourne. The rescue party split into three parts. Four men, including Tadgh, used the barricades as cover as they made their way to the Fusiliers' Arch. From there, they took up firing positions on the Shelbourne. Carrying the two stretchers, four more Volunteers followed the first group. Finally, Commandant Mallin and three others flashed by and dove headfirst into the foxhole halfway to where the Countess and her men were pinned down.

Morgan saw that this last action drew some machine gun fire from the Shelbourne. She rushed to the barricades. From there she could see Mallin and the other Volunteers crouching down in the hole to avoid being shot. He couldn't even lift his head. Morgan saw that the commandant's calls to Constance remained unheeded due to the persistent rat-a-tat of the combatant fire.

Concentrating on what to do about the British machine gun, Tadgh did not see Morgan. The Volunteers seemed to be at a stalemate.

Finally, she watched as the scene unfolded before her. Mallin reached down and grabbed a sizable rock. He threw it at the nearest entrenched Volunteer. The rock pinged off the fighter's rifle and into the street. He swung around and acknowledged Mallin's gesture, looking up toward the rescue party crouched behind the arch. Mallin pointed his rifle at the Shelbourne and waved the Volunteers toward the arch.

The Volunteer nodded his head and passed the message down the line to Constance who turned around and spied the rescue party. "*Now*, boys. It's time to go," she cried out. "Run for the arch!"

Morgan watched as they popped up and ran for cover. Constance stayed behind, firing her single-shot weapon up towards the snipers. The three rescuers at the arch opened fire on the snipers.

Tadgh could see past the temporary barricade on the roof. He took aim and fired the Mauser at the glint off the machine gun. A sniper fell forward off the roof presumably to his death on the cobblestones ten stories below. The machine gun went silent for a minute until another sniper could take up the position. This gave the Volunteers precious seconds to reach safety.

It also enabled the medics who streaked out onto the killing ground to find survivors among the fallen. Morgan counted four bodies. Then she saw a fifth man hit and drop before he could reach the arch.

At the same time, the commandant came up shooting and ran eastward, then dove into the foxhole beside his deputy. Morgan could see that the two of them were providing covering fire from their location nearer the Shelbourne while their comrades ran for the safety of the arch.

Four British soldiers burst out of the hotel's entrance, shooting at Mallin and Constance. Tadgh sprang up and ran down North St. Stephen's Road in the direction of the hotel with his Luger ready. When he was in range, he fired three shots, downing two of the attacking soldiers. The remaining two turned and fired at Tadgh. Mallin stood up and shot one of the enemy dead before crouching back down in the trench.

Tadgh lunged at the remaining soldier just before he got another round off. Striking him with the quickness of a champion hurler, Tadgh knocked him off balance. The soldier attempted to run Tadgh through with his bayonet. Tadgh deftly sidestepped the thrust, then raised his Luger, and shot the soldier between the eyes. He knew they only had moments before the machine gunner would be replaced and death would rain down on them again.

"Time to save yourself, Countess!" he shouted, upon reaching her. "Your men should be safe now."

Together they ran for cover with the commandant bringing up the rear. Both men stayed between the countess and the Shelbourne, chivalrously protecting her with their bodies. The Volunteers at the arch fired a volley at the Shelbourne. The three retreating rebels reached the arch just as the machine gun came to life once more. Bullets pinged off the east face of the monument as they dove for cover, unscathed.

One of the stretcher bearers wasn't so lucky. Hit high in the chest, he dropped his end of the litter as he fell. The remaining bearer struggled to drag the litter alone with the weight of its wounded comrade slowing him down, still seventy feet from the protection of the arch.

Morgan rushed out to help.

Tadgh saw her. "Stop!" he yelled. Lunging for her arm, he missed. As Morgan picked up the downed end of the stretcher, she urged the bearer to run. Bullets stitched the ground around them.

Tadgh rushed out to assist, firing at the wicked source of death as he sprinted. Thirty feet from safety, he reached the stretcher. Turning and shielding his beloved, he kept his body between her and the Shelbourne as they ran. About ten feet from shelter, a bullet whizzed past his chest. Morgan cried out and dropped to the ground, holding her right leg. Tadgh scooped her up and set her on the stretcher on top of the other wounded comrade. Then he picked up her end of the litter and pulled them the last ten feet to the arch.

The machine gun sniper must have been angry at having missed his intended target. He unleashed his fury on the stonework. Chips flew, but no one else was wounded.

Tadgh could see blood squirting out of Morgan's lower right thigh. Constance immediately applied a tourniquet and direct pressure to Morgan's wound. Still pressing on the wound, she leaned down and tried to find a pulse on the Volunteer lying beneath Morgan on the stretcher. Dead.

Tadgh aimed his rifle, and with two well-directed shots, silenced the menace once again, temporarily. He would have liked to have stormed the Shelbourne, eradicating the machine gun nest once and for all, but he realized that would be a suicide move.

"She'll be fine if we can get her to the college quickly," Constance assured him. "Thanks for coming to our rescue. We'd have been overrun by those four bastards if you hadn't showed up. Your friend here also showed great courage in charging out to save the fallen. We'll take good care of her, you can be sure."

As dark settled in, the Volunteers were holed up in the college. One of the medical students had remained when the institution had been seized, and he assisted the triage nurses, performing surgical intervention on a few of the wounded. Although blood was available, anesthesia was not. The college, unfortunately, did not have supplies of antibiotics as far as the Republicans could determine, and their own supply was meager.

From her position propped up near where they were operating, Morgan gave instructions based on her experiences in the battlefield hospitals of Belgium.

"I assume that the British will have advanced at least as far as the barricades," the commandant told Tadgh as they worked to fortify the college against assault.

Tadgh slipped out the south door long enough to confirm Mallin's assumption.

"Can't we turn up the heat in this place?" the countess demanded. "My patients are shaking with cold."

"There is no heating available," the medical student admitted.

"Well, at least we aren't out in the elements," Morgan whispered, her voice raspy now, as a light rain began to fall outside.

Tadgh was worried, but not about the battalion. They would be able to hold off the British from within this strong fortification, but they were trapped and Morgan was gravely wounded. She was no longer able to help the others, being instead slumped over by her vertical pillar.

"How are you feeling, aroon," Tadgh asked, bending down to prop her up and feel her brow. She was burning up.

"About the same as when you were shot in the B&C loading yard, I expect. I think I've lost quite a bit of blood. I'm really woozy."

Tadgh unwound the bandaging from her wound and took a look. The bleeding had stopped but the area looked infected already. He quickly rebound the leg. "Constance tells me that the bullet passed right through without hitting bone, Morgan. That's good, isn't it?"

Morgan was slow to answer and her voice was slurred. "Better than the alternative, I guess, Tadgh. But I don't feel so good."

Tadgh wanted to admonish her for jumping out onto the killing field, but he decided against it and kissed her forehead instead. "You're in much better shape than when I first found you at sea, my love. You survived that tragedy and I'll make sure you survive this mishap, if it's the last thing I do."

She reached out to hold his hand but her arm was shaking too badly.

Tadgh steadied her arm and leaning down, kissed her fingers. "I love you, aroon. You are not going to be buried with my people anytime soon, do you hear me?"

Morgan moaned and weakly pressed her fingers to Tadgh's lips. Then she murmured almost too faintly for him to hear, "But we will be married, mavourneen, won't we?"

"Absolutely, my love. Now rest."

As the night progressed, Tadgh agonized over Morgan's worsening condition. Her fever spiked higher. She kept moaning and calling out his name in a fitful sleep. Cold compresses did not seem to help. This now reminded him of when he first rescued her from the Celtic Sea, when she was essentially unconscious and frozen. He had almost missed her there, hanging off that broken transom among the flotsam, miles from where the *Lusitania* had gone down. It was almost a year ago now, yet such a watershed of his young life. Thank God for her. He vowed that he wasn't going to lose her this time, either. When Constance stopped by around midnight with the medical student to check Morgan's condition, Tadgh could see by the squint of her bloodshot eyes that she, too was worried.

"Tadgh, we've done everything we can for Morgan here. We have precious few antibiotics to go around to all the wounded. I'm afraid your partner may get gangrene if she isn't taken to hospital at first light."

Tadgh had already decided as much, but he knew that he could not take her there. Then it dawned on him that the only person he could trust to do so during this Rising was his mentor, the pacifist Sean O'Casey. And that meant going to the women's Rotunda hospital near Sean's home.

The commandant joined them at that moment and added his two cents' worth. "We're hemmed in here, but we are under control in this fortification. I don't think that we can influence the outcome of this Rising much from this location. We have to assume that the authorities have put the city under martial law with a nighttime curfew. So, Tadgh, I want you to get your lady to safety." He continued, "Then I am requesting that you scout out the situation at the GPO and report back here. Also, you need to tell them that we have retrenched here in the college. I have a feeling that the planned courier communications may have broken down completely. You are resourceful, so I am counting on you to be our courier from now on."

Tadgh could see from their sidewise glances that the commandant, Constance, and the medical student had talked about this already and planned to get Morgan some additional medical assistance. He concluded that they must think, like he did, that she was in mortal danger. "Well then, on one condition, if ye please."

"What's that, Tadgh?" Constance put her hand on his shoulder.

"That you live long enough to attend the wedding of this gorgeous woman and me," Tadgh answered. Taking Constance's other hand in his own, he gazed at her and then at the commandant.

"Why, of course," they both chimed bravely. Tadgh could see from the faces of these two patriots that they knew that the probability of their survival was very low indeed.

Chapter Three
Easter Rising

*M*ercifully, the rain had stopped before the sun rose that cold Wednesday morning. Tadgh had monitored Morgan's condition as it deteriorated overnight. He was very worried, even more so than when his younger brother had been gravely wounded by Boyle's henchman near Tralee the previous Friday. God, it seemed like an eternity since that fateful day when the German ship with the critical arms shipment had been apprehended by the British dogs, and then scuttled, essentially sinking any chance of success for the Rising.

Tadgh looked out of an east-facing, second-story conference room window toward the Fusilier's Arch some six hundred feet away. The enemy had moved their machine gun and eight or ten soldiers to the barricades. It didn't look as if they had any reinforcements yet that could attempt to encircle the college. By the same token, the Volunteers could not overwhelm their enemy as long as the machine gun was operative. Bullets spattered against the impenetrable stone facade of the college's eastern wall, one bullet shattering the window where Tadgh stood, nearly taking his head off.

The Volunteers opened fire from the other windows and a gun battle ensued, no combatants drawing blood.

Tadgh returned to the temporary infirmary on the main floor. Morgan's thigh wound had turned ugly. As the dressing was changed, Tadgh glimpsed swelling, blisters, and oozing pus at the wound site.

He had mapped out a northward route to O'Casey's home on Mountjoy Square on the other side of the River Liffey, one that he hoped would avoid both Trinity College and the area of the GPO where he knew British forces would be active. He had to get Morgan to the Rotunda Women's Hospital in Parnell Square, a quarter mile north of the Post Office and only five blocks west from his mentor's digs. Although they specialized in maternity at the hospital, he knew they would not turn away a seriously wounded woman.

Tadgh hoped that the gun battle on the other side of the building would give him the cover he needed to get Morgan safely away from the college. He wore no uniform and carried his concealed Luger and Webley handguns. Matching the lettering on the hotel sign he had seen through his binoculars, he affixed the crudely-made sign reading 'Shelbourne Hotel Courier Service' to the frame of his motorcycle.

Tadgh carried Morgan, wrapped in a blanket, through the south doorway out of sight of St. Stephen's Green, then gently lowered her into the wicker sidecar of the Kerry. They escaped undetected and skirted the south end of St. Stephens Green, heading east just as the gunfire near the college intensified. Tadgh hoped that the British didn't bring more forces to bear on Mallin's battalion. He could see no sign of British troops advancing on the park from this vantage point.

When he guessed he had traveled far enough to the southeast, Tadgh turned northeast on Fitzwilliam Place, passing first Fitzwilliam, and later Merion Squares before reaching Mount Street. He could hear single-shot gunfire in the distance off to his right. Eamon de Valera's battalion must have encountered some northbound advancing British forces, meaning that reinforcements had arrived at Kingstown Harbour from England. *I'd better hurry.*

Tadgh reached the south bank of the River Liffey on City Quay at Holles Street. He had passed two armored vehicles whose occupants had given him a look but had not stopped him.

Reaching the Quay, a quarter mile east of Trinity College, ahead on the left in the river, a British war ship loomed opposite the

Custom House. *Damnation. So much for Connolly's belief that they won't destroy the city infrastructure with artillery.*

Tadgh checked with his binoculars. The HMY *Helga* was a one hundred and fifty-foot, single stack, armed auxiliary patrol yacht. Tadgh could see sailors already yawing twin twelve-pounder guns in the direction of Liberty House, less than 500 feet away to the northwest. He hoped to hell that there was no one left inside the ICA headquarters.

The big guns belched fire, pounding the air with concussive force. Even a thousand yards away to the east, Tadgh's eardrums popped. He watched as the western top corner of Liberty Hall exploded. The front entrance doors and surrounding structure disintegrated. Tadgh stood, mesmerized as the *Helga's* crew dismantled the top of the rebel fortress, piece by piece. He watched as the "We Serve neither King nor Kaiser but Ireland" banner shredded. Their line of fire was somewhat obstructed by the adjacent railway Loop Line Bridge and parallel Butt Bridge over the Liffey. Thank God they stopped this floating menace from sailing farther upriver, closer to the GPO. The enemy was going to raze the city to get at the brave rebels. *Maybe the martyrdom will work after all, but with a terrible toll on Dublin and its citizenry.*

Looking above and northwest of this scene of destruction with the binoculars, Tadgh saw the Republican tricolor and Green Irish Republic flags fluttering in the breeze on top of the GPO, up O'Connell Street, three hundred yards from the river. The headquarters of the New Irish Republic could not be more than a half mile away, and that structure would be next. Tadgh wondered if the *Helga's* guns could be elevated high enough over the bridges to attack the GPO. He hoped not. But heaven help them. He felt sick at heart.

This attack on Liberty House proved Connolly wrong. If the *Helga* couldn't do the job, other artillery would. Tadgh hoped to hell that those shells were not packed with Lyddite. If so, each one would kill many from the concussive force alone. He knew from his training that these lethal guns had a range of at least six miles, hardly needed for this engagement. As if this wasn't bad enough, he could hear the staccato bursts of deadly machine gun fire erupting in the distance. A few outdated single-shot rifles, pitchforks, and pikes in the hands of the rebels, against powerful artillery. *Defenseless.*

Tadgh was helpless to change the course of this attack, and he had dallied too long. Morgan desperately needed medical attention. He knew that he would have to risk crossing the bridge directly under the artillery barrage causing the architectural carnage. He headed west along City Quay to the Butt Bridge over the Liffey at the western end of the Customs House. As he approached, he could plainly see the temporary checkpoint that had been set up at the south side of the crossing, and quite a few soldiers stood at the west rail on the bridge intently watching the fireworks upriver. They pointed and laughed as Liberty Hall crumbled.

Smart move, Tadgh thought. *They're establishing control along the river to split our forces north from south and cut off our supply lines. That's probably why the courier information from the GPO has dried up already.*

There was no way around it. Tadgh had to get Morgan to the north side of the river. Earlier in the morning, she had been delirious, but in the last hour, she had gone silent. He hoped that she stayed that way at least until they got across the bridge. It would be disastrous for her to blurt out rebel information. Despite this risk, Tadgh made sure that Morgan's head was visible and then drove right up to the checkpoint.

"Good morning sir," he addressed the corporal in charge. "I need your help, if ya please."

"What's your business here?" the corporal asked, eyeing Tadgh and Morgan closely. "Don't you know there's a war going on and that Brigadier General Lowe has just imposed martial law? There's been looting, so we have imposed a curfew."

"Please, sir. I must get my sister to the Rotunda Hospital," Tadgh explained. "We were staying at the Shelbourne Hotel as visitors to your fine city. Then, yesterday this war started, and the rebels shot my sister in the leg. They tried to help us at the hotel, but this morning I was told her situation is desperate, and she needs to get to the hospital. So, they lent me their motorcycle."

"Show me your papers or some other identification," the corporal demanded, leveling his carbine at Tadgh's chest. "How do I know that you aren't rebels, yourselves?"

Tadgh shrugged. "We left the hotel in a hurry and I forgot my identification."

"Show me the wound, then."

Tadgh uncovered Morgan's leg wound, which was festering and oozing. She moaned in her semi-conscious state. He was relieved that she did not inadvertently give away their affiliation. "Can you give me an escort to the hospital? It does not seem too safe out there, does it, now?"

"We can't leave our post, son. You'll have to find the way on your own. I don't like your chances in the war zone."

With that, he summarily shooed them through the checkpoint, forgetting that they had not provided any identification whatsoever. When he left the north end of the bridge and turned east on Custom House Quay, Tadgh felt the blast from another shell as it found its mark. It was all he could do to keep the bike under control as shards of stone from the hall rained down on them.

They arrived intact at Number Thirty-Five Mountjoy Square[2] at nine in the morning. The only sound Morgan had uttered since they left the college was that moan when Tadgh uncovered her wound for the corporal. He could see that her condition had worsened.

Tadgh hoped that Sean O'Casey would be at home since *an Stad* pub, which his friend habitually frequented, was likely closed if not damaged. Tadgh pulled up at the fine Georgian row home at the southeast corner of this magnificent square and knocked. The eighteen stately two-story homes on each side of this open park were each distinguishable by a unique colored front door. Another elite neighborhood. At least this one wasn't under siege, yet.

Sean came to his hunter green door in pajamas, disheveled as usual.

"Good God, Tadgh, you'll get shot driving around in the open like that," he blurted by way of a greeting. Then he must have seen the look of anguish in his pupil's eyes. "I'm too late for that warning, aren't I?"

"Morgan's been shot, and I desperately need your help, Sean." Tadgh opened the blanket to reveal his stricken colleen. "She's got to get to Rotunda right away, and I can't go there, that's for sure." In Dublin, he had been a wanted man even before the Rising.

Sean knew without asking what that meant.

"You've got to take her and say she's your younger sister from out of town," Tadgh pleaded, grasping Sean's hand and placing it on Morgan's fevered brow. "They'll believe you, Sean. They know you're a pacifist."

"Do I have enough time to get dressed, lad?" his mentor asked.

"I guess it might look suspicious if they saw you driving my motorcycle down Grenville Street in your nightclothes. Although I'd like to see that myself." Tadgh tried to grin, but his mouth went slack. "Seriously, Sean, this woman means more to me than life itself."

"Consider it done, me boyo," Sean said, as he rushed off to get ready.

Tadgh tried to make Morgan understand what was about to happen. Her delirium had worsened, but he thought from the flicker in her eyes that she was cognizant of the trouble they were in. He could not lose her. Not now, not ever.

Sean was ready to go in five minutes. "You have a telephone, Sean?"

"Aye. Yeats at the Abbey Theatre insisted I have one. But I'm not sure it still works with this insurrection."

"I need to go to the GPO, but I'll wait here until I hear back from you. After that, I'll find a way to call you to get Morgan's status. I owe you one, Sean."

"Mark my words, you'll owe me more than that before this Rising is over, lad."

"That's certain, Teacher."

"It's been years since I drove one of these contraptions," Sean said, as he deftly slipped the Kerry into first gear. A moment later, before Tadgh could instruct him, Sean and the motorcycle were already out of sight.

Tadgh felt terribly alone and helpless. He wasn't about to go to the GPO until he knew that Morgan would be all right. He already had a brother being treated near Tralee for a gunshot wound, and now, his beloved seriously wounded. These were dangerous times that they were living in. *Dangerous yet necessary.* If Pearse and the others could martyr themselves, then he, Morgan, and Aidan had to do their part. *Although, losing Morgan is unacceptable.*

For the first time since his parents were murdered, there was something at least as important as the revolution in his mind, and it was driving him crazy.

Rather than letting his thoughts get the better of him, Tadgh had to do something. He checked the phone, expecting it to be disconnected, and amazingly, an operator responded when he cranked the handle. Tadgh realized that the British still had control of the telephone exchange. If the Volunteers had captured it, then there would have been no service. The Limey bastards probably cut off service to the Republican strong points. *No wonder we have had to rely on couriers.*

"I'd like to call St. Patrick's Teachers Training School at Drumcondra, on the north side of Dublin, ma'am."

"I'm not supposed to place personal calls because of the fighting, sir."

"It's an emergency, ma'am. My son is at the school and his mother has been killed. I must reach him."

"Oh, all right then, sir. I am truly sorry for your loss."

Tadgh could hear ringing on the line and asked for his compatriot Peader O'Donnell when the school operator answered. As he waited on the line, Tadgh pictured Peader, a serious senior student with wiry, short brown hair, strong chiseled features, and a prominent nose. Tadgh remembered that Peader was a civil activist, a Larkinist, not yet committed to the need for armed insurrection. His deep-set piercing eyes and strong forehead revealed a determined character.

The headmaster came on the line and told him that the student was attending a political science class. *Great timing for that.* He said that they would have Peader return the call when he was finished and Tadgh gave him the number.

A few minutes later, the telephone rang. It was Sean.

"Tadgh, they admitted her. No questions asked. I told them she was caught in a cross-fire on O'Connell Street but managed to limp to my home."

"Can they help her, Sean?" Tadgh asked, twisting the cord on the receiver into a tangled knot.

"They say they have drugs to combat the infection. She'll have to stay there. It's too early to say if they can save the leg, but they are pretty sure that she'll live. Don't worry about the cost. I'll handle it. Can't let my younger sister down now, can I?"

"You're a godsend, O'Casey, to be sure!"

"You can write me another of your infamous plays some time, me boyo," Sean quipped, and then rang off.

Jaysus, what have I got her into, losing a leg?

The telephone rang again. Tadgh answered unsteadily.

"Tadgh, is that you?"

"Peader, it's great to hear a friendly voice, comrade," Tadgh said. "Do you know what's going on?"

"Of course. Your damned revolution."

"Our revolution, you mean."

"No, Tadgh. It's *your* revolution. It's more than civil unrest strikes, isn't it, now. You sound like you're in trouble. Want to tell me about it?"

"Not over the telephone, my friend. Can you come right now to the place we talked about?"

"On my way, Tadgh."

"Peader lad, bring your student card."

"Got it, Tadgh," Peader confirmed, and then he hung up.

Tadgh looked for Sean's supply of Jameson and found it in the kitchen cupboard. Then he remembered Mick's gesture before they left Liberty Hall. He had smashed a whiskey bottle in front of the Volunteers yelling, "Not like Ninety-Eight, my boys!" Apparently, the insurgents in Tones' rebellion of 1798 needed more than intestinal fortitude. He put the elixir back and slammed the cupboard shut.

Then he made another crucial telephone call and asked the man to hurry.

Peader pedaled his bicycle south to Mountjoy Square, arriving before Sean returned.

"Any sign of British forces, lad?" Tadgh asked, clapping his compatriot on the shoulder, ushering him into the kitchen.

"They're gathering up north. I overheard one of them say that about eighteen hundred arrived from the Curragh and Belfast yesterday, with Brigadier-General Lowe taking charge. They said that a lot more are arriving from England at Kingstown and heading north towards the city. They mean to cordon off your rebel positions from the north and south, splitting you up by gaining control of the Liffey."

It amazed Tadgh that Peader had gotten through the gauntlet and overheard such critical intelligence of British activity.

"Did you have to use your student card?"

"No, I managed to stay out of sight behind buildings as I traveled south."

"As I expected. Peader, they're shelling the city with a gunboat on the river."

"My God, Tadgh. They'll destroy the historical buildings. And that will mean a loss of life, civilians as well as military."

Tadgh slapped his friend on the back. "Come into Sean's kitchen for a minute, Peader. Your man Connolly's the Dublin Commandant in charge of the Volunteers."

"He's not my man, Tadgh. Too militant. Larkin was my man."

"You sound just like Sean, lad. Can't get the British out with words and labor strikes, I'm afraid. Connolly realizes that."

"The might of the British army will crush you, Tadgh. And that's the truth, to be sure."

"I think that's Pearse's plan, at this point." Tadgh left it at that. Peader shook his head in confusion.

"Well, then," Tadgh pressed. "Didn't your political science class teach you anything about the value of martyrdom?"

"I see your point now. It's a sad day for Ireland."

"Nonsense, it's a glorious day for Ireland." Tadgh rummaged through the kitchen cupboards. "I haven't eaten in a day. I wonder what Sean has got hidden away, here. Are you hungry, son?"

"No, what you've just said has turned my stomach."

Tadgh found a half loaf of bread and a block of Dubliner cheese, and brought them to the table. He sliced off a piece of cheese, paired it with a ripped hunk of bread, and urged Peader to sit and eat. "Where we're going, I'm not sure when we'll have our next meal."

Tadgh took some of the food and chewed. "This war has turned personal, now. Morgan's been shot in the thigh, and Sean O'Casey has taken her to hospital." Tadgh wiped his eye with the back of his hand, clearing tears that welled up. "I couldn't take her myself."

"Oh, no. How bad?" Peader leaned forward, putting his hand on Tadgh's shoulder.

"Don't know yet. Let's hope for the best."

"It must be hell for you to be separated from Morgan at this dangerous time."

"Yes." Tadgh coughed and changed the subject. He took a deep breath. "I have a mission to fulfill at the General Post Office, and then I think we should make a visit to the Royal Irish Academy."

"Now? In the middle of a Rising? St. Columba's *An Cathach*, right? Our little adventure."

"Yes, Peader. I think I will be sent back to St. Stephen's Green as the only courier left. That's where I came from, with the ICA forces, Mallin and Countess Markiewicz. They are under siege in the Royal College of Surgeons and won't be able to influence the outcome of the Rising. The Academy is only a couple of blocks from there. I'm sure that Mallin will approve it if we do some scouting along the way."

"You're all mad as hatters, you know. But all right, let's go, then. I'll come if the Clans Pact is involved, but just don't ask me to fight." He tore off a piece of bread. "I'd better have more cheese. It may be my last."

Tadgh handed him another slice and took some for himself. "We have to wait for Sean to get back first for an update on Morgan's condition, lad."

They waited an hour before Sean returned home.

He entered through the kitchen doorway and greeted them. "Tadgh, I've left the Kerry back in the alleyway behind the house. Hello, Peader." Sean clasped his hand. "It's been awhile since we met at *an Stad*. What are you doing here in the middle of a war?"

Peader shrugged. "Tadgh asked me to come and help him."

Turning to Tadgh, Sean's eyes rolled. "Can't you leave us pacifists out of it?"

"It's a non-war matter, Mr. O'Casey," Peader said, in defense of his friend.

"With Tadgh, it's never a non-war matter, me boyo. Be careful, lads."

"How is Morgan?" Tadgh asked, grabbing Sean by the lapels of his jacket.

"They admitted her and will get her a bed, but they are keeping her in the triage room so they can monitor her condition. At least she is resting comfortably now after they gave her morphine along with infection drugs. She woke up, and I told her why you couldn't be there with her. She knows that she is my younger sister."

"Thank God for that and your help, Sean." Tadgh let go of his mentor's jacket.

"She told me to tell you that she loves you desperately and that she won't let you off the hook just because you proposed in the heat of battle." Peader and Sean exchanged glances.

"Just like her, so it is." Tadgh laughed, breaking the tension. "That's why I'm crazy about that colleen, don't ya know."

"After this is all over, we'll help you keep your promise to her," Sean said.

"Good man, Sean." Tadgh picked up his jacket, then his gloves. "We have to go out now, but we'll be back. Sean, you're going to stay put here, I hope."

"Except for venturing out to check on Morgan."

They stepped out the kitchen door and Tadgh took the crude Shelbourne sign off his vehicle. "I'm going to leave my motorbike for you, Sean. If anyone asks, say it's yours. I'll call you when the time comes."

"Time for what, Tadgh?"

"Why, time to come get me, of course."

"Not into the inferno, me boyo."

"No, Sean. It will be in the opposite direction. Thank you, by the way, for looking after my girl."

"No problem, son. Just make sure I get to give the bride away at your wedding."

"It would be Morgan's delight," Tadgh exclaimed, as he and Peader headed west towards the gunfire in the distance.

Chapter Four
Easter Rising

Day Three - Return
Wednesday, April 26, 1916
Mountjoy Square, Dublin

*T*adgh took the long way around to the GPO. Peader gave him directions based on what he had seen earlier that morning. The route on foot first took them north, then southwest on Dorset Street, where the trams were not running. They passed the Rotunda Hospital in the distance on their left. Tadgh would have loved to get in to see Morgan to make sure she was safe, but the armed guards he spied at the entrance convinced him not to try. He realized that he could not help her if he was captured. He trusted Sean, but it maddened him that he would not be able to communicate directly with Morgan. It made him think of just how much he counted on her now, and how empty he felt without her.

"Don't go any farther this way, Tadgh," Peader advised, pointing towards the Four Courts off to the west. "Brigadier General Lowe must be moving southeast into the city with his men by now."

"I think we can still get through the back way down Moore Street, comrade." They headed south on Domenick Street Lower, jogging at Great Britain Street. "This is likely the only possible retreat route for our GPO boys when the time comes," he said, stopping at the intersection of Henry Place.

"For obvious reasons, the Moore Street market is deserted," Peader said, as they turned toward the GPO.

Tadgh put up his hand and stopped them when they were northwest and back of the post office, so they could take in the situation. Eastward beyond the massive edifice, and to its right

71

towards the Liffey, he heard the first shell hit the building just to the south on the O'Connell Street side. Debris flew skyward and the smell of cordite filled their nostrils. The concussive force made their ears ring. The bombardment by the gun-ship on the Liffey had apparently begun.

"This is getting dangerous," Peader said, ducking behind a building on the corner of Henry Street.

Tadgh drew his Luger and flicked off the safety. "Welcome to the war. Easy, lad. Just follow me."

They trotted towards the back door of the GPO. It was one in the afternoon.

When they tried to open the barricaded door, Tadgh heard a woman's voice he recognized as Elizabeth O'Farrell call out, "Mick, there's men at the back door." Rifles pointed through broken windows and Peader thought that they were going to be shot on the spot.

Tadgh glared at the barrels of the guns pointed at their hearts and then pounded on the door, "Mick. It's me, Tadgh. I bring news from Commandant Mallin."

Finally, the door cracked open long enough for them to be dragged inside. "Tadgh, for the love o' Mike. You almost died here today, my friend," Michael Collins scolded. "Who is this with you?"

"A friend, and an ally of James Connolly, don't ya know?" Peader shot his companion a dirty look.

Tadgh holstered his Luger. "A little trigger happy, are we?" he teased, with a slap on Collins' clean-pressed epaulet.

Tadgh glanced around at the disheveled condition of the once stately three-story post office. Tables, chairs, cabinets, coat racks, books and myriad other paraphernalia were stacked in jumbled fashion against all the doors facing O'Connell Street. Mail was strewn about like so much confetti, undoubtedly dropped in haste by patrons who ran when the Republicans commandeered the building for their headquarters.

The cavernous expanse of the main foyer was crowded with

the chaotic occupation of three hundred harried souls. Tadgh could hear the ICA Leader, James Connolly barking orders somewhere in the distance. The garbled sound of his shouts echoed off the walls and lofty ceiling like an announcer's voice crackling over a crystal set radio. Many of the men who had rifles stood guard at the windows facing O'Connell Street. Others huddled in small groups, their pikes and pitchforks stacked up against the wall. Padraig was writing furiously at a table in the far corner with Tom Clarke and Joseph Plunkett hovering over him. An anxious anticipation of the Grim Reaper pervaded the hall, so much so that it raised the hair on the back of Tadgh's neck. He could see from the horrified look in Peader's eyes that he sensed it, too.

"This must be what Colonel Custer's men must have been feeling just before they were ordered to charge into the battle of the Big Horn in America," Tadgh commented, stepping forward into the tumult. Clearly, that direct hit on the building next door by cannon fire was causing this commotion.

Mick overheard the comment. "Next time it will be guerrilla warfare, Tadgh. Attack and run. This sardine can approach is suicidal at best. But I take orders from Plunkett, so here we are."

"The situation's the same at St. Stephen's Green, Mick. They machine-gunned us from the top of the Shelbourne and forced us to hole up in the Royal College of Surgeons. It's a strong fortification, but we're helpless to attack."

"How many men lost, Tadgh?" Collins needed to know.

"I'd say twenty out of a hundred. They got my partner in the leg when she jumped up to save one of the wounded men."

"I'm sorry to hear that, Tadgh. We haven't lost but a few here, as yet. Elizabeth and the other ladies have yet to be challenged with their nursing skills."

"Where are the couriers, Mick?"

"We can't get the couriers through at this stage. The bastards have set up machine guns at the end of O'Connell Street. They are systematically driving us back out of the businesses."

"I think that artillery you just heard is from a gun-boat in the Liffey opposite the Customs House, Mick. I saw it raze Liberty Hall earlier this morning with two twelve-pounders when I was on my way here."

"We've been hearing it. Connolly still can't believe that they will destroy the city."

"Believe it, friend! You're an easy target."

"I think this was part of Pearse's plan."

"I know that, Mick."

"So, how did you get through?"

"My job is communications and transportation, remember? I'm an apparition snaking through enemy lines, don't ya know? The men seem resigned to their fate, Mick."

"It's a glorious but sad day, if you know what I mean, Tadgh. Some of us have to survive, to rise like a phoenix from the ashes of this martyrdom. Our leaders believe that this is a necessary steppingstone to freedom. I believe it will ignite our people to act next time. But not now."

"What's the backup plan?"

"If necessary, withdraw to the west and hook up with Ned's battalion at the Four Courts."

"That's not much of a plan, Mick. We heard gunfire to the west on the way down here. I expect that Ned has his hands full at this point." Tadgh relayed everything that he had heard from Peader. "The bastards are coming from the northwest and southeast, obviously starting a campaign to isolate and destroy each of our strongholds. They've already cut our communications lines, so they will soon completely choke off our supply lines as well."

"We know, Tadgh. The mood here is to hold our Republic free for as long as possible so that we can prove our point."

"And what point might that be?" Peader asked, stepping up to Collins' face. "To upset the population when their city is destroyed?"

"No, to show our people that they can be free of the tyrants if they will only rise up and throw them out," Collins stated emphatically, his eyes blazing at Peader.

Tadgh changed the subject. "I've got to talk to Padraig to find out what he wants me to do now."

"Not now, friend. He's busy writing some follow-up proclamation."

"What good will that do?" Tadgh questioned, glancing across the main room to see his boss still furiously writing at the desk. "He already issued the main one at the outset."

"Messages for the next war, I suspect," Mick slapped his forehead. "That's what you get when academics lead a revolution."

"But Connolly seems to know what he is doing."

"He's the salt of the earth, Tadgh. I'd follow him to hell itself. Listen, boys. You can't help us much here. We have enough martyrs for one building. You should return to the college, if you can, and take them the message that we are still in control here. Tell them that we heard on this side of the river that Ned—"

Wham! The eastern windows rattled and lit up from an explosion. They rushed to look out, seeing Clery's Department Store across the street ablaze, a gaping hole where the shop's front windows used to be. The Easter fashions display had vaporized. Looking south, they saw a barricade fully engulfed in flames.

"Damn, it's really started." Tadgh could see the puzzled look on Michael's face. Tadgh reasoned, "That incendiary artillery shell didn't come from the gunship. Trajectory's all wrong. Looks to me that it came from Trinity College." The reality of defeat had already set in. *At least Morgan is safe at the hospital.* He prayed that would remain true.

Just then, looking right down O'Connell Street, Tadgh saw another flash light up the sky as the Imperial Hotel took a direct hit.

"Go on, get out of here!" Mick ordered them, turning on his heel to find his boss, Plunkett.

"Take care of yourself, Mick. Tell Padraig I admire his courage." Tadgh saluted as they headed for the back door.

"We're heading into the lion's den, don't ya know," Tadgh exclaimed, as they ran west on Henry, turning south on Liffey Street towards the river. "I sure hope we're still holding City Hall."

When Tadgh and Peader approached the Ha'penny footbridge, Tadgh expected a British blockade, but no one was manning the turnstiles.

"We've got to be careful now," Tadgh cautioned, as they crossed over the Liffey. "We'll be passing between the Castle and Trinity College, both known British strongholds. If we're challenged, we are students caught in a war zone while visiting Temple Bar pubs. You'll need to show your student card."

"Got it. I sure hope that we get useful information about *an Cathach* after all this craziness."

"Revolutionary war is not crazy, my friend. Just bloody dangerous," Tadgh muttered, as they padded across the bridge.

Tadgh sensed the enemy's presence. Looking left down Crampton Quay on the south side of the Liffey, he saw two British Highlanders marching in time towards them.

Thinking quickly, Tadgh whispered, "Walk slowly west along Wellington Quay. Remember, we're students. I've got a plan if we're challenged."

The soldiers caught up to them before they got to Fownes Street. "Halt, you two," the older soldier ordered. "What are you doing here?"

With the attitude of an arrogant student, Peader slurred, "We're just students from St. Patrick's College looking for a pint and tryin' to stay away from all that gunfire." Peader produced his student identification and showed it to the officer.

"Are you two stupid?" the younger soldier scolded. "There's martial law, and you are breaking it. Show me your identification," he demanded of Tadgh.

Tadgh reached into his pocket, as if to get his identification, and cocked his Luger. He didn't think they heard the sound of it.

"We've been caught here for two days, ever since the fighting started, sir," he responded, weaving from side to side. "Can you show us a safe route back to our college?"

"The only route I'll show you is the road to the Castle," the older man sneered. "You're lucky we didn't shoot you on sight. Them's our orders. Now where's that identification?"

Tadgh signaled to Peader with his eyes. Then he calmly drew his gun from his pocket and pointed it directly at the younger soldier's forehead.

"I would advise you both to put your weapons on the ground in front of you."

They appeared to comply, but at the last second, the younger soldier scooped his revolver back up and fired from the hip. The bullet grazed Tadgh's cheek as he jumped back. "Down," Tadgh yelled at Peader, as he rolled to his left and shot the younger soldier between the eyes.

The older soldier had grabbed his rifle in the commotion, and Tadgh turned to shoot him. Click. The next bullet in the Luger jammed in the breach.

"Run," he commanded, and he and Peader took off like rabbits, zigzagging west down Wellington Quay.

The older soldier stood his ground while he tried to shoot them down. Bullets went whizzing by their heads as they darted left, then right down the quay. The Highlander stopped firing long enough to blow a shrill whistle for assistance and reload his Enfield rifle.

When they reached Fownes Street, Tadgh looked back and saw the soldier hot on their heels. He yanked Peader around the corner, and they ran south. When they reached Temple Bar, Tadgh pushed Peader through a pub's swinging doors. The establishment was empty of patrons, and the lone barkeep had stayed to clean glasses and protect her bar from looters.

"Well, I'll be. If it isn't Tadgh McCarthy," Deirdre shouted, motioning them in with her arms. "You still on the run, are you? Get over here, you two."

They ducked behind the bar at her feet.

It took the older soldier a minute to assess the situation when he turned south on Fownes and found they had disappeared. A minute later, he entered the pub after he failed to see them running down Temple Bar.

"We're closed," Deirdre growled at the man. "Thanks to your war."

The soldier ignored the remark. "Did you see two blokes come through here a minute ago?"

"I told you, we're closed," Deirdre answered, pointing at the sign on the door. "Of course there's been no one in here. No customers and no money." She shrugged her shoulders.

"What if I said that I don't believe you?"

"Then I would say, look for yourself if you want to waste your time."

As the soldier approached the high bar, Deirdre lifted her floor-length skirts and dropped them over the two fugitives. Fortunately, there was no mirror behind her.

"Do you know the penalty for harboring a rebel, one that just killed my partner?"

"You don't scare me," Deirdre shot back, not intimidated. "I told you there is nobody here, except you abusing me."

"How dare you talk back to an officer of the Royal Army," he snarled, and slapped her across the cheek, making it bleed.

Deirdre's eyes blazed with disgust.

"Stay right where you are," he ordered her, "while I search the premises."

Tadgh could hear him ransacking the kitchen, then heavy boots thudding upstairs.

"You know where to go," Deirdre whispered to Tadgh. He wanted to wring the soldier's neck but he was afraid that that might incriminate Deirdre if the soldier got away. So, they crawled out from under the woman's skirts, and he led Peader through a hole in the pantry wall, pulling a barrel back to cover the opening behind them. Once seated on the cold floor, he cleared the jammed weapon in the dark.

A minute or so later, the soldier bounded back down the stairs. After scanning the pantry from its entrance, he strode back into the pub. Stepping behind the long, walnut bar, he pushed Deirdre aside and proceeded to carefully examine the cubbyholes underneath.

"I told you that no one came in here," Deirdre commented calmly, as she resumed washing the glasses.

Without a word of apology, the soldier rushed out of the pub blowing his whistle and the sound echoed down Temple Lane.

The pub owner waited until the whistling faded away before bringing the men out of the hole. "What's going on, Tadgh?" she asked, as he administered a cold compress from the bar to her cheek.

"This Rising—a call to arms for all true Irishmen," Tadgh responded. "Not now, but shortly."

"They're tearing up this town, you know."

"That's the British bastards' doing," Tadgh said, vehemently. "Bullies don't like to give up their turf."

"And who's this with you, if I might ask?"

"I'm Peader O'Donnell, ma'am, a colleague of Tadgh."

"And why were you running?"

"Because that bastard was going to arrest us. Is your telephone working, my dear?" Tadgh motioned to the instrument behind the bar.

"It was a while ago. Try it."

Tadgh contacted the operator and gave her Sean's number. He answered on the third ring.

"Where are you?" Sean asked, through a crackling receiver.

"We're south of the river and safe for now. How's Morgan?"

"I just got back from the hospital. She's in her room, recovering. The doctor thinks he can save the leg."

Tadgh let out a loud sigh of relief. "Thank God."

"But she's still running a high fever, Tadgh. By the way, she thinks I'd make a very distinguished father of the bride."

"That you will, O'Casey. That you will."

"If you don't get yourself killed, that is, me boyo."

Tadgh had to take the chance that the operator was not listening. "Listen, Sean, I'm having my fishing boat brought to a dock at Howth Harbour. She's a Galway hooker with a dark gray mainsail. Her current name is *Morgan's Quest*, and you can't miss her. The captain's name is Martin Murphy, an old salty dog. Assuming your telephone continues to work, I will call you when it's time to come and get me from there. Can you get Peader's bicycle into the sidecar?"

"Yes, no problem. When?"

"Don't know, dear friend. It depends on how quickly the bastards close the net. I suspect Friday or Saturday. The hooker should be at the dock by tomorrow night. If you don't hear from me again, go there at six in the evening on Friday."

"Will do. Stay alive, lad." Sean hung up.

Turning to his brave female compatriot, Tadgh gave her a big kiss on her bruised cheek and a squeeze with his muscular arms.

She kissed him back, lingering in his embrace.

"You are an angel from heaven, Deirdre. We will repay you in kind someday, my dear," he promised, encircling her shapely waist.

She shrugged off the compliment. "I heard what you said on the telephone, Tadgh. Is Morgan going to be all right?"

"Yes, God willing. She's at Rotunda with a leg wound right now."

"Serious?"

"Serious enough."

"Boys, you are going to get yourselves killed, you know. They'll be watching for you if you've murdered one of 'em."

"Self-defense," Peader countered, coming to Tadgh's aid.

"Meaningless distinction," Deirdre countered, placing two shot glasses on the bar and reaching for the Jameson. "Where are you headed?"

"St. Stephen's Green. No whisky for us, thanks, lass."

"Well now, there's a switch. Tadgh McCarthy—a teetotaler."

"We need our wits about us now, don't we."

"Your brother Aidan's told some tales about you to my waitress Aileen, I can tell you."

"All in the past, Deirdre. And Aidan's a changed man, a staunch supporter of our revolution."

"Is he, now." The voluptuous pub owner's eyes flashed with skepticism, remembering his character when she first met Tadgh and Morgan. "Is he with you, then?"

"He's incapacitated in Tralee, lass. Shot in the leg less than a week ago saving Morgan and me from being murdered by that foul RIC bastard who was here in this very pub searching for Aidan last July, as you'll remember."

Deirdre's eyes darkened. "Are all the loves in your life shot in the leg now?"

Tadgh realized it was true. *What a week.* "Sadly, yes, but it's all for a glorious cause. How did you know about Morgan and me?"

"I'm a woman, Tadgh. I could see the love in your eyes last year, how you protected her." Deirdre put away the Jameson.

Tadgh remembered. It was the morning after he and Morgan had first made love at the rebel-frequented *an Stad* hotel, when that Fenian patriot O'Donovan Rossa lay in state before his funeral. So long ago, so much had happened here and in Belgium. And now she lay in serious trouble in the hospital because of him. He ached to go to her.

Peader checked his watch and brought them back to the present. "They may come back for us."

Tadgh remembered Boyle coming back to the pub in search of Aidan just before Rossa's funeral. "Yes, right, Peader. We must be going."

"The Green, is it?" Deirdre looked worried for them. "So near and yet so far. You've got to get past the Castle-Trinity strongholds, don't you. Can you wait until dark?"

"We've got to go now."

Deirdre put her hand on Tadgh's forearm and said, "Come with me."

Ten minutes later, Deirdre left the pub by the back door with two other women. It was five in the afternoon. All three had broad-brimmed hats pulled down to shield their faces, and Deirdre carried the Good Book in her hand. Tadgh felt the undersized corset pinching his lower back and the top of this torture contraption stuffed with socks made him a comical, mustached spectacle. Yet he had newfound respect for womankind and the agony they went through to look appealing for their men.

"Come on, Peader. It's not that bad, is it, lad?" Tadgh could see that his compatriot was less than pleased with their disguises.

Peader adjusted the padded bustier. "Putting on these long dresses over our clothes is damned uncomfortable." He laughed. "I'm going to trip over the hem and break my neck. How can women possibly wear these things?"

"You lads have no idea how we women suffer for you."

Tadgh flashed her a smile. "Deirdre, you've done wonders with these flowing wigs and floppy Easter bonnets, but this face paint doesn't cover my stubble," he said, rubbing his cheek with his knuckles.

"They're looking for two men, not three women," she suggested. "You two look a fetching sight, I must say. That flower print dress of mine does something to light up your dour eyes, Peader."

Deirdre locked her establishment up tighter than a drum to deter looters, and they headed out.

Tadgh hoped they wouldn't run into the same soldier who would undoubtedly recognize her.

Walking briskly down Fownes, the trio came to Dame Street, the main conduit between the Castle and Trinity. Tadgh could see the intense activity of soldiers coming and going from the Castle and City Hall.

"Stop a minute," Peader said, hiking up the waistband of his dress.

Deirdre turned to him and smiled. "Being a woman isn't that easy, is it, Peader?"

"Damn, the capital building has already fallen to the enemy," Tadgh announced sadly, turning his compatriots east, away from the danger.

From the direction of College Park just north of Trinity, the artillery was bombarding O'Connell Street, filling the area with smoke. The smell of cordite permeated Dame Street and caused their eyes to water. They could hardly make themselves heard over the din of the booming guns. Tadgh noticed that all the firepower seemed to be focused northward toward the GPO.

Tadgh thought that they had safely bypassed the trouble after they had jogged east on Dames Street and south on Great Georges Street to the South City Market. This Victorian-style arcade with its myriad shops and stalls, rebuilt after the city fire of 1892, housed everything from cutting-edge fashion and curios, to fortune tellers and restaurants. Tadgh had spent time there during his Dublin days. It thrived in the shadow of the Great Castle to its west.

"Normally this market would be teeming with patrons looking for a good buy, or their evening supper," Deirdre commented, peering into the cavernous interior. "Today it's like a morgue."

At a side entrance that had either been broken into or inadvertently left open, they observed empty stalls devoid of life, and there was some evidence of looting. So much for their ruse of being hungry women looking for an evening meal, blending in with the surge of humanity.

They were isolated in a city at war under martial law. They had just emerged from the market to turn south down Great George Street when three Sherwood Foresters came swaggering down from the Castle's east side. The three women saw that they were already well into their cups as they approached, weaving unsteadily up the street. Tadgh guessed that Deirdre was experienced in handling these sorts in the confines of her own pub, but out here, she could have her hands full.

When they got close enough, he could see that they had lust in their eyes and in their hearts. They joked with each other about how these tarts would help erase the memory of seeing their friends gunned down earlier that day. Each of the Foresters singled out a woman and moved to grope her. Tadgh realized that he and his friends had the element of surprise on their side, but an open street fight directly below the battlements of the Castle would be disastrous.

"This way," he beckoned to the group in a falsetto voice, as he led them back through the open door and into the arcade. Deirdre could see Tadgh's reasoning, but Peader was bristling at the thought of what might come next.

The Foresters took the bait, likely thinking that these women were willing whores. When they were inside the arcade and out of view from the Castle, Deirdre held up her Bible and said, "Will you handsome young gentlemen accompany us to St. Patrick's Cathedral? We were just on our way to Evening Mass."

"A likely story, whore," the biggest soldier laughed as he grabbed her arm and ripped off her hat. "I like a girl with a sense of humor. Come and show me your wares, me darling." With that, he started to tear at her blouse.

"What—?" a second infantryman said, tearing at the bodice of Tadgh's dress.

Tadgh sprang into action. Pulling his knife from the top of his boot, he sliced the second soldier just below the jugular, and the man dropped without uttering another syllable. The third soldier went for his rifle, but Tadgh's throw was on target as the knife lodged in the man's chest, likely piercing his heart. He fell silently at Peader's feet.

By this time, the remaining Forester must have realized his predicament. He was holding Deirdre by the throat with his left arm and using her as a shield. The man raised his rifle. Tadgh could not let the soldier fire his weapon. The sound would bring reinforcements from the Castle.

He shot a look to Deirdre and gestured with his foot. She nodded and kicked her right leg back and up. Her heel caught the soldier squarely in the balls. Not the reception that he had been hoping for a few minutes earlier. He squealed and let go of the real woman.

She dropped and rolled away, and Tadgh came in for the finish. Still struggling with the sudden pain, the attacker tried to aim his weapon.

"Bastard!" the soldier shouted, as Tadgh lunged and ripped the rifle out of the soldier's right hand. Tadgh heard the man's wrist snap. The gun discharged, the bullet missing Deirdre by inches. The muscular soldier, taller than Tadgh, desperately fought for his life, which made him even more dangerous. With his good arm, he clawed at Tadgh's face and got him in a choking headlock. Peader came to Tadgh's rescue and kicked the soldier's legs from under him. As he fell, Tadgh reversed the headlock, and the Forester's neck broke with a sickening crunch.

"Damn, now we're in for it." Tadgh planted his boot on the corpse and pulled his knife free, blood splashing onto the hem of his dress. He stepped over the other soldier's body sprawled in the doorway. Peering from the arcade, he saw activity on the battlements. Soldiers were looking and pointing in their direction. No time to drag the Forester back out of sight.

"Let's go," Tadgh ordered, grabbing Deirdre by the arm and pulling her out into the street.

The three women walked briskly south on Great George Street. The east door of the Castle gate burst open and several soldiers emerged at a trot.

"Run!" Tadgh yelled, and the three took flight. He was not going to risk hand-to-hand combat again with enemy numbers like that. Tadgh knew that they were only three blocks from the back of the Royal College of Surgeons. He hoped that the Republicans still had control there.

When they turned east on Stephen's Strand, the soldiers were about three hundred feet behind them. "It's damn hard to run in women's clothes," Tadgh shouted, pushing Deirdre out ahead of him. "No wonder men can chase you colleens down at will."

"It's no wonder we let you catch us," Deirdre quipped, not looking back.

"As you should," Tadgh shot back, as bullets whizzed past them. He wished that he hadn't dragged Deirdre and Peader into this dangerous situation. But she had insisted on accompanying them, adding credibility to their womanly ruse.

Sprinting down Mercer Street, they came to the back of the College situated to their left. One of the soldiers closed to about a hundred feet behind the three, so the other pursuers stopped shooting. Tadgh could see that Deirdre was running out of steam, so he grabbed her arm once again and urged her onwards. They turned left on York Street, rounding the college just as the fastest soldiers neared to fifty feet.

Damn. "Keep going," Tadgh urged his compatriots. "The door is just ahead on your left." He stopped to deal with the first soldier to give them time to reach safety. When the four other soldiers rounded the corner of the building, they knelt down to take aim and fire at Tadgh. *At least my friends will make it.* Tadgh drew his Luger and prepared for the worst.

The door to the College burst open. Strong arms yanked Peader and Deirdre inside, and six Republicans rushed out, guns drawn. Tadgh turned towards the oncoming soldiers, dropped down prone on the cobblestones, and shot the first soldier in the chest.

When the shooting stopped, the five soldiers and one of the Republicans lay dead in the middle of York Street. Republicans rushed out of the College, gathering up the British weapons and ammunition and laid the contorted, bloody bodies in a row, out of respect. The British would have to risk being shot themselves to retrieve their dead comrades. Then the rebels withdrew with their fallen warrior. Unscathed, Tadgh picked himself up and helped a wounded comrade back into the building, thankful to be alive.

Tadgh was the last courier to reach Mallin's trapped battalion. Inside, he could see misery in the men's exhausted faces. Cooped up in the stone mausoleum with no heat and little food, they remained at their stations, defending the building at all costs. A few of the men turned from their posts and mustered grins at Tadgh's unusual uniform.

"Thanks for saving our lives," Tadgh told the men who had protected their arrival.

Constance was already tending to the wounded Republican that Tadgh had dragged to safety. "Thank *you* for saving mine," the man murmured, through clenched teeth.

Commandant Mallin strode up. "Well, you made it back to us," he boomed for all to hear. "What news do you bring?" He grinned. "And quite the disguise, I must say. Don't tell me what possessed you to transform yourselves."

Tadgh took him aside to speak privately. "Sir, you will not be pleased when I tell you what I know. You may wish to censure what you tell the troops at this stage."

As he explained the situation to the commandant, Tadgh could see Mallin's facial expression go from curious anticipation to abject disappointment. This was not lost on the Republicans who were watching their commander at that moment.

"We heard the artillery but didn't know what was being shelled," was all he said, the bitter military truth of the matter sinking in.

"That's why the courier system has broken down," Tadgh concluded, staring intently into his commander's eyes. "We're all isolated strongholds without outside assistance, ordered to hold out as long as possible to demonstrate for future generations of true Irishmen that freedom can be won through blood sacrifice."

"So be it, then," Mallin said.

Constance had overheard the conversation and approached her defiant commandant. "The men and women deserve to know the truth."

Mallin nodded agreement and then went off to tell his troops the unhappy news. Tadgh marveled at the rebellious reaction from the men. They would not surrender. He was quite proud of them at that moment.

"How is Morgan doing, Tadgh?" the countess asked.

"She's in hospital, Constance. They think they may be able to save her leg. Thank you for letting me get her there. She would have died, to be sure."

"Glad to hear it." The countess smiled at Tadgh's feminine getup. "I won't even ask what necessitated your gaudy plumage, Tadgh. Please introduce me to this fine lady who has bravely accompanied you through the gauntlet." Countess Markiewicz fingered the silk bodice of Peader's disguise. Impressed by the countess's poise under fire, Tadgh made the introductions for Deirdre and Peader, who were both recovering from the ordeal. While Constance chatted with Deirdre, the men doffed their getups, and breathed great sighs of relief.

"You are both welcome here," Constance offered, taking Deirdre by the hand. "We know that this is currently not your fight, but as true Irish citizens, you will come to realize the importance of this Rising."

"I am beginning to see the necessity of this sacrifice in order to achieve our freedom," Peader announced, taking in the cluttered room and haggard faces.

Tadgh was shocked at Peader's change of heart. "I thought that Larkin was your man."

"That was before I witnessed the British destruction of our beloved Dublin and its people, Tadgh."

"I'm just a shopkeeper who loves her country, her God, and her friends," Deirdre shared solemnly. "The Crusaders fought and died to protect the faithful, so it is fitting that the righteous battle should be continued here today."

Deirdre's words gave Tadgh new insight into the fervor of her religious beliefs. He realized that there was more than met the eye to the spunky lass.

After he had informed his ICA troops, Commandant Mallin returned to the temporary infirmary. "Tadgh, you have done us a great service at significant peril to yourself and your friends. Thank you all for your contribution to the cause."

"I'd like to continue in the capacity of courier, sir. I can see that we are being hemmed in by soldiers at the St. Stephen's Green barricades to the east, but I don't know whether they will also attack from other points of the compass. Tomorrow, Peader and I would like to scout north towards Trinity College. We have a personal stop to make along that route."

"That would be very helpful," Mallin agreed, clapping Tadgh on the shoulder. "Please bring us more news. Meanwhile, can we get your lady friend to help us with the wounded?"

Chapter Five
Splitting Asunder

Wednesday, April 26, 1916
New Brunswick, Canada

*C*ollin hadn't slept a wink on the train ride from Toronto. The same could be said for the raw Canadian troops heading to the Front in Belgium or France. Glancing in the window glass, he noticed that his hazel eyes were more sunken than usual beneath thick black eyebrows. His thinning hair, and rounded, now heavily perspiring Irish pate, attested to his stressful upbringing in Brooklyn and Toronto. At five foot ten, even in a sitting position, he was dwarfed by many of the soldiers, yet his muscular frame resulting from rigorous street fighting and his thickened arms from years of competitive rowing, meant that he could hold his own with any man present. He had fought his tendency to lash out when provoked, as had been his wont, especially in deference to his lover and new wife Kathleen and their baby son, Liam. But now, he had to take matters into his own hands. He tried to sleep, but the loud talking of soldiers jarred his reverie.

The reasons for the train passengers' insomnia were varied. After talking to several of the men, Collin realized that their boisterous exuberance was a defense mechanism against the news they had been hearing.

About two in the morning, the soldier sitting across from him, who had spied Kathy on the train platform in Toronto, extended his hand. "Marshall, here. Collin, is it? Missed your girl back there on the platform, did you? That's a shame."

"Collin O'Donnell, glad to know you."

Marshall extended a flask. "Maybe this will help. We all need it."

91

"Tough business, this war." Collin took a sip and licked his lips. "You on leave?"

"Reporter, covering the troops."

"I've got a story for you. Ever since the second Battle of Ypres, when the Germans used chlorine gas for the first time on our Canadian troops, there had been never-ending reports of the terrible toll of atrocities by the Germans. The damned Bosch."

Another soldier leaned toward him. "You mean depravity, pestilence, and gruesome death awaiting us at the front. The British would not have imposed conscription in January if losses at the Front hadn't been devastating."

"Hold on now, Joe. We are going to make the difference and pay the Germans back for their travesties. We're teachers, parents, railroad workers, miners—we've all had to leave professions and loved ones to fight the brutal Hun. It has to be done. Otherwise, the bastards will overrun Europe and America."

"We've been trained to shoot and bayonet human beings, but that weighs heavy on my soul, Marshall. I'm not sure I can do it, even if I see your head blown off or guts spread all over the battle-field, our eyes and lungs burned out by hydrochloric acid from the gas attacks, or skin incinerated by flamethrowers. Dreadful visions keep me from sleeping."

"C'mon, Joe. Snap out of it. You're not helping the men's morale with that talk. You've got to believe that you will be one who survives. Otherwise you're doomed. We have to know that we'll rid the world of this scourge."

Marshall took another slug from his flask, then both soldiers fell silent as the train jerked along through the farmlands of New Brunswick.

Collin studied the men. In most cases, their wives, girlfriends, and children had just seen them off with great anguish. The Canadian Club whisky the officers had previously rationed, now flowed freely as each soldier dealt with his demons in his own way. Maybe they would be the ones to survive.

Collin saw Marshall's flask lying in his lap and noticed a photo taped to it, Marshall hugging a young woman holding a baby. Collin thought of his own family. Here he was heading off to Ireland and not the Western Front just because he had a hearing problem in one ear. Sure, he had just left his wife and newborn son to fulfill his obligation to find his younger sister Claire, but not to go to a horrible death in the killing fields of Europe. His stomach twisted inside.

Collin rationalized that his mission was just as important— for him. His mother had entrusted him with his younger sister, and he had failed her miserably back in Brooklyn. His Mam had already suffered enough since his Da had been brutally murdered by that RIC goon in Donegal so many years ago, and then her terrible death. He could not let them down, would not let them down, come what may. Now he knew that young Claire had been abducted and sold into the slavery of a textile mill in Rhode Island, where unspeakable things may have been done to her during her tender years. Now, more than ever, he was convinced that Claire had survived the *Lusitania* tragedy, but she was in mortal danger in the midst of the Irish insurrection in the company of a proven, murdering rebel. The Cunard manager in Queenstown, Jack Jordan had said as much when he organized Collin's passage on the troop ship *Aquitania*. Wasn't Claire's involvement with a rebel just as dangerous as the German soldiers in their trenches?

Collin regretted this separation from his family and the pain it caused his beloved wife, but it couldn't be helped. Her anguish was no worse than that of all the other womenfolk who had just been left to fret while their men headed into the horrors of war. She and Liam would be safe at home in Toronto; Sam and Lil would see to that. He wasn't worried about his own safety. He would not be going to the trenches, nor was he a rebellious Irishman begging to be shot by the British in the streets of Dublin.

A stabbing pain had started overnight in his right thigh. Damn hard seats on this train. Or was it something else? He ascribed the gnawing ache in his stomach to the bully beef he had consumed, the main portion of military rations that they were all subjected to. A frightening sense of foreboding consumed his thoughts, causing a pounding in his temples. It wasn't like him to feel this helpless. He was convinced that there was something terribly wrong in Dublin, and with Claire. He could feel it.

The train rattled into the Moncton Station at ten in the morning. Marshall was jarred awake when it jerked to a stop and shunted into reverse. "Where are you headed, Collin?"

The soldier didn't look as if he could push over his own grandmother. "Queenstown, and then Dublin. I work for the *Toronto Evening Telegram* newspaper, and my editor is sending me there to report on the insurrection."

"Insurrection? Don't tell me that our British comrades are squabbling amongst themselves. That can't be good."

Collin realized that these Canadian recruits, being sequestered in their training for war, might not have heard of the Easter Rising. "The Irish rebels have risen up, as I understand, and want their freedom from British rule."

"But aren't the Irish fighting for our side in Europe? That's what I heard."

"Yes, we have been reporting that fact at the *Tely*."

"The *Toronto Evening Telegram?*"

"Yes, that's right. I guess the politics is complicated. That's what I'm going to try and find out over there." Collin knew in his heart that his prime focus would be finding Claire, even though the official position from the ocean liner company was still that she was lost at sea. He wasn't going to talk about that with these men.

The train came to a stop on a siding, linking up three more cars full of New Brunswick recruits. There had been little time for hand-to-hand combat training before shipping them out to Europe. The dead had to be replaced if they were going to hold the line.

At three o'clock that afternoon in central Nova Scotia, they switched locomotives to the recently acquired Dominion Atlantic line, which had opened up rail access to the eastern port of Halifax for Canadian Pacific. This now allowed year-round shipments to Europe, thereby avoiding the winter shutdown in Quebec City and Montreal.

"We've got more company," Marshall observed, leaning out of the window and looking forward towards the new cars that had joined the train. "From their insignia I would guess they are from the Aldershot Military Camp near Kentville. We were told they might come with us. The more the merrier, I guess."

His comment fell on deaf ears. They would be in Halifax in a couple of hours and sailing away from safety to Europe on the evening tide.

They rolled into Halifax North Street Station at five. The men scrambled off the train and out into the main street. From the outside, the station looked like one of CP's elaborate stone-pillared hotels, but it seemed to Collin that the soldiers were oblivious to the beautiful architecture and surroundings of Nova Scotia's main port city. Far in the distance, the Cunard RMS *Aquitania* lay at anchor along the wharf. Collin could clearly see its crazy grey zigzag camouflage paint job. This vessel would carry him finally to Ireland and his sister Claire.

Collin watched as disciplined officers lined up the thousands of soldiers and efficiently brought them to attention, checking their condition and that of their equipment. For the most part, the newly arrived men had made themselves presentable, although a few still showed the effects of a night and day of carousing. The officers dealt with those stragglers harshly. Collin hung back as the soldiers fell in and marched down to the quay, hefting their duffels past Citadel Hill. He could see flag-waving well-wishers lining the street to see them off. Life wasn't going to get any easier for these men, to be sure.

Collin dreaded what he needed to do next, as he headed back into the station and to the telephone center that he had noticed earlier. But he had to do this. The *Aquitania* did not sail until seven.

When the telephone rang, Samuel Finlay was home in his studio at Number Ten Balsam Street in the Beach, finishing a watercolor that he had sketched of the family around the Easter dinner table. He loved the Easter break from teaching school.

"I'll get it," Lil called out from the kitchen where she was preparing leftovers from Easter for their evening meal. Food was scarce during this deprivation time of war, especially after the winter months. Busying herself with domestic chores and caring for the dear children helped her to subdue the pain she felt for her best friend Kathleen. The agony that Kathy felt before she finally let Sam drive her to the train station a day earlier paled in comparison to her anguish when they returned empty-handed without Collin. That knucklehead was gone on his crazy goose chase, leaving his poor wife and wee son. She wished that she had smacked him on the head to knock some sense into him when she had the chance. While reaching for the wall telephone, Lil picked up her rolling pin with the other hand and gave it a swish through the air.

She had managed to convince Kathy to stay over with baby Liam last night. Her friend was in no shape to be at home alone in that house where she and Collin had argued so violently about his intention to go to Ireland. Kathy had finally headed home after lunch, just as the cold April rain stopped. She had calmed somewhat, yet seemed totally dejected, poor girl.

"Hello."

"Lil, is that you?" Collin's voice came through faintly from eleven hundred miles away. "Are Kathy and Liam there?"

"Collin O'Donnell, you numbskull. Don't you dare get on that boat. Come right back home, you deserter." Lil rapped the rolling pin viciously onto the porcelain sink edge. "No. They've just gone home in tears, you—" she hesitated, then blurted out, "callous oaf."

Samuel rushed to the kitchen when he heard his wife's end of the conversation. "Give me the telephone, dear." He gently muscled the telephone receiver away from her ear. "Sit down, Lil, please. I will handle this."

Lil shot him a look of defiance but acquiesced and sat down at the kitchen table. "You order him back."

"Collin, my boy. Where are you, lad?"

"In Halifax, at the train station, Sam. I'm feeling awful about all this."

"As well you should. We want you to reconsider what you are about to do. Kathleen is beside herself. It's unconscionable for you to leave at this time with baby Liam to care for."

"You tell him to come home," Lil reiterated, drumming her fingers on the oak table.

"They saw her on the platform, Sam."

"Who saw who?"

"From the train window. A soldier named Marshall said he saw Kathy, heard her crying out my name. I tried calling out to her, but we had left the station by the time I got to the window. Was she there?"

"Yes, I drove her. She didn't see or hear you, Collin. You can imagine her anguish."

"I'm in agony too, you know. Don't you think that I know how my wife would be feeling?"

"Then come home, lad. Just do it."

"I can't, Sam. I believe that Claire is in mortal danger, and now I have a path to find her."

"We've talked at length about this, Collin. I saw the telegram that you got from Jack Jordan. I think it is just wishful thinking by a man who is obsessed with a girl he interacted with for only a few minutes when his ship was sinking. Come home, lad."

"With Claire in terrible danger and Kathy and Liam safe at

home, my choice is clear. I called to ask you to protect my family while I am away, Sam. I don't know if I could bear to call her directly, even if we had a telephone at home."

Sam knew the boy wasn't listening, or else he just refused to see the reality of this blow to his marriage. "You are on a dangerous path, Collin."

"I know that the rebels are raising a ruckus."

"That's not what I'm talking about. You are splitting your family apart, lad."

"It can't be helped, boss. Tell Kathy that I love her and I will be back soon. It will be all right."

"You're an *idjit*, Collin, and I don't use that term lightly."

"I have to go now, Sam, or I'll miss the boat. Will you take care of them for me?"

"Of course I will, lad. Just come back as soon as you can and keep us informed."

"I will be filing my reports to the *Tely*."

"I'm not talking about the Rising. Your progress, I meant, and when you'll be home."

"You're not letting him go, are you?" Lil had stood up and tried to grab the receiver away from Sam. He held it out of her grasp, but she shouted into the wall transmitter. "You come home, Collin, or Kathy will divorce you." She knew that was unlikely. It just wasn't done. But the threat was real.

Collin had hung up, and Sam didn't know if his young friend had even heard that last outburst.

Four-year-old Norah and her two-year-old sister, Dot, came bounding down the stairs when they heard their mother cry out.

"Everything all right, Mommy? Ernie's awake and crying."

Lil could hear the month-old baby bawling in the crib upstairs and put down the rolling pin. "Mommy's fine. Let's go see what Ernie needs." Lil tried to calm her nerves as she took her daughters' hands and led them back upstairs.

Sam went back to his painting, having first grabbed his pipe from the sideboard, lighting it, filled with his favorite Prince Albert blend. A smoky haze encircled him as he swirled his No. 2 brush in the vermilion and gently stroked paint onto the canvas. *I'd better give this development some thought before I talk to Kathy.*

Collin checked his watch, almost six. He rushed to the telegraph office in the station and sent a brief note. "Sorry darlin'. Stop. Keep Liam safe. Stop. I will be home soon. Stop. Love Collin. Stop."

The ship sailed on time with Collin at the stern rail amongst a crowd of soldiers. As the Halifax skyline receded behind the steel gray of the Atlantic, at his elbow Marshall moaned, "Farewell, my love."

Collin wasn't sure if he personally meant the love of his life or his country, but it was as if he spoke for all of them on board.

Chapter Six
Easter Rising

Day Four - *An Cathach*
Thursday, April 27, 1916
Royal College of Surgeons, Dublin, Ireland

*T*hursday morning dawned cloudy and gloomy, befitting the mood of the Republicans. A faint light filtered in through dusty windowpanes.

"Deirdre, I want you to stay here today," Tadgh suggested, having already reconnoitered to confirm that the British were still content to keep the rebels pinned down without attacking. "You will be safe with my comrades until we get back. I promise that I will see you safely home, lass."

"I won't let you down, either," Peader added, taking a more active role in their adventure.

Deirdre stood up from where she ministered to a wounded Volunteer, smoothed the bloody smock over her dress and swept her hair back out of her eyes. "I can't leave my pub unprotected for very long, but I will help with the wounded for the time being."

Before Tadgh and Peader left that morning through the York Street exit, Deirdre gave Tadgh a smooch on the cheek for good luck. Tadgh felt wickedly aroused and then ashamed. Morgan, the love of his life, was in serious condition and he had no current knowledge of her condition. He had no business paying attention to another woman.

When they came out into the street, both men noticed that the bodies had been removed during the night, most likely by the Republicans. "It doesn't look as if the British Army has followed up. Those five soldiers must have acted on their own cognizance," Tadgh surmised, as they circled west and then north up Mercer

101

and onward onto Williams Street between Trinity and the Castle, unchallenged.

"You see those bastards behind the barricades at the northwest corner of the Park?" Tadgh pointed past the Wolfe Tone Memorial that for the most part blocked their view.

"I'm glad to hear that Wolfe is still protecting us more than a hundred years after his death," Peader joked.

Tadgh's raised his eyebrows at the comment.

They worked their way up to Wicklow Street, near the south quay of the Liffey, with the George Street Arcade now on their left side, blocking the view from the Castle.

"We need to do our scouting duty first," Tadgh explained, leading Peader east. He saw some British rangers turning the corner up ahead. "Hide in here." They entered the Wicklow Hotel, a well-known Dublin establishment. "Wait here in the lobby," Tadgh requested, carefully studying the nearly empty foyer. He slipped into the main floor eatery and emerged a moment later with a waiter who he introduced as Paddy O'Shea from Kerry.

"Paddy and I go way back, so we do, Peader. He's agreed to grant us access to the roof, haven't you, lad?"

Paddy took them to the deserted staircase before answering. "Anything for the Cause, Tadgh," he murmured quietly as they climbed. "On Monday noon, I was holding a reservation for Captain John MacBride and his brother who is about to be married. He never showed, and I heard he hooked up with Thomas McDonagh on his way to fight at Jacob's Biscuit Factory."

"Battalion Two's rendezvous point was St. Stephen's Green, Paddy. I saw them there together before they marched off."

"It's a grand day, isn't it, Tadgh?"

"Not today, my friend, but soon." Changing the subject, he asked, "Does your telephone still work, Paddy?"

"Yes, I believe it still does, which is amazing, given what's going on out there."

"Will you still be here this evening, my friend?"

"Yes, I'm afraid so, Tadgh. We're very short-handed today. Those of us in the hotel must stay here, workers and guests."

"We'll see you then, Paddy," Tadgh assured him, clapping him on the back.

The top floor of the hotel was deserted. Paddy unlocked the keyed door to the outside metal landing and its ladder to the roof, which was located on the northern back side of the building facing the Liffey.

"I've got to get back to the few breakfast patrons that we have today. Just pull the door closed when you're done," he called out, as he excused himself.

From the roof, they had an unobstructed three-hundred-and-sixty-degree view of the city, what was left of it.

"This is terrible," Peader moaned, as he looked past Trinity College and up O'Connell Street. "Those big guns down there on College Street are destroying the Hotel Metropole and the GPO next door to it. And look at those buildings on fire across the street from them."

They could hear the concussion of the whomp-whomp every time another shell was launched and landed. Looking through his binoculars, Tadgh narrated the action. "Our boys are trying to take back some of the buildings next to the GPO." They could hear the machine gun fire from somewhere on Lower O'Connell Street.

"They've got our boys pinned down now," Tadgh relayed, squinting to center his eye in the reticule. "Is that Connolly out there leading them on Abbey Street?" He paused, quiet, then cried out, "Damn, he's gone down."

"Look," he pointed. "He's alive, grabbing his ankle. Now he's crawling back towards the GPO."

Tadgh saw some brave Volunteers rush out of the GPO. They picked up their leader, shooting as they ran, and dragged him back into their headquarters.

"Now that is terrible. He's the only real military leader we've got."

Scanning northwest, Tadgh could see clouds of smoke north of the Four Courts, where undoubtedly Ned Daley and his boys had their hands full.

"There's no way that we are goin' to cross the Liffey here, that's for certain. I can see khakis on all the bridges and linin' the south side of the river. They are making damn sure that our forces are split north and south."

They turned their attention to the southeast. In the distance, past the National Museum, Tadgh could barely make out the lower end of the Grand Canal Docks where he knew De Valera and his men would be trying to stop the enemy from advancing north into the city.

"It doesn't look to me that the Boland's Bakery and Mill at MacQuay Bridge are under fire, but the houses around the McKenna Bridge at the end of the Northumberland Road are being pummeled and they're catching on fire. They'll be breaking through across the bridge and tightening the noose soon, the bastards."

To the south they could see the Royal College of Surgeons and the occupied barricades at the northwest corner of St. Stephen's Green. Mallin's boys seemed to be holding the enemy back from attacking the college building itself.

Sickened by what they saw, the two men headed back down. Tadgh left a small pencil wedged in the hinge of the door to the roof ladder so that it wasn't fully latched shut.

"We've got to report all this to Mallin. But first let's check out the Royal Irish Academy on the way back to the college."

"Finally, we are getting to the action that I've been waiting for," Peader said, as they left the Wicklow.

"I agree, but I must follow orders, comrade. The war comes first."

"I am beginning to understand the bravery of those boys, but I still can't justify this destruction," Peader said, as they cut across Duke Street to Dawson.

"Try thinking about who is causing the inferno."

They arrived in front of the RIA at about eleven in the morning without having seen any soldiers. What a difference from their escapade the night before, farther west.

The Academy at 19 Dawson Street was a three-story brick building, regally decked out with Corinthian pillars flanking the entrance. Peader said that this was the home of the premier learned society for science, humanities, and social science in Ireland, with such illustrious honorary members as Charles Darwin, William Wordsworth, and Louis Pasteur.

Tadgh commented that Eoin MacNeill was a member. "But I don't hold that against the Academy."

"Since it was established in 1785, the RIA has been the center for serious study of Irish civilization," Peader recounted from his recent studies. "No wonder they acquired *an Cathach* when it became available in the 1800*s*."

At first glance, Tadgh thought that the building was deserted. Then Peader said he noticed movement in one of the front office windows on the second floor.

"There are at least a couple of people in there. Perhaps some of the academics were trapped inside when the Rising erupted on Monday afternoon."

"On Easter Monday?" Tadgh questioned, eyeing the second-floor window.

"I've known some of my professors to work through Christmas Day if they're doing some critical research."

Tadgh noticed that the RIA was sandwiched between Mansion House and St. Ann's Church, with no side entrances.

"We'd best stay on this side of the Academy," Tadgh suggested, peering south on Dawson. "The Shelbourne is just a block to the east at the south end of Kildare Street. The bastards can't be far away."

"In that case, we must put our best foot forward, and there's no time like the present," Peader announced, stepping up to ring the front door bell. "I can hear someone at the door, but they're not opening it for us," he said, after several rings had failed.

"Slip your student card under the door."

That did the trick. Someone pulled the card inside. After a brief debate, the occupants cracked open the big front door.

"You aren't rebels, are you?" came the quivering question from within.

"I'm a student at St. Patrick's looking for some expert information," Peader answered truthfully.

Tadgh remained silent.

"Come in, quickly, and close the door," the voice pleaded, and an arm motioned them inside.

Tadgh counted five occupants huddled in the foyer. Students, most likely, with blue and gold Trinity cardigans and Oxford loafers. One of them, sporting horn-rimmed glasses, stepped forward. "I'm Henry Hollingsworth. Who are you? Why are you here?"

"We heard that Professor Lawlor was working on some research regarding an ancient document that relates to my ancestors," Peader responded, taking back his student card and pocketing it. "We understand that *an Cathach*[3] resides here in the Academy Library."

At that moment, they looked up to see a distinguished-looking gentleman descend the winding marble staircase from the second floor. In tweed and flannel, the man sported a bright orange cravat. His bespectacled, sunken eyes suggested a bookish scholar.

"I couldn't help but overhear your conversation. My name is Hugh Jackson Lawlor, professor of ecclesiastical studies at Dublin University and a member of this Academy. I am in the middle of some important research, so the President of the RIA asked me to care for the building during this crisis. My students arrived with me on Tuesday to protect this venerable establishment and its treasures from the rebels and potential looters. We are not militant, and we hope you are not, either. How in heaven's name did you manage to get here during the martial law curfew?"

"We were caught down here examining the *Book of Kells* in the Trinity library when the war started. We've been unable to get back to Drumcondra ever since. We dare not try to cross the Liffey," Peader responded quickly.

"An excellent tome, *the Kells*, is it not? Best in the world, I should think." The professor reached the bottom step and rested his hand on the banister.

"They want to examine *an Cathach*, Professor Lawlor."

"Do they, Henry? Do they, indeed?"

Tadgh was concerned the man might start asking them questions they couldn't answer about the famous illuminated manuscript.

"Young man, may I see your student card, please?"

"Aha," he exclaimed, when he saw the name O'Donnell. "*An Cathach* was a family treasure, was it not?"

"That's right, sir. We realize that this is a bad time to be inquiring, but we are studying my ancestry and learned that this family relic is housed here at the RIA," Peader said, taking his identification back. "My friend here, Tadgh McCarthy, doesn't get to Dublin often, so we took the chance of visiting the Academy when we could manage it."

"Well, well. O'Donnell and McCarthy. What an historically interesting combination. Hmmm, north and south. You've come to the right place, and your timing couldn't be better," Lawlor responded enthusiastically. "I am currently examining the document as one of my major projects."

"We know, sir. We saw the notice in the paper last Sunday," Tadgh offered. "That's why we're here now, in the middle of this insurrection."

"Yes, I see." The professor adjusted his glasses. "Well, now that you're here, I'd be glad to show you the document and tell you what I have found out about it. It will help get our minds off the ghastly business going on outside."

"That would be wonderful."

"Henry, if you'll hold the fort, here, I'll show these fine students my work."

Henry double-locked the massive front door and led the other students back up to their second-floor lounge.

Lawlor walked them through the back meeting and reading rooms with the open double floor library shelves and Vierpyl bust collection of Roman emperors and empresses. Finally, he came to a restoration laboratory set off beside the rare book stacks.

"This is the holy of holies," he explained, relishing the opportunity to show his work. "Here we examine and repair ancient manuscripts."

"Are you repairing *an Cathach*?" Peader stepped forward to part the examination area curtains.

They all stepped through.

"Trying to. Let me show you. But first we must don these lab coats, shoe covers, and gloves. And Tadgh, you must wear a moustache cover."

"*An Cathach* is over here on that hooded worktable," he explained to them, once they were all garbed. "I am convinced from the cursor signature provenance that this document was written by St. Columcille himself. Carbon dating puts its creation at about 560 AD, which closely aligns with his copying of St. Finnian's Psalter." They could see that Lawlor was ecstatic about his discovery.

Tadgh and Peader looked at each other in shock as they viewed the misshapen blob that was once a beautiful set of the Psalms from the Bible. Tadgh sensed that Peader felt as he did, that this part of their adventure was going to be a disastrous waste of time.

Lawlor must have noticed their profound disappointment. "I know it doesn't look like much now, with all its folio pages dog-eared and stuck together. But you have to remember that it was bounced around inside its *Cumdach*[3] on and off the battlefield by your ancestors, Peader, for five hundred years or so, and by itself, before the creation of the box, for another five hundred years before that."

"Is it salvageable?" Peader wavered and reached out to touch one edge.

"Don't touch, son." Lawlor pushed O'Donnell's hand away. "I think it can be saved. We will be carefully employing a very mild solution of vinegar and lemon juice to help us separate the folios and restore the legibility of the written word."

Tadgh noticed that the top page was written in a language that he didn't understand. "This must have been new for its time."

"Yes, yes, Tadgh," Lawlor gushed, taking off his spectacles and twirling them near his temple as he peered closer at the folios. "Illuminated Latin Vulgate with interpretive headings in old Irish. Isn't it marvelous? It's the second oldest surviving collection of Psalms. And the story goes that St. Columcille copied it in one night by the light of angels."

"What's that written on the top folio?" Peader pointed at the inscription.

"Well, it starts with Psalm 30, Verse 10. Those are the Roman numerals you see."

It was so faint that it looked like sooty scribbles to Tadgh, but he didn't say so. Lawlor would have been deeply offended. "Isn't that an odd place to start such an important religious Psalter?"

Lawlor seemed jubilant that Tadgh had picked up on that fact, as he looked at him with an expression of newfound respect. "Good. Tell me, Mr. McCarthy. Can you see what I have discovered?" the learned scholar asked expectantly. He appeared to be challenging his neophytes to use their gray matter.

At first, this stumped Tadgh because he couldn't decipher the language of the enigmatic blob. Then he realized that Lawlor referred to his earlier question. This focused his observations. When he saw what Lawlor was getting at, Tadgh turned his head to hide a smile.

"Well, McCarthy?" the professor questioned impatiently.

"The left side binding is in bad shape. The folios are more glued together by the grime of time, but I can see some slight threads protruding out of the muck on the front side of that binding."

"Excellent, my man. Excellent. What does this mean to you?" Lawlor asked.

Peader jumped into the conversation. "That there were more folios in front that somehow were separated and lost."

"Yes, that's it," Lawlor agreed, clapping them both on the shoulder. "It is *acephalous*."

"What does that mean?"

"Headless. It is missing the beginning. Lost in antiquity due to the rigors of battle, I should think."

Tadgh couldn't help himself. "Or those folios could have been purposely removed by someone."

Lawlor laughed. "Now why would anyone do that?"

Tadgh and Peader exchanged glances but said nothing.

"What about the ending of this ancient tome?"

"It's the strangest thing, Tadgh. It ends at Psalm 105, Verse 13," Lawlor answered, glasses spiraling around his index finger. "Again, incomplete. It's confusing."

"Can we turn the document over, Professor?"

"Not at the moment, I'm afraid. But I can assure you that there are also tiny threads protruding from the binding on the back side of the book."

"Curious." A possible reason occurred to Peader. "Perhaps, someone removed them so *an Cathach* would fit into its *Cumdach*, Tadgh."

Remembering their inspection of the *Cumdach* in the National Museum, Tadgh said, "I don't think so, Peader. The inside of the jeweled box is deeper than the height of this manuscript. And that container would have been made to fit the document in the eleventh century and not the reverse."

"You've seen the *Cumdach,* then?" Lawlor asked. "It is beautiful, is it not?"

"Yes, we saw it in its case at the National Museum last year."

"But how could you tell how deep it is from an outside inspection?"

Tadgh dove in. "I guessed the thickness of the metal sheeting sides we heard about when I made that remark."

"I've seen it myself and would have to agree with you. Why do you have such an interest in these relics?"

"Family heirloom is all, Professor," Peader offered. "Is there anything else that you can tell us about this document, sir?"

"Nothing very technical, I'm afraid. I haven't been able to separate the folios yet. But I do know from the first folio that this is the first insular Christian manuscript in which graphic decoration became a major feature. It is amazing to me that it has survived at all, given its history of abuse."

"But it ensured victory on the battlefield in the name of God for the Domhnaill Clan for centuries," Peader exclaimed triumphantly.

"So it is told, my man. So it is told. Clearly, Columcille gave it to his royal relatives for that purpose before he left Ireland for Hy."

As they left the laboratory on their way to the entrance, Lawlor asked, "Peader, have you ever heard of the *Book of Ballymote*?"

"No, sir. What is it?"

"I thought you would have. It's another ancient manuscript, which we also have here at the RIA. It was written in Sligo back in about 1390, commissioned by Tonnaltagh McDonagh. It contains segments ranging from religion to secular subjects of history and language."

"That sounds interesting. But why mention it to me?"

"Because, as I understand it, this priceless document was purchased for one hundred and forty milch cows by your ancestor, Aed Og O'Donnell, in 1522. Then it was turned over to the Chancellor of Trinity College by your ancestors in 1618, more than a decade after the flight of the Earls. The story goes that it was partially copied by a student there in the early 1620s before it was stolen from Trinity. Eventually this important codex was turned over to us after a long absence on the Continent when the RIA was founded. I haven't had a chance to evaluate it yet, but it's on my list of projects for the future."

When they realized that Red Hugh possessed this manuscript in the 1600s, Tadgh's and Peader's ears perked up.

"Could we see it, please?" they said in unison, hooking their little fingers and chanting the good luck saying.

"I'm afraid not. It's locked carefully away in a special sealed compartment in the stacks. It is in the same place that *an Cathach* resided before I got permission to examine and repair it. Maybe someday soon I can show it to you. Unless we are all destroyed by this revolution."

"We will definitely take you up on that offer, sir," Peader stated, as they passed through the reading room.

As a final aside before they departed, Lawlor asked Tadgh, "Which sect of the McCarthys are you from son, do you know?"

"MacCarthaigh Reagh from Kilbrittain, sir."

"Then you'll be interested in the *Book of Lismore*, won't you?" the professor suggested, looking for some reaction.

"Never heard of it, sir."

"It's another ancient compendium of historical literary prose stolen from your ancestors and taken to Lismore Castle."

Again, a wave of relevant recognition swept over the visitors as they locked eyes and smiled.

"When, do ya know?" Tadgh asked, nonchalantly.

"From what I've read, it was compiled in the 15th century to commemorate the marriage of the Gaelic Lord Finghin MacCarthaigh Raibhaigh and Caitilin, daughter of the seventh Earl of Desmond. It is written that it was removed from Kilbrittain in 1642 when Lewis, Lord of Kinalmeaky, seized the castle during the start of the Confederate Wars. There's a letter that shows he sent it back to his father at Lismore Castle, and it was found inside a walled-up section of the castle along with the Lismore Crosier in 1814 during renovations. Some say it was hidden in 1643 when the McCarthy Mor of Muscry attacked Lismore in retaliation for the Kilbrittain takeover."

"Do you have this document here, too?" Tadgh asked, looking over at Peader as they returned to the front foyer.

I understand that the original is still kept by the Earl of

Chatsworth at Lismore Castle," Lawlor replied. "I'd like to get my hands on it as well someday, though. But we do have a couple of copies here in the controlled stacks, one by Eugene O'Curry and collated by John O'Donovan, the man who also compiled the Annals of the Four Masters."

Tadgh could not believe their good fortune at having run into Professor Lawlor. This scholar was a font of knowledge that they needed. What had, at first, appeared to be a dead end when they first spied the ancient *an Cathach* was fast becoming a treasure trove of possible leads for further investigation in their search for the truth of the Clans mysteries.

"Did those manuscripts also have a *Cumdach*, sir?"

"Not as far as I know, Peader. But there is apparently a secret pouch sewn into the inside of the leather cover of the *Book of Lismore* that might have held a family relic. We don't know because the stitches had been opened, exposing the empty pouch, when the book was found in the castle wall."

"We need to look at your copy of that manuscript, if you please, sir."

"As I say, for the original, you would need to go to Lismore Castle." Lawlor thought for a moment. "You know, I started looking into those two documents years ago. I remember compiling a list of the contents of each of those early literary collections. They should be in my office files. Wait here for a moment."

A few minutes later, he returned to the foyer with two scruffy looking pieces of paper. "I found them," he announced jubilantly. "I scribed you a copy. At least from these topics you may decide if it's worth coming back to examine the copies of the documents themselves."

"Thank you, sir," Tadgh said, as he tucked the pages into his trouser pocket for safekeeping. "Is that why you called us an historically interesting combination when you met us earlier?"

"Yes, Tadgh. I'm glad you picked up on that. McCarthy and O'Donnell. Owners of two of the most important, and in some ways, similar anthologies of ancient Irish history. Curious, is it not?"

"Or coincidental, sir," Tadgh responded, wondering whether there was more than meets the eye about the learned professor. Thank you for showing us *an Cathach.*"

"Not at all, lads, not at all. Come back any time." His students appeared, descending the stairs leading to the foyer. "Hello, Henry and crew. Any problems while we were gone?" the professor asked.

"Some soldiers came to the door an hour ago looking for rebels. We convinced them that we are bona fide graduate students from the University, here to help protect this establishment, sir."

Tadgh's ears pricked up. "Did you happen to mention our visit to them, Henry, lad?"

"No. It didn't seem relevant. We're all just students, right?"

"Of course I am," Peader responded without hesitation.

Tadgh and Peader thanked the professor for his time and insight and requested a future audience when the hostilities died down. As they left the Academy, coming out onto Kildare Street, Tadgh couldn't believe they had been there for nine hours. Night had already fallen.

Chapter Seven
Easter Rising

Day Four - Return
After Sunset, Thursday, April 27, 1916
Outside the RIA, Dublin

*T*hroughout the afternoon, even during the fascinating conversation with Professor Lawlor, Tadgh had been thinking, God, how he missed Morgan and worried about her recovery and whether infection would resurface. Now he wondered how he could meet his Republican duties while saving his friends and himself. To make matters worse, based on what he had seen from the rooftop that morning, he knew it was just a matter of time before the damned British quelled the Rising. Mick's words, when they last spoke, rang true in his mind. *Those who survived Pearse's martyrdom would live to fight another day.*

"I need to take another detour on our way back to the Royal College of Surgeons," he told Peader, as they started north on Dawson away from St. Stephen's Green. "You can head back the way we came if you would like. I would appreciate it if you would check up on Deirdre for me."

"I think it's better if we stick together, Tadgh," Peader said.

"True, comrade. It's all for one, then." The reference to that salutation was an acknowledgement of Peader's socialist tendencies. Yet his compatriot was changing right before Tadgh's eyes and he knew it. Tadgh realized that he had another ally in life, and then he thought of Morgan again. He wished he could be with her to protect her.

"We need to check out the condition of Eamon de Valera's forces at Boland's Mill and Bakery," Tadgh said, turning east on

Molesworth. "Therein may be our salvation in the near future, make no mistake."

They reached Kildare Street, just opposite the National Museum. Tadgh knew they were entering very dangerous territory. The street lamps were lit in this area, and any civilian out at night would definitely be shot on sight at this point. A block and a half to the south was the Shelbourne Hotel. A block and a half to the north was Leinster Street, the western extension of Lower Mount Street, where he had seen advancing British forces breaking through de Valera's forces earlier in the day.

"I can hear soldiers marching," Peader whispered, clutching Tadgh's arm.

"This way, his partner said, darting across Kildare and slipping behind the museum façade for cover.

"We need to get closer without being seen," Tadgh suggested. "But not in the lamplight of Kildare Street. Come on, lad, this way."

They scurried east in the darkness through the museum grounds and across Leinster lawn, slipping through the shadows close to the south edge of the National Gallery until they came to Merrion Street at the west edge of Merrion Square and Park. From there, the sounds of marching men grew significantly louder.

"We need to get closer, Peader. I remember a dense grove of walnut trees in the northwest corner of the Park. Let's head there." They dashed across Merrion Street and found cover in the trees. Creeping north, they got to within forty feet of Leinster Street.

"My God, Tadgh. There's a continuous stream of soldiers from the canal all the way up to Trinity College."

"Thousands, I'd say. Look at that artillery rolling through."

They heard a shout from behind them. "Down!" Tadgh whispered, instinctively pushing Peader to the ground.

A Sherwood Ranger ran by, not ten feet from where they were lying exposed. He must have been heading north out of the Park to intercept the column on Leinster and didn't see the two men. Tadgh had pulled his knife out of his boot, but the ranger didn't look down as he plowed on through the trees and reached the road, merging with the mass of deadly humanity. That oversight saved the man's life. Or maybe Tadgh's.

"This way," Tadgh murmured, as he cautiously led the way southeast, crawling towards the center of the park.

When they got to the south edge of the trees, they stopped abruptly. Ahead of them, they could see an extensive military bivouac filling the open spaces.

"I was right. At least five thousand here, alone. This Rising's going to end very soon, I would imagine. We're not going to cross at this point, to be sure."

"Cross what?" Peader asked softly.

"Cross over to de Valera at the Grand Canal Docks area."

"Why do we have to go to see him?"

"Like we observed earlier, we can't get across the Liffey. We were lucky yesterday before all these troops arrived. I have an alternative plan."

"What plan, Tadgh?"

"You'll see later tonight," Tadgh replied, and that's all he would say.

"No trust?"

"Later, Peader."

They silently backed farther into the trees and retraced their steps until they were in front of the Wicklow Hotel once more.

"We've one more stop on our way back to the RCS," Tadgh announced as they entered the hotel foyer. He led Peader up the back stairs without incident and opened the door to the roof stairs, removing his pencil from its position as he did so. Once on the roof, he took out binoculars and surveyed the city. O'Connell Street between the river and past the GPO was ablaze. He couldn't look at the conflagration without needing to retch. He saw other fires in the Four Courts area to the northwest, in the southwest in the direction of where Ceannt's Battalion Number Four had been holed up at the South Dublin Union and to the east, at the Westland Row Train Station.

Turning his attention toward the southeast, Tadgh could see that the fires he had spotted earlier at the houses near the Lower Mount Street Bridge were still burning bright. In their light he could just see the stream of military personnel crossing the canal and moving northwest in waves toward Trinity. He focused most intently on the darkened Grand Canal Docks area.

"Looks like the bastards have bypassed de Valera at Boland's Bakery now that they have a crossing at Lower Mount Street. That's good for us."

"Can we leave, Tadgh?" Peader pleaded. "Our city is being destroyed, to be sure. This is making me sick."

"Me too, comrade. Let's go."

Through the doorway, Tadgh noticed that there were several khaki uniforms in the eatery. They were well into their cups and paid him no mind. Paddy looked dead on his feet, as he pandered to one of the loudmouths. He finally saw Tadgh and came to the door.

"You still here, friend? I thought you'd be long gone by now."

"We've been busy, Paddy. Could I use the hotel telephone for a minute?"

"The kitchen telephone is through this way."

"Thanks, Paddy. This is more help than you can imagine."

"It's bad out there, Tadgh, isn't it."

"You're best to stay here in the Wicklow, Paddy, until it's over."

"Will that be soon?"

"Yes, I'm afraid so, lad. And I don't advise going up on the roof, neither."

Giving the operator Sean's number, he hoped that the circuits were still connected. He was about to give up after ten rings, when Sean finally answered, breathing hoarsely.

"Sean, you all right?"

"Tadgh, is that you? I wondered if I would ever hear from you again. Have you seen what's happening out there? It's tragic."

"I've seen it, Sean. The British destroying the city."

"They wouldn't be doing it, me boyo, if you rebels hadn't started it."

"Let's agree to debate this later, Teacher. I'm tired and dying to know how Morgan is doing."

"Just got back from Rotunda when I heard the telephone ringing." Sean paused on the line, as he was wont to do for theatrical effect. Dead air.

"Well?"

"She's much better. The infection in her leg is clearing up, and her temperature is almost back to normal."

"Thank God!" Tadgh exclaimed. "You are a lifesaver, Sean. Morgan might have died, or at least lost a leg, if you hadn't helped her."

"It was nothing, lad. They say that she can come home tomorrow. But she must have bed rest for a few days before she will have the strength to go any distance. You're welcome to stay at my place as long as you don't wage your war from here."

"It's a promise, to be sure. But getting to you is a challenge we face at the moment."

"Why, where are you?"

"That's the problem," he lowered his voice in case anyone had come into the kitchen. "We're on the south side of the Liffey and can't possibly get across it now. So I need your help again, my friend."

"Anything I can do to execute my duties as father of the bride." Sean hesitated. "Unless it means I have to fire a gun."

"Pick another verb besides 'execute,' Sean. That one strikes too close to home, don't ya know." Then he outlined his plan in quiet tones.

When he finished, Sean said, "Piece of cake, my boy. I'll pick up Morgan in the morning beforehand. She'll be fine here on her own for the rest of the day."

Tadgh rang off after thanking his mentor profusely again.

Paddy waited for him with Peader in the foyer. He had a bag, which he handed over.

"Here are some sandwiches, cheeses, and fruit for you fellows. You look like you haven't eaten in days."

"Close to the truth, my friend," Tadgh admitted, thankfully taking the provisions.

"Listen, Paddy, could you do us another big favor, lad?" he went on, taking his friend aside to a quiet corner of the lobby where he made arrangements for Deirdre.

"I'd be glad to do that for you and your friend," O'Shea responded. "I can house her here until the hostilities die down."

One less worry for Tadgh. Deirdre would be safe.

Cheers greeted Tadgh and Peader when they arrived safely at the side door of the Royal College of Surgeons at eleven that night.

"I see you have been holding the British at bay all day," Tadgh said to Commandant Mallin.

"They seem happy enough just to keep us pinned down here. What's the status outside?"

"Disastrous, I'm afraid, sir."

After he had finished reporting on what they had seen evolving over the day, Mallin and Constance exchanged sorrowful glances.

Constance took Tadgh aside. "We had guessed as much, given no other communication. But this is much worse than we had imagined."

Deirdre rushed over and asked, "How is Morgan doing?" her bloodstained hand brushing his arm.

Tadgh handed over the bag of food, saying, "Distribute this to those in greatest need," staving her off. He looked the woman directly in the eye, and asserted, "Thanks be to God she's doing much better." He hesitated, then asked, "How are *you* faring, my dear?"

"I'm fine compared to everyone else here. But I need to get back to the pub, Tadgh." She reached for his arm again, and he didn't pull away.

Constance chimed in. "Deirdre's been a big help tending to the wounded."

"That's grand," Tadgh added, giving Deirdre a squeeze around her shoulders. "She's a fair colleen, to be sure. I'm going to get you back home safely, lass."

"Oh, Tadgh, that would be grand."

Stepping away from Deirdre, Tadgh addressed his superior. "Commandant Mallin, I think I can be of best use to the Cause if I continue as your courier. It looks like de Valera may be cut off from getting news. I propose that we take him some, grim as it is."

"That would be of great service, Tadgh, if you think you can get through. It sounds as if that may be problematic given what you've told us. There is no need for you to return here. We can hold out as long as is necessary."

"Thank you, sir. I have a plan which, God willing, we can implement tonight."

"What? Tonight?" Peader asked. "We just got here, and I'm famished."

"It's now or never, comrade," Tadgh answered, pulling out a small stale roll that he had saved for his exhausted friend. Looking around he saw what was left of the proud ICA battalion, eighty determined men and women now worn down, cold, and hungry. Close by were the blanket-covered bodies of six brave Volunteers.

"May God be with you," Tadgh offered to this group of staunch Republicans, whom he could see were committed to their cause for freedom and resigned to their fate.

Twenty minutes later, the trio set off for the Wicklow, with Peader bringing up the rear where Tadgh finally delivered Deirdre to Paddy near midnight.

"I completely trust this fine Kerry gentleman. Paddy's arranged for you to have a room here at the Wicklow, Deirdre," Tadgh said, when they were all standing in the deserted lobby. "The British know him well, and that should give you safe passage as soon as the hostilities die down. It's a much safer approach than if I took you, lass, I can assure you."

"What's to become of you, Tadgh?" Deirdre asked, her voice wavering.

"We'll have to see, won't we now," Tadgh responded, giving Peader a sideways glance. "I will see to it that Peader, Morgan, and I survive to fight another day in our own way. I promise you that we will see you again when times are less dangerous."

"God speed to you all," Deirdre exclaimed, as she gave Peader a hug. Then slowly, and deliberately, she kissed Tadgh hard on the mouth. He let her, and reasoned that she was a woman distraught, and nothing more. In the dark foyer, he thought he saw tears on Deirdre's face as she turned away, but maybe he had imagined it.

"We owe you our lives, to be sure," Tadgh called out, as she ascended the stairs to bed without looking back.

Chapter Eight
Easter Rising

Day Five - Boland's Bakery
Friday, April 28, 1916
Outside the Wicklow Hotel, Dublin

*A*s they left the Wicklow, Peader stood his ground and demanded, "Where are we going now, and how are we going to get there? Since my life is on the line in a war I never planned to fight and still don't completely believe in, I think you owe me that information."

"Well, now. We're going to visit de Valera at Boland's Bakery to give him our intelligence report. Then I'm taking care to get us all home safely when this Rising is over. I hadn't shared these details in case we were captured by the enemy."

Tired and more than a little irritated, Peader jabbed back. "What does that matter?"

"Because if you knew nothing under questioning, and with your student card and honest looking face, you might be set free, my friend. I know it's not your fight yet, and I wouldn't want to be the cause of your incarceration or worse."

"I see," Peader muttered. "We both saw the column of troops and the huge bivouac of soldiers that block our way east to the Grand Canal Docks, Tadgh. It seems to me as impossible to cross that line as it would be to cross the Liffey."

Tadgh turned to look at Peader, hiding his smile under his thick moustache. "I saw earlier that there are troops and the *Helga* on watch to make sure rebels don't get across the Liffey, especially anywhere from the Grand Canal Basin area, west to the Four Courts, but probably beyond. I agree that we wouldn't stand a chance at this point. But they aren't worried about, or expecting, a crossing by the canal at night, are they now."

"What do you mean?"

"Are you a good swimmer, comrade? Can you tread water?"

"Yes, I swam for the college swim team last year. Why?"

"Because we are going to cross that troop line by swimming down the canal and under the McKenna Bridge at Lower Mount Street."

"Isn't that where fierce fighting was?"

"Yes, but now I suspect that the British have complete control. They've finally crushed the resistance there, otherwise they wouldn't be marching in such numbers up Leinster Street. They won't be expecting anyone to cross under their lines in the water at night."

"I sure hope you're right. But how will that get us safely home?"

"All in good time, comrade."

This time Peader didn't push the matter. He had confidence in Tadgh's ability to find ways to survive. He trusted his friend.

Tadgh circled them back past the western side of the RCS and down into Wesley College grounds south of St. Stephens Green.

"I can hear them up there in the park, Tadgh," Peader whispered, as they headed east.

"Sounds as if there is a significant troop encampment there, doesn't it. It's good we didn't try to go through St. Stephens," Tadgh replied, leading them away from this British contingent.

"I wonder why they haven't attacked the RCS in force."

"I'd guess that with the Mount Street access open, they don't need to come by St. Stephens. So they are content to just contain us."

Having passed the park, they continued traveling east through the back streets until they passed by Fitzwilliam Square. Tadgh was astonished that the stubborn British had concentrated on the route north through the stiff resistance at the Northumberland Road and Lower Mount Street crossing. There was no sign of troop movement ahead on Lower Baggot Street. If they had only shifted three streets southwest to the Pembroke Road and Baggot Street crossing, they could have marched straight on to St. Stephens where the resistance had been weak, at best.

Tadgh led the way southeast until they intercepted the canal just west of the Mccartney Bridge at Baggot Street. Climbing down the embankment, Peader put his hand in the water. "Holy Mother, Tadgh. It's like ice."

That brought back the painful memory of a similar night almost a year before for Tadgh, when he had pulled Morgan from the icy grip of the Celtic Sea after the sinking of the *Lusitania*. If she was able to survive that prolonged ordeal and the ensuing amnesia, then he and Peader could handle this brief immersion in a puny canal. He couldn't believe that in such a short time, his life had changed so much. He wanted, more than ever, to be with Morgan again. *Tomorrow, my love.*

"We'll survive, Peader," he responded, checking the water and gauging it to be about fifty degrees. "Trust me. I've been there before, lad."

"So far tonight we've only seen a few soldiers off in the distance to the east," Tadgh observed. "But as we get closer to Lower Mount Street, there's going to be a lot of them. Just follow what I do, and we'll communicate with hand signals." He demonstrated the signals, and then they darkened their faces with mud from the canal.

"I hope one of those bastards doesn't throw a lit cigarette into the canal, Tadgh. I can smell gas. We could go up in flames."

"Probably not a good idea to put our heads under water unless it becomes absolutely necessary, comrade."

They climbed back up, and Tadgh led the way across the Mccartney Bridge, crouching below the stone railing. There was no other traffic at two in the morning.

"Fortunately, on this clear night we only have a crescent moon." Tadgh knew that without cloud cover, the temperature had to be dropping to the freezing level. They made their way northeast along the southern embankment of the canal until they reached the Huband Bridge, being careful to stay out of the light of the bridge's lamp.

Tadgh held up his hand. Across the canal on the northeast side of the bridge, he clearly saw the round top spire and clock tower of St. Stephen's Church high above the surrounding buildings. Called "the pepper canister" church, it stood at the center of the crescent of Upper Mount Street and commanded an excellent view of the canal on the east side of the bridge and Beggars Bush Barracks to the south.

Using his binoculars, Tadgh could see movement in the shadows of the spire pillars, high above ground level. He signaled to Peader and pointed at the spire. Peader nodded acknowledgement.

Tadgh had to think quickly. If they came up from the embankment to cross over the roadway at bridge level, they were likely to be seen. There was only one way to proceed.

Holding his Luger above his head, Tadgh slipped into the canal on the southwest side of the bridge so that its structure would block the view of their movements from the church. Crossing over to the northwest, he swam a clumsy sidestroke under the bridge, pressing closely to the reeds on the north embankment. The water was dirty and frigid, but the cold was tolerable. As his clothing became saturated, he felt like a lead weight was dragging him down, but he managed to maintain buoyancy through limited movement. Peader struggled right at his shoulder as they passed east of the bridge.

A military open-bed truck rumbled onto the bridge above them heading north. Over his shoulder, Tadgh could clearly see the glinting of weapons in the glow of the bridge light, the lorry's headlights illuminating the scene ahead. He pressed closer into the reeds as they passed, holding his Luger above the waterline. He thought it was a good thing that the soldiers concentrated on their task and didn't look down, or else Tadgh and Peader would have been caught. *Just like the day of Rossa's funeral with the Dublin Metropolitan Police in the tram on the O'Connell Bridge, where we were nearly discovered. God grant us the same outcome.*

"Hail, there," he heard one of them call out.

"Hail, yourself," came a yell from somewhere near the top of the church steeple.

Just after the truck cleared the bridge, he heard it grind to a halt, and boots hit the ground. *Damn. They must have seen us.* Tadgh cocked his Luger and waited, expecting them to rush down the embankment. The noise of the men subsided as they moved away from the canal, possibly to relieve the lookouts in the church steeple.

He wasn't going to wait around in case more men descended from the waiting truck. But there was a gap in the reeds ahead. After motioning to Peader, Tadgh gripped the Luger in his teeth. Leaving the relative safety of the cattails, he used the heads-up breast stroke to swim northeast towards McKenna Bridge, about five hundred feet ahead, keeping the gun just above water level. They moved silently, but they couldn't avoid making ripples on the otherwise calm water.

What Tadgh saw ahead burned into his soul, fodder for future nightmares. On both sides of the canal, homes at the McKenna Bridge were either in smoldering ruins or lit by the glow of fires. A jumble of khaki bodies were laid out along the top of the embankment, shoulder to shoulder, if they still had their shoulders. Exposed heads were horrifically wounded, and appendages were missing or terribly mangled. The sickening smell of burning flesh mingled with the gas vapors rising up from the canal. Through all this carnage, the waves of British soldiers were still marching over the bridge and up into the city, lit up by the flames beside the roadway.

Tadgh thought it was an eerie, ghoulish scene—the aftermath of a bloody battle that the enemy had finally won. My God, he thought. Those few brave rebel comrades from de Valera's battalion had inflicted terrible losses on the Limey bastards before they had succumbed. He knew that these heroic Volunteers would have fought on, to the last man.

As he and Peader slowly approached the bridge from the west, having slipped over the last lock about a hundred and fifty feet away in the dark, they swam cautiously through reeds along the edge of the embankment. Tadgh realized that they had to cross No Man's Land—the battlefield ahead. They could hear army sergeants barking orders to their men as they marched. They could see Red Cross orderlies flitting back and forth on the top edge of the embankment among the wounded, their moans agonizing. Worst of all, the firelight lit up the canal for fifty feet on the west side of the bridge, and the foliage there had been razed to the ground.

There was no way around it, they had to proceed. Realizing that his Luger would be useless against these odds, Tadgh took the scarf from around his neck and wrapped his gun tightly in it. To succeed they must avoid detection. He could clean the weapon later. Turning towards his companion, Tadgh held his nose and closed his eyes as a signal. Without waiting for a response, Tadgh turned forward and slipped under the water along the embankment. Propelling himself forward with awkward frog kicks he headed for the bridge, his wrapped gun in hand. When his air ran out, he surfaced silently and realized he was under the bridge. Tadgh wiped his eyes to clear them of the putrid canal water. Moments later, he saw Peader surface in the open, five feet short of the bridge. Tadgh extended his right arm and grabbed his friend by the collar, yanking him to the shelter of the bridge.

"What was that?" an orderly above them on the bank called out to his mate. "Down there in the canal by the bridge."

From his dark vantage point under the bridge, Tadgh could see several military figures in the macabre glow of the house fires, peering down from the top of the embankment. A torch clicked on and swept its light on the surface of the water. Tadgh pulled Peader farther under the bridge just in time to avoid discovery. *Damn.* They were trapped, with nowhere to run or swim.

He saw it as soon as the flashlight found it. An officer's cap floated past them under the bridge and Tadgh heard a voice saying, "I threw a bloody cap with bullet holes in there. This dead zob don't need it no more anyway." Laughter from others followed. Peering out from his position behind a column, Tadgh saw that the soldiers had gone back about the business of tallying up the dead and trying to salvage the wounded.

Tadgh could tell that Peader was in bad shape, shivering and having trouble treading water quietly. Tadgh could no longer feel his toes when he wiggled them in his boots. Moving to the eastern side of the bridge, he rejoiced to see that the fires were barely flickering on the water.

He knew that it was a matter of life and death for Peader whose student card would not save him now. When Tadgh dove, he dragged his comrade along underwater, and they swam for their lives. He kept his mouth shut tight.

They managed to stay hidden for a good minute, having moved to about thirty-five feet from the bridge in relative darkness. They were tangled in reeds by the embankment, and finally able to touch bottom, with their heads above the water. Behind him, Tadgh saw that the soldiers marching across the bridge were focused on the west side where their fallen comrades lay.

Tadgh thought of the trenches in Belgium where they had safely crossed over another No Man's Land just like here between the British forces and de Valera's Boland's Bakery Volunteers, but the danger wasn't over here. They could still die later of a typhoid infection from the dirty canal water. Tadgh swam another hundred feet before he pulled Peader up onto the dry land of the embankment. Surprisingly, there were no British soldiers in their path. Exhausted from their ordeal, Peader needed to rest.

Tadgh checked his Luger, which was wet. He realized that they needed to get to de Valera's stronghold to warm up before frostbite set in.

Half dragging his ailing comrade, Tadgh managed to make it to the MacQuay locks and bridge along the bottom of the embankment undetected. He was struck by how linear the British thinking was. Establish one beachhead at all costs and move through it. Definitely guerrilla warfare next time. The boys at Lower Mount Street had proved that, once and for all. He pushed Peader into a sitting position alongside the bridge to catch a breath.

Too tired to drag an exhausted Peader any farther, Tadgh left him at the foot of MacQuay Bridge. At three in the morning, Tadgh arrived at Boland's Bakery, just across the bridge and up Grand Canal Quay. De Valera's troops must have seen him, hobbling the last few hundred feet, and they rushed out to meet him.

"Our comrade is back at the bridge," Tadgh informed them. "Take care of him first."

Once he was safely inside the Battalion Number Three stronghold, Commandant Eamon de Valera greeted him, saying, "We made a foray to the Westland train station and saw the destruction of the city from the hill. It was very demoralizing for the troops, so I ordered the men back here." The man shot Tadgh a piercing glance. "I started to sabotage the station but then stopped it before the flames got out of control. Please tell us what you know," de Valera asked.

Tadgh told him what he had observed and relayed the message from Mick Collins that they were to hold their ground as long as possible. "How have you managed to avoid a sustained attack from the British?"

"On Tuesday we flew our gold harp flag from the water tower of the Guinness Distillery north of the railway line near the Grand Canal. That has drawn the enemy's fire and mostly kept them away from us."

"Good thinking, sir. Your boys did a hell of a job at the Northumberland Road. Looks like one to two hundred British bastards killed or seriously injured, I should think."

"Yes, Malone led them, all twelve of them. I suspect that they're all gone now."

"We just went there, and I think you are right. It was a valiant stand that could be called the Irish Thermopylae."

"An apt description, McCarthy," de Valera said. "I'll have to use it if I survive. The Greeks who held that pass would be proud of my lads."

"You should be proud of them yourself, sir."

"I am, of course."

Tadgh had been briefed by Collins on the planned deployment of the battalions, but he wanted details. "What has been happening here?"

"We've been holding off snipers here at Boland's Mill on the east side of the Grand Canal Basin during daylight. With the exception of some fire, we have been left alone, guarding the eastern access from Ringsend and up the rail line."

"Likely because they have opened up the Northumberland Road and Lower Mount Street corridor." Tadgh needed to know what awaited them when they withdrew. He wondered if he would be considered a deserter but then he remembered what Mick had said. The outcome of this insurrection was a foregone conclusion. Many thousands of fully equipped soldiers against less than fifteen hundred poorly supplied academics. *We need to live to fight another day.* "I thought that they might have attempted an attack by boat from the Liffey through the Grand Canal Basin."

"They tried to blow a hole in the mill on Wednesday with cannons and demolished the top floor, but we sustained minimal personnel injury. We think the attack came from a ship in the river."

"I saw that gunship in action. It's the *Helga*, sir. It destroyed Liberty Hall and has likely been part of the barrage on the GPO."

"How did you get through, McCarthy? From the hill we could see columns of soldiers moving northwest across the canal once they broke through."

"Well, now. In the canal under Mount Street Bridge. Not a pleasant duty down in the muck, I can assure you."

"Clever. Right under their noses where they wouldn't expect it, lad. Let's see if you can get cleaned up. I don't understand why they haven't attacked us here. So close to Beggars Bush Barracks, too. We are ready for them."

"Based on the lambasting I've seen at the other stronghold points, you and your men should consider yourselves lucky, sir."

"This is not an honorable way to fight for our convictions, holed up in a few buildings, waiting for the end," the commandant blurted, clearly distraught.

"This is not the end, but only the end of the beginning," Tadgh assured him.

"I hope you are right, lad. If only the populace had come out to support us with pitchforks instead of providing tea for the British soldiers." He was guessing that was the case since he hadn't seen any support from the nearby Dublin citizens.

"Next time, sir, next time."

The Volunteers brought Peader in on a stretcher and set him down beside Tadgh, addressing their superior officer. "He's just exhausted, sir."

"You lads have shown us that we need to stay put. You almost didn't make it to us. The enemy is closing in." De Valera seemed resigned to his fate.

"The same for Battalion Number Two at the Royal College of Surgeons, sir. Those are brave boys."

"Are Mallin and the countess still alive?"

"Yes, sir, and just as committed to the Cause as you all are here."

"Good. It is God's will."

Within the hour, Tadgh and Peader were feeling much better. Although there was no central heating, de Valera had fired up the bakery's ovens. His one nurse offered them blankets and draped their sodden clothes on the outside of the ovens to dry. They gobbled down some bread, hardly noticing its toughness. Better stale bread than nothing at all, like the ICA contingent.

While they were waiting for their clothes, the two men rested in an isolated corner of the bakery near the ovens. Just as at the GPO, the rebels had barricaded the doors with furniture and the windows were knocked out. In the distance, they heard single shots, staccato machine gun fire, the pounding cannon shots.

None came near, although the Volunteers continued to man the window openings. It didn't look as if any of these men had slept since Monday. This was a much smaller contingent and facility than they had seen at either the RCS or the GPO. Despite the macabre condition, these soldiers were rock-steady in their determination to fight for freedom.

To take their minds off the awful situation, Tadgh and Peader kept themselves alert in the hour before dawn, talking about the information they had received from the professor. Peader kept trying to wipe his mouth on the blanket, a vain attempt to cleanse the inside of his mouth from the vile canal water. Finally, Tadgh scrounged up an almost empty canteen with enough water to swig a mouthful each.

Then as they sat propped up against the warm wall of the kitchen, Peader munched on the last piece of bread and asked, "How can we determine any potential clues from *an Cathach* in its severely damaged condition? It's still a glued-together mess. Maybe after Professor Lawlor gets finished with it, we can get some useful information."

Tadgh tucked the blanket around his companion's body. He was still shivering, as the wind whistled through the broken windows, adding to the cold. "I have an idea, but I have to check something in my family Bible. Do ya remember what was written in the Clans Pact, lad?"

"What? That *an Cathach* contains at least one clue?"

"What else, Peader?"

"It forms a bridge to the ancient past."

"Quite correct. But there is something else."

Peader couldn't remember anything else.

"'Blessed be the Alpha and Omega,'" Tadgh said, remembering that the phrase had bothered him earlier. At Peader's quizzical expression, Tadgh added, "I have a notion based on what we heard from the professor that Alpha and Omega could stand for the beginning and the end. What if it *was* Red Hugh who removed the folios for the early and late Psalms from *an Cathach* in 1600 to establish clues for us to find at the new extremities of the manuscript?"

"That would be a sacrilege, Tadgh. And anyway, wasn't the *Cumdach* in the possession of the saintly one, MacGroaty?"

Tadgh got up and paced the floor, stopping to warm his hands on an oven. "MacGroaty was under the command of Red Hugh. The Clan Chieftain could have demanded to have it brought to Donegal Castle when Florence visited. And what if the order to not open the *Cumdach* was issued to stop prying treasure seekers from examining *an Cathach* and determining its secrets, and to keep the Clan Pact from falling into the wrong hands?"

Peader rubbed his forehead. "Your idea is farfetched, Tadgh, but it's all we've got. What did Lawlor say were the beginning and ending Psalms?"

"In the Psalter, it was Psalm 30, Verse 10, and then Psalm 105, Verse 13."

"I wonder what is written in those verses?"

Tadgh went out into the bakery shop where de Valera and his men were congregated and asked around, but none of the Volunteers carried a Bible. When he returned empty-handed, he said, "I need to check my family Bible."

Peader appeared more alert, having stood up to follow his leader by warming himself at one of the ovens in Tadgh's absence. "What a novel idea you have, Tadgh McCarthy, suggesting that there are clues in, or rather around, *an Cathach*. Do you think that the *Book of Ballymote* could be linked to our mystery?"

"Lawlor says it would have been in Red Hugh's possession in 1600, all right. But we have no information that links it to the Clans Pact riddles. I think we should concentrate on *an Cathach* at the moment."

"What about the *Book of Lismore*, Tadgh? It was in the hands of Florence in 1600 as well, supposedly a very important MacCarthaigh Reagh relic."

"Well, now. I've been thinking about that since this afternoon, comrade. I don't see the connection yet, if indeed there is one. Of course, my brain is a little foggy. Maybe three days without food and sleep might be factors and being shot at could be a distraction. All of this is quite intriguing, the anticipation of unraveling ancient mysteries, especially those affecting our own clans."

Before Peader could reply, the nurse brought in their dry clothes. After dressing, they were joined by some of the Volunteers who wanted more news from the outside. That cut off further discussion of ancient matters. While he talked, Tadgh disassembled, cleaned, and dried his Luger before reassembling it and confirming its functionality without firing it.

De Valera insisted that they get some sleep, and he called off his troops.

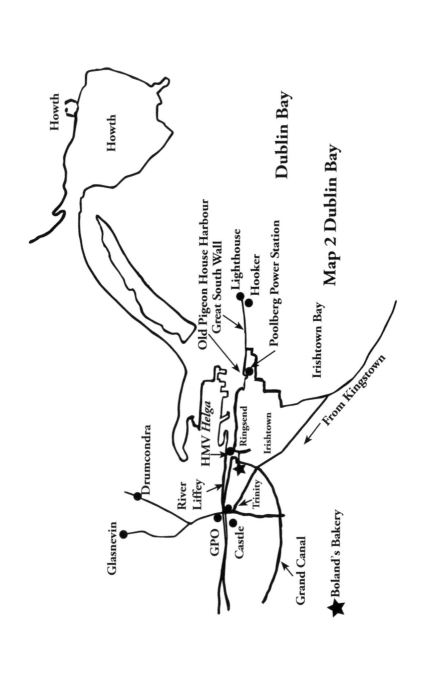

Howth

Howth

Dublin Bay

Old Pigeon House Harbour
Great South Wall

Lighthouse

Hooker

Poolberg Power Station

Irishtown Bay

Map 2 Dublin Bay

From Kingstown

HMV *Helga*

Ringsend

Irishtown

Drumcondra

River
Liffey

Trinity

Glasnevin

GPO

Castle

Grand Canal

★ Boland's Bakery

Chapter Nine
Easter Rising

Day Five - Rendezvous
Friday, April 28, 1916
Boland's Bakery, Dublin

*T*adgh was dreaming about living with Morgan and their future children in a seaside cottage when an errant shell missed the Guinness Distillery and hit the gasworks five hundred yards north along the Grand Canal Basin. Shards of glass still lodged in the broken windows in the kitchen broke free and rained down on the stone floor. He instantly awoke, adrenalin pumping. Jumping up, oblivious of the glass beneath his feet, he could see a mushroom cloud of smoke and fire lighting up the Grand Canal Docks through the broken north windows of the bakery.

Eamon rushed to his side. "McCarthy, you and your friend better get out of here now. You're resourceful and the only courier that we've got. Get a message to Connolly to tell him we are coming under attack from a ship in the Liffey. Tell him we got Collins' order to hold our ground as long as possible and that we will do just that."

Tadgh's gaze turned east from the gasworks to Boland's Mill on the southeast side of the basin. "The gasworks are mighty close to our troops at the Mill."

"Yes, lad, they are. Get going."

Pulling Peader awake, Tadgh thanked the commandant and wished the battalion Godspeed.

"C'mon!" he yelled to Peader, as they scampered north out onto Grand Canal Quay. A second small coal gasholder station tank blew, spewing balls of methane flame into the water.

"Jaysus, Tadgh! Out of the frying pan and into the fire," Peader screamed, as they ducked into the shadow of the adjacent buildings.

"You call this a safe haven?"

"We'll get there!" Tadgh yelled back, and they moved more cautiously north, just west of the canal docks. "But we first need to go to the gasworks." They passed under the rail line with no resistance.

"Through that inferno? I don't think so."

Tadgh had assessed the situation. Two of the smaller lift holder stations were now burning, but the adjacent four-lift gas holder tank, at two million, nine hundred cubic feet, and the biggest in Ireland, was still intact. Tadgh had worked there as a coal tender while he was eking out a starving playwright existence in 1913.

He knew that if the gas fire moved down the connection pipes into the large holder tank, the whole Grand Canal Docks area would be incinerated, including de Valera and what was left of his gallant Battalion Number Three at the bakery and the mill. He had no way of knowing how much time he had before that would happen, but he knew he had to stop it.

"Follow me, Peader. It's a matter of life and death, ours included," he commanded as he sprinted towards the gasworks.

"What isn't, these days?" Peader yelled back, following his compatriot's lead, matching him stride for stride.

They reached the maze of pipes, valves, and tanks in the span of three minutes. Tadgh expertly maneuvered away from the smoke and fire of Holder Number One and darted under the parallel asbestos-covered conduits leading to the big tank. There were no other workers to be seen.

"Over here, lad," Tadgh urged his comrade. "I need you!"

Peader ran through the smoke towards Tadgh, who was now standing beside a massive gate valve about a fifty feet from the huge four-lift tank. It controlled whatever flowed through the connecting conduit.

Tadgh saw that the other end of this conduit connected to the Holder Tank Number One, which was on fire. The black smoke billowing high into the sky produced a toxic cloud. The conduit itself was hot, and smoke spread towards the gate valve. He hoped that the likely flash fire within was not instantaneous, being somewhat controlled by the limited oxygen only becoming available as the pipes zippered open.

"Hurry. Help me close this valve before it's too late!" Tadgh pleaded, as Peader reached his side and gripped the wheel with him.

With all his might, Tadgh struggled to turn the massive red wheel that would close the valve. Peader felt the heat in the valve as he tugged, but it would not budge. He knew they were in grave danger as the smoke shooting out of the rupturing conduit accelerated toward them.

Peader frantically scanned the area and then let go of the wheel.

"No!" screamed Tadgh, putting all his muscles into moving the valve. He hoped to hell that the control gate was not already warped from the heat. "Help me."

Peader returned with a pipe. "We need a lever arm and fulcrum. Stand back!" Then, jumping up onto the conduits on the large tank side of the valve, he inserted the pipe diagonally through the wheel spokes. Holding the pipe out in front of himself, he lunged off the conduit, pushing the pipe ahead of him. The valve screeched as metal-to-metal contacts that had not been moved in years gave way.

Tadgh cheered as the valve cracked in the direction of closing. He jumped in and started to spin the wheel. "Hurry!"

Peader recovered from his fall and rushed to assist his comrade. The smoking asbestos was now only a few feet away from the valve, and the fire crackled in their ears.

Together they worked frantically to get the valve closed. They were tiring fast from this labor. Just as the smoke reached the valve, Tadgh heard it clank shut.

"Jump!" Tadgh commanded, pushing Peader aside. They both fell backwards, crashing into the four-lift holder tank. Tadgh knew the consequences if the flaming gas in the conduit got past the valve. "God save us." They turned away, bent down, and covered their heads with their arms, as if that could protect them.

The tank didn't explode. The worst that happened was a minor scald mark on Tadgh's forearm. "Thank God and yourself, Peader. You saved many lives today, my friend, including our own, to be sure."

Still breathing heavily from the ordeal, Tadgh took stock of their situation. Through the smoke, he could see in the distance that the *Helga* was moored at the Sir John Rogerson's Quay in the River Liffey just west of the Grand Canal Docks. The elevated Dublin-Kingstown Railway line impeded the barrage of Eamon's headquarters. He checked his watch, almost noon. "We're late." He knew they would miss the rendezvous if they didn't hurry. "Time to move on."

"Where are we after going now, Tadgh? To hell, or have we already been there? I can't figure it out."

"Well, now. You are going back to school, and I am going to meet my beloved, God willing."

"I must be missing something important. It seems to me that we're boxed in and on the run, with only the Irish Sea at our backs."

"Precisely, comrade. How observant of you. I have arranged for a friend to pick us up and bring my hooker offshore at Irishtown Park away from the Liffey. It should be in a cove there at two o'clock, so we have to get going. Sean won't wait around more than an hour. There may be British patrol boats offshore, and I don't want him arrested."

"Sean?"

"O'Casey. He's with my friend."

"How did you arrange that, since you didn't even suspect that the British were out of the coastal area until our rooftop observations last night?"

"Let's go," Tadgh replied, as they skirted the gasworks and headed east on Ringsend Road. "I'll tell you en route."

They evaded sniper fire as they zigzagged across Ringsend bridge, heading east. Republicans high up in Boland's Mill leaned out briefly and cheered them on, in recognition of their efforts to stop the conflagration at the gasworks. Tadgh wondered if the men understood how close they had come to being incinerated.

♣ ♣ ♣ ♣

Morgan was very happy to be back at Number Thirty-Five Mountjoy Square. The doctor at the Rotunda had lanced her thigh to drain away the poisons building up there, and she had twelve stitches to prove it. The terrible pain and swelling in her leg had dissipated leaving her as weak as a kitten. They had needed her bed for the critically wounded. Morgan had not been told just how close she had come to losing her leg. But she knew from her Belgium experience that in times of war, overworked surgeons often removed an arm or leg that was seriously infected and then moved on to the next casualty rather than spend precious time trying to save each patient's limbs.

God how she missed Tadgh and worried what had become of him. Morgan deeply regretted having gotten wounded so she could not be at his side through this dangerous period. At least Sean had told her he had talked to Tadgh the previous evening, and he was alive at that point.

Her so-called elder brother had left for Howth, joining Captain Murphy in taking *Morgan's Quest* to Irishtown to pick up Tadgh. Morgan didn't fully understand why Martin had gone to Howth first, but that didn't matter. Tadgh was coming back for her. *They say that a cat has nine lives.* She prayed that was true for her betrothed.

Morgan could hear gunfire in the distance. En route from the hospital, she had seen the conflagration to the south. Oh, the devastating fires! Things must be getting bad for Tadgh's comrades.

She could vaguely remember the grueling trip from the college and how Tadgh risked his life to get her professional help. It was ironic that her doctor was an obstetrician since she had been fantasizing about having Tadgh's children to get her mind off their troubles. Her thoughts all jumbled together, and her mind clotted in a fog. She wondered if the drugs she took caused the fuzziness and wished she had been able to find out what they had given her.

At this same moment, another wounded soul slowly rolled over in his bed in the Tralee Union Workhouse. RIC Head Constable Darcy Boyle had barely survived his own ordeal, driven in great measure by his hatred for the McCarthys—a hatred that consumed his very being. The men had killed Gordo and deprived him of the gold that was rightfully his. He had to live to avenge these injustices and deal with that clan once and for all.

Yet, in the depths of his critical condition, when the outcome was still in doubt, his mind recalled a kaleidoscope of his life experiences. It was then that she had come to him, his mother. He remembered the beatings she had endured from her husband, yet her resolute belief in God and doing good works kept Beth alive for a time. Eventually she had succumbed to his violence when he cracked her head against a stone wall for trying to turn his son into a do-gooder. After that, young Darcy was at the mercy of his father, driving him to seek what was rightfully theirs at all costs. He still had the scars from whippings to remind him of the family expectations.

His father had died, yet his relentless pressure to recover the Clans Pact treasures for the family remained the immutable force behind all Boyle's actions. Yet faced with possible death, it was his mother's face he saw and voice he heard, if only for a fleeting moment.

Boyle had been given a leave of absence until his wounds healed. There was a risk of his chest wound opening up again if he tried to lift anything heavier than a beer stein, or so he had been told. He hated being tied down, yet it had its advantages during this abortive Rising. He hoped that the newly-arrived General Maxwell would exterminate the vermin.

Boyle prayed that Tadgh would stay alive long enough so that he could flush out his knowledge of the prize and finish the bastard off.

♣　♣　♣　♣

Meanwhile, not thirty miles from Boyle, at the Barrow Bay home of Maurice Collis and his wife Margaret, a third wounded warrior was still recuperating from his gunshot wound.

"I'm worried," Aidan McCarthy told his benefactor that Friday morning after breakfast, "We haven't heard from Tadgh and Morgan for a week."

"The newspapers are full of information about the Rising in Dublin, all of it bad news for the Republicans," Maurice commented, picking up an empty tray from Aidan's bedside. "They're probably very busy right now. The news is that General Sir Grenfell Maxwell has arrived in Dublin to take charge throughout Ireland and rout the rebels from their nests. Birrell and Wimborne now report to him. He's a feckin' ruthless killer, just like the bastard British who slew our countrymen during the Desmond Rebellion. He's responsible for the slaughter of Allied troops, including Irish soldiers, by the Turks at Gallipoli last year. My brother was killed there, rest his soul."

Aiden shot him a look, and Maurice added, "My brother was not as deep in the Cause as I am. Listen to this pompous proclamation from the General." Maurice read aloud from the *Tralee Liberator*—

> 'The most vigorous measures will be taken by me to stop the loss of life and damage to property which certain misguided persons are causing in their armed resistance to the law. If necessary, I shall not hesitate to destroy any buildings within any area occupied by the rebels and I warn all persons within the area specified below, and now surrounded by HM troops, forthwith to leave such area.'

Aidan thought this to be just restating what General Lowe had already done in establishing martial law in Dublin earlier in the week.

"That Maxwell's a blowhard with venomous teeth," Maurice added, tearing the front page into bits, throwing them onto the floor.

Aidan knew that his brother and Morgan would be in the middle of this fight, and he feared for their lives.

Sean O'Casey was not a mariner. The windswept chop on Dublin Bay was enough to curdle his stomach after they sailed south past Howth Head. "How long until we reach the rendezvous point, Captain?" he asked, leaning over the side of *Morgan's Quest*.

"That depends on that armed patrol yacht sitting in the Liffey just west of the Grand Canal Dock. Can ya see her?" Martin Murphy replied, pointing to the west.

"Looks to me that they are pretty busy destroying those docks," Sean coughed out, hanging over the starboard gunnels. "I never did like those gasworks. If that big holding tank explodes, there will be nothing left of the whole basin."

"We'll be skirting to starboard round that lighthouse at the entrance to the Liffey. So twenty-five minutes give or take, lad, if the Brits don't intercept us. But I don't think Tadgh reckoned the tidal condition accurately."

"What have the tides got to do with it?" Sean challenged, between retches.

"You said we are to rendezvous at the southeast corner of Irishtown Park, right?"

"Yes, Tadgh said that it would hopefully be away from the fighting and the British on the River Liffey." Sean leaned against the side rail.

"Well, I'll bet that we won't be able to get within a half-mile off shore there at this time of day because the tide is out."

"Well, can't they walk or swim out to us then?"

"See there, on the south side of the mouth of the Liffey, lad. To get to Irishtown, we will be sailing around the Great South Wall that juts out eastward about a mile from shore to the Poolbeg Lighthouse. That breakwater was built to control the silt, which would otherwise push into the mouth of the Liffey from the southeast, clogging the harbor. So, the area south of the wall and into Irishtown Bay, called White Bank, is too shallow to bring the hooker near the shore at this time of day even with our keel. The water is only about four to five feet deep. They would have to swim to us and the sea is still pretty frigid at this time of year."

"Go there, anyway. That's the rendezvous."

"Will do. Twenty minutes now, lad."

After crossing Ringsend Bridge and now coming down Thomas Street to the sea off Irishtown, Tadgh could see they had a problem. Not the British this time, but Mother Nature.

"Damn," he muttered, "I should have known that the tide would be out. The hooker will get stuck offshore."

"Can we swim for it?"

"No offense, comrade, but in your weakened condition, you would never make it in the cold sea. Come on. We still need to get to the rendezvous."

Using his spyglass, Murphy could make out two figures running along the shoreline path, nearing the east end of Irishtown Park. It had to be Tadgh and his compatriot. He couldn't see any British soldiers. Anchored a half-mile off the rendezvous point and looking north, he could easily see the Poolbeg Power Station with its two distinctive tall smoke stacks on the isthmus north of the small scruffy park and south of the River Liffey. [7.1] He could also see the fire and smoke on the western cityscape, coming, he guessed correctly, from the Grand Canal Docks area. The fighting was not that far from the south shore.

"Give me that torch under the gunnels, lad."

"Is that them?" Sean asked, pointing shoreward.

"I think so. I'm going to signal them," the Captain announced, and he started flashing Morse code shoreward through the cloudy air.

High up on the roof of the Electric Power Station office building that until recently had been the Poolbeg Hotel, company security officer Lewis, an ex-naval officer, was on the lookout. Although they had no soldiers on site, he knew that the military was worried that the rebels might try to take over the facility, enabling a shutdown of electric power to the city. Since the rebel strongholds were nowhere near the Station, he was proud that his small private security team was considered adequate, even though they were unarmed. They had been given new-fangled ship-to-shore wireless sets to communicate with the *Helga* gunship, in the unlikely event that they came under attack.

Scanning with his binoculars northeast out over Dublin Bay, he had seen a fishing vessel heading south from Howth Head until it rounded the Poolbeg Lighthouse. Then the hooker disappeared, hidden by the power station smoke stacks, until it reappeared, sailing southwest into White Bank to his south. He could see two men on board, and one couldn't be much of a sailor, with his head hanging over the side, seasick probably. *Why are they moored there? They're not fishing.*

"They don't look like rebels. But who knows what a rebel should look like."

"What's that flashing light?" his partner Ernie asked, squinting to see.

"Probably just reflections off the water," Officer Lewis commented, without looking.

"No, I don't think so. Too cloudy. They're too regular."

"Let me look. Jeez, Ernie, get me the ship-to-shore."

"They're signaling us, Tadgh," Peader exclaimed, as they reached the eastern end of the park. "Do you know what they're saying?"

"As I expected, they cannot get closer. They are awaiting instructions."

Tadgh worried that the longer they waited, the riskier the situation would become as the enemy took control of the Grand Canal Docks area. When he had worked at the gasworks, he had frequented the Irishtown bars with fellow workers at the new Poolbeg Power Station. Both utilities were coal-fired, and he had toured the power facility three miles east of the gasworks with some of his drinking buddies.

"I wanted to stay away from a rendezvous on the Liffey side of the Great South Wall, but now that seems the only possible place."

Taking out the torch that de Valera had given him, Tadgh signaled to the boat. "Understood. Glad to see you, Murphy. Hold for instructions." Without waiting for confirmation, Tadgh set off north at a trot towards the power station perimeter.

Tadgh returned, out of breath, minutes later. He signaled, "Change of plans. Rendezvous in twenty minutes at Old Pigeon House Harbour. Watch out for gunship at the Dodder River entrance to the Liffey to your west."

Murphy signaled back. "Understood. Twenty minutes. OPHH. Avoid gunship. Proceed with caution."

Peader didn't understand the code. "What now, Tadgh?"

"We have a new rendezvous point a quarter mile north of here at the old harbor in the power station complex. We'll still be two miles or so downriver from the gunship," Tadgh answered, as he started loping north along the eastern boundary footpath of the Irishtown Park.

Peader had no choice at this point but to follow his lead.

Lewis saw them on the run when they reached the south perimeter of the facility. He was convinced that there was a rebel attack in the making and had notified the gunship.

"The *Helga* is just deploying a launch with four armed marines. They should be here in ten minutes," Ernie assured him, getting off the radio. "The gunship cannot change its position and orders. We are requested to hold our position and continue to report movements."

They watched as Tadgh and Peader crossed through the power station yard, passing just west of their office building and disappearing down to the wharf at the power station harbor on the Liffey. Simultaneously, they tracked the fishing vessel as it swung around north of the Poolbeg Lighthouse, heading west towards them down the Liffey entrance channel.

Looking west, Ernie reported, "I see the launch from the gunship now. I'd guess that they will be here by the time that the fishing boat draws up."

"Notify the *Helga* of the suspects' position," Lewis ordered his subordinate.

Chapter Ten
Easter Rising

Day Five - Escape
Friday, April 28, 1916
Old Pigeon House Harbour, Poolbeg Power Station

Tadgh could also see the unfolding drama from his vantage point on the harbor wharf. "Damn. Somehow, the *Helga* got wind of our activity. She's not moving, but she's sending a launch to investigate." Through his binoculars, he saw the aft twelve-pounder gun on the *Helga* swing in their direction. "Surely they're not going to fire on the power station or their own launch." Then he remembered the destruction on O'Connell Street.

"Your boat is almost here," Peader reported, looking east.

Tadgh turned and watched as Murphy tacked into the westerly wind to come about and berth near them on the wall. They were about two hundred yards out, and he could see Sean waving to them.

A megaphone voice boomed out from the launch no more than three hundred yards upriver to their left. "Ahoy there, *Morgan's Quest*. Can't you see that this is a restricted area? Do not land. Heave to and prepare to be boarded."

Sean made a command decision. "Land anyway, Captain." He had promised Morgan he would bring Tadgh back to her.

Murphy swiftly brought the hooker about and headed for the point where Tadgh and Peader stood on the iron stairs leading down to the water at the seaward end of the small harbor. A hundred yards to go.

"Heave to. Prepare to be boarded." One of the sailors on the launch fired his handgun across the hooker's bow.

Tadgh knew they were cutting it too close. The hooker was still too far out for Peader to swim for it, and if they landed to pick them up, the launch would catch them. He could see from the speed of the approaching launch that the hooker couldn't outrun it for very long, anyway. Four armed sailors were pointing rifles shoreward. *Damn.*

There was only one thing to do. They'd have to hope that the four marines would split their forces. His team was clearly outmuscled and outgunned.

"We have to lure those bastards on the launch out of sight of the *Helga* and then dispose of them," he said to Peader.

Tadgh could clearly see Murphy eyeing the launch and the shore and shaking his head, looking to Tadgh for direction.

Tadgh yelled out, "Poolbeg Light South," and gestured east.

He could see Murphy nod his head as he trimmed the sails and heeled over, racing eastward out along the South Wall.

He saw the launch veer towards them, and the men seemed to be arguing. Tadgh thought of a way to distract them.

"Run, Peader," he commanded, pointing east through the power station.

They were already headed past the smokestacks by the time the launch had landed and two sailors hopped ashore. Looking over his shoulder, Tadgh could see the armed sailors already giving chase. *Good. We've separated their forces with this distraction.*

Sean had seen all this action and then watched the launch cast off again to catch up to the hooker.

"We got a head start on them when they stopped at the wall, Captain. They're about a half mile behind us now."

In the stiff breeze, the hooker was already east of the power station at the end of the shore. Murphy judged the length of the offshore wall to the lighthouse to be a mile.

150

He looked over his shoulder. "We'll make it round the lighthouse just before the launch catches us. But it will take Tadgh a few minutes longer to get there. We may have to deal with those marines on our own. When the time comes, I want you to lie down flat on the deck, lad."

Earlier, when he had picked up the hooker at Tadgh's home at Creagh on the Ilen River, Murphy had known that they might run into trouble. Though he held himself a pacifist, he hated the British, so if push came to shove, he would fight to save Tadgh. Now, he took his old naval rifle from under the blanket that lay by the rudder and flicked off the safety. Then he returned it to its hiding place.

"C'mon," Tadgh urged Peader when he lagged behind. Tadgh knew that his compatriot's endurance limit was being sorely tested. "A few more feet and we'll be through the production yard and into the sewage treatment field."

As they ran east along the edge of the south wall, Tadgh knew they were exposed but it couldn't be helped. Looking back, he could see the two fit marines with their bayoneted rifles at the ready, gaining ground about a hundred yards behind them. Looking ahead, he could see they would be completely vulnerable once they were on the offshore wall. He had to neutralize these two adversaries before they left the sewage processing tanks area. Then he'd have to figure out how to deal with the two sailors remaining in the launch.

Four tanks stood ahead of them on their right, each at one hundred and forty feet in diameter, positioned two by two, and each separated by about twenty-five feet. The Liffey was lapping at the wall to their left. Before reaching temporary cover, Tadgh and Peader had to cross a narrow fifty-foot long catwalk over the sewage exit sluice where it emptied into the river.

"Peader, after we cross this walkway, we are going to run behind the farthest tank. I want you to stay there on its east side while I circle back around the tank. Understood?" He hated to do it, but he had to take the risk and use Peader as a decoy.

"Understood."

Just as they started to cross the catwalk, Tadgh looked back and saw one of their pursuers stop and kneel down to fire. The other one veered away at an angle, maybe to stay out of the line of fire. *Good. That will split them up.*

Bullets bounced off the catwalk just behind them, and Tadgh felt a sting, and then a throbbing in his left calf, thinking a ricochet may have nicked him. The next shots would most likely find their mark.

"Jump off, now!" he commanded, at the end of the walkway.

They both leaped, landing hard on the tarmac. Bullets whizzed just above Tadgh where his head had been only a moment before.

"Run for the last tank," Tadgh directed his comrade, and he literally pushed him forward as they dove for cover.

Bullets twanged off the tank behind them as they reached the safety behind it. The air was filled with a repugnant stench from the sewage tanks. Tadgh pulled out his Luger and snapped the safety off, hoping to hell that the gun would actually fire after their swim. He only had six bullets left without reloading. Then he drew his knife from its sheath in his boot.

"Stay here," he ordered Peader, as he circled around the south side of the tank to where he could barely see the advancing marines. As he suspected, the first was just crossing the catwalk on the run. The second one had gotten up and was following a distance behind him. Tadgh knew instinctively what he had to do. Split-second timing would be critical.

Tadgh saw the first marine running on the tarmac toward the location where Peader hid. As he passed by, Tadgh circled the tank until he was behind him, taking a chance on exposing himself to the second marine who was just approaching the catwalk.

The first marine encountered Peader when he came around the tank. Peader dove to his left as the first marine fired, and the bullet missed him by inches. Now only ten feet away, the attacker's gun jammed. He momentarily paused to check his bayonet for a hand-to-hand attack on Peader.

The second marine saw Tadgh's attack and called out to his comrade, only too late. Tadgh's knife plunged through the Tommy's back and into his heart just before the bayonet found its mark. The dead marine and his weapon fell harmlessly on top of Peader.

Tadgh dropped and spun around, Luger in hand, and caught the second marine running across the catwalk. Tadgh fired wildly and the shot missed its mark. His second bullet caught the man on his side, under his firing arm. He imagined that the projectile punctured the marine's lung before entering the man's heart. The bullet's force toppled the man into the swift moving sewage water that flowed into the River Liffey.

"You all right?" Tadgh asked, as he pulled the marine's body off his comrade.

Peader didn't answer right away. Tadgh could see him shaking. He was covered in the seaman's blood. Finally he murmured, "I've never been that close to death before, mine or someone else's."

"You're alive, comrade. But we've got to get going. There are two more sailors to take care of. Let's move out now."

Back at the power station, Ernie lamented to his superior, "I can't see them anymore. They're in amongst the sewage processing tanks, and the smokestacks are blocking my view. Now—wait a minute. The two suspects are running out onto the Great South Wall, sprinting toward the lighthouse. I don't see the sailors in pursuit."

"What about the rebels' boat and the patrol launch?" Lewis demanded, grabbing the ship-to-shore.

"The hooker led them a merry chase out into the harbor past the lighthouse. Both boats are circling back south of it, now, and have gone out of my view."

The supervisor got on the wireless. "*Helga*, this is Lewis at the power station. They are saboteurs, for certain. They have gotten the better of two of your men on land and are now trying to escape, heading east on the Great South Wall towards the lighthouse. Your men are not pursuing. Your launch caught up to their hooker out of view east around the lighthouse. We will stand by and report."

"Did they disable any of your operations?" *Helga's* captain demanded.

"No."

"How long until they reach the lighthouse?"

"About six minutes, it's just a mile."

"Affirmative."

"Power station saboteurs attempting escape. Requesting permission to shell the Great South Wall," Captain Thompson notified his superiors by wireless.

"What of your launch, Captain?"

"Out of sight, chasing the rebel vessel, sir."

"Hold for General Lowe's decision. Do not divert from your station or primary target."

"Enemy could escape in six minutes."

"Understood, Captain."

"Get under this tarpaulin now," Murphy ordered Sean, as the military launch closed on the hooker. He had maneuvered his vessel around the end of the south wall to the best rendezvous point some three hundred feet west and about a hundred feet south of the Poolbeg Lighthouse where the sea was deepest. He felt the keel scrape the rocky bottom when he brought her to a halt, so he couldn't get any closer. Then he dropped the main sail in response to the launch's demands to lay-to and tried to look innocent.

Murphy surmised that the sailors wouldn't shoot him outright, since the hooker had complied with their orders, and he was an old unarmed sea salt. But he could be forced to tell them what he and his compatriots had been planning to do at the power station.

They brought their launch alongside and laid to.

Murphy knew that he had to stall them until Tadgh could get there. He had heard the gunshots but had no way of knowing whether Tadgh and his compatriot had been apprehended or killed. This pickup was turning into a nightmare. He wondered how the *Helga* had been able to spot them from its location two miles west of the power station. The old captain watched closely as one marine tied off the launch's bow to the hooker while the other kept his rifle trained on the captain's chest. The senior officer jumped over onto *Morgan's Quest,* and the one holding the rifle stayed on the launch.

"Get up from under there," the senior marine ordered, lifting the edge of the tarpaulin.

Sean stood up, brushed off his coat, and addressed the marines in a formal manner. "This is all a misunderstanding, sir. I am Sean O'Casey, the playwright. The captain and I were just picking up two colleagues at the power station harbor. It seemed the safest place to do so, given the war you are waging upstream."

"Then why did you run when we asked you to heave-to back there?" the lead marine demanded, poking Sean in the ribs. "I know your name. Your job at the ICA is General Secretary, is it not?"

"I quit that group when they became militant in 1914, sir. I believe the pen is mightier than the sword."

"Not today, with this city in flames." The younger marine shifted his weapon to point at Sean's heart. "Why did you run?"

Sean employed all the false bravado that he could muster. "You had guns with bayonets pointed at us, that's why. We have nothing to hide."

"Then show me what else is underneath the tarpaulin."

Sean pulled the cover aside to reveal an empty deck. "Nothing, as you can see."

"I don't believe it," the leader snarled, slapping Sean across the face and knocking him to the decking. "This Rising is caused by you crazy academics and literary sorts. Now, one of you will tell me the truth about your plot to sabotage the power plant."

Murphy rose and spoke calmly, staring down the marine. He had to keep the fellow talking. "We had no intention of sabotaging the power plant. Where did you get that absurd idea?"

"The security detail at the facility observed you and your friends."

"Well, they are mistaken. Obviously, we are not carrying explosives of any kind. You can see that for yourselves."

The leader knocked Murphy down. "That's enough impudence from the both of you. What's in the cabin?"

"If they're not going to talk anyway, should I shoot them?" the younger sailor asked.

"If they clam up, yes." The senior officer continued his questioning of Murphy when he made no effort toward the low cabin. "You're clearly part of the rebel forces, or you wouldn't be here. You've one more chance, or I'll have him put a bullet in your brains."

Murphy had to think quickly and come up with a credible story, or they were dead.

Behind them, a quarter of the distance down the sea wall, the first shell from the *Helga* hit the wall at the Liffey, momentarily deafening them. It took a three-foot gouge out of the walkway and spewed river water southeast over the wall into the sea.

The senior marine turned to his compatriot and yelled, "Leland, take the launch to the breakwater and scout out the top of the seawall. Stop any approaching enemy. Shoot to kill."

Leland loosed the bowline and motored over to the wall. After tying the bowline off around one of the large granite boulders that formed the base and protected the wall from easterly storm surges, he scaled eight feet to the top of the wall.

By the time Tadgh and Peader were nearing the lighthouse, Tadgh could see the two boats tied together ahead at the rendezvous point. The figures on the vessels seemed to be in conflict and were not looking his way. Behind him, a twelve-pounder shell hit the Liffey River, throwing water and a portion of the rock wall high into the air.

"Jump!" he ordered, and they both lunged down amongst the granite boulders as water and rock debris flew over their heads and into the sea.

Tadgh saw Peader grab his right ankle in obvious pain. Tadgh dragged his comrade behind one of the larger boulders, just as the armed man on the hooker looked in the direction of the aerial bombardment. He wasn't sure if they had been spotted. Then Tadgh saw the two boats separate and the launch move towards the wall.

"Stay here, out of sight," Tadgh whispered. He knew that Peader could go no farther in his condition and regretted getting him involved in this fiasco.

He saw a marine reach the top of the wall, and then he heard him shout, "There's no one up here, lieutenant. Maybe the shell got him."

"Very good. Return to the launch."

Tadgh had already walked into the water, heading east along the underwater base of the breakwater. He made his way behind boulders, his leg throbbing. The sea was no warmer than the canal.

He knew this was his chance while the two boats were still separated, and with the shore marine still pre-occupied. But he hadn't come up with a plan of attack that wouldn't further jeopardize their lives.

"Captain, your first shell landed on the wall about a quarter mile from the lighthouse and short of the saboteurs," Lewis yelled into the wireless. "They disappeared to the south side of the wall, out of sight."

"Roger, thank you for your spotting."

The captain then shouted his order, "Gunner, one degrees up elevation, a half degree left azimuth." He gauged that the next shell would land several hundred feet short of the lighthouse. "Fire!"

The second shell whizzed over his head while Tadgh deliberated his course of action. He heard the blast and then watched as the launch and sea wall vaporized, taking with them the junior marine. He saw the hooker blasted with water and debris and its occupants dove for cover. In the confusion, Tadgh swam directly for his boat as swiftly as he could.

Ahead, he saw that the boat listed badly, and its jib sail was partially shredded. Two figures onboard scuffled for control of a weapon.

With a final adrenaline-fueled effort, Tadgh reached the gunnels undetected. His biceps felt like they were tearing, his breath came in spasms. The remaining marine had his back to him and was preoccupied with fighting for possession of an antiquated rifle. Murphy put up a good fight, given his age, as both men grappled for the weapon. Tadgh knew his Luger was waterlogged and probably would not fire, so he had to do something else.

When Murphy spotted Tadgh in the water, he forced the marine back against the gunnels with the rifle and pushed with all his might. Tadgh slashed his knife into the marine's leg, just above the knee. With a grunt, the man let go of the weapon, and it clattered onto the deck.

"Get the rifle, Murphy," Tadgh yelled, as the marine bent down to recover it. Murphy pushed him back. In desperation, the sailor unholstered his sidearm and turned to fire at the man who stabbed him before finishing off the rest. Just as Tadgh saw him start to squeeze the trigger, a shot rang out that dropped him to the deck. Both Tadgh and Murphy looked up to see Sean, standing white-faced and open-mouthed, with the antiquated rifle in his grasp, the end of the barrel smoking.

"Help me get Tadgh into the boat," Murphy shouted to Sean, who sagged back. With the last of his strength, the old man groaned as he dragged Tadgh from the water into the hooker. The marine was crumpled on the deck with a bullet lodged in his brain.

"So the pen is mightier than the sword, is it?" Tadgh breathed heavily and collapsed at Sean's feet. He looked up and said in a quiet tone, "I am forever in your debt, Teacher."

From a distance, Peader had witnessed the entire event as if it was a theater performance, concluding with the disposal of the marine's body over the side of the boat. Then he saw the three men sit on the gunnels and the old mariner take a pipe from his slicker and fill it as if he had not a care in the world.

Tadgh embraced both men, thanking them profusely. Then Murphy and Sean set to work hand bailing so Tadgh could right the hooker. Finally, he was able to unfurl the mainsail, which fortunately showed little damage.

"Lovely day for a sea voyage, don't ye think," Murphy quipped in a jocular tone. "What say we pick up Peader and head home?"

It took only a few minutes for Murphy to bring the hooker as close as possible to the breakwater so Tadgh could swim in and bring his compatriot in a rescue-carry back to the boat.

"How's that ankle, comrade?" Tadgh asked, as he helped lift him into the boat.

"I'll live, thanks to you, although I don't know how you did it," Peader replied weakly.

All the while Tadgh kept an eye on the top of the wall and the lighthouse for any sign of life, but he didn't see anything. He took charge and kept the main sail trimmed tight. "We will travel due east just south of the wall until we are over the horizon. Someone's been spotting us, and I want to either stay out of sight or at least present a minimal profile during our departure."

Murphy brought out a blanket and fresh water for Peader while Tadgh took the helm.

"That second shell almost hit the lighthouse," Lewis reported to Captain Thompson. "I can't see any sign of the saboteurs or their vessel. Hope you got them."

"What about our launch?"

"I can't see it either, I'm afraid."

"Your facility was not harmed?"

"Only some damage offshore at the Great South Wall, as far as I can tell."

"I have been ordered to cease fire and hold position so we don't destroy the wall or the lighthouse," the captain informed the security officer.

"My man and I will check our facility and the lighthouse and report back on any findings."

"I have notified Central Command to get military vessels into the area, but most are stationed at Kingstown and can't be here for at least an hour."

"In retrospect, it might have been easier just to swim the Liffey right in front of the soldiers at O'Connell Bridge," Tadgh joked, as they drifted into Howth Harbour six hours later. He wanted to arrive as dusk settled into night, should there be any activity at the landing.

"Taking the long way around seems to have saved us from military contact." Captain Murphy said, observing the lack of British presence in the harbor.

It had killed Tadgh to be away from Morgan so long. After racing east toward the horizon into the advancing fog bank, he had ordered a northerly looping course to reduce any risk of detection. He suspected they would be after him, and he knew that most of the British warships were stationed south of the coast along U-Boat alley. He guessed correctly that any chase vessels would not think that they would head north towards Belfast.

Tadgh heard Peader and Sean in animated conversation, trying to understand how they got dragged into this war with such a risk to life and limb. Their allegiance with Tadgh had made it all worthwhile.

"How's the ankle feeling now, Peader?" Tadgh asked, as they berthed the hooker at the most remote dry dock in the western reaches of the harbor away from its entrance.

"I'll live, which is more than I thought seven hours ago."

"But can you bicycle home to St. Patrick's, lad?"

"Yes, I'll be fine. After what we've been through, that will be easy, even if I were to be attacked by lions escaping from the zoo," he shot back.

Sean led them to the Kerry motorcycle with Peader's bicycle precariously perched in the sidecar, which he had hidden in the foliage surrounding the dry dock area.

Tadgh drew Peader aside and quietly said, "Well, now. We have much to discuss regarding our adventure at the Academy, to be sure. There's been no time to think about it since last night. I will examine my Bible, and we will talk further, agreed?"

Peader rubbed his ankle and then retrieved his bicycle. "Yesterday seems an eternity ago. Assuming we all survive this ordeal, we should meet in Donegal once I graduate in early July. At least there we can be away from whatever fighting may be going on."

"Agreed, lad," Tadgh said, and they rejoined the others.

"I am truly sorry to have dragged you into all these troubles," Tadgh confessed. Although he directed the comment to Peader, he was apologizing to them all.

"Wouldn't have missed it for the world," Peader replied with gusto. It was evident that he now believed in the Cause and the need for military action. He had seen first-hand the commitment in the rebel forces and the viciousness of their enemy.

"That's easy to say now, lad," Sean scoffed, rubbing a bruise on his hand. "After all, I killed a member of the Royal Navy, but in self-defense. This was a first, and hopefully will be the last time that I am forced to employ physical violence."

"Yet for this act of heroism, I owe you my life, Teacher, so I do. I owe my life to all of you, my friends. Thank you."

In turn, Peader thanked Murphy and Sean for helping to save them and pushed off towards his school, pedaling slowly, favoring his right foot.

"Captain Murphy, do you have any way home except by this fine ship?"

"Normally, I could pick up a ride from several of my mates, but not during this Rising. On the other hand, there's no rush to get back to delivering stout, neither, me boyo. And besides, this fine ship has seen better days. I would like to get her back in shape for you while your partner is recuperating. We should repaint her name. I suggest that we should replace the main sail with a traditional dirt-red color one, since we were spotted during the escape and the dark gray sail sticks out like a sore thumb, so it does."

"My thumb is sore," Sean chimed in.

"Fair enough," Tadgh agreed with Murphy's recommendation. "Let's call her *Survivor.*"

"Good name, lad. "

"How long do you think Morgan will have to stay at your place before we can leave Dublin, Sean?" Tadgh asked, as he fired up the Kerry to head west toward the fires on the horizon.

"The doctor said bed rest for five days, lad. But she looked much better when I picked her up this morning."

Tadgh guessed the Rising would be quashed well before that. He certainly hoped that Morgan would be healed enough in the next few days because the damned enemy would move to control the city, ferret out the conspirators, and close off all exits by land and sea.

Tadgh turned to his sea captain. "We will be here six days hence, God willing, on May fourth at noon."

"I'll be here with your hooker in tip-top shape, Tadgh."

Sean gave Murphy his address and telephone number in case of trouble.

Tadgh clapped the crusty old captain on the shoulder with affection, which the B&C sailor reciprocated. Then they were off, Tadgh in the driver's seat of his Kerry, with a cantankerous and an exhausted Sean in the wicker sidecar. Thoughts of Morgan drove him on, and he longed to finally be with her once again.

The darkness of Dublin played tricks with Tadgh's weary eyes as he drove the streets without a headlight. Sean snored in the sidecar. The playwright had warned him of the khaki patrols that were out looking for those who ignored the martial law curfew. As if Tadgh needed a warning. Twice, at a distance, he had seen lights, and when they got closer, he could hear the staccato of gunfire coming from the west. The night sky was marred by the sickening glow of smoky orange on the horizon to the south and west, an indication that the city was still burning. He could smell death.

Tadgh finally wheeled safely into the back courtyard of Number Thirty-Five Mountjoy Square just before midnight.

163

Morgan lounged on the chesterfield in the drawing room, looking out the darkened front window. She had been there, keeping vigil, since ten that morning when Sean left. She had imagined all manner of dire circumstances that could have befallen her lover and his mentor. Fortunately, she couldn't know the truth of what was happening. When she heard the distinct rumble of the engine and saw Tadgh finally appear on his Kerry, she rubbed her eyes in disbelief.

Leaving Sean sleeping in the sidecar, Tadgh burst into the house in search of his partner.

"Morgan, aroon. I'm back!" he called out from the kitchen door. "Anything exciting happening with you? My day's been a dreadful bore." He heard her voice nearby and followed it into the room.

"Oh, Tadgh," she cried out with relief. "You made it back to me!" It seemed to her as if he had been gone a month and not just two days. She held her arms out to him in welcome.

"Well now, lass. You look a sight better than when I last saw you, my dear." Rushing across the drawing room, he took her passionately into his arms and kissed her long and hard on the lips.

He lowered her down on the chesterfield and adjusted a pillow behind her head. "How is your leg?" He touched the bandage underneath her nightdress.

"Much better now. It doesn't burn anymore."

Tadgh lifted her garment, bent over, and kissed the bandage. "It doesn't seem hot."

"The doctors were so good to me, Tadgh. Once I woke up, I was sure I was going to lose my leg."

Tadgh brushed the dampened black ringlets out of Morgan's eyes. "I'm so glad that you didn't. But if you had, it wouldn't matter. I love you with all my heart."

Morgan pulled him down on her and hugged him fiercely. "I knew you'd come back. You promised me."

"Oh, Morgan, I've missed you," he murmured, stroking her

forehead. "Being without you is like being only half a man."

"Looks like your half a man kept you safe enough, my dear," she chided him.

"If only you knew, darlin'. If only you knew."

"Tell me how you got here. The fighting's so fierce—explosions and gunfire have driven me mad."

"Let's not spoil this moment, my heart. I think that a drink is in order, Rising notwithstanding."

"Mmmmm. That would be nice," Morgan purred. "But having you back is elixir enough, my love."

"First, I'd better bring Sean in. He's sleeping so deeply in the sidecar he might not wake before he freezes to death. It's bloody cold out tonight, to be sure."

Well-fortified with Jameson, and with their host tucked in, Tadgh carried Morgan to the guest bedroom. He gently removed her nightdress and lay her on the eider comforter. Lovemaking was out of the question. After undressing, he used the wash basin and towel in the room to remove some of the grime from the last five days in the trenches of the Rising. When he finished, the white towel looked ashen gray.

Then climbing in beside her, Tadgh stroked Morgan's black ringlets with his hand. In this bed, no jagged tree roots stabbing them in the back, no soggy cold blankets, and most importantly no enemies shooting.

"I was afraid that I might lose you, aroon. I couldn't have gone on if you had lost your leg and hated me for it." Tadgh kissed her behind her earlobe.

"That tickles. Do it again."

Tadgh obliged, this time hovering there, intoxicated by the scent of her neck.

"You wouldn't lose me even if I had lost my leg, mavourneen. I am yours forever. Don't you know that?" Morgan reached out and took his hand. Her green eyes were smoking again, just like when she first opened them in his own bedroom all that time ago . . .

"And I am yours no matter what happens, my love." Tadgh patted her wounded leg above the bandages.

Before relinquishing their tired brains to slumber, Morgan drew him down on her nude body and wrapped her arms and a leg around her lover. "There now. I've put them all to good use, except one that's still mending. You can never escape my clutches."

"I never want to." Tadgh brushed his lover's lips with his own and immediately drifted off to sleep. He had a dream about their life together in the Queenstown cottages to finish.

For her part, Morgan's liveliness had been a burst of energetic rush rather than a sign of robust health. She sank into the eider, holding fast to her sleeping man. Without another word between them, Morgan drifted off, resuming her dream of dancing children and feeling safe for the first time in a week.

Chapter Eleven
Aftermath

Saturday, April 29, 1916
O'Casey's Home, Thirty-Five Mountjoy Square, Dublin

*W*hen Tadgh came down to the kitchen the next morning, he found Sean seated at the table, muttering and frowning as he read the newspaper. It surprised him to see that it was *The Irish Times* their host was reading, since its printing facilities were still at Number Four Lower Abbey Street, just off O'Connell Street, in the middle of the fighting. It was reported that the insurgents had stolen large rolls of newsprint from the premises to form a barricade. Nevertheless, the paper was still printing Unionist-favored articles about the revolution.

"Why so glum, Teacher?"

"They drove them out of the GPO late yesterday, Tadgh. Burned it out. Many were killed," Sean lamented, pointing at the headline story. "They've got the leaders trapped in Moore Street. It won't be long now."

Tadgh grabbed the paper and read the lead article aloud,

> "'Last evening, British forces closed in on the rebel headquarters after incendiary shells burned the General Post Office. Twenty-one out of thirty advance guard rebel fighters were killed leaving through Henry Street, including prominent Dublin lawyer Michael The O'Rahilly who had thrown in his lot with these ruffians. General Maxwell, who arrived and took charge yesterday, has vowed to swiftly drive these bullies from their nests at all costs.'"

Tadgh paused and remembered all the brave men and women he had seen in the GPO and how terrible it must have been there in the end. "I wonder if Pearse, Connolly, and Mick survived?"

"Don't know. There's nothing said about their fate in the newspaper."

Tadgh's zeal for freedom from English tyranny was subdued but not dulled. His committed heart still burned as a result of the British brutality in dealing with the Volunteers. "I hope that this ignites not only our city, but the hearts and minds of all true Irish men and women, to finally drive the British bastards out of our country."

"With the pen and not the sword, Tadgh."

"With pikes, if that's all we have." Tadgh thrust his arm out, as if stabbing the enemy with a pitchfork, and the sugar bowl went flying across the kitchen, shattering into a thousand pieces.

"You just tried that and look where it's got you," Sean said, getting up to sweep up the mess." The city is already ignited and the common man is paying for this. No food. No transportation. Our city is in flames."

"Because only fourteen hundred were brave enough to rise," Tadgh said angrily, dusting the spilled sugar on the table into his cup. "I'm talking about the millions who are oppressed."

"The millions are worried about having enough to eat today, not resurrecting the ideals of an extinct Clan system," O'Casey replied, getting his ire up.

"Tell that to the millions who died of illness and starvation in the Famine while the British overlords sent all the food back to feed their own bellies."

"Point well taken, my boy," Sean said.

"Will you two men shake hands and make up?" Morgan called down from the upstairs landing. "You'll wake the dead."

"Would that were true, aroon," Tadgh lamented, as he watched her try to manage the stairs, gripping the rail, and favoring her right leg.

"Morning, older brother," she said, giving Sean a peck on his forehead and a squeeze.

Tadgh noted with satisfaction the bond that had formed between his mentor and his love. Both had saved him. "Where's my kiss, love?"

"If you must, you overgrown jackass," Morgan joked, and gently kissed his ear.

"Have you given any thought to feeding our own bellies this morning? I've had a lovely sleep and now I'm hungry as a bear."

"Point well taken," Tadgh replied, turning to her and wrapping his muscular arms around her for support. "We'll fix you up something to eat, won't we, Sean?"

"Absolutely. There's not much in the larder, but I still have a couple of eggs left. How do those duds fit, lass? You are a fair sight in that frock, on that I can see Tadgh agrees."

Morgan enjoyed that the men noticed her outfit accentuating her form nicely, though she had grown thinner since her injury. "I feel like a girl again, thanks to you, my brother," Morgan said, smoothing the navy-blue skirt over her slender hips. "This white blouse with the flowers, how long has it been since I wore anything so feminine? Well, I couldn't have worn my uniform as it was in shreds, only fit for rags." Morgan paused, then said, "So who is she, Sean? The one who is so generous with her clothes?" She straightened the belt at her waist and fastened the top button at her throat.

"Just a friend who comes to see me from time to time, lass."

"Does she now, Sean? From time to time? She must be a well-born lass to wear such beautiful things."

"Well, she's a caretaker."

"What kind of care does she take, of you, if I might ask, Brother?"

"You can ask all you want, Morgan, but we aspiring playwrights need to maintain suspense, don't we, Tadgh. So I'll not be telling *you*."

Tadgh let her go and Morgan hobbled over to give Sean a big

kiss on the cheek. Tadgh realized what he had suspected all along. Beneath Sean's curmudgeon shell dwelt a romantic softie. He would have to watch out for his mentor, who seemed to be making inroads with his girl.

"I was planning on getting to the GPO this morning to give Pearse my report before this disastrous news."

"I'd lie low here if I were you, lad. He's not there anymore, is he. The paper states that the British now have eighteen thousand soldiers in Ireland, the majority in Dublin."

Tadgh remembered that Mick had encouraged him to survive to fight another day. At this juncture, it seemed pointless to try to report de Valera's status, which undoubtedly would have changed for the worse anyway.

Morgan wasn't so reticent in her recommendation. "You're not going away from me again, Tadgh McCarthy, and that's final."

Tadgh abandoned any idea of further support for the Rising. The outcome was in God's hands, or rather those of the ruthless General Maxwell.

The evening paper told the story. Sean read to them,

> "'The rebel Pearse surrendered to General Lowe this afternoon at 3:45 after sending a nurse, one Elizabeth O'Farrell, with a white flag of truce. The Government insisted on unconditional surrender of all the rebel forces. James Connolly, the proclaimed Dublin Leader had been very seriously injured, so he was taken to Royal Hospital Kilmainham. It is reported that gangrene has set into his leg. Rebel forces at the Four Courts, St. Stephen's Green, and Boland's Mill have not yet received the word to cease hostilities. Good citizens of Dublin threw refuse at the rebel leaders as they stood, lined up outside the GPO, for causing the destruction of our city.'"

Sean continued reading for a few minutes, then tossed the paper onto the table. "Damn those British," he shouted. "It says here that after Ned Daly surrendered to Colonel de Courcy Wheeler in North Street this afternoon, a Colonel Taylor shot and killed fifteen unarmed civilians. Apparently, Taylor said he was operating under orders from General Lowe to take no prisoners. I'll wring his scrawny neck, the sniveling coward!" Sean roared, lifting and balling the paper with his fists. 'Unarmed citizens', indeed!"

"Will you use a pen on his neck, then?" Tadgh remarked.

Sean shot daggers at his former pupil, but Tadgh noticed that he kept any further remarks to himself.

"The witch hunt will be on now," Tadgh offered, smoothing the paper to read for himself. "You mark my words."

The Sunday newspaper came late in the afternoon the next day, one week after the countermand notice by MacNeill.

"The Rising is over," Sean announced. "It says here that 'all battalions have surrendered including Thomas Ashe and his forces in Asbourne north of Dublin. General Maxwell has ordered all the leaders to be detained at Kilmainham Prison, including the seven signatories of the Easter Rising Proclamation. He has vowed swift retribution for the evil caused by these traitors of the Crown.'"

He paused for a moment and then continued, as if to himself, "'Lord Wimborne, Sir Matthew Nathan and Augustine Birrell have all been recalled to Britain and are being questioned by intelligence leaders there regarding their failure to act in a timely manner to prevent this atrocity.'"

Tadgh could see that his mentor was gradually being won over to the Cause, not so much due to the actions of the freedom fighters, but to the punitive actions of the British leaders. *Maybe the strategy of martyrdom will work after all.* He feared for his captured compatriots, yet he was curious to see this drama played out and how the Irish masses would react. He decided that Sean would be a pretty good bellwether of that when the time came.

After they finished the meager supper Morgan cooked that evening, she commented, "My leg is aching, so I need to rest. Sean, would there be enough hot water that I can enjoy a bath?"

"Certainly, lass. But mind you are careful to keep the dressing dry, like the doctor said."

There he goes again, Tadgh thought, as he helped Morgan up the stairs. *He cares for her as if he is her older brother, and I'm glad of it. Morgan deserves his attention.*

Tadgh followed Morgan into the bathroom with a steaming copper kettle. As she slowly removed her clothes and left them on the tiled floor, she could barely keep her eyes open. She followed his directions to sit on the lip of the tub so he could take a look at the condition of her leg wound. His touch was gentle but clumsy when he unwound the dressing.

He was pleased to see that the site was dry and already knitting together nicely. The bruising had faded, and he saw her tremble from pleasure when he bent his mouth and covered the spot with a gentle kiss. She slipped into the bath carefully, drawing her legs up to her breasts and resting her head on his strong arm so Tadgh could avoid soaking the wound as he poured water over her head and down her back. Her breath slowed when Tadgh took up the flannel and massaged her shoulders, then worked his way all along her back in a firm circular motion to take away the aches that had settled into her body.

"Turn your lovely face to me, lass, and I will wash your hair," he breathed into her ear. He lost himself in the sweet curve of her neck and buried his fingers in the riot of black ringlets tumbling unbound over her shoulders. He saw her cheeks flush with sudden heat when he trailed his hand to tease her nipples, and her green eyes flew open to catch him in his naked desire. He reached for the towel at his elbow and rose, holding Morgan close so he could wrap it over her. Gathering her into his arms, Tadgh brought her to the bed in the next room, toweling her hair and body. All the while her smoky eyes were fixed on him. Tadgh took it as a silent dare to forget their exhaustion, her wounded body, and to take her with the force that fed her obvious hunger for him.

He was already awakened, his hardness pushing up in its burgeoning insistence. They burned kisses into each other's skin. Morgan loosened his belt and buttons, and his trousers slipped from his loins, leaving him aroused and unfettered. "My, oh, my," she murmured and reached down. "What have we here?"

Tadgh leaned in and kissed her on the mouth, enveloping her lips. The air fairly crackled with the sexual tension. He slipped into her embrace and moved her so he would not bear down on the wounded thigh.

"I was so afraid that you—"

"I'm here now and we're safe, aroon. I came back as I promised. But I am so sorry that you were wounded." Tadgh stroked her right thigh just below the affected area.

Morgan pulled his hand away and placed it on her breast. "It was my fault for jumping up into the battlefield."

He could feel himself pulsing as she tightened her grip in response. How her long legs and arms fit him so perfectly astonished him. She arched her body toward him in her greed.

He opened her wide with his fingers, felt her hot dampness, and steered toward her sanctuary. Morgan shuddered as he penetrated and filled her, drawing her hips into a closer embrace and rocking more deeply into her body.

"Oh, Tadgh," Morgan moaned as his movements intensified. At her peak of excitement, she cried out as waves of ecstasy rolled over her, and her legs clamped shut.

Morgan's surrender spurred Tadgh's passion, and he felt the warm rush of his release into her body. His groan of spent pleasure sang into her ear, and she held him tight in their complete union.

173

As they had done so many times before, the two fell into a slumber even the angels would be loath to disturb.

Tadgh and Morgan woke up in each other's arms, content for the first time in weeks. For Tadgh, this bliss pushed the horrors of the last week to the back of his mind. For Morgan, the war was over for the time being, and they were still alive. More importantly, she had a firm marriage proposal from the man she so desperately loved.

When they descended together in the morning, they found Sean still brooding over taking the life of another human being. He read them the grim news. "*The Irish Times* reports that:

> 'The state has struck, but its work has not finished. The surgeon's knife has been put to the corruption in the body of Ireland, and its course must not be stayed until the whole malignant growth is removed.'"

Chapter Twelve
Convoy

Tuesday, May 2, 1916
In the Celtic Sea, South of Ireland

As usual, **Collin** awoke Tuesday morning in the midst of three hundred sweaty men. The bunks on B deck were stacked three high to his left and right in columns of fifty. Only two latrines. There were a dozen similar dormitories on the *Aquitania*. He realized that these were the best conditions the soldiers would see for many months, and for unlucky millions of them, the rest of their lives.

They were finally going to arrive in Liverpool at two the next morning, after six and a half days at sea. This is what he had been waiting for and what all the other men on the ship had been dreading.

Corporal Robert Johnson had been assigned to make Collin as comfortable as possible. After breakfast, they met at the rail on A deck and struck up a conversation.

Collin told him, "We've published stories in our Toronto paper of the atrocities caused by chemical warfare at Ypres."

"Yes. Ghastly business, the blighters. We've got better masks now."

"I've read that they're developing even more toxic and undetectable chemical weapons."

"As if the trenches aren't bad enough," Johnson remarked.

When Collin saw Marshall and others approaching, he quickly changed the subject. "I understand that the Germans are resuming U-boat warfare[4] on merchant marine ships in the war zones as of the beginning of March."

"There's a fight on within the German General Staff, son,"

Johnson said. "The chief of the army general staff, General Erich von Falkenhayn, desperately wants to weaken the Allied supply lines ever since he started the Battle of Verdun in February, which, by the way, is where these troops on *Aquitania* are headed. Our military intelligence found out that the army general convinced Admiral von Holtzendorf to intensify U-boat activities to sink Allied shipping without warning."

"But I thought they were supposed to operate in cruiser mode. That's what I reported on for the *Tely.*"

"It's true that after the *Lusitania,* the Kaiser ordered the U-boats to surface and warn their enemy prior to torpedoing our ships, but their navy refused to fight that way because it put their U-boats in grave danger."

"Aren't they worried that these renewed underwater attacks will bring the United States into the war, Corporal?"

"That's Chancellor Bethman Hollweg's argument to Kaiser Wilhelm II. But our blockade of the North Sea is choking off their supplies, and they are desperate to strangle our import of all materials including troops. On April 18, the cross-channel steamer *Sussex* was torpedoed without warning."

"When do we enter the U-Boat attack corridor?"

"We've been in it since twenty-one hundred hours last evening. We'll be reaching Ireland's coast in a couple of hours where the probability of an attack doubles."

"Isn't that where the *Lusitania* was torpedoed?" Collin had a personal interest.

"Yes, lad, but she wasn't being escorted like we are here in our convoy. The Huns aren't likely to attack this group."

Collin looked out across the sea to where the convoy was steaming in formation. The *Aquitania* had rendezvoused two hundred miles off the Nova Scotia coast with ships from New York and Boston the first night of their voyage.

Although he wasn't a mariner, Corporal Johnson showed Collin the difference between an armed merchant cruiser like the *Aquitania* and a destroyer. It was obvious, since the cruisers were generally larger civilian ocean liners that had been outfitted for convoy duty. Collin counted two destroyers on each side of the cargo ships interspersed with three other armed merchant carriers port and starboard. The *Aquitania* and two other troop ships, the *Carmania* and *Teutonic*, as well as several cargo vessels including the *SS Mount Temple*, made up the fleet of twenty ships, all powering along in close formation.

"Did you know that the CP cargo ship, *Mount Temple,* received the *Titanic's* distress call and steamed to her assistance through an iceberg field? Unfortunately, she was more than fifty miles away when she got the call and didn't get there in time to save anyone in the frigid ocean."

Referring to the number of ships in the convoy, Collin remarked, "I suppose there is safety in numbers." He moved from the port to starboard rail.

Johnson crossed with him. "Yes, but the Admiralty didn't initially agree with the convoy approach." At Collin's quizzical look, the corporal continued, "They thought that a convoy would present a larger target for the U-boats.[4] Convoys have proved their worth. The Germans are sinking much less tonnage since we instituted this process."

"What's the story about that destroyer just off our starboard beam, do you know?"

"That's the HMS *Contest*, Mr. O'Donnell, an Acasta K Class destroyer. We've sailed with her many times. She's stopped attacks before."

"How is that?"

"With depth charges. We had to invent those timed bombs to blow up U-boats. They are launched from the aft deck, landing in the wake of the ship. Can you see?"

Collin could see metal ramps on the aft deck, each with a large barrel on its base. "Are they accurate?"

"They're hit and miss, but they stop the attack. We travel at about twenty knots and U-boats can only move at about nine knots under water. So, we can often outrun them. They had the advantage at the start of the war, but we are now successful in finding ways to destroy them."

Collin thought that this was a newsworthy item for the paper. "But all of this is after they fire one torpedo so we know they are present. And that might be too late for some poor vessel."

"True. That's still a risk. That's why the escorts flank us at all times."

"I know someone who was on the *Lusitania*, Corporal."

"Terrible business, so it was. You had a friend. Did he survive?"

"I believe she did. She's my sister Claire, and I am going to Ireland to find her before it is too late."

Johnson was intrigued. "She was saved after the *Lusitania* sank?"

"I believe so, even though the official records show her as lost at sea. I think she is in Dublin and has been hurt in the uprising."

"Do you, lad. Terrible business," he reiterated. "What's wrong with those Irish? Don't they know we are dying in the trenches of Europe desperately trying to save their country, as well as our own, from the Hun invasion?"

"That's what I am going to find out."

Marshall overheard this conversation and stepped to the rail as the corporal moved away to address one contingent of the troops. "I heard that the *Lusitania* sank in eighteen minutes." He scanned the ocean ahead of the ship.

"I suspect that the dangers you face in the next few months are greater than those posed by this voyage," Collin offered, turning to face the private.

"Look!" someone yelled from the port side. "Land."

Marshall and Collin drifted over to the port side of the ship. Beyond the escorts, Dingle Peninsula was coming into view. "We must be about ten miles offshore," Marshall guessed, holding his hands up in a triangle to gauge distance, a trick artillerymen used to determine the elevation to set for their heavy weaponry.

"All hands on deck," Captain Haig announced through the loudspeaker. "Keep a keen eye out for U-boat periscopes from now until we reach Liverpool."

"How long would that be?"

"They told me seventeen hours now, Collin."

Collin returned to the starboard rail, assuming that an attack, though unlikely, would come from the seaward side. The HMS *Contest* was running parallel about two hundred yards away.

At two in the afternoon, a light rain started to fall, and Collin grew uneasy. Off the port side in the distance, he could see a lighthouse on a spit of land.

"Old Head, Kinsale," someone yelled out.

The klaxon on the *Contest* sounded shrill in the heavy afternoon air. Collin raced to the starboard rail where he could see seamen scampering to quarters as the destroyer nosed to starboard.

"Why is he leaving us?"

"He's not, Collin. He must have seen a periscope and he's trying to block the fire angle."

"To what, Marshall?"

"To us. That's his job."

A torpedo, intended for the troop ship, slammed into the destroyer just below the water line, slicing through its aft rudder controls. Its deafening percussive force incited turmoil onboard. The *Contest* veered left on a collision course with the *Aquitania*.

Soldiers on the deck of the *Aquitania* squashed Collin against the rail as they all crowded to observe the commotion on the destroyer.

"Full speed, port thirty degrees!" the captain of the *Aquitania* yelled from the bridge wing. "Brace for impact."

The huge liner swerved to port and surged ahead, trying to avoid the oncoming vessel. A collision with the *Contest* was inevitable.

Collin felt it first and then heard the grinding impact. The bow of the destroyer sliced into the starboard side of the troop ship aft of where Collin stood amidships. Men on the troop ship were thrown to the deck, and some fell overboard. The ship initially rolled to port from the violent impact and then listed to starboard as torrents of water gushed through the slash in its hull.

A klaxon sounded and from the deck, Collin could hear bulkhead doors below him slamming shut. He jumped up to see the destroyer drifting off behind them, its bow crumpled. It appeared to be disabled.

Water gushed in through the damaged hull of the *Aquitania,* and the stricken ship was slowing, but still under way. The captain on the bridge bellowed to his men. "All ahead full. Come starboard to bearing one seven zero degrees."

The *U-boat* had missed its intended target. In the conning tower, its captain cursed at the destroyer that had gotten in his way. He saw the troop liner turning to attack. *Damn. We drifted too close to the convoy.* "Full speed to starboard. Dive, level one hundred," he yelled at his helmsman, pushing the button to retract the periscope. "Brace." He knew too well the sluggishness of his vessel's response. At least this attacker would have no depth charges. They would be all right.

A minute later the *Aquitania's* bow struck the diving U-boat, shearing off its conning tower and flooding the control room. The submarine rolled over, violently tossing the crew against its bulkheads just before the submarine ripped open. Most of the men in the control room died before they could drown, chewed up by the *Aquitania's* four steam-driven propellers. As if by Divine intervention, the U-boat Kapitan and his crew, entombed inside the broken hull of their mangled submarine had plowed into the Celtic Sea bottom less than a quarter mile from the *Lusitania's* carcass.

♣ ♣ ♣ ♣

Holding fast to the railing, Collin cried out, "Did you feel that?" as Marshall stood up and rubbed his neck.

"We hit something."

Corporal Johnson rushed over to the rail. "You boys all right? Our captain rammed the U-boat. I think we got him."

They looked overboard, but all they could see was the smashed-in hull of their own ship.

"Now hear this," the Captain announced from the bridge. "We have spotted debris in our wake. We destroyed the U-boat, a first for an armed merchant cruiser."

All the escorts in the flotilla blasted their horns in unison.

The scowl on the corporal's face showed he was not impressed. He headed off to assemble his men and check on their condition. Marshall followed behind him.

The *Aquitania*, still afloat but moving at reduced speed, doubled back, looking for survivors from the U-boat and for the soldiers who had gone overboard at the initial collision. By this time, sailors on the HMS *Teutonic* were fishing soldiers out of the sea. The *Aquitania* limped back into formation as the convoy stopped to assess the damage. Collin saw that the *Contest* still seemed seaworthy but clearly had steering and engine difficulties.

An hour later, the captain announced over the loudspeaker, "Fortunately, we closed the bulkheads in time and prevented further damage. The housing fore and aft was not affected, just the cargo hold. We still have propulsion and steering. But we will be putting in at Queenstown for repairs. We are circling to search for the fourteen men that your officers have determined were lost overboard. The forty-five soldiers who were injured below decks are being treated in sick bay. Unfortunately, three of our crewmen died in the hold at the time of the attack."

This was terrible news for the ship's complement and for the officers of the troops, but the soldiers were thankful of any diversion that would postpone the inevitable. Collin felt sorry for those who had lost their lives or were injured, but this was good news for him. He would be arriving in Ireland sooner, at the port where Jack Jordan would be waiting for him. He returned to his bunk to write his first war report. This would be a scoop.

Chapter Thirteen
Dublin Bound

Tuesday, May 2, 1916
Queenstown Harbour, Ireland

*J*ack Jordan had his hands full. The Cunard dock overflowed with troops bound for Liverpool, and his prize Cunard liner, *Aquitania,* was tied up, showing a great gash in her side and a flooded main cargo hold. The White Star Line's *Teutonic* lay at anchor in the harbor, preparing to load *Aquitania's* troops, despite having a shipload herself. The soldiers would be crowded for the nine-hour trip to their destination at Liverpool.

Collin finally stepped off the gangplank and onto his native Irish soil after an eleven-year absence. What a relief. He clearly remembered fearing for his life as his mother hustled him and his sister Claire onto that fishing boat in Killybegs Harbour near Donegal Town back in '05. Left everything behind. They needed to escape the night after his Pa was brutally murdered by the rogue RIC devil and his underling. God, he hated that monster. His Pa had protected him when Collin tried to save him from the evil Britisher. But he was only twelve then. Did Pa get buried? He didn't know. Some day on this trip he'd find out, and then he would avenge his Pa's death.

"Line up, you men!" Corporal Johnson yelled, above the din of his rowdy troops. Collin could plainly see that they were trying to ignore their leader.

Collin bumped into Marshall in the crowd. "I guess this is it, my friend. This is where I get off," he said, reaching out to shake the soldier's hand.

"Lucky you." Marshall meant it and shook the Irishman's hand vigorously. "We've already had a taste of battle today. Now we must go to the Front." He looked grim, the lines around his mouth deepening.

"God be with you and your comrades, Marshall." Collin clasped the soldier around the shoulder and then let go. Marshall waved as he moved off and was soon lost in the sea of troops.

Collin set off to find his benefactor and only ally in Ireland, Jack Jordan. He figured if he could find the ship's captain, he would locate Jack. He had seen Captain Haig disembark along with the troops. Scanning the dock area, Collin glimpsed the captain through the throng of soldiers and saw him disappear into a building with the Cunard sign over the door.

The boats from the *Teutonic* were starting to ferry the troops over to their ship as Collin reached the Cunard shore office. The ship's bosun intercepted him at the door.

"I need to talk with Jack Jordan," Collin stated, hoping for support from this officer.

"Do you, now? He's busy with our captain. We have a slight dent in our boat, if you didn't notice."

"I was on board, sir. I realize he's in a critical conversation, but I must talk to him."

"What's your name?"

"Collin O'Donnell."

"Wait here, I'll inform my captain." The bosun stepped through the open door and approached a man sitting in a wheelchair conversing with the captain. Collin saw him wait for a break in the conversation before speaking. When the bosun finally got their attention, he pointed back toward Collin at the door.

The officer in the Cunard cap swiveled his chair to face Collin, revealing a carefully trimmed moustache below a pair of sparkling blue-green eyes. His face broke into a wide smile as he motioned to Collin.

"Excuse me, Captain."

As Collin approached, he said, "Mr. Jordan, I presume. I'm so glad to finally meet you."

"Call me Jack. Collin, isn't it?"

"Yes, that's right. Claire's brother." He clasped Jack's hand and shook it vigorously.

Jack returned the handshake with tremendous strength. It was as if two long lost friends or brothers had been reunited after being years apart.

"I need to talk to you, but I've got urgent business with the captain. Can you come back in half an hour?"

"Yes, yes, of course. This must be putting a monkey wrench in your day, Jack."

"You can say that again. But our ship sank a U-boat today. That's a first. I hope we got that damn Kapitan Schwieger who sank our beautiful *Lusitania* last year. So many brave souls lost."

"That would be justice, right enough. I'll see you later." Collin returned to the dock to watch the embarkation of the troops.

He joined Jack an hour later after the captain departed for his ship.

"Sorry for the delay, Collin. The damage is worse than we thought and the whole cargo's ruined. Worst of all, I must contact the relatives of our lost crew members and attend to their needs." Jack waved a list in front of Collin's face. "But first, let's get you sorted. The Rising is over, in case you didn't hear on the ship. They've rounded up most of the rebels and are holding the ringleaders in Kilmainham Jail. Much of Dublin is in ruins, and the citizens are angry."

"Who are they angry at?"

"Initially at the rebels, but now I'm not so sure. The British are taking a hard line. The papers are full of it all." Jack tossed over a pile of newspapers that he had been saving for Collin. "Here, read for yourself."

"Thanks, but what about Claire?" Collin opened his valise and tucked the newsprint inside.

185

"No news there, I'm afraid. But here's what I do know." Jack proceeded to fill Collin in on what he had found out and what he surmised in a way that his curt telegrams could not have done. He left out no detail.

"So, you're telling me that this RIC head constable named Boyle from Cork swears that Claire is in cahoots with two German spies."

"He's gone further than that. He now calls Claire a murdering foreign spy after their gun battle down near Tralee a little more than a week ago, when Roger Casement was captured."

Collin wondered if his sister had been brainwashed by radicals and worried about the possibility of her having changed so completely. She had been a sweet, caring child before her abduction, but he hadn't seen her in almost ten years, since that fateful June day in '06 when he had left her alone in Brooklyn to go and street fight. He did know she had survived her incarceration in that terrible orphanage and workhouse with great charitable character. He clenched his teeth in frustration. "But you're sure that we're talking about *my* Claire?"

"I believe so. I've seen her twice in the company of that Irishman. Once on his motorcycle just leaving this Cunard facility and once on his hooker ship right off the end of my dock here."

"Both times right here?" *That seems a little odd.*

"It's the only place I've been since the *Lusitania* went down, really. Until recently, I've been wheelchair bound. My back, you know."

"How close were you when you saw her?"

"Close enough."

"So, you're sure it was her. You only saw her for a few minutes on the *Lusitania*, Jack."

"But I'd know her anywhere. You should have seen her, Collin. She was amazing. No thought for her own safety. So heroic."

Now Collin was worried. Maybe Sam was right. Jack seemed obsessed. But wait a minute, wasn't he obsessed, too? She does that to people. He owed Jack the benefit of the doubt.

"You care about Claire, don't you, Jack."

"It's a strange thing, but I do, Collin. I only met her for five minutes and yet she inspired me."

"Inspired you, did she?"

"Yes. I jumped off the *Lusitania,* breaking my back just as it sank out from under me. A broken piece of lifeboat was within reach, or I'd have sunk like a stone. I clung to it until I was rescued. During that time, the vision of Claire filled my thoughts and kept me alive. And after I saw her that day on the Cunard docks, she motivated me to eventually get out of my wheelchair, walk again and find her. I have some of the feeling back in my legs now. Watch."

Jack locked the wheels of the chair and strained his arms to stand.

"Here, let me help you."

"No, Collin, let me be. I've been practicing."

Collin could see Jack's biceps twitch as he pushed to stand. Then, all at once, the man was up, tottering, but upright. Collin jumped to assist, grabbing Jack's left arm for balance.

"All right, let's walk now." Jack took a tiny step, then another, and another.

Collin could feel the man start to sag and strengthened his grip to prop him up.

"No, I've got to do this on my own. Turn me around."

Collin noticed that Jack's spine straightened as if in a second wind.

"All right, now. Let's walk back." Jack returned to his wheelchair, shaking like a leaf. They had only gone twenty feet, but it was a monumental achievement, propelling him from invalid toward self-sufficient human being.

"She's a saint, Collin, really. I was thinking of her now with every step I took. A step closer to Florence Nightingale. We've got to find her."

Collin remembered now—Florence Nightingale—as the orphan Lucy referred to her at the remembrance service. *My God, it is Claire. It's got to be her.*

Collin felt a kinship for this man. "Jack, I am as determined as you are to find my sister."

"Obviously, or you wouldn't be here, would you."

"I left her alone in a really bad place ten years ago when she was my responsibility and she was kidnapped. My Ma and I never saw her since. I've got to find her." Collin grasped the Cunard manager's hand and shook it with vigor. "All right then, Jack. Let's find her together." He felt his eyes burn. "What's this Irishman's name?"

"I don't know, and the RIC didn't tell me. Maybe they don't know."

"All right. Then where's this Boyle fellow? I need to talk with him."

"I spoke to Inspector Maloney, his boss at the RIC office in Cork City. Boyle's still in hospital outside Tralee in critical condition from the chest wound that he says the German spy gave him. You won't be able to question him at present."

"I don't suppose they know where the Irishman lives. I want to go and confront him."

"I have no idea and neither does Head Constable Boyle, I believe. It's a mystery."

"Well, I'm here to solve this mystery and to save Claire from these thugs. My newspaper credentials should help, as I can be in places and ask questions that will open up the information. You would be surprised by what a press pass can do."

"Good. I'm here to help you. I'd like to offer you lodging tonight, and tomorrow you can start your search. As I said in my telegram, my best guess is that Claire and her Irishman would have gone to Dublin for the Rising. It makes sense since they were apparently part of the gun-running scheme, and the Rising was centered in Dublin."

"I have to report to the publisher of *The Irish Times* tomorrow in Dublin for my assignment. I'll take you up on that offer, Jack."

"Good. I'm going to be tied up here for another two hours sorting out the plan to repair the *Aquitania* and then we can get a drink at the Seafarer's Bar. It's down on the wharf, about as far as I can go for the time being."

"Do they have O'Keefe Ale?"

"Beer? Not here, my lad. It's B&C Stout or Guinness in these parts. Puts hair on your chest, it will."

"I don't need any more hair, Jack. Just Claire. Can you direct me to the telegraph office while I wait?"

"A block down on your left. I'll meet you at the bar, then."

Collin sat in the bar and scribbled out a note he would telegraph to his boss about the U-boat attack. *That should get their juices flowing.*

Then came the shorter, yet more difficult missive—

> Kathy and Liam. Stop. Miss you. Stop. Arrived Queenstown safely. Stop. See my news report. Stop. Met Jack. Stop. Tomorrow Dublin to find Claire. Stop. Love you. Stop.

After finishing his stout, Collin sent off the telegrams. *There that should do it.* He felt exhausted, but at least he was on his native soil and not heading into the jaws of hell like Marshall and the rest of the soldiers. God save them.

Still ensconced at Sean's home, Tadgh noticed that Morgan had gained strength by the day. Soon it would be time to try to escape the clutches of the British bastards and thus limit the risk of exposure to his benefactor.

On Tuesday evening, a hundred and sixty-five miles from where Collin and Jack were making plans for the search, Tadgh read General Maxwell's tally of the casualties in the dailies of *The Irish Times*. Sixty-four rebels had been killed out of a total of four hundred and fifty dead.

Morgan put on the kettle and pretended not to hear. "Who wants sugar in their tea?"

Tadgh read on and then blurted out, "What started on Monday with fourteen hundred rebels and four hundred British military in Dublin has ended with over eighteen thousand well-equipped British forces less than a week later. Hardly a fair fight, do ye think, Sean!" Tadgh threw down the paper.

Their host sat down in his favorite chair facing the kitchen window, pinching the bridge of his nose. "The saddest statistic is that two hundred and fifty-four civilian bystanders have been killed."

The kettle started to whistle. Morgan attended to it, then snatched the paper from her partner and scanned it. "My God, Tadgh. I told you. No distinction between rebel and civilian clothing in many cases. Awful."

"Aye, lass." Tadgh turned to his bride-to-be. "How many civilians wounded, then?"

Morgan read on to the end of the article. "It doesn't say, but two thousand, six hundred and fourteen is the total tally of the wounded."

Tadgh paced the kitchen. "Connolly was wrong, Morgan. The bloody British destroyed the city and brutally murdered our citizenry. The bastards." He realized that he was helpless to strike back at the moment. They all were. But it made him mad as hell.

Morgan poured the water into the teapot and added Darjeeling black, Sean's favorite blend. Then she opened the icebox door and pulled out some cheese, scraping off a bit of mold. "Look at the positive side. The war is over and no more people will be killed."

Tadgh stopped pacing and stared at his mate as she sliced away. "The war is not over, lass. Just the first skirmish. You mark my words."

Morgan flinched and he could see her heart wasn't in it. It never had been.

"Tadgh, me boyo, we can all agree with you. The British have just made matters worse. But just as Morgan says, *The Times* reports that the city is slowly returning to normal, with food becoming available and some trams back in operation."

"That's all fine and good, Teacher. But the citizens need to be angry enough to revolt en masse next time."

Morgan's green eyes turned dark, but she pretended she hadn't heard Tadgh's last remark. "Tea, anyone?" she said, pouring the boiling black liquid into Sean's kitchen cups adding what was left of the sugar. "We've no biscuits, I'm afraid," she announced, setting the tray down on the kitchen table. "I'm taking mine to bed. Coming, love?"

Tadgh didn't need a second invitation. He picked up his cup and headed upstairs right behind her.

Before he reached the top step, he turned and called out to his host. "This is only the beginning, Sean. You mind me. We will exterminate the British here in Ireland."

O'Casey pretended not to hear.

They awoke on the third of May to terrible news.

Sean's voice broke as he read the newspaper. "They've executed Pearse, Clarke, and MacDonagh by firing squad before dawn today at Kilmaimham Gaol, and they've thrown their bodies in a lime pit in Arbour Hill Prison. They're calling them traitors. They did this after a closed military court martial." Sean couldn't read anymore, and he covered his eyes as if to block that awful sight.

Tadgh slammed his hand on the table, snarling, "The British are the traitors and the cowards. Those three are the martyrs for our Cause, by Jaysus."

"Martyrs or not, they're dead and gone, so they are." Sean shot

Tadgh a look of agony.

"Dead, yes, but now forever alive in our hearts as the advance guard for our freedom," Tadgh assured him.

"I guess we'll see about that, me boyo. But I'll grant you that the British are taking too heavy a hand on the common man for my liking."

At the same time at the Cunard office in Queenstown, Jack Jordan was making final arrangements with Collin. "A Cunard car is at your disposal. Just remember to drive on the left-hand side of the road. While you are in Dublin, I will try to get you access to Head Constable Boyle. If he's not well enough, I can get you in to see Inspector Maloney."

"It's Boyle I need to see. He's the only one who has seen Claire, right?"

"Far as I know. Except me, of course."

"Of course. Wish me well."

"Godspeed, Collin. I am excited at the prospect of seeing Claire again."

"I'll keep you informed, Jack," Collin said, as he drove off.

Six hours later, Collin encountered a roadblock in Clane twenty miles from Dublin. When he finally got to the checkpoint, a belligerent officer demanded to see his papers. Collin suddenly shivered and he sensed a presence. *Claire must have been here.*

"I'm a reporter for the *Toronto Evening Telegram.*" Collin showed his identification. "I am expected by the publisher of *The Irish Times* this afternoon, sir."

At the mention of the Unionist newspaper, the policeman chose to bypass the car search. "Long way from home, lad. You know that the newspaper is in the impact zone of the rebellion, don't you, O'Donnell?"

Collin thought that was a quaint description of the complete devastation levied by British artillery, as he recalled from seeing newspaper photographs.

"You can't park down there, and the public tram system is not yet working at full capacity," the officer stated.

It took Collin two hours to navigate the complex one-way road system in Dublin, having to backtrack on several occasions because of the police presence in the war zone. Finally, in desperation, he left the locked car in the yard at Portobello Barracks due south of St. Stephens Green across the Grand Canal with the approval of the compound sergeant.

He had to hurry. Jack had arranged a call that morning to the publisher at *The Irish Times*. His secretary said that he would be leaving work at five in the afternoon due to the curfew imposed in the wake of the Rising.

Collin headed north at a trot, passing by Jacob's Biscuit Factory where Thomas MacDonagh had been commandant, then running alongside St. Stephen's Green past the Royal College of Surgeons where Mallin had held out. Finally, he circled Trinity College and crossed O'Connell Bridge over the Liffey. Breathless, he stopped to take in the sight.

Sackville, which the rebels called O'Connell Street, was a shambles. North of the Liffey River, the buildings on both sides of the street were either burned-out shells or cannon-peppered hulks. He saw work crews attempting to clean the roadway so that the trams could start running and commerce could return. Farther up on the west side of the street, one colossal stone building with six pillars was completely destroyed. Its roof had fallen or burned away. The Union Jack flew over this hulk, replacing the rebel tricolor. *That must be the General Post Office.*

Although he was short on time, Collin couldn't resist snapping a few pictures with his Brownie before quickly turning east on Lower Abbey Street, the first street north of the river quay. There it was, *The Irish Times* at Number Four. Collin couldn't believe this eyes.

The stone edifice stood, alone and undamaged, while the buildings all around were in various states of destruction. Maybe there was something to the adage, *freedom of the press.*

"I'm here to see Mr. Healy," Collin said to the receptionist in the front foyer. "I believe that he is expecting me."

"I'm sorry, sir, he is not here. We just do the printing here these days. You will find our editor in the executive offices at Thirty-One Westmoreland Street. It's just a block south of the O'Connell Bridge and west of Trinity."

"Thank you, miss. I just came by there, not much damage."

Ten minutes later, Collin presented himself to the receptionist in the executive office.

"Your name, sir?"

"Collin O'Donnell from the *Toronto Evening Telegram*, ma'am."

"Oh, yes. You've come a long way, then. We wondered if you would be able to make it through. Such a mess here in Dublin."

"Yes, ma'am, I noticed."

She disappeared up the nearby stairs and returned a few minutes later with a bespectacled, round-faced gentleman who introduced himself as John Edward Healy, publisher and editor of *The Irish Times*. It seemed to Collin that his waistcoat buttons were about to pop.

"May I offer you tea, lad? Come up to my office." He turned to the receptionist, "And we'd like scones and clotted cream too, please."

Collin noticed the girl scurrying off as they began the climb up the curved mahogany staircase to the inner sanctum. What a difference from the cubicle arrangement at the *Tely*, where even the editor was out among his journalists.

Bookshelves with works on every subject imaginable lined three walls of the opulent wood- paneled office. Collin saw one rather large section titled "Union Policy." Framed front-page articles lined the fourth wall. Collin noticed one that read, TITANIC HITS ICEBERG ON MAIDEN VOYAGE - 1517 DEAD, dated

April 15, 1912. Alongside it was another that read LUSITANIA TORPEDOED - 1300 FEARED DEAD, dated Saturday, May 8, 1915 with a large photograph of the super liner. Collin shuddered.

"Sit down, sit down, Collin. Are you cold, lad?" Healy motioned to a padded leather sofa and chairs set in front of a massive fireplace.

"No, sir." The Canadian pointed at the wall. "I was just noticing your articles on the sinkings."

"Very nasty business, those, I can tell you. Now then, your publisher, John Ross notified me that you were coming to represent his paper over this Rebellion. You've come a long way, lad, but I'm afraid the show's over. We have the perpetrators in custody, and they will get swift justice, to be sure."

Collin was impressed. John Ross Robertson had not only established the *Tely* to be the voice of the common man in Toronto in 1876, he had also been editor-in-chief since 1888. Collin had no idea that he would have taken an interest in him and his assignment. No wonder this chief editor was giving him the royal treatment. This fellow obviously had no sympathy for the Republicans.

"There are millions of Irishmen living in Canada, sir, most of whom had to leave under troubling circumstances. They want to know what is happening in their old homeland."

"Do they now, lad? You can be their witness then to how we maintain civility and social justice here in the United Kingdom."

The receptionist knocked and entered with the tray of tea, placing it on the table between the two men and taking her leave.

"One lump or two, Collin?"

"None, sir. I prefer my tea black."

"No cream? Not civilized in the colonies, then."

Collin didn't want to offend his host. "It was the way my Ma served it back in Donegal Town before . . ." He realized that he'd gone too far.

"Before what, lad?" Healy was the consummate investigator, always searching for a story.

"My Da was killed back in '05, and my Ma whisked us off to

America, me and my sister Claire, that is."

"You must have been young then, Collin. What killed him, if I might ask."

"Not what, but who, sir."

"Oh, murder, then. Your Ma must have been awfully frightened for your safety to cross the ocean and leave her country."

"Yes sir, we all were. We left the next night. I hesitate to say who was responsible."

"Nonsense boy. Out with it."

"All right, then. It was a rogue RIC constable and his underling, sir. I don't suppose that he was ever brought to justice."

"And your father?"

"An honorable shopkeeper, sir. Shoes and boots."

"A cobbler, then."

"Yes."

"We can check the records at the time and see what became of your Da's body and who might have attacked him."

"That would be appreciated, so it would. Thank you."

"Have you never been back before this?"

"No, sir."

"Your Ma and sister. Are they well in America?"

"Ma is dead. I saw her killed on the Toronto waterfront. My sister Claire was apparently lost on the *Lusitania,* but I am convinced she survived and is alive here in Ireland."

"If that's true, wouldn't she have contacted you?"

"According to the Cunard manager in Queenstown, she has amnesia and can't be found. It's a long story."

"It's complicated enough to confuse an old newspaperman."

"Yes, sir, it taxes my brain and heart most of the time."

"Whoa, lad. What a tale. You must follow up on all this while you are here. I insist upon it." Healy leaned over and offered the plate of scones to Collin. Then he forked one onto his own plate and slathered it with the cream.

Collin saw the gleam in the man's eye. He obviously sensed a big, human-interest story. He had another ally here, one who could unleash resources to aid in his search.

Collin took a bite of the raspberry scone. "My editor sent me here to report on the Rising and its aftermath, so that's my priority, sir."

"Fine. So be it. John Ross asked me to facilitate your time with us. I am assigning a local journalist to work with you and show you our fine city. She will provide background information and transportation."

"I already have a Cunard car, sir, parked at the Portobello Barracks."

"Yes, transportation is still disrupted and security is tight, but we are returning to normal. I'll make sure that the military holds that vehicle safe until you need it."

Based on what he had seen outside, Collin wasn't sure that the city or its citizens would ever return to whatever was normal before Easter Monday. "Thank you, sir."

"Also, I have arranged for you to stay at the Shelbourne Hotel, which just reopened to the public. It should give you a central location from which to operate."

"Thank you again, sir." *Mr. Robertson must carry some weight with his counterpart.*

"I only have one request, that you keep me informed of your activities and the content of your reports before you send them home."

"Yes, sir, except that I hope you will not censor my reporting."

"Wouldn't think of it, lad."

Collin knew that this was a lie. Healy didn't get where he was without controlling everything he touched.

With that, the meeting and the tea were over. The receptionist reappeared to usher Collin out. As he turned to leave, the publisher and editor-in-chief said, "My reporter will meet you at your hotel at eight o'clock tomorrow morning. Have a good night."

Chapter Fourteen
Witch Hunt

Thursday, May 4, 1916
Shelbourne Hotel, Dublin

*C*ollin had slept fitfully in his elegant room at the Shelbourne. Sure, it wasn't the presidential suite at the Knickerbocker that Governor Lippitt had arranged for him and Kathy in New York's Times Square, but it was a darned sight better than the rocking berth with all those sweaty men on the *Aquitania*. Being back in such a marvelous hotel suite brought back memories of that magical night in New York when he and Kathy consummated their love for the first time, and he was sure that was when beautiful baby Liam had been conceived. God, he missed them now, and he felt awful about his behavior the night before he left them alone in the world. To be sure, he had come far since the days in the Ward, when he was so lost and alone. Yet now, when the chips were down with Claire's life on the line, he had reverted to his old ways. *Shame on me. But I'm here now, and they will be safe at home under the guidance of Sam and Lil, so get on with it. But where to start?*

"Mr. O'Donnell, sir." Collin heard a voice at the door. He checked his watch. Six o'clock.

He saw through the sheers that the sun was just rising. *Damn, I thought he said eight o'clock.* "Yes?"

"There's a pretty woman named Maureen O'Sullivan from *The Irish Times* waiting for you in the lobby, sir."

"Is she, now. Tell her I'll be right down."

O'Sullivan, eh? Now there's an ironic name.

Collin descended into the lobby to find that Miss O'Sullivan was a dark-haired beauty, five foot eight with lustrous brown hair framing a sensual, inviting face. She wore a gray business suit that was unsuccessful in hiding her ample curves.

"Miss O'Sullivan?"

"Yes, Mr. O'Donnell, from *The Times.*" They shook hands, and Collin could feel the warmth and slight moisture in that touch. She smiled, and her amber eyes twinkled.

"Looks like it will be a fine day, sir."

"Please, call me Collin. I thought we were going to meet at—"

"Eight o'clock, yes, but something's come up that we should be privy to. I thought you wouldn't mind."

"Not at all, lass." Collin was not minding this duty in the least, but he thought that God must be warning him. "What a coincidence. My wife's maiden name is O'Sullivan, from Belfast. Could you be related?"

"Highly unlikely. It's a common enough name. My family is originally from Tipperary. Are you from Donegal then?"

"Yes, a long way back. I've been away. What do you have to tell me?"

"I presume you haven't had breakfast."

"No, I've barely had time to shave. I'm starved." Collin had been so tired that he had fallen into bed the night before without eating supper.

"Good. Let's eat while we talk." Maureen led him into the main dining room off the lobby, facing St. Stephen's Street North.

The room was furnished in splendid French provincial style with Versailles-type chandeliers and padded velvet chairs. There must have been room to seat at least a hundred and fifty patrons. But not today. They were practically by themselves.

The waitress escorted them to a window table that looked out onto the park, and Collin pulled the chair out for Maureen. Her smile showed him that she recognized his chivalry. He thought of Kathy back at home with little Liam, and a twinge of guilt crept in.

"I noticed that the park across the street is cordoned off, Miss O'Sullivan."

"Call me Maureen, Collin, please."

"All right, Maureen. This was one of the sites of the Rising, I understand from your newspaper reports."

"Yes, we occupied this hotel and pushed the rebels back from the Green into the Royal College of Surgeons to its west where we contained them until hostilities ceased last Saturday. They've just re-opened the Shelbourne yesterday and the authorities are still examining these sites."

Collin felt a chill. He thought of Claire in danger and the hair on his neck stood on end.

"Are you all right? You look like you've seen a ghost."

"Just thinking of the terror this uprising would have caused, lass."

"Yes, but it's over now."

"Are you sure about that?"

"Yes, quite."

After their waitress brought tea and took their order for breakfast, Maureen started in, "I'm a reporter who covers political affairs here in Ireland. Just so you know, we're a Unionist paper."

"I gathered that, speaking to Mr. Healy yesterday afternoon."

"Did you, now." Maureen seemed surprised, "He's staunch, you know."

"Yes, that's very clear."

"Mr. Healy wants me tell you what has happened regarding local politics and then tour you around as the situation develops."

"Isn't the term 'local politics' understating what's been happening? It's a revolution, for God's sake."

Collin could tell that she was mouthing the party line. "You need to be candid with me if we're going to work together, lass."

Maureen looked around and then lowered her voice. "You're right. Listen, Collin, you're not from around here. May I speak frankly?"

"Yes. It will help me to gain an impartial view if you would do so. You can trust me to keep our conversations confidential, and

I will show you any reports that I plan on sending to Canada. I know that Mr. Healy can be an overpowering leader, just like my editor-in-chief back home in Toronto."

"Right, then. This Revolution was instigated and carried out by very brave men and women who care deeply for their country and its people. Their Rising was destined to fail militarily, and they knew it as soon as their gun-running scheme failed, maybe sooner. Heaven knows they are not military men. Word is that James Connolly, the only man with any military acumen, counted on the British not bringing artillery to bear on the city, whereas Pearse hoped they would."

"Martyrdom?"

"Exactly. And it seems to be working."

"What do you mean?"

"When the Rising commenced a week ago Monday, and the British began shelling the city, Dubliners were outraged at the rebels. When they surrendered last Saturday, they threw garbage at them. But in the short span of time since then, I have observed a change in the Dubliners' attitude. Maxwell has been quite vicious with the organizers. He had the soldiers strip poor Tom Clarke naked in public while he was being lined up before being taken to Kilmainham. And the executions yesterday without a public trial."

"Executions?"

"Yes. By firing squad. Pearse, Clarke and MacDonagh yesterday at dawn, and then their bodies dumped in a lime pit. And that's just the beginning, I'm told."

Collin could imagine the grisly scene, made even more horrific for loved ones looking on. *God, what if Claire's been captured?*

"Collin?"

"Sorry. Lost in thought. The British are very harsh, aren't they?"

"Yes, playing into the rebels' hands. That's why our reporting has to be accurate and fair to all parties."

"Indeed, if Mr. Healy allows it."

"Point taken, sir."

"Thank you for clearing the air, Maureen."

Their talk was interrupted by the waiter bringing a full Irish breakfast for Collin and a croissant and fruit for Maureen. "So what have you planned this morning?" Collin asked, as he wolfed down two sausages.

"We got word from Lowe's office that they plan a raid on some known collaborators this morning at nine o'clock. We're going to follow them. Then we'll go to Kilmainham Gaol for the latest on the executions."

Collin knew from his work back home that leaks from government sources were like gold for the journalist. "Sounds ghoulish, but we have to go where the action is developing. Where's the raid supposed to take place?"

"Mountjoy Square [2], northeast of the GPO. On the way, we can stop so you can see the condition of that post office. At least martial law has been lifted this morning so Dubliners can go about their business."

"Who are they after?"

"Walter Leonard Cole is a Republican who lives at Number Three Mountjoy Square, North. It has just come to light from notes taken by a Glasgow Volunteer that secret meetings of the Republicans, including James Connolly, and three who were executed yesterday were held at Cole's home this last winter. He was a founding father of the Sinn Féin organization and publishing company. Beyond that, we learned that twelve rebels of Company D, commanded by Captain Sean Heuston, marshaled in that square before heading out to commandeer the Mendicity Institute across the river from the Four Courts. So, eat up. I have a lorry waiting outside."

Morgan came down for breakfast at eight o'clock. "The smoke has cleared and the sky is blue. I want to go for a walk in Mountjoy Square Park. May I, please?"

Sean and Tadgh had been up early to check the news. It was terrible, they told her, with four more men executed in the same brutal manner, or as Tadgh would say, murdered. Joseph Plunkett, Edward Daly, Michael O'Hanrahan and Willie Pearse. This made Sean furious. "Poor Willie didn't have much to do with the Rising, except for his last name and sticking close to his brother."

Tadgh thought that some fresh air might do them all some good. Opening the front door, he noted the tranquil atmosphere of the deserted park, so he bundled Morgan up and out they went, Tadgh close at her side every step of the way.

The park was about six hundred feet square with eighteen three-story Georgian row homes on each side, although, for some reason on the south where Sean's home was located, there were nineteen. The northeast section of the park contained a ballfield, while the remainder was grassy, with low hedges, flower beds and bordered walkways winding through treed serenity. The Scottish standard electrified lampposts situated all around the park provided an elegant touch.

They stopped their languid stroll for a breather at a bench in the flowerbed area opposite Sean's home at the east end of the park. Inside the house they had been holed up like rats. Now, outside in the morning air, Tadgh thoughts veered to their adventure. He recounted to Morgan what had happened with Professor Lawlor at the RIA, and the subsequent conversation he had had with Peader on this subject.

"Intriguing, isn't it, lass?"

"Fascinating. There's certainly a lot of food for thought there. At least it explains why Boyle knew what he knew."

"What do you mean, aroon? What did I miss?"

"The obvious, dear. The *Book of MacCarthaigh Reagh* or *Lismore* is the key."

"Is it, now?" Tadgh still wasn't following.

"From what Boyle said in Kerry, we wondered how he knew so much about the Clans Pact, didn't we."

"Yes, that's right."

"And we speculated that the McCarthy Clan would have kept an original signed copy of the pact somewhere safe in their relics, didn't we?"

"Go on," Tadgh requested, gaining interest in her reasoning.

Morgan looked at him as if to say, figure it out yourself.

It finally struck him. "Of course, why didn't I see it earlier? I knew that I was missing somethin' but couldn't put my finger on it."

"So—?"

"So Florence had the McCarthy copy and placed it in the sealed pocket in the revered *Book of MacCarthaigh Reagh* in 1600 for safekeeping." Tadgh was twisting his moustache. "Just like Red Hugh put his copy in the *Cumdach.*" *It is all falling into place.*

"Precisely, Tadgh. He was incarcerated before the Battle of Kinsale, but their plans had been laid. Then in 1642 at the start of the Confederate Wars, when your MacCarthaigh Reagh's Kilbrittain Castle was taken by Lord Kinalmeaky on behalf of his father, Richard Boyle of Lismore Castle, the son confiscated the book and sent it to the elder statesman."

Tadgh stood up and started pacing while he thought. Then he said, "Lawlor told us there was a letter to that effect. Somehow, the Boyles must have discovered the pact and vowed to find the Clans treasures. They've presumably been searching for centuries for them, without adequate clues. Now their descendant, the malevolent head constable, is likely the lone remaining Boyle in the search. He finally employed extreme force to extract the clues from *us*, the descendant McCarthy Reaghs, clues that my immediate ancestors didn't know existed because they were not aware of the Clans Pact. And somehow, over the eons, the Boyles, with all their efforts, came to believe that these treasures are rightfully theirs."

Tadgh sat down beside Morgan and gave her a squeeze.

"Exactly, my love," Morgan beamed and kissed him on the cheek. "You are such a brilliant man, you know."

"But there are three things that I still don't understand other than where the treasure is hidden."

"Only three things, my love?" she laughed and started counting on her fingers.

"Why did the Book of MacCarthaigh Reagh get walled up in Lismore Castle? And two other things—what became of the McCarthy Clans Pact copy, and when did the McCarthy treasure disappear?"

"You already told me two of the answers, love. McCarthy Mor of Muscry attacked the Boyles at Lismore Castle during the following year, 1643, in retaliation for the defeat handed to their other family Clansmen a year earlier. Remember when you told me that?"

Tadgh grasped her shoulders with both hands. "They must have been motivated to regain the *Book of MacCarthaigh Reagh* to protect its secrets. Which means that while he was in prison, Florence secretly confided in the McCarthy Mor of Blarney. He must have told him that the *Book of MacCarthaigh Reagh* was a crucial family heirloom that held a Clans Pact, one to be protected at all costs. He probably wanted to protect the fortunes of the whole McCarthy family clans and instructed the Mor where to hide the MacCarthaigh Reagh and McCarthy Mor assets if the English were about to defeat them."

"You don't think that he would have hidden his assets before he was incarcerated, Tadgh, do you?"

"No. He wouldn't have done that while he was still in firm control of his lands. Then in 1601, he was arrested by Sir George Carew, the new governor of Munster, likely with no time to react. Also at that time, the Muscry McCarthys had a policy of passive defiance and they did not fight with the clans against the British in the Battle of Kinsale the following January."

"All right. Then what happened, do you think?" Morgan stretched her right leg out to ease a sudden cramp.

Tadgh knelt in front of Morgan on the lawn and massaged her

right calf. "There, aroon. Is that better?"

"Mmmm."

He got up and looked around the square for any dangers. When satisfied that they were safe, he continued his line of thought, twirling his moustache as he spoke. "Later, before Florence's death in 1640, when both McCarthy Clans still had control of their lands and castles, the McCarthy Mor of Blarney took a leadership role in the planned Confederate Wars insurrection. That was when Florence would have confided in him, when he was out of the Tower of London and living under his own cognizance in London but prohibited from returning to Ireland."

Morgan pulled him down onto the bench beside her, saying, "Those were certainly turbulent times."

"Aye, lass." Tadgh stroked the black ringlets away from Morgan's face so he could see her eyes. "When their hand was forced during the Confederate Wars, I think that the McCarthy Clans united. They had to fight the British or have their lands, treasures, and culture forfeited. At least that's what my father taught me. Hopefully my ancestor would have been able to get his treasures to Blarney before Kilbrittain fell to Boyle, known as Lord Cork."

Morgan turned her lovely eyes on him. "If what you say is true, Tadgh, then we know something else important."

"And that is?"

"The Boyles had discovered the Clans Pact and removed it when Lord McCarthy Mor of Muscry attacked his castle, right? Otherwise, the pact would still have been in the book when it was discovered buried in the Lismore castle wall in 1814. Boyle must have assumed or known that the McCarthy Mor branch knew about the pact. He hid the book so that the McCarthys couldn't regain it and find that the pact was missing. Clearly, they thought that the pact was more valuable than the book itself, don't you think so, Tadgh?"

"I suppose you are right, aroon. Don't you think that we should go back inside now? That's enough sunshine for this morning."

"No, dear. Let's stay a little while longer. This fresh air is just what I need right now. I have more questions. What about the fact that the clues were in the possession of the firstborn male descendants of your McCarthaigh Reagh branch only? Why would the McCarthy Mor agree to hide his treasure where only Florence's descendants could find it?"

Tadgh had to think hard about that. "How about this—by the time of the Confederate War, the situation was dire for the McCarthy Clans. They really did have their lands and cultures taken by force and their castles badly damaged, especially when Cromwell arrived with his deadly troops. With Kilbrittain gone and Blarney Castle under siege, and the McCarthy Mor and his sons fighting to the last man as they retreated to Ross castle in Kerry, Florence's plan was in place and could be implemented, and at least there was one McCarthy Clan line that could eventually recover the treasures for all of them when the time was right, by Divine intervention."

"That's a bit of a stretch, but it's a plausible explanation of what we know so far, Tadgh."

"I wonder if there are clues in the book itself, just like there are clues likely in *an Cathach*?" Tadgh pondered, smoothing his thick moustache. "If so, the Boyles would probably have recognized this possibility. But did they find them? Might that be the reason they walled up the book, to protect it?"

"In other words, does Boyle already have more information than we have?"

"There's no way to know now, lass. But maybe it's a moot point if Darcy Boyle died in Kerry. We need to find out what happened to the monster, to be sure."

They had just agreed that this adventure was becoming more complex and fascinating, when Tadgh noticed the arrival of a squad of khakis pulling up at Number Three, near the northwest corner of the square. They fanned out into three groups, three to a house, and these squads forced their way into the residences. In addition to the soldiers, he saw two civilians, a man and a woman, talking to a captain who appeared to be in charge of the operation. Tadgh didn't like the look of the situation. "I knew it. A witch-hunt. We need to go in now, dear," he coaxed Morgan, not wanting to cause any alarm. But he sensed her unease as she looked in the direction of the raiding party. Her arm trembled beneath his hand.

She shivered. "I'm drawn to those people for some strange reason, Tadgh."

"Nonsense, lass. There's danger there. Let's go in now, love."

Tadgh had to hurry Morgan along, given her still-weak condition. By the time that they had mounted the steps of Number Thirty-Five, Tadgh could see that the goons were selectively choosing houses. The initial group had led an older man out of Number Three and the other two squads were checking out houses on the east side already. They moved with lightning speed.

"What's your hurry, me boyo?" Sean asked when they stepped inside the foyer.

"Army goons with what looks like RIC constables are searching some of the houses on this square. Undoubtedly looking for rebels, I should think."

"Number Three, right?"

"Yes. That's where they started. Why?"

Sean quickly explained the Mountjoy Square history with Walter Leonard Cole and Heuston who had been executed, just that morning.

"Do you have a place where we can hide until they're gone, Teacher?"

"Don't be absurd, Tadgh. The local police know me to be a pacifist. They won't search my house, surely." Then he thought for a moment. "You don't think they know we killed those sailors, do you?"

"I don't think so. We dispatched them out of the sight of any witnesses."

"What?" Morgan exclaimed, turning to face Tadgh with a scowl on her face. Tadgh had not briefed her on the details of their narrow escape.

"I'll tell you later, aroon. We need to get out of sight this instant."

"There's one place, but I don't know if you'll fit." Sean showed them a removable horizontal grate covering the front of the hot water radiator enclosure in the wide, front window seat. "There should be just enough room on each side if you lie flat."

After trying it out, Tadgh realized that there was barely enough room to squeeze them both in there, one on each side of the bulky radiator. In fact, its relief valve knob pushed up against Tadgh's forehead in a most uncomfortable way. He worried that Morgan's injury would cause her too much pain.

"Maybe you could just leave on the Kerry, Tadgh. Stay here, and I'll scout out the inquisition's progress."

Sean went back to the open front door. "Damnation. It looks like a squad is heading this way across the park. Another group just dragged two men out of Number Thirty. They broke down its front door. A wagon just drove up and they're herding them into it. They're coming here, Tadgh, the bastards. There's no time for the Kerry, now. You'd be apprehended."

Collin and Maureen followed the squad across the park. Collin stopped for a moment in the middle to take a couple of Brownie snaps of the violent extraction at Number Thirty.

"A mite brutal, don't ya think, Maureen? Why don't you have a seat on this bench? This will take a few more minutes."

After she sat down, Collin asked, "Did you see the man and woman hurry over to the house near the southwest corner a while back?" Collin asked. "The woman was limping."

"No, I didn't. Is that important?"

"I don't know, but it happened just after the soldiers removed

Mr. Cole from his home. That fellow in the doorway they entered looks familiar. Where have I seen that face before?"

Maureen looked up from note-taking. "Why, that's O'Casey. The budding playwright, Sean O'Casey."

"Is he, now? Yes, that's right. The *Tely* did a piece on him a year ago, about him dropping out of a militant organization."

"The Irish Citizens Army. He resigned from it when Connolly took over from Larkin."

"Yes, that's right." Collin sat down beside Maureen to see what would happen next. It seemed suspicious to his journalistic brain. "This squad is going directly there. Maybe they saw them."

"I think it's prudent to hide, Teacher. Got your pen ready?" Tadgh said, after Sean closed the door and raced back into the parlor. Tadgh shoehorned Morgan into her hiding place as gently as possible. "Are you all right, aroon?"

"Yes, Tadgh, but it's a tight squeeze. Don't leave me in here for very long."

"We'll be out in no time, right, Sean?"

"As soon as I get rid of those raiders."

"With your pen? Give me a hand here, Sean," Tadgh requested, as he tried to get into his own cramped space after pulling his Luger out of its holster.

"You're not going to discharge that weapon in here."

"I hope not. Only if your writing implement fails to stop them. Now close this grate."

"There you go," Sean grunted, as he gave his former pupil a shove with his boot and then slid the grate into place, locking it on two sides. "I may never let you out if you don't stop reminding me of my pacifist beliefs."

Tadgh heard Morgan's muffled voice. "You keep telling him, Sean. Just don't leave us in here, please."

211

♣ ♣ ♣ ♣

Collin watched the lead raid team as they approached O'Casey's front door. "Do you think I should tell them?"

"Up to you, Collin. It's probably nothing." Maureen didn't stop him when he jumped up and headed to the home. Instead, she rose and followed.

Sean heard a scuffling outside the door, and then a loud knock.

"Sean O'Casey. Are you in there? This is the military. Open this door immediately, or we'll break it down," the group leader roared.

"Hold your horses. I'm coming," Sean growled back. He knew his rights. They needed a warrant, didn't they? The next knock broke a pane of glass. *Apparently not, under these circumstances.* When he opened the door, three goons burst in and raced through the ground floor, guns drawn, looking everywhere.

"What is the meaning of this intrusion?" Sean saw that the soldiers were tossing his belongings, shoving them aside to search every nook and cranny. So far, they hadn't approached the window seat.

Their leader, a sergeant from the Black Watch, returned from the parlor to the foyer, list in hand. Consulting it briefly, he barked, "You were the Secretary of the ICA, were you not?"

"Under Larkin, yes. But not since Connolly became militant. I don't believe in violence. Only peaceful labor disputes," O'Casey explained, although he secretly wanted to wring this sergeant's neck.

The sergeant was talking again, jamming a meaty forefinger into Sean's chest. "Do you know a Tadgh or Aidan McCarthy?" he asked point blank.

How could they know that Tadgh is here? Sean could feel his face flush. Then he realized it was a trick question.

"Yes, I know Tadgh McCarthy. I mentored him a couple of

years back when he was a playwright student. But I've lost touch since then."

"Really? One of our informers said that he saw you talking to Tadgh McCarthy and his girl a week last Sunday in *an Stad* pub."

"Oh, that's right. We spoke briefly about his literary career, that's all. He wants to write another play."

"I could have you arrested for consorting with murdering rebels."

"I'm a pacifist, sir. They're not here. Search if you must."

"He is a criminal and a fugitive, you know. He maimed a member of the DMP during the Rossa funeral weekend a year ago. And there have been other problems according to the RIC from Cork," the sergeant quoted from his list. "And then there's his subversive play, *A Call to Arms*, that you helped him write."

"I helped him with technique and not content." Sean was getting really mad at this insulting inquisition.

The journalists overheard snippets of this conversation as they walked up to the open door. Maureen handed Sean her press identification card. "It's an honor, Mr. O'Casey."

"I told you to wait in the park," the sergeant snapped, reaching out to push Maureen away.

Collin stepped in between them. "Move back. You seem to be harassing this well-known playwright, a known pacifist, and now this lady, a member of *The Irish Times*. We're here to be witnesses to your actions. Freedom of the press, sir."

"Not here, not today."

It looked to Sean as if a fight would erupt, or worse. "Get on with it, Sergeant, if you must. I'll deal with these reporters."

The sergeant glared at Collin for a moment, then turned on his heel. "Come on, lads, let's look on the second floor."

Moments later, all three officers bounded up the stairs.

"Thank you, Collin," Maureen said, batting her long eyelashes in his direction.

"My pleasure, I assure you, lass. We journalists must stick up for each other, especially now in troubling times. Do you mind if we come in, Mr. O'Casey?"

Sean had stepped further into the foyer so he could see the parlor and its window seat. *These reporters might just be the distraction that could get the bastards out of my house.* "Not at all, lad and lass."

Collin followed and asked quietly, "Where is the couple that came in a few minutes ago?"

Damn, he saw that. "Oh, Henry and Marg? They're good Irish neighbors. Their home on Gardiner Lane backs up to my yard. Salt of the earth. They came for a visit and a stroll in the square. They went out home through my kitchen back door."

Collin stepped into the kitchen and peered out through the glass in the door. Sean watched him closely as the reporter observed the open gate in the wall at the back of the garden. The houses on the next street to the south were more modest than the Mountjoy Square Georgians.

"That your motorcycle, Mr. O'Casey?"

"Why, yes. Yes, of course." Sean walked Collin back to the foyer and Maureen. "Your way of speaking pegs you as being from the northwest."

Collin looked shocked. *I didn't think that I had any dialect left.* "Donegal, sir."

"I thought so. And you are reporting for *The Times?*"

"No sir, the *Toronto Evening Telegram.*"

"Canada? A mite far from home, aren't you, son?"

"My paper sent me to cover the Rising. We have many Irish folks in Canada interested in what is going on in the homeland, as you know. They're lucky ones whose ancestors escaped the Great Hunger sixty years ago."

"Isn't it hard to get across the unfriendly Atlantic these days? There must be something more than our little insurrection, surely."

"Little doesn't describe it." Collin swept his arm toward the stairs.

"Your point is well taken, lad. And to my question?"

Collin didn't respond.

"You're the escort then, lass?" Sean shifted focus, turning his attention to Maureen, looking her up and down.

"We work together, sir," Maureen replied, returning Sean's stare.

Switching his gaze to Collin, Sean said, "From the weakness of your accent, Collin, I'd say you left Ireland at an early age."

Why, yes. I was thirteen, my sister eleven."

"Is she here with you in Dublin, your sister, I mean?" Sean was keeping a watchful eye on the window seat.

Collin spoke in hushed tones maybe so as not to disrupt O'Casey's obvious concentration. "I hope so, sir. Claire was lost in the *Lusitania* sinking but is purported to have been seen on at least two occasions in Queenstown in the company of an Irish motorcyclist with a boat. I desperately want to find her."

Glass broke on the floor above. Sean flinched, but he didn't leave the foyer where he could keep an eye on the parlor. "What are those damned Britishers doing to my bedrooms? So that's it, then, Collin? I thought there was more."

"My main focus is for my paper."

"Of course, lad. She's only a lost sister after all." Sean shot what he hoped was a steely look at his unexpected visitor.

Holding his tongue, Collin smiled, and Sean realized that his visitor understood his understatement.

Maureen seemed intrigued by the conversation.

One of the khakis pounded down the stairs and into the parlor. He poked his head in a closet before sitting down on the window seat, obviously fatigued from the house-to-house search. The seat directly over Tadgh sagged under his weight. Sean, feigning nonchalance, stepped forward into the parlor.

The sergeant had returned to the main floor and was rummaging through the kitchen and pantry. There was no need to empty drawers other than to upset Sean.

Collin snapped a picture with his Brownie.

Tadgh needed to sneeze. He couldn't touch his nose to stop it. *Damn.* He resisted the sensation with all his might.

Just then, the relief valve on the radiator under the seat belched trapped air, a periodic annoyance that embarrassed polite visitors.

Although she had heard it before, at this close range the rude noise startled Morgan, and she gasped.

Tadgh, about ready to burst from holding his breath, sneezed loudly despite his attempt to stifle the sound. Fortunately the sneeze mingled with the rattling sound of the radiator. The result was a strange symphony of sounds that made the khaki jump off the window seat in alarm.

"What the hell was that?" The soldier leaned down toward the grill.

Sean moved quickly toward the window seat to block the action. "Haven't you ever been in a house with hot water pipes, man? It's still cold enough to have the heat on. There's a coal boiler in the basement and bubbles of air get trapped in its pipes. It's a damn nuisance, I can tell you."

Still suspicious, the corpulent soldier tried to peer through the darkened grate. "It sounded like more than that to me," he grunted, picking at the grill with a stubby finger. "How do you get this grate off?"

Tadgh flipped off the safety on his Luger and slowly cocked the weapon.

"Sergeant Sanders," a voice called from the front steps. "Are you about done here? I'm waiting to take Walter Cole from Number Three in for questioning. Finish the search of these damn houses now so your group can escort him to the Castle."

"Roger, sir." The sergeant called back from the kitchen and came the parlor door. "Get a move on, Bailey, no time to stand around." Sergeant Sanders then stepped smartly to the front door, calling out to his squad, "All right, men, let's go."

Sean watched Bailey hesitate and then reluctantly turn to obey the order. But not before he gave the grate a vicious prod with the butt of his rifle, which caught Tadgh in the solar plexus. The grate cracked, and Sean could see the glint of Tadgh's drawn Luger behind the opening.

Bailey complained to Sergeant Saunders about the suspicious noises he had heard, but the sergeant was too concerned with following orders and he paid no attention.

"Let's go, men. We're going to have some fun interrogating Cole. He's the founder and director of the Sinn Féin Printing and Publishing Company, you know."

They slammed the door with a vengeance as they rushed out into Mountjoy Square South, without any apology for the disruption of Sean's household.

Collin drew a sigh of relief at the squad's noisy departure and turned to shake Sean's hand. "We'd best be going. It has been an honor to meet you, Mr. O'Casey."

"I hope you find your sister, lad," Sean said, as Collin and Maureen followed the raiding party out into the sunshine.

Sean watched from the door as Collin and Maureen climbed the steps and disappeared into Number Thirty-Seven on the left. Old Shaughnessey would give them holy hell. As he expected, the khakis, Collin, and the girl soon hurried out onto the street as if being shooed away. He watched until they left the square.

"That was a close call," Sean announced, closing the door and returning to the parlor. "But they're gone for now, the bastards. Are you going to stop with the jabs about my pen, Tadgh?"

"If it gets us out of this torture chamber." Tadgh's reply was muffled.

"All right, then. I'll let you both out," the playwright agreed, while he tried to pry the damaged grating from its wooden frame.

He pulled Tadgh out from around the radiator. It was like trying to carefully unwrap a crumpled piece of paper without tearing it.

After rubbing the cramps and bruise on his stomach so he could breathe freely again, Tadgh then extricated Morgan from her hiding place. She threw her arms around his neck, as much for support for her weakened legs as it was for their narrow escape. "Oh Tadgh." She gave him a fierce and tearful kiss on the lips.

They both fell gratefully onto the sofa and stretched, after which Tadgh checked on Morgan's leg to make sure the stitches had not torn.

"I feel like a twisted pretzel. Can you rub the feeling back into my feet, Tadgh?"

Tadgh massaged gently and turned to Sean. "Thank you for handling this dangerous situation."

"Yes, you were quite ferocious," Morgan chimed in.

"With your pen," Tadgh added, massaging Morgan's toes.

"I was going to stab that khaki with it, see?" He pulled a fountain pen from his waistcoat and handed it to Morgan.

"Were you now, Teacher?"

"Yes, well. Who's going to help me clean up this mess?"

Morgan thought. *He doesn't handle compliments very well, does he?*

The excitement of the raid, combined with her first outing in the fresh air, took its toll on Morgan. She could hardly keep her eyes open to eat the meager supper of boiled beef and cabbage. Afterward, Tadgh carried her up to bed, sound asleep, before returning to talk to their host.

"Do you have a Bible, Sean?"

"Need some Divine spiritual guidance, me boyo?"

"Yes, for all that."

"Fine then, lad. It's on my bedside table. Help yourself."

"Thank you. That was too close for comfort today, Sean. We need to get out of here and leave you in peace."

Sean knew what he meant.

"I have a question, though. It was hard to hear from inside that cage, everything muffled, but it seemed to me that there were more people in your house than just those raiders."

"Right you are. I want to talk to you about that, Tadgh. Two newspaper people showed up, following the proceedings. Woman and man. Strange young man."

"How do you mean?"

"He said he has a sister lost on the *Lusitania*, called her Claire. He's looking for her and says he has learned she is travelling with an Irishman who has a motorcycle and a boat. That's a strange coincidence, don't ya think?"

Tadgh was dumbfounded. "Brother, is it?" *Could this be the man from the newspaper article, the one I thought was Morgan's husband or lover? He called her Claire. How could he have tracked us here? So many questions.* "What's his name, Sean?"

"The lady reporter called him Collin."

"Did she now? What's his last name, then?"

"I don't know, but he's from Toronto."

"What, from Canada?"

"Yah, newspaper man. But originally from Donegal, Tadgh. And his fetching associate, Miss Maureen O'Sullivan, is from *The Irish Times*. I have her card. We could call and ask her."

"Shush now, Teacher. You're always the one for makin' a mountain out of a molehill, to be sure. Did those reporters know we were here?"

"I don't think so, lad."

"I think it's just a coincidence then, Sean. Let's not bother Morgan with this."

"Whatever you say, lad." Sean exclaimed, slapping his former student on the back. "I just hope that you have Morgan's best interests at heart. Now I'm going to bed. And yes, you'd best leave as soon as possible. My heart can't take much more of this."

If this is how Tadgh wanted it, he wouldn't interfere. It was no coincidence, but maybe Divine intervention. Collin seemed like a smart reporter and that shaky story about the neighbors could be easily checked. *Let the Lord sort this out, not a poor playwright.*

Tadgh shook his mentor's hand firmly. He knew that Sean was just worried about them. The teacher would have given his life for his friends, and almost did, against his core principles.

Morgan woke up when Tadgh returned to their bedroom.

"Did I nod off at supper?"

"Yes, my love. I carried you up. How's the leg?"

"Better."

"Do you feel like talking, Morgan?"

"About what, sweetheart?"

Tadgh undressed and got into bed, handing Morgan Sean's Bible. "Let's check out the wording in the beginning and ending verses of *an Cathach* Psalms to see if they could be clues from Red Hugh and Florence."

"Didn't you tell me that the first verse is now Psalm Thirty, Verse Ten?" Morgan asked, sitting up in bed, turning on the light, and flipping to that location in the book.

"That's right. What is the wording, lass?"

"'Hear Lord and be merciful to me. Lord be my help.' And the last verse?"

"Psalm One Hundred and Five, Verse Thirteen," Tadgh replied.

"'When they went from one nation to another, from one kingdom to another people.'" Morgan looked perplexed.

Tadgh hung his head in his hands. "These verses aren't obvious clues as far as I can tell. Maybe the idea that our ancestor chieftains removed the front and back folios of *an Cathach* as a clue was only wishful thinking on my part. The clue riddle, if there is one, could still be buried in the glued-together folios, or worse, lost in the missing folios. Presumably the manuscript was in much better shape the last time Red Hugh had it."

"I just think that we don't have the full context of all the clues, Tadgh. Don't give up on this idea yet."

220

"Okay, then. Maybe, my old family Bible will be able to shed some more light on this conundrum."

They left it at that for the time being. Morgan turned out the light and pulled Tadgh down to snuggle. "I can't wait to get home, mavourneen."

"Now that's a term I haven't heard in a long time. Come here, you vixen."

After their gentle lovemaking, Morgan returned to a peaceful slumber.

Tadgh wasn't so lucky. He couldn't sleep for all the thoughts whirling in his brain. If this Collin really was the man from the newspaper inquiry he found in Baltimore, then mustn't he be told about Morgan, so she could finally know who she really was? It would be so easy to find him through that Maureen O'Sullivan.

Collin would not have come all this way just to check on his sibling. He would fight to take her back to Canada. I can't allow that. Morgan has stopped talking about her former life, so why stir it up? We've been through so much, and we belong together. I need her. He may be Irish, but he's not a Republican. So he's the enemy. To hell with this brother, Collin.

With that sorted, he dropped off to sleep just before dawn.

Chapter Fifteen
Turmoil

Thursday, May 4, 1916
Number Ten Balsam, Beaches, Toronto

*S*am stepped through the door from work, needing a quiet sanctuary after a long, hard day at school and a tough drive home in the rain. What he saw and heard was a household in commotion. Lil was doing her best to calm all the children down.

"Thanks to Jesus, you're home now. The dinner's boiling over on the stove, Ernie's got colic, and the girls won't behave. And, you're going to have to deal with Kathy who is on her way over with little Liam. I can't cope anymore right now." Without waiting for a response, she retreated out of sight into the kitchen.

Sam could feel his chest constricting. That wasn't good. He removed his rain boots and shook out his umbrella before closing the front door. With stooped shoulders, he leaned down and picked up a bawling Ernie from his bassinette in the front room. Holding him against his chest, Sam patted the tyke's back and heard a frightful burp explode from the boy.

"What's all this about, Norah?" he asked, just as Ernie stopped crying and immediately threw up all over his father's blue suit.

"Here, Daddy." Norah found the burp cloth and handed it up.

Sam carefully placed a much quieter Ernie back in his bed and wiped his suit front. "Thank you, princess. How are my little girls this evening?"

"Dot took my dolly, the one with the brown hair, and won't give it back. Make her, Daddy."

"Mine needed a sister," Dot said, appearing at the door and holding her sister's doll in a stranglehold.

"Dot, do the dollies love each other and play well together?"

"Yes, Daddy, see?" Dot mashed the two dolls together in a hug.

"Just like your dollies need to be friends, so do you two, you know. Why don't you hug and make up?"

Sam pulled gently on a reluctant arm of each daughter until they were face to face. "Now, hug girls, just like the dollies. Good. Now Dot, give Norah both dollies to play with for a while. Then you can play together before supper."

Sam took two wrapped sweets out of his jacket pocket and handed one to each girl. "Don't tell Mommy." He put his index finger to his lips.

"Thank you, Daddy," they said in unison as they sat on the floor to unwrap their treats.

No sooner had Sam gone to the sideboard to pour himself a tot of Jameson than Kathy flew through the door with Liam bundled in her arms. She was in such a hurry she didn't stop to shake the water off, so raindrops splattered onto the hardwood floor.

"My suitcase is on the porch. I rolled it on my dolly all five blocks over here."

"No wonder you look like a drowned rat, lass. Come and sit down." He pointed to his favorite chair, the one he'd been looking forward to all the way home in the rain.

"Here, take Liam for me, Sam. I've had him all day."

"Of course you have. You're the mother." *How bad could that be?* Kathy had been looking after thirty of them before she had to take maternity leave from teaching at the school.

Thrusting the wee lad into Sam's arms, she said, "I mean it. You men." Then she collapsed into the easy chair.

Sam handed her the dram of whiskey. "Drink this. Now then, what's this all about?"

As if he didn't know. Kathy had been completely downhearted and disoriented since Collin deserted her on Easter Monday morning. When she got his telegram from Halifax and realized he was really going, she fell apart. His own wife Lil had to care for her and Liam for a week. Ever since, she had veered from anger to anxiety and back again.

"I got this telegram this morning. He's in Ireland and going to Dublin." She waved the paper and threatened to throw it in the roaring fireplace.

Sam grabbed the telegram and read it. "At least he got to Ireland safe and sound, girl."

"But did you read his first report today in the *Tely*?"

"No, I've been at work, teaching."

"Well, one of the ships in his convoy was torpedoed and it ran into his troop ship. They were leaking and had to limp into Queenstown Harbour. He could have been killed."

"But he wasn't. Look, he's all right."

"I don't know, Sam. Sometimes I want to kill him and sometimes I am deathly afraid for him."

"That's natural, lass."

"But I can't forgive him, not ever. And I can't stay in that house on Lee Avenue anymore. Too many bad memories." She started to sniffle and the girls came over.

"Don't cry, Auntie Kattie." Norah and Dot crawled up on her lap and lay their heads on her tummy. "You can stay here with us again, can't she, Daddy?"

Sam sorely needed some peace and quiet. "Yes, I'm sure she can, Norah. We'll ask Mommy."

Lil came into the parlor to announce that supper was ready. She smiled at Kathy and turned back to the table to set another place.

Kathy was quiet during dinner, and Sam steered the conversation to local post-Easter events at the Beach.

When the conversation wound down, Lil said, "You girls need a bath this evening, so go get ready. Tonight you'll sleep together in Dot's room, so Aunt Kathy can have your room, Norah."

"Can I sleep in your bed, Mommy?"

"No, Dot. You'll sleep with your sister. Now get going. I'll be right up."

Sam herded the girls up the stairs.

"Thank you, Lil. I just can't go back home. I just can't." Kathy's face crumpled with sadness.

"There now, no need. You sleep here tonight, and tomorrow we'll talk about what we need to do, dear. We will all have fresher heads then."

"All right. Thank you, Lil." Kathy seemed comforted by Lil's words, and she lifted baby Liam to her breast for his own supper. Ten minutes later, Kathy ascended the stairs with him and closed the bedroom door for the night.

"This is getting very serious," Lil told Sam as she put Ernie down in the crib in their bedroom and closed the door. "Can't you talk to your old boss at the paper and have Collin recalled?"

"I doubt Collin would return at this point."

"I know Kathy—she's my best friend, and she is reaching the breaking point. Something bad is going to happen. You mark my words."

"Something bad has already happened. What could be worse?"

"Divorce. She feels abandoned. And has been."

"That just isn't done, Lil. Not unless he's been unfaithful."

"But he's run away and left her with a newborn baby. This is nonsense, Sam. It's just not right."

Sam debated whether to bring up his own problem. Better out in the open. "I had some chest pains again today, on the way home in the rain."

"Why didn't you say so earlier, *creena*?" Lil came over and insisted that Sam get undressed and slip into bed. "Does it hurt now?"

"No. It stopped after your chicken and dumplings dinner, *astore*. You are my treasure chest, and the children are my jewels."

"Go on with ya. It's the stress of Kathy and our loud children, isn't it?"

"The children are my joy, lass. I'll be all right."

Lil tucked him in as she had just done for the girls before she read to them about Humpty Dumpty. Minutes later, Sam was snoring soundly.

At last the house was reasonably quiet. Lil got ready for bed and slipped beneath the cotton sheets. Then she moved over gently until she curled up around her man with her breasts against his back and her right arm draped across his stomach. Putting her ear against his shoulder blade, she could feel his pulse against it. *Comforting.* Every once in a while his heart skipped a beat, same as last night. *That can't be good.*

But what could she do about it? He had a tough job and a long drive to get there. At least he could count on the Model-T. She would call and talk to Doctor Stewart, their family physician. Heavens, he was everyone's doctor and mentor in the Beach. He would tell her the truth.

But what was she going to do about Kathy and Liam? Sam was right. Collin wouldn't come home anytime soon, maybe not before it was too late to reconcile his marriage. She couldn't worry about him. Lil wondered if Kathy's problem was that she was separated from all the children that she taught and the profession that she loved, as well as from her husband. *What if I take care of baby Liam during the day and she goes back to work? I'm sure that the school would love to have her back and release the substitute. Get her busy again with less time to dwell on her problems.*

And if she can't stand to be at home with Collin gone, she can stay with us. That way she will be on a more even keel and less stress for the rest of us. I owe this to my best friend and my husband. That's what we'll do.

Chapter Sixteen
Departure

Friday, May 5, 1916
Sean's Home, Mountjoy Square, Dublin

*T*adgh had made his decision before coming down to breakfast. "Morning, Teacher," he greeted his host in the kitchen. "Morgan's feeling decidedly stronger this morning, despite our Houdini episode yesterday. We need to get out of your way today."

"What? And deprive me of my daily dose of hair-raising mayhem?"

"I think you have enough grist for that fertile playwright mill of yours, don't ya think."

"I am getting mad enough to write tomes about this despicable era we find ourselves in."

"All kidding aside, you go ahead and fight this war with your pen, Sean. I mean it. You're great at it. I was just mediocre."

"You are too modest, me boyo."

"My playwrighting days are over, Teacher."

"It's none of my business, lad, but what are you going to live on now that the IRB has been quashed? I presume that they were funding your livelihood."

"I'm a fisherman, Sean. I'll go back to what I know best."

Sean looked askance. "You and I know that you're a soldier and that you won't rest until the British are driven from Ireland."

"But I could be a fisherman. Morgan and I will be all right. I have some funds locked away in my ancient desk back in Creagh."

Sean took out a bulging envelope from his bread box and slid it across the kitchen table to Tadgh.

"What's this?"

"A little something that I've had stashed away for a rainy day. And it seems to me that the country's mood couldn't be rainier than it is today."

Tadgh opened the envelope and looked at the contents before pushing it back across the table. "I can't take your money, Sean."

"Seriously, Tadgh, I believe in the pen. That doesn't mean that I don't have the same goals that you do. This is my contribution to the Cause."

Tadgh knew that this was meant to be payment for the Cause. He also knew that Sean had guessed correctly. He had no funds at the moment and very little opportunity to earn any in the near term. But the envelope contained over a thousand pounds, if he had estimated correctly and this sum would surely sustain him and Morgan over the coming months.

Sean pushed the envelope back over to Tadgh. "I insist you take this, Tadgh. My needs are met. We can't have Morgan going to her wedding destitute, now can we?"

Tadgh thought for a moment. "You are too kind, Teacher." On the spur of the moment, he decided to confide in his mentor. "There is a possibility that I will be coming into an inheritance soon, if things fall into place."

"An inheritance, eh?"

"Yes, Sean, an ancient one. Maybe the funds can help with the Cause, if they come through. I'll pay you back for your generosity."

"Well then, me boyo, I'll hold you to that pledge. Now put that envelope away before your lovely betrothed joins us."

Tadgh slipped the envelope under his shirt and thanked his benefactor.

Later, when Morgan entered the kitchen, she noticed the two men in close conversation, with Sean rattling the newspaper pages. "You two seem to be playing nicer this morning," she smiled.

"MacBride, the one they called Foxy Jack, was shot at Kilmainham this morning," Sean said, reading from *The Times*.

"I heard just last Thursday from Paddy that the man joined MacDonagh at Jacob's Biscuit Factory, almost by accident."

"Did he now, Tadgh? Maybe he deserved his fate for what Yeats said he did to Iseult Gonne."

Morgan turned to face their host. "Iseult who?"

"MacBride's former wife Maude's daughter by an earlier marriage."

When Morgan heard Sean say that Foxy Jack may have had his way with the girl, who was only eleven at the time, she curled her lip in disgust.

Tadgh joined the conversation. "Yeats [5] must be pleased, since Maude was his muse who refused to marry him on several occasions before being smitten by the callous lout, MacBride."

"Yeats is the best poet of our times, Tadgh."

"Not my opinion, Teacher."

"I know that he fought against your play at the Abbey Theatre two years ago. You shouldn't hold that against him, Tadgh, just because he has a different ideology than you."

"Siding with the British."

"He's a fair man, is our William. Here, I'll prove it to you."

Sean got up and went into his office, returning with a handwritten letter. "He brought me a letter with a draft of a poem he'd written about John and the Rising after he heard his adversary had laid his life on the line for a cause near and dear to Maude's heart."

"He came here, Sean?"

"Last Thursday, lad, while Morgan was still at the Rotunda. Braved the curfew, he did. Here, read the poem." Sean thrust the paper into Tadgh's hand.

Morgan leaned over Tadgh's shoulder to see what was written. "Read it aloud for us, mavourneen."

Tadgh examined the text and then surmised, "He must have anticipated MacBride's death along with our heroes. He titles it '*1916*.'" Tadgh began to read,

> "*'This other man I had dreamed*
> *A drunken, vain—glorious lout.*
> *He had done most bitter wrong*
> *To some who are near my heart,*
> *Yet I number him in the song;*
> *He, too, has resigned his part*
> *In the casual comedy;*
> *He, too, has been changed in his turn,*
> *Transformed utterly:*
> *A terrible beauty is born'.*"

"That's a great turn of a phrase," Sean said, repeating the last line for effect. "You mark my words. That line will be famous once he publishes the poem, despite the temporary ruination of our city."

"As will your literary works, Teacher. I must admit, though, 'a terrible beauty born' pretty much sums it up, doesn't it?"

Sean nodded agreement, and Tadgh went on, "The illegal executions so far are just the beginning. Mark my words, they'll all be dead soon. It's the British mentality. By all accounts, our boys fought a clean and fair fight for freedom. They deserve to be treated as prisoners of war, not like vermin to be exterminated, Sean."

"What will happen to the Countess Markievicz?" asked Morgan.

"She was a leader, lass. So unfortunately, I would guess that Constance's head is also on the block, that's certain."

"Oh, God, no."

"Morgan, we're leaving today."

"But Captain Murphy hasn't called yet," Morgan objected, just as they heard the telephone ring.

"Speak of the devil," Sean said, picking up the wall receiver and hearing Murphy's voice. "It's the captain for you, Tadgh. Do you think he heard us speaking of him?" He handed the phone to his protégé.

"Well, Murphy, you ready to go south?"

"That's why I called this morning, son. The hooker's ship-shape. But there's a catch. That armed yacht that shelled us off Poolbeg has been docked at the mouth of the harbor since early this morning. I can see that they're looking for something or someone, lad. I've got your boat backed into a dry dock and covered with tarps and they haven't seen her yet. A sympathetic friend of mine here at the dock yard helped me."

"Where are you calling from?"

"The harbormaster's office. He's out at present. He told me that the *Helga*'s put in here for provisioning for the next few days instead of going back to Kingstown. He says they're lookin' for the saboteurs what killed their men a week ago off Poolbeg. We can't stay here much longer without being exposed, lad."

"Can we slip out by night, Martin? We've no other way home. The witch hunt is on here in Dublin."

"Tricky, Tadgh. The *Helga*'s moored at the entrance by the light. There's a path by 'er, but we'd stick out like a sore thumb."

Tadgh knew they shouldn't have berthed her in the harbor with its narrow entrance. He couldn't stay at Sean's any longer. Collin would likely be back poking around, and it wasn't safe in Dublin. "We're coming out to Howth now, Captain. We'll be there by two, but we'll have to go home around Ireland's north shore. Too many enemy ships in the Dublin-Cork corridor."

"Aye. That's a six-day voyage at best if the winds are favorable, lad. I'll stock provisions before you get here. But I can't be away from my duties at B&C for that long. I'll check for a ride to Queenstown from one of my mates and let you know when you get here."

"Fair enough, Murphy. You have been of great service already, my friend. Stay out of sight."

"Aye, sir. I'll be waitin'." Murphy hung up.

"Problems, love?"

Tadgh had postponed telling Morgan about his adventures since she went to hospital. They still had enough problems with the

British, and she needed to have a positive spirit to mend her leg.

"Let me tell you a story, aroon," Tadgh said, as he put his arm around Morgan and led her toward the parlor chesterfield.

"I've heard this tale," Sean called out from the kitchen. "You two go along."

For a half hour, Tadgh detailed their adventures from the time he brought her to Mountjoy Square until he and Sean returned.

"What an adventure! Tadgh, I feel so badly that I wasn't there to help you."

"Everything worked out, lass. As you can see, I am here and whole, if you please."

"Dressed as women? Really? Accosted by soldiers? I would have loved to have seen that."

"It didn't seem funny at the time. What if I had lost my virginity?"

They both collapsed entwined in much-needed mirth.

Tadgh finally admitted, "Lookin' back, we survived an outrageous situation, to be sure."

"I'll just have to get the juicy details from Deirdre when next I see her, won't I, now. So you just happened into the Temple Bar Pub by coincidence, did you?"

Tadgh saw her eyebrows go up and her smoky green eyes widen when she said that. *Deirdre is a fine-looking buxom girl. Could it be that Morgan is jealous? And then there was that kiss. No match for Morgan's, but even so.*

"Yup. Purely by coincidence. Soldiers showed up right near there."

Well, you and Peader were lucky then, weren't you."

"Very lucky, indeed. She was a big help to us, so she was."

"So it would seem, my dear. I'm just glad that you made it back to me without being killed, or having your flower plucked." With that, she pulled him to her, and she made sure that her breasts pressed up against his muscular chest as she kissed him long and slow.

Aroused, he wondered if this was her way of marking her territory. Truth be known, he was crazy about being her territory.

While Tadgh and Morgan were involved in their intimate conversation, Sean had gathered some clothes from which they could fashion disguises. Half an hour later, Tadgh packed a satchel onto the back rack of the Kerry, and Morgan slipped gingerly into the sidecar. "We are forever in your debt, Teacher."

"Don't you forget it, Tadgh. You owe me another play."

"Do I, Sean? One where the sword is mightier than the pen?"

Morgan reached up, pulling Sean down to kiss him. This time he accepted her affection as an older brother would embrace his sister.

"Come on. Admit it, Teacher. You're a softie at heart, aren't ya, now?"

"Get off with you," Sean chided, as Tadgh goosed the throttle of the Kerry and they sped away from the alley behind O'Casey's home.

"Write when you get a chance," Sean called after them sternly. But they were already gone around the corner of Mountjoy Square and out of earshot.

Heading northeast out of the city, Tadgh kept an eye out for potential trouble. "We're fortunate there were no Republican strongholds on our route to Howth Harbour," he commented as they passed Clontarf Castle. "The authorities combing the roadways may be on the lookout for our rather easy to distinguish Kerry." In fact, he knew they were, since the RIC bastards had given chase back in Cork City and earlier, during their last escape from Dublin. *We always seem to be on the run from tyranny.*

"Surely they will stop looking now that the Rising is over," Morgan yelled over the noise of the screaming motor.

"I'd be willing to bet good money that they will initially incarcerate thousands of innocent Irishmen, if I know the British mentality. Mark my words, lass. The witch hunt has just begun. Look at poor Willie Pearse, a teacher and sculptor by trade. He was caught in the crossfire and executed just because of his last name. We need to get away from it all for the time being. And you still need to recuperate from your wound, my love. So I have the perfect solution for us, an invigorating sea voyage for two."

"Heading home, I hope, Tadgh."

"Yes, in a roundabout way, aroon. Think of it as a getaway from mayhem. I'd like to show you my homeland. The real one that we're fighting for. We'll fool the bastards and go north."

"Where you go, I go, my love," Morgan knew that mayhem followed Tadgh wherever he went. She realized that, to a certain extent, she loved him for that, as long as it didn't involve killing people.

They sped along the Howth Road without being challenged, eventually nearing the harbor.

"Look, Tadgh. That's the captain flagging us down up ahead."

Tadgh pulled over to talk with Murphy less than half a mile from their destination.

"What's the situation, Martin?"

"Everything was quiet when I called you, lad. Most of ship's crew have since come ashore and gone into town. As I told you, she's tied up to the East Pier just down from the Howth Harbour Lighthouse, at the narrow harbor entrance." [7.2]

Tadgh remembered that the small harbor looked like a crab from above, claws pointing north, with the east and west piers as its closing pincers and its sea entrance at the end of the east pier. "Is the hooker where we left her?"

"In the dry dock area shoreward on the west pier. They haven't seen her under wraps, and I left the new red lug sail exposed to throw them off if they came lookin'."

Tadgh realized that the *Helga* would have tied up on the Liffey if all they wanted was provisions.

After they had driven slowly to the harbor and inspected the hooker under wraps, Tadgh quickly took stock of the situation. "We've got to assume that the *Helga* is still looking for us and will search this harbor thoroughly by tomorrow. We killed three of their sailors, after all."

"You said it was in self-defense," Morgan interjected, looking worried.

"Yes, and they blew up the fourth sailor themselves," Tadgh confirmed. "But they probably don't know that, do they now."

Martin interrupted. "I changed the hooker's name and the foresail was shredded, of course, so I replaced it. Now it's red like the others."

"Thank you, Captain. But I'm still concerned that all Galway hookers will be suspect and boarded."

"The sail was shredded, Tadgh?" Morgan stuttered.

"Yes, it happened when the *Helga's* shell hit the breakwater. It's over, lass. Forget it."

"You missed telling me that minor detail, Tadgh." Morgan pounded on her partner's chest. "Don't you ever do that again, Tadgh McCarthy."

Tadgh stilled her hand. "I certainly intend to stay away from being shot at."

"That's not what I'm talking about."

"Yes, aroon."

Morgan limped to the aft bulkhead and sat down by the tiller. "Don't you *aroon* me."

Tadgh sat down beside Morgan and put his arm around her. "I promise that we will survive this war."

Morgan rubbed her injured leg above the knee and moved his arm away.

Tadgh encircled her and pulled her in.

She wiggled a little but didn't resist. "Just don't keep secrets from me ever again!"

That speared Tadgh's conscience. His brow furrowed as he

decided how to answer. This wasn't the time or place. "We'll be together, forever, my love. Where you go, I go."

"That's my line," Morgan replied, finally smiling.

Tadgh got up paced the deck for a minute. The only plan he could come up with left them no margin for error. "All right you two, we've got to be gone before dawn. This is what we're going to do. They usually change the watch at two in the morning on a military ship, so we'll slip out of the harbor past the *Helga* at one-thirty when they are getting sleepy. It looks like we'll have cloud cover tonight."

"What about the lighthouse beam at the end of the east pier?" Morgan asked.

"It's going to blink out mysteriously just before we make our run out of the harbor," Tadgh said matter-of-factly.

"Isn't that going to attract attention?"

"I'm counting on that diversion." Tadgh grasped Morgan's hand to assure her.

Crazy like a fox, Morgan thought. *That's another reason that I love this man, infuriating as he is. Look at him taking charge of the situation. Heaven knows how he's going to accomplish that while we are sailing out to sea.*

"Let's get this motorcycle onto the hooker and out of sight before we are spotted," Tadgh advised. "We're sitting ducks out here on the dock, to be sure." Soon, they had the Kerry battened down under the tarpaulin on the forward deck.

Tadgh thanked the captain. "You've done a great job with her, Martin. She looks like new with that red mainsail."

"It's a used one, me boyo. I figured a new one would stick out."

"It's a marvel you could get one at all for this boat. They don't get many Galways on this side of the country."

Morgan sighed as she saw the new name, *Survivor*. "I was very fond of *Morgan's Quest*."

"Martin, I'm going to need your help once more, my friend.

You'll have to stay tonight. Morgan, here, cannot run the ship by herself." He outlined the new details of their departure.

At twelve thirty, still dressed in his disguise as a dockworker with long scruffy beard, Tadgh left Murphy in charge of maneuvering *Survivor* out of the harbor. Earlier that evening he had done some reconnoitering and determined that the bulk of the warship's crew had not returned from the city. Likely on shore leave, he surmised. But there were several sailors and officers still onboard. He gauged the separation distance between the *Helga* and the hooker would be fifty feet or less at closest approach during the departure if Martin could maneuver to within three feet of the opposing entrance wall. There was no way that Morgan could have done it alone without smashing into the warship.

Now, as he walked down the east pier towards the enemy ship, he was sure that they could never get out of this narrow harbor undetected with the lighthouse lamp illuminated, no matter how sleepy the watch. He wondered if there was an onsite keeper at this hour of night. He was glad that Murphy knew this harbor like the back of his hand, because he was going to have to navigate through the entrance in near dark. He was thankful for the fresh offshore breeze that would blow the hooker out to sea.

The running lights on the merchant yacht *Helga* and a low intensity glow from the wheelhouse cast a pale light close to the ship, moored to the east wall a hundred yards from the lighthouse. Tadgh calculated that the hooker could stay outside their light pattern if Murphy maneuvered right up alongside the exit pier when he passed. It would all depend on how observant the sailor on watch would be, if he could detect motion in the near darkness, or hear the boat's wake and the creaking of rigging in the breeze. The risks were high.

As he approached the *Helga*, Tadgh found crates on the pier to sneak behind as he passed. There was no one in sight on the dock but he could hear the strains of a music box coming from the wheelhouse playing some sleepy English country tune. *Good. That will help.* From behind the crates, Tadgh could see a lone sailor's head in the dimly lit bridge wheelhouse. He appeared to be reading a newspaper.

Tadgh turned his focus to the lighthouse [7.3], just a stone's throw beyond the *Helga* at the pier's end where the main building stood behind a fortified stone wall. He could see it was a two-story cut stone structure, with an attached circular granite lighthouse tower looming up behind it. Its lamps were more than sixty feet above the waterline. They shone red and white bright lights in all directions, fully illuminating the *Helga* and the Howth Harbour entrance.

From the yellowed color of the light, Tadgh decided that it must be an Argand-style set of lamps, likely burning coal oil or paraffin. He had been taught about these devices as part of his guerrilla warfare training for an event such as this, when Volunteers might need to disable lighthouses for the purpose of confounding the British Navy.

Tadgh knew that these systems operated on storage tanks of combustible fuel set a distance away to prevent catastrophe in the unlikely event of a detonation or fire. The downstream piping of it, located in the watch room just below the glassed lantern room would either be pressurized by means of a manual hand pump or gravity-fed to force the fuel up the circular wicks to the lantern room combustion chambers overhead. He knew that if there was a pump and he could disable it, the pressure would drop, causing the lamps, starved of fuel, to simply go out.

He wasn't sure how to disable a gravity-fed supply without leaving evidence of sabotage, since he didn't know that much about the detailed mechanisms involved. But he knew that a keeper had to be in the loop for this process on a round-the clock basis; thus the need for his accommodation on site.

Get moving. Timing was critical. After quietly circling the facility, staying in the dark, he realized that he would have to go through the keeper's living quarters to gain tower access because the one door on the waterfront, and the few windows, were all locked.

He needed to temporarily disable the light as if by natural accident at precisely one thirty since Murphy would have left the berth on the west pier at one twenty-five, heading for the harbor entrance and the *Helga*. Then, having caused a problem that would draw immediate attention, he needed to slip away undetected, with the enemy warship just a hundred yards away and the keeper undoubtedly onsite. If that wasn't enough, he would only be able to determine how to disable the lamps when he could examine the system.

As he approached the facility door, a rogue thought interrupted his concentration. He wondered just how many of his cat's nine lives he had already used up. He knew he was vulnerable while picking the lock. The lamps threw enough light down at the base of the building to illuminate him, an obvious intruder, if the sailor on watch in the wheelhouse happened to look in his direction. This time his skills did not fail him. The lock tumbler quickly fell into place, and the door opened inwards into the darkness with only the faintest creak.

Stepping gingerly inside, Tadgh closed the door behind him and listened. The only sound he heard was a ticking clock. He presumed that the sleeping quarters were upstairs, so he took out de Valera's torch and turned it on. His quick scan revealed that he stood in a cramped galley kitchen and to his right was a living room with an open fireplace on the far wall in the direction of the *Helga*. To his left he spied an inward opening door that should lead to the spiral staircase of the lighthouse tower. Straight ahead were the second-floor stairs, presumably to the sleeping area.

After turning off his light, he moved with catlike grace to the tower door. Turning the torch back on, Tadgh saw the lighthouse daily service schedule pinned to a tack-board on the wall. The service frequency was every thirty minutes, including one fifteen in the morning. He glanced down at his watch. It was one fifteen.

Then he heard footsteps coming downstairs. Dousing his light once more, he plastered himself to the wall behind the tower door as he listened. Were the footsteps coming from the house or the tower? He couldn't tell. If the keeper was in the house, he would turn on the living room light and trap Tadgh in its light. Then he heard grunting definitely coming from the cavernous tower stairwell beyond the door.

Through the hinge crack, he could just make out the boots of a large old man dimly lit by a small lantern he carried. He was cursing something fierce in Gaelic. When the rotund keeper reached the bottom step, Tadgh saw him stop and prop himself against the newel post, panting. He was dressed in a nightshirt that strained against his corpulent torso, and he mopped his sopping brow with a grimy handkerchief.

When the doddering man had gathered himself, he shuffled through the open doorway into the living quarters, past the door where Tadgh hid. The old man muttered something about how he was getting too old to navigate those stairs all the time while he paused to scratch his initials on the service sheet. Tadgh held his breath while the keeper, not three feet away, wheezed. Tadgh's thoughts raced. What would he do if the keeper stopped to close the door? He couldn't possibly kill the aged Gaelic Irishman, so he would lay him low with a blow, that's all, not a permanent injury.

Tadgh drew a shallow breath of relief when the keeper shuffled off across the living room towards the house stairs without touching the door. He could hear the man curse again as he began climbing to his bedroom. Tadgh waited until the sounds of the keeper signaled that he was in his room before he moved.

He stepped quietly over the threshold into the lighthouse tower before turning on his torch, leaving the door partially open. *Damn.* It was one twenty-two already. The hooker would be starting up in three minutes. Tadgh couldn't avoid some creaking as he ascended the spiral staircase leading to the watch room. He guessed he had climbed twenty feet before he reached its open door.

Stepping into the room, Tadgh was instantly relieved. Before him he saw a Heap air pressure pneumatic lamp fuel delivery apparatus. It was just like the one that he had been trained on. It was feeding fuel up through the ceiling into the burners above. Its hand pump and round pressure gauge were plainly visible. It was a simple mechanism really. This is why the keeper had to check every half hour—to maintain feed pressure at all times.

Moving over to the equipment, Tadgh could see that the gauge read the normal twenty pounds per square inch. The pressurization system was plumbed above and into an inverse truncated metal cone base that housed the local fuel tank. On the other side, outlet plumbing carried the fuel up to the lamp burners. In that plumbing there was a clear sight-glass and a shutoff valve in the open inline position. Using his torch, Tadgh could see a flow of what looked like paraffin through the sight-glass.

He thought for a moment. If he just closed the shutoff valve, the lamps would go dark. The keeper would immediately know it had been tampered with. Then the sailors might realize that someone had sneaked out of the harbor, and the *Helga* would come in pursuit. There was also the chance that the keeper might get there fast enough to turn the valve back on before they had cleared the harbor.

Looking at his watch, he saw it was one twenty-eight. The hooker would have left its berth and started towards the narrow entrance. He had to do something immediately.

Then it came to him that if he could loosen the pressure line connection to the gauge, the pressure would drop and the fuel would cease to flow. That could take the keeper a while to find, and he might think it a natural occurrence as long as Tadgh didn't leave any scratch marks.

Tadgh tried to twist the connection by hand, but it wouldn't budge. He looked vainly around for a pipe wrench. Time had run out, and Morgan and Murphy were counting on him.

Just when he decided that he would have to turn the shutoff

valve, he spied a toolbox under a small workbench in the corner. Rummaging through it, he found a wrench, just what he was looking for. When he noticed the tool's sharp jaws, he quickly stripped off his shirt and forced its folds into the jaws before he grabbed the connection. As he applied the wrench's full leverage, the connection loosened and compressed air escaped from the tubing with a loud hiss. Tadgh could smell the paraffin as he watched the gauge needle plummet to zero.

Donning his shirt, he was satisfied that the connection did not appear to have been gnarled in any way. Within a few seconds, Tadgh returned the wrench to the tool box and turned to go. It was one thirty exactly. That's when he noticed the small casement window facing back over the keeper's house.

Tadgh could see that the outside light was waning. Starved of fuel, the lamps were going out. Peering out, he saw that the keeper's window was just above the flat roof-line of the housing building.

Must go now. He raced out of the watch room and down the spiral staircase on the run. When he was ten steps down the stairs, a klaxon bell erupted. *Damn, it must somehow have been triggered by the loss of light or stoppage of fuel flow.* Then he could hear the loud footfalls of the keeper lumbering down his house stairs. He wasn't going to make it through the house without being detected. He wouldn't be able to squeeze through any windows in the tower, they were too small.

Then he remembered the rear window off the watch room, and he ran back up the tower stairs. When he reached the room, he could hear the keeper starting up the stairs behind him, panting. Tadgh saw that he could squeeze through the casement window, but the edge across the horizontal casement frame interface was painted shut. He whipped out his knife and quickly scored the painted edge, pulled up on the lower window. It wouldn't budge. He could see the glow from the keeper's lantern coming up through the stairwell. The blighter was getting close. He had to get out now or prepare to attack the man.

Tadgh pushed up with all his might once more and as the side paint seal cracked, the window jumped open an inch. Another mighty heave and it opened fully. Tadgh pushed himself through and fell onto the roof with a thump. Turning, he managed to pull the window down closed just before the keeper lunged into the watch room.

Tadgh saw the old man turn the klaxon alarm horn off, flipping a switch, and then sag against the wall, wheezing.

Tadgh watched from the darkness while the keeper caught his breath and then advanced on the machinery. "What the hell?" he heard the man yell when he saw the pressure gauge reading.

Just as Tadgh turned to get away from the tower, he heard a shout and banging on the keeper's house door below. He cautiously crept to the front harbor edge of the roof above the door and peered over to see the dim outline of a sailor twenty feet below him. He was pounding on the door and yelling, "You all right in there? Open up." He wasn't going to get off the roof that way. Then the sailor opened the door and entered the building. Tadgh remembered that he had left it unlocked to facilitate his exit. It would only be a matter of seconds before the sailor would join the keeper in the watch room. They could possibly figure out what went wrong and restart the lamps. Tadgh turned left, away from the harbor, heading for the rear of the flat roof in the darkness.

Suddenly he was blinded by a piercing light coming from the *Helga* to his right. He dove behind the chimney top on the end of the roof nearest the warship, hoping that he hadn't been spotted. He could see the narrow beam of a searchlight lighting up his end of the building farthest from the tower as well as the harbor door side of the building. Thankfully, it didn't illuminate downwards towards the water where the hooker might be.

Squinting off to his right, in the darkness beyond the light, Tadgh barely detected movement coming from the west pier in the harbor entrance waterway. It must be the hooker and right on time. The sailors on the *Helga* were focused on the lighthouse.

Murphy had been intent on navigating the hooker within three feet of the exit channel's west side as they silently passed by the *Helga*. Tadgh had been successful in dousing the lighthouse lamp. The klaxon alarm from the lighthouse hid any sound of the lugsail in the breeze as the warship loomed high above them.

So far, so good. But the siren was also disturbing since it could be signifying that they had detected a saboteur. The sailor in the wheelhouse was not looking their way. Neither Murphy nor Morgan dared move a muscle as they floated by.

Morgan saw the sailor standing at the forward window, peering out ahead of his ship. Suddenly, he moved his arm above his head and a bright spotlight shone out catching the lighthouse in stark relief against the ink-black sky. *They know Tadgh's there and they're trying to capture him.* She wanted to dive in and try to save him. But he had been clear. Their job was to get the hooker out to sea without detection—period.

When they came abreast of the lighthouse, she saw that Murphy was being careful to stay out of the reflection of the spotlight that was vectored off the lighthouse onto the widening entrance channel water. At least, with the light blinding the sailors, the hooker would be more invisible as long as they could stay in the darkness.

Morgan saw a sailor at the front door yelling to the lighthouse keeper. Then movement on the roof caught her eye. From her vantage point, she could see a figure move from behind the chimney and drop out of her sight. If that was Tadgh, he was trapped. *God help him.*

Tadgh had to hurry. He had to take the chance that he could make it undetected to the rear edge of the roof and then survive a twenty-foot jump off the building wall onto God knows what. *Damn*, he should have checked that escape route earlier. Moving crabwise across the roof, Tadgh saw that the searchlight did not follow him. When he reached the back edge of the building, he lay prone and looked down into the darkness. At the end, he saw a pipe running vertically down its side. *That won't support my weight.*

He could barely make out a low structure behind and below the middle of the building, one with a flat roof up against the wall above ground level. He dared not turn on his torch. A vertical supply line and vent attached to the wall with clamps ran almost to the roof. A paraffin storage tank, he surmised. *It's a better risk than jumping and possibly breaking a leg.* He had to move quickly to make the rendezvous. Morgan and Murphy had been ordered to keep going out to sea if he missed the one fifty-five deadline. Turning his timepiece to catch the light from the watch room window, he saw that it was already one forty.

Crawling back towards the tower, Tadgh realized that he was fully exposed in the light from the *Helga*—not likely to those on the ship, but certainly to the keeper and sailor in the watch room. All they had to do was look out the window. Tadgh could see their backs as they appeared to be working on the machinery.

Returning to the center of the building, away from the harbor, Tadgh carefully lowered himself over the edge feet first, until he was able to hold on to the roof. He shifted his legs to secure a foothold on the pipe when he heard the keeper cry out, "I can't find where the damn thing's lost pressure."

Keep moving. Throwing caution to the wind, Tadgh grasped the top of the vent pipe with his hands and shimmied down the pipe at an accelerating rate of speed. There were no footholds. The friction stung his knees and hands. When he hit the top of the metal storage container at the bottom, it clanked in the night air. His knees buckled and he was thrown clear onto the stone courtyard, the wind knocked out of him.

Lying on his back in the darkness, he heard a window open

above him and a voice call out, "What was that noise out here on the roof, keeper?"

"Damned if I know. I'm busy trying to get this lamp lit."

Tadgh dragged himself five feet over to the wall on the side of the storage container farthest from the tower and pressed himself hard against it. He heard the crunch of footsteps on the roof above, and then he could see the sailor, caught in the spotlight from the *Helga*, standing just above him.

Tadgh dared not breathe. At that moment a feral cat jumped over him and up onto the container where it was barely visible from the roof. The sailor caught the motion and fired his sidearm at the animal.

"What are you doing?" The keeper yelled from the watch room, "You want to blow us up? There's a paraffin storage container down there."

"It's only a stupid cat!" the sailor exclaimed, and he disappeared from view. Moments later, Tadgh heard the window slam shut.

I guess I have at least one life left. Must go now. The lighthouse lamp could come back on at any second. From his first step, he knew he had a problem. His right ankle hurt like hell.

As the hooker cleared the harbor boundary and headed out to sea, the sailor's shot startled Morgan. Murphy told her they had miraculously avoided detection because of Tadgh's diversion at the lighthouse and their cover of darkness.

"Do you think that they're shooting at Tadgh?" Morgan whispered to the captain.

"Only time will tell," Murphy whispered back anxiously. "All we can do is head for the rendezvous, lass."

There was no doubt in both their minds that they would wait there for Tadgh until just before dawn or until the lighthouse lamp came back on. They could do no more.

Staying close to the back wall of the building, Tadgh circled to the offshore side of the tower. Keeping the lighthouse between himself and the *Helga*, Tadgh painfully scaled the seven-foot high stone sea wall, then scouted the dark water beyond the harbor. His right ankle throbbed, and he couldn't see or hear a thing. Was he too late? He couldn't see his watch in the dark, so he really didn't know how much time had passed.

Then he heard a faint signal out on the water like the mournful call of a whip-poor-will. It was Morgan, all right. He needed her to keep calling, indicating the direction he was to swim. He clambered down over the breakwater and its rock base to the water. There was a sizeable chop on the Irish Sea outside this barrier. Tadgh's side stung from his encounter with the metal paraffin container and stone courtyard, and his right leg had gone numb. The rendezvous point was seven hundred yards offshore just outside of the illumination of the lighthouse beam, a challenging task at this point. He was exhausted, but he could not rest or make a different choice.

It's now or never. He dove headlong into the cold, dark Irish Sea and the shock of the icy water jolted him. Treading water, he could hear the mournful sound ahead of him. He started a crawl stroke rate of two seconds, pausing every thirty seconds to get his bearings. He dared not call out to his colleagues for fear of detection. They had agreed to leave the hooker's running lights off. After swimming ten minutes, he knew he was well beyond the time limit and running out of steam. The fifty-degree water temperature was getting to him. Yet, bless her heart, Morgan was still making sounds that were getting louder.

The lighthouse lamp suddenly blinked on. Tadgh could just make out the hooker a hundred yards northeast of his position and Morgan beckoning to him. The light spread out over the water capturing him in its beam, but the hooker was only barely visible. He could hear the sailor calling goodnight to the lighthouse keeper.

A charley horse seized his right calf, and he floundered in the waves. It was all he could do to keep from screaming. He tried to straighten his toes, but that only made the cramp tighter. He was caught in a vice and could hardly keep his head above water.

♣ ♣ ♣ ♣

Morgan was relieved to see Tadgh swimming toward them and apparently not being pursued. She had to admit that she had had some black thoughts prior to seeing him. But now she could tell that he was in trouble. "Martin, she exclaimed softly. "We've got to go get him, now!"

Murphy saw that they would be caught in the lighthouse beam if they did that, but he couldn't hesitate. Deftly swinging the main sail boom around, he made headway back to shore and reached Tadgh in little more than a minute. Despite her leg injury, Morgan slipped overboard without a splash and swam the last fifty yards to him. She towed him along with a carry backstroke, until he broke free clutching his right calf muscle. He slipped under. Morgan dove, pulled him back up out of the freezing depths. Her right thigh burned, sending shooting pains down to her toes. By the time the hooker arrived, both Morgan and Tadgh were in danger of drowning as Tadgh went under for a second time.

"Help me, Martin," she croaked when he came alongside. While Murphy pulled and Morgan pushed as best she could, they managed to hoist their barely conscious leader into the boat. Then, with his last bit of strength, the captain dragged Morgan from the water.

Swiftly, Murphy flipped the mainsail, and they headed back out into the darkness. After he had reefed off the tiller, he got blankets to cover the shivering couple. This time Morgan was using her body to warm her mate. "This is a sudden turn of events," she murmured. She was in excruciating pain, but she clutched his body close to her.

The captain set the course, and they sailed off northeast in the darkness as the Howth Harbour light grew fainter and fainter in the distance. Thankfully, no following lights.

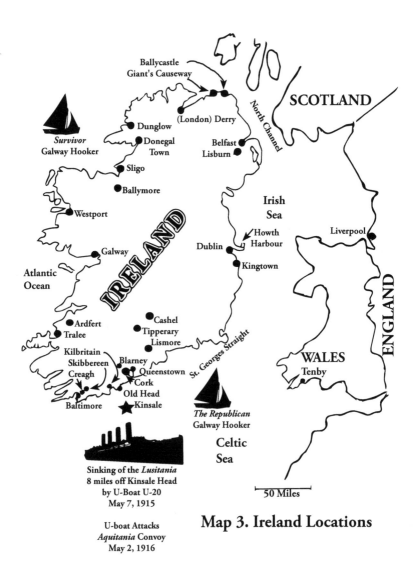

Ballycastle
Giant's Causeway

SCOTLAND

Dunglow

Survivor
Galway Hooker

(London) Derry

North Channel

Donegal Town

Belfast
Lisburn

Sligo

Ballymore

Irish Sea

Westport

Liverpool

Atlantic Ocean

Galway

IRELAND

Howth Harbour

Dublin

Kingtown

ENGLAND

Cashel

Tipperary

Ardfert
Tralee

Lismore

St. Georges Straight

WALES

Kilbritain
Skibbereen
Creagh

Blarney

Queenstown

Tenby

Cork

Baltimore

Old Head

Kinsale

The Republican
Galway Hooker

Celtic Sea

Sinking of the *Lusitania*
8 miles off Kinsale Head
by U-Boat U-20
May 7, 1915

50 Miles

U-boat Attacks
***Aquitania* Convoy**
May 2, 1916

Map 3. Ireland Locations

Chapter Seventeen
Brutality

Saturday, May 6, 1916
Irish Sea, North of Dublin

*T*he provisions that Murphy had brought aboard included a change of clothes, a first aid kit, and an ample supply of Jameson. Thus fortified, Tadgh began to thaw from the inside out. Morgan took care of the rest, including the bandaging of his bruised ribs and right ankle. Then, as her leg pain subsided, she re-bandaged her thigh after checking that the closed wound did not seem to be much affected by her strenuous swim. She and Tadgh sat huddled together for warmth just aft of the cabin, thankful to be free and on their way home.

"Well now, Martin. Didn't you tell me that Old Gus Tanner was going to take you to Queenstown after we left?" Tadgh asked, as the sun crept up over the horizon of the Irish Sea.

"Last night, I figured that you might need my assistance longer than you planned. So I told him that I wouldn't be joining him. I can catch a ride from one of my friends out of Belfast."

"Thank you for everything, Martin. You saved the day, my friend, to be sure."

"We all did our part. If Morgan here hadn't dived in to rescue you before I got there, you'd have gone down for the third time. And that's the truth of it."

"Where you go, I go, mavourneen. I didn't fancy a trip to the bottom of the Irish Sea."

Tadgh turned to look deeply into Morgan's eyes. "Thank you, my love. Shoe on the other foot, that's certain. You know, I think that my cat was also instrumental in saving the day."

"What cat? And after you answer that question, tell us how you got away. We couldn't see what was happening, and I thought that you were trapped up there on the roof."

Tadgh walked them through what happened starting with his entry into the light keeper's house.

After all that, Morgan asked, "Did the cat get shot?"

"I don't think so. He didn't squeal. I think I've used up six of my own nine cat lives, though."

"So who's counting, my love?"

"Well, you've saved me three times, including just now. I think that cat just saved another of my lives, Sean saved us from the raiders, and Aidan and Maurice saved us both from Boyle."

"You'd better take it easy from now on, then."

"No worries, aroon. I remember part of a poem that suggested more lives than nine. It seems fitting, particularly tonight. It goes something like this—

> '. . . *Yes, we go into the night as brave men go,*
> *Though our faces they be often streaked with woe;*
> *Yet we're hard as cats to kill,*
> *And our hearts are reckless still,*
> *And we've danced with death a dozen times or so . . .*'"

"Well said, lad. Always the adventurer, eh? I remember that poem by the English pioneer and poet, Robert Service, too. Isn't it from the 'Rhyme of the Restless One'?[6.2] The preceding verse is even more pertinent to our current dilemma," he added, reciting,

> "'. . . *We are fated serfs to freedom—sky and sea;*
> *We have failed where slummy cities overflow;*
> *But the stranger ways of earth know our pride and*
> *know our worth,*
> *And we go into the dark as fighters go . . .*'"

"You two are a font of all literary knowledge, to be sure. Does

Mr. Service know of our plight? He seems to be writing about it."

"I doubt it, aroon. He wrote it in the Klondike searching for gold in 1907, I believe."

"As true tonight for us, here, as for him in the Canadian Arctic back then, Tadgh."

They all marveled about how perceptive those lines were of the Irish Republicans' current condition.

This repartee was hurting Morgan's head, so she changed the subject. "Do you think that the *Helga* will come after us?"

"I don't think so, but we need to keep a lookout all the same. I'm pretty sure that they don't think the lamp outage was sabotage. And, as far as I know, we weren't seen last night," Tadgh said.

"So we are all really like the cat in the poem, then."

"What cat, Morgan?"

"Didn't that line in the poem go, *'we're hard as cats to kill'?*"

"That we are, lass, that we are."

They all had a good laugh.

Belfast had a major deep-water harbor, perfect for its main industry of shipbuilding. Martin easily maneuvered the hooker into the labyrinth of piers, slips, and dry-docks just as the sun reached its zenith, directly over the mast.

"Ahoy, Danby," Murphy called out to one of his scruffy shipmates as they passed the east jetty.

"Murphy, you old barnacle. Where's that old B&C scow of yours?"

"Tied to the dock in Cork due to the Rising. You don't happen to be shipping out for that neck of the woods, are you?"

"I'm headed south for Shannon, by way of Kingstown. I could drop you off at your home port if you have a mind to come with me."

"Obliged if I could. By the way, Danby, was there a Rising here last week like there was in Dublin?"

"You know Dennis McCullough from here. He led a minor

gathering of about a hundred in Coalisland, County Tyrone just to the west. They never fired a shot as far as I know."

Padraig had already told Tadgh that Dennis was the figurehead president of the IRB's three-man executive, but they didn't want fighting in Belfast where the religious fervor would be the highest. They certainly did not want the well-equipped anti-Home Rule Ulster Volunteers brought into the conflict.

Tadgh brought the hooker up alongside Danby's supply ship at the jetty and Murphy jumped onboard.

"Anytime you need me, just let Jeffrey know," Murphy called out, with a wave of his hand.

"Give him our best regards," Tadgh replied, as he pushed off.

Tadgh could see the captain's face blush when Morgan blew him a kiss.

"Murphy, that old scrounger, is worth his weight in gold," Tadgh chuckled, examining the rolled-up tent and blankets stored neatly inside the small cabin of the hooker after they tied up at a nearby dock.

Collin and Maureen met under the big clock at the entrance to *The Irish Times* offices as prearranged at one o'clock.

"They've cleared a desk for you next to mine, Collin. We can work better that way. Come, I'll show you." She walked him up to the third-floor newsroom where he saw reporters and support staff in a flurry of activity at a dozen row of desks, even on a Saturday.

"I write alone, Maureen."

"Not while you're here getting support from Mr. Healy and *The Times*. And besides, when else do you get a chance to work with a beauty like me?" Maureen did a pirouette and sat demurely on her desk with her ankles crossed.

She was very cute, Collin had to give her that. "I'm married, lass, with a son."

"Funny, you haven't mentioned them before this. They're not in Ireland with you, are they now. These are tough times, Collin. As you said yesterday, we need to stick together."

"That's not what I meant, Maureen." Collin noticed that their two desks had been arranged in an alcove, somewhat away from the maze of employees.

Maureen put on a business face and changed the subject. "Shall we get on with our report on the raids yesterday, then?"

"I have some camera shots that show the brutality of the raiders," Collin said, producing a roll of film and handing it to Maureen. "Can I get these developed today? The military is unnecessarily cruel."

"I can have these pictures and their negatives printed for you, but we will need to tone down the article in keeping with the paper's policies."

"What policies are those, exactly?"

"As Mr. Healy explained, we are a conservative Protestant voice here in Ireland."

"I refuse to make light of this atrocity, girl."

"Look, Collin. I agree with you, but the editor will change it anyway."

"Fine, then. You write for your paper, and I will write for mine."

"Could I co-author with you for your *Telegram,* Collin? That way I can express my real views on these heavy matters that are shaping our destiny."

"That's fine with me, but double work for you."

Three hours later, they had hammered out a scathing article for the *Tely* and Maureen had prepared an orderly piece about how the military was efficiently rounding up the rebels for *The Times.* They had met the deadline for the Sunday editions.

"How about some dinner, Collin? I know a place that has re-opened. It's good *craic.*"

"Well, I could use a good meal. Just dinner, lass."

"Of course, silly."

There she goes batting those eyes again.

On the way to Peadar Kearney's Pub on Dame Street just opposite the City Hall, Maureen took Collin on a tour of the burned-out General Post Office and other recent ruins on what the rebels called O'Connell Street.

"The British certainly caused a lot of destruction with their artillery, didn't they?"

"Wouldn't have happened if the rebels hadn't risen, Collin."

"Overkill, I'd say. I read where they had eighteen thousand well-armed soldiers by the end of the week plus artillery and machine guns. The rebels had twelve to fourteen hundred poorly equipped men and women. Surely, they could have put down the rebellion with a lot less destruction, even if it took longer. It's their city too, isn't it?"

"Yes, of course."

"And what about the civilian casualties? Your paper says they counted two hundred sixty dead and most of the two thousand six hundred wounded were Dubliners caught in the crossfire. How many fighting men and women died?"

"We reported two hundred sixty civilians, eighty-two rebels, one hundred twenty-six British troops and seventeen police killed, Collin. I see your point."

They walked the same route the GPO rebels had taken when they retreated northwest from the burning GPO across Henry Street, burrowing into Moore Street where they made their last stand. As fate would have it, this is where The O'Rahilly died holding the British momentarily at bay, but Michael Collins survived the fight.

The couple crossed the Ha'penny Bridge as rain started to sprinkle. They hurried toward the restaurant, pulling their coat collars up around their ears. As Maureen darted down Fownes Street Lower and across Temple Bar, pulling Collin after her, the rain turned into a soaker.

"In here." Maureen yanked Collin out of the deluge and into the warm and cozy pub.

"Drowned rats, are ye?" Deirdre exclaimed, as the two reporters stood near the door, dripping on the sawdust floor.

"Any port in a storm," Maureen replied, taking her Macintosh coat off and shaking it out.

"I like to think of my Temple Bar Pub as more than just a last resort, lass."

"I'm sure that the lady meant no disrespect. Right, Maureen? Given the storm, why don't we eat here?" Collin moved to a table and held a chair out for his companion. Maureen glowered but acquiesced. Collin guessed she didn't like being called a waterlogged rodent.

Collin couldn't help but notice the well-endowed blond waitress serving the next table. Maureen seemed miffed that his attention was being diverted.

"You're fortunate that your establishment was not damaged during the recent uprising," Collin said when Deirdre approached their table with two glasses of B&C Stout.

"You don't know the half of it, lad. I could tell you stories."

"We're reporters, lass. We would be all ears."

Maureen cut them off. "Another time, perhaps. I'll have the Irish stew."

"Yes, ma'am."

During dinner, Maureen remarked, "Speaking of rats, with all those burrows on Moore Street, the rebels have come to a sad end, haven't they now?"

"Or a glorious beginning, lass." Collin remembered Kathy's emphasis on the glass half full when he was so down on himself. *Why wasn't she taking that attitude when the shoe was on the other foot? But she had been so good to him. And innocent baby Liam . . .*

"We'll have to wait to see how the history is written about this tumultuous Rising."

"It's ours to write, lass. Just you remember that."

The rain had stopped when they finished their evening meal, leaving slippery puddles in the street. Before they bid each other good night and went their separate ways, Maureen suggested,

"Would you like me to give you more of a tour of Dublin tomorrow?"

"I think that I'll just take the day off completely. I have to catch up on my sleep before we get back to work. Thank you for this afternoon."

"How about a visit to the jail on Monday morning, then?" She gave him her address near the Kilmainham Gaol. "Pick me up at six."

"At your place? Why so early?"

"I have a feeling that there will be more executions."

"This is cozy," Morgan remarked from inside the tent that they had erected on the aft deck, at the Clarendon dock in the center of the shipbuilding quarter for the night. The deck was still sopping wet from the rain, but the tent's canvas floor kept them dry and comfortable. "We haven't been completely alone for over a week, mavourneen. I'd like to talk now about the most important thing on my mind."

"How does August fifteenth strike you, Morgan? It's my birthday."

"What do you have in mind, lover?"

"Well now, aroon. I am for making an honest woman of you so we can go out together into polite society."

Morgan gasped in mock horror. "It's a little late for that, don't you think?"

"Ah, Morgan, it's never too late, my love," Tadgh murmured, as he carefully slipped her blouse from her shoulders and bent his head to her breast.

"And lovers must have their due," she said, as her fingers unbuttoned his pants.

Tadgh was true to his word. They spent most of Sunday walking Belfast's streets, first visiting the Falls Road, largely inhabited by oppressed Catholic families. Then he took her to the Shankill area where the Ulster Volunteers and Protestants lived and marched.

Tadgh steered Morgan around a group amassing on Agnes Street as Protestants poured from their church. "If we don't get Home Rule for all of Ireland, then this area will become a hotbed of strife for our country, Morgan. You mark my words, lass."

"I'm surprised that Republicans didn't rise here, Tadgh."

"I'm not. Too much of a hornet's nest here in Edward Carson's bailiwick."

"I'm not following you."

"That bastard hawk-nosed Carson is the senior government anti-Home-Rule bully. The worst Britisher. And that damn Prime Minister Asquith allows his Ulster Volunteers to have weapons. They'll fight if Home Rule gets approved."

"So the Prime Minister may allow that such a law to be passed and then condone arming the very people that will create a Unionist revolt to oppose it. That's political corruption at its worst, isn't it."

"Yes, and diabolical."

"Then this is a good place to stay away from."

"I thought you should see what's here, aroon."

They were up and out early on Monday morning. Dock workers had threatened to invade their sanctuary with their crude language, so Tadgh placated them and quickly loosed their moorings before the boisterous ruffians could cause them harm. As they glided out into the channel, hearing the heckling and wolf whistles from the dock, Tadgh announced, "Best get dressed, love. We've a hundred and twenty-five miles to go before we reach Derry. I'll be more careful where we moor for the night from now on."

Collin fretted as he made his way to Maureen's apartment. There had been no word back from his telegrams to Sam and Kathy. He had checked numerous times at the front desk. Surely, they were happy to know that he had arrived safely in Ireland.

He found Maureen's apartment building on Bulfin Road after an arduous predawn trek on the south circular road. Jack's car was still impounded at Portobello. Although still spotty, the tram service was returning, but not yet here.

"C'mon up," Maureen called down when he rang her bell.

"I'll wait here for you," Collin replied, waving to her as she leaned out the window.

"I wanted you to see my place," she said, as they walked the three blocks to the gaol.

"Some other time, perhaps." Collin had no intention of letting that happen.

"I heard four volleys of rifle fire earlier," Maureen muttered as they approached the gaol. "That means the firing squad has likely been spitting unholy death."

A small gathering of women waited patiently in the front stone courtyard outside the walls of the heavily-defended penal fortress. The reporters approached two grieving women who each clutched the hands of two small children. The women's faces were pale and the children whimpered and sobbed. Maureen and Collin discreetly eavesdropped on what the women were saying.

"He's dead. I know it," the younger woman wailed.

"You don't know that for certain, Agnes."

"You're Michael's mother. Can't you feel it, too?"

Collin could see from the look on the older woman's face that she was just trying to be brave. He knew it would be improper to bother them for information at this terrible time.

Maureen interrupted the women. "Excuse me, madam. I'm with *The Times*."

Collin put his hand out to hold her back, but she had already stepped into their circle of grief.

"I apologize for bothering you at this time, but I have a responsibility to my paper and the people of this city to report on how the rebels are being treated. I heard you say the name Michael, so I assume you are talking about Michael Mallin. Am I right?"

Collin could see the younger woman recoil from this insensitive intrusion, so he stepped in. "Excuse me, ladies. Come on, Maureen. Leave these women and their children in peace."

Maureen was reluctant to back off, so Collin grabbed her wrist forcefully and turned her away.

"Just a moment, young man," the older woman said, taking an envelope out of her bag. "I have something to say."

Collin let go of Maureen, and they turned around to face the pair.

"I am Michael Mallin's mother. My son is a hero, not only by fighting for his conviction that we must free Ireland, but also for his spirit of fair play and decency in the face of barbarous adversity and defeat."

Collin stepped forward and put his arm on the older woman's shoulder. "I'm sure he is, ma'am."

"They let us see him last night, you know, all seven of us, before . . ."

Maureen looked puzzled.

"Agnes is pregnant with their fifth child. He didn't get a real trial, you know. None of them did. They are a scurrilous lot, that Brigadier Maconchy who presided for the rogue General Maxwell, and all the rest. We heard that they called Michael terrible false things to impugn his character."

Collin saw that Agnes was about to break down, but the mother was going to speak her piece. He touched the wife's elbow gently so she would know she could lean on him.

Maureen took notes, listening to the older woman.

"There was one soldier who spoke the truth, though," the

mother continued. "He was the arresting officer, Captain De Courcy-Wheeler. He said that Michael came forward to surrender on behalf of his garrison and saluted politely, taking full responsibility. At his court martial, Michael told the tribunal about the kindness and consideration the captain showed during the surrender."

Collin tried to separate fact from the poor woman's grief-stricken vitriol. "Your son seems to be a strong and compassionate leader of his cause."

"Yes, he is, and you can print anything I'm telling you."

"Is there anything else you would like people to know?"

"Yes. I know why they are being so hard on my son."

"Why is that, madam?"

"Agnes read to me from the paper that General Maxwell says Countess Markievicz is certainly guilty and dangerous. 'A woman who forfeited the privileges of her sex,' he says. The man hates the Countess, and he's making the case for executing her."

"How is that?" Maureen asked for the first time.

"If they discredit my Michael, then it makes the countess look more important in their garrison. Maxwell wants her dead, but we heard that Asquith insists that no woman should be executed."

"Were you going to show us something, ma'am?" Collin pointed to the envelope in the mother's hand.

"Oh, yes. This is a note that Michael wrote to all of us just before he surrendered. I think it speaks to his character." She retrieved a small sheet of paper and handed it to Collin.

"Read it," Maureen urged, her pencil at the ready.

Collin looked at the mother and Agnes and they both nodded their consent. He cleared his throat and read aloud,

> "'My darling wife, all is lost. My love to all my children, no matter what my fate. I am satisfied I have done my duty to my beloved Ireland and you, and to my darling children. I charge you as their sole guardian now to bring them up in the

national faith of your father, and of my faith, of
our unborn child may God and his blessed Mother
help you and I. I said all is lost, I meant all but
honor and courage. God and his blessed Mother
again guard and keep you, my own darling wife.'"

"I would just add one thing," Agnes spoke for the first time,
emboldened by her mother-in-law's discourse. "Last night, on the
eve of his death, Michael told us that he found no fault with the
soldiers or the police. And for us to pray for all the souls who fell in
this fight, Irish and English." Agnes took a breath, "The last thing
he ever said to us in this life, 'So must Irishmen pay for trying to
make Ireland a free nation.'"

They all realized that they were talking about a man who had
likely been executed in the few hours since he had spoken those
solemn words. Collin wondered if he would have as much intestinal
fortitude and fair judgment if he was in that terrible situation.

The side door to the prison opened, and a stake-sided truck
drove out with canvases covering its cargo. Agnes collapsed in
Collin's arms. He had a fair idea what was under those covers.

On a written notice the sergeant posted on the front door,
Maureen read to the others,

> "'After a fair court martial, the following rebel
> leaders have been found guilty of treason and have
> been executed this morning. Eamonn Ceannt,
> Sean Heuston, Michael Mallin and Con Colbert.
> God rest their souls.'"

Collin muttered, "Damn those English bastards." He
reluctantly left the heartbroken women. There was nothing he nor
Maureen could do to lighten their sorrow. He asked Maureen as
they moved down the street, "Where are they taking the bodies
for burial?"

"Haven't you heard? They are not even getting a decent burial. They are taking them to Arbour Hill Cemetery and dumping them in a quicklime pit."

Collin was so revolted by the morning's events and revelations that he returned to the Shelbourne unescorted and spent the rest of the day planning his next steps. He couldn't get out of his head an image of Claire's body decomposing in quicklime.

Chapter Eighteen
Chance Encounter

Monday, May 8, 1916
North Channel, Off Ballycastle, Ireland

*T*adgh was delighted to be at sea once more, on a bright sunlit day no less, with billowy white clouds and a brisk easterly breeze in the rigging. Finally, they were away from the madness and travesty of the last three weeks, at least for a little while. His boss and mentor, Padraig Pearse, and many of the IRB leaders were dead and gone.

He had heard from dockworkers before they left that Mallin was dead, shot that morning. Morgan was really worried about the countess. They agreed not to talk about it since they couldn't do anything to change the outcome anyway. No one could. The damned English were in punitive and destructive control, grinding the common man under the heel of their boots. Tadgh swore to himself that the bastards would eventually pay for this infamy.

After they had traveled north along the coast, Tadgh pointed to the land. "You see that town and harbor to the west? It's called Ballycastle."

"Yes, it looks pretty windswept."

"Aye, lass, a northeastern outpost for our fair land. Did you know that Marconi sent one of the very first wireless transmissions from there to Rathlin Island over on your right? That was back in '98, three years before he managed to send signals all the way across the Atlantic."

"Did he, now? Am I supposed to be impressed with him or with you for knowing about this?"

"Just a simple fisherman, that's for certain."

"Go on with ya."

"You see that castle on those white cliffs ahead?"

"You mean that shell?"

"Called Kinbane Castle. Means 'white head.' Fellow by the name of Colla MacDonnell built it in about 1550. The English attacked the castle and eventually destroyed it. That's a Scottish derivation of a name we know well."

"O'Donnell, is it? Like Peader?"

"Right you are. The contemporary Irish name would be Collin O'Donnell. It looks like the O'Donnells branched out from Donegal in medieval times."

"We're going to moor *Survivor* here for a spot of lunch," Tadgh announced half an hour later as he tacked and came about in the calm leeward harbor of a tiny fishing village. "This is Portballintrae."

"You know every nook and cranny of your country, don't you, skipper?"

"*Our* country, you mean, aroon."

"Ah, yes. Our country. Why are we stopping here?"

"For lunch and another mythology lesson."

"Do tell."

"In good time. This was just what the doctor ordered. A sail, a ride, and lunch."

After tying up at the jetty, Tadgh took Morgan to the mercantile store where he bought soda bread, slices of lamb, local Blue Rathgore goat cheese, and early harvest strawberries. Then he grabbed a bottle of red wine. Any wine. It wasn't usually to his taste.

"We're going for a picnic and a ride into history."

"Really, Tadgh. You surprise me." Morgan grabbed her lover's arm, as he guided her up into a rented horse-drawn cart. After a two-mile ride eastward along the rugged coast, he stopped and helped her down. Walking to the edge of a cliff, Tadgh pointed to a strange geological formation down at the rocky shore.

"What is that, Tadgh, all those vertical interlocking blocks?"

"That's the Giant's Causeway, my dear, with forty thousand vertical hexagonal steps, as they're called." Tadgh explained the mythology. "You see, Finn MacCool was a very fierce leader of the Fianna. They were the supposed inhabitants before Saint Patrick brought us Christianity. Finn built these steps as a causeway to Scotland so that he could fight and be victorious over his adversary Benandonner. Can you see Scotland, lass?"

"Yes, I see it." She stood on her tiptoes and pointed to the northeast where a land mass seemed to float, wreathed in mist.

Tadgh spread a blanket on the grassy knoll high above the steps and laid out their lunch, as he continued, "When Finn saw the size of his opponent, he fled back to Ireland pursued by the Scottish leader. So Finn's wife dressed him as a baby. When Benandonner saw the size of the 'baby' and imagined the size of the father, he fled back to Scotland, ripping the causeway up so that Finn could not follow him. There is a similar geological formation on the island of Staffa in Scotland, northeast of here."

When Morgan's eyes widened, Tadgh held his hand over his heart and said, "It's told by the *seanachai* nomadic storytellers of old. I believe it's the gospel truth, so it is." Having spread the gospel according to the ancients, Tadgh proceeded to feed his love her lunch, one strawberry at a time.

"This is just what the doctor ordered, mavourneen," Morgan murmured, as she sipped a second glass of wine.

It was worth the time to divert to pleasures of the mind and body, but they were delayed in reaching Tadgh's goal that night of Derry, or Londonderry, as the English oppressor called it. At about midnight, they finally berthed at Lisahally in Foyles Bay. Although still very active for the import and export of goods, the Foyle Harbour and its shipyard, which had proudly built famous clipper ships over the ages, had fallen into disarray, giving them a perfect spot to anchor undetected.

"I've been worried about what's happened to your brother, Aidan. What if the British have gone back to Barrow House. When will we get to Tralee, Tadgh?"

Tadgh had also been thinking about Tralee. Maurice could probably handle the RIC, but there might be a witch-hunt there, as well. With a bullet wound in his leg from his valiant effort to save them from death at the hands of Boyle in Rathoneen just seventeen days earlier, Aidan would be in no shape to flee the enemy. *God help us, it seemed an eternity ago.* Beyond that, Boyle was still the biggest threat. Tadgh wanted to kill him before he could get away. *If he was still alive, that is. He wouldn't have gotten far with the injuries that he sustained.*

"Yes, lass. I want to get to Tralee as soon as possible, too. It should take us another six days."

"Aidan was not in good shape when we left, Tadgh."

"I am sure that he's in good hands."

"I'd feel better if we were there."

"So would I, Morgan."

Sam had liked Lil's idea of getting Kathy back to teaching. They broached the subject with Kathy. On Monday evening when he returned from work, she balked. "I can't leave baby Liam. He's all that I have left."

"Nonsense, lass. Collin will soon tire of traipsing around Ireland looking for his long-lost sister," Sam replied, pulling on his pipe.

"He'll be back with his tail between his legs, dear."

"I'm not sure I want him back, Lil."

"I'd beat his hide before I'd let him back, Kathy, I can tell you."

"Really, ladies. Listen to you. Remember who we're talking about. The man who saved your life or at least your honor, Kathy. The father of your son. It isn't his fault that he feels responsible for his sister's disappearance and loss, surely."

Lil looked askance at her husband. "Shush, Sam. You don't have the whole story."

"That comment doesn't become you, love. Educate me, then."

The evening paper was strewn on the parlor floor where Norah had been looking at the funnies. Kathy picked through it to find the news article she was looking for. "There's a report from him in the *Tely* this evening."

"Show me. What does it say?"

"It's not what it says as much as who it's from."

"Why, what do you mean?"

"There are two reporters for the article. Collin and some woman named Maureen."

"So? I don't understand why the problem's worse this evening than last."

"Maureen O'Sullivan?"

Sam was taken aback. All right, he could see where associating with another O'Sullivan woman might stoke the fires of envy and anger.

"Maybe he has found a relative."

"That's ridiculous. He sure doesn't seem to miss me and Liam."

"What about that telegram you got from him a few days ago?"

"Actions speak much louder than words, Sam. Isn't that what you always preach?"

Sam could see that there was male condemnation going on, and nothing he could say would deter them. Both of them. He wanted to change the conversation's direction, "Would you care to join me for a drink before dinner's ready?"

Lil scowled and led Kathy toward the kitchen. "Go take care of the children, Sam. Dinner will just be soup tonight."

Sam took charge of the situation Tuesday morning, dropping in on the public-school superintendent for east-end schools before heading to Riverdale. "Rita, how's the Kingston Road substitute teacher doing?"

"The children are struggling, Sam. It's hard to come in near the end of the year. And Joyce has her own problems with her husband away at the war."

"What would you say if Kathy were to come back this week until year end?"

"That would be wonderful, Sam. But what about her baby boy?"

"My wife will look after the tyke. There's a catch, Rita. The request has to come from you, without my involvement."

"Could I count on her, Sam?"

"Yes, unequivocally." Sam hoped he was right.

"All right. I'll call in on her tomorrow before school."

"Come to my house, Rita. Number Ten Balsam Avenue. She's staying there."

"Please tell her I'll drop by."

"I think it best that you just show up. Don't take no for an answer, Rita. She may balk at first, but she really needs to be with her schoolchildren."

"I see. Tomorrow then."

"Did Sam put you up to this?" Kathy abruptly asked Rita, during their conversation at Sam and Lil's the following morning before school.

"No. We have been having a problem with the children, Kathy—without you, I mean. When Sam mentioned your interest in your students' well-being, I seized on the opportunity to talk to you about it."

"What's the problem?" Kathy had to admit feeling a surge of energy, thinking about her students once again.

"Joyce is struggling, trying pick up where you left off. And it is now so close to the end of the year, I truly worry for her."

"How's Michael Jacobs doing? You know, the one who gets everything backwards. And Nancy, the bright little girl who loves science?" All the individual quirks and capabilities of the students she loved came flooding over her, thoughts she hadn't allowed herself to think about since baby Liam was born.

"That's just it, girl. I don't really know, since Joyce has been having trouble communicating with the children and with me."

"But that's terrible! The children like Michael won't pass and they'll be held back a whole year."

"That's what I'm worried about, dear."

Kathy started to see that she had been prioritizing one child, her own, at the expense of thirty.

"Could you come back, Kathy? I mean, would you?"

Lil was excited by the prospect. "Liam will be all right with us here, Kathy. Norah and Dot love having him as a 'cousin' along with baby Ernie."

"But I'm worrying about the load on you, and all."

"Nonsense, girl. There's not much difference between three and four, and I am still nursing."

"I do miss them, the students."

Lil pulled Kathy from her seat and shooed her to the bedroom. "Of course you do. Now run along and change your dress. Where's your coat and hat? Supper will be at six o'clock." Lil wasn't going to take no for an answer. Fifteen minutes later, after a tearful goodbye to her Liam, Kathy climbed into Rita's roadster and they disappeared up Balsam Avenue.

Sam came down the stairs, still adjusting the knot in his tie.

"You did it, *creena*. She's off with a twinkle in her eye at last."

"We all did it, Lil. But it's only a stop-gap success, I'm afraid. Worse storm clouds are gathering to the east that threaten to engulf Kathy if the real problem is not solved."

"But, for now, Kathy has something to occupy her, my love. Now, your breakfast is getting cold and you'll be late for school yourself if you don't get a move on. Honestly, lad, you're worse than the children some days."

Sam sighed as he sat down to eggs and bacon, not relishing the long drive to Riverdale School. He had hoped that the success of his initiative might elicit a playful suggestion of a romantic night ahead. *Maybe when I get home this evening.*

Meanwhile, in Dublin that Wednesday evening, Collin struggled over taking a course of action. He had spent the last three days walking through the rubble that was downtown Dublin, snapping photos for his reports.

He had checked the jails for anyone named Claire O'Donnell, with no success. The head of the RIC and Dublin Metropolitan Police were too busy to see him about his quest. He had no concrete knowledge that she was still alive, and if so, if she even was a fugitive. He still had to check the hospitals, but he was beginning to think that she never came to Dublin and the Rising after all. Maybe it was all a figment of Jack Jordan's vivid imagination like Sam had suggested. But he couldn't leave it at that, not while there was a chance of finding and saving her.

Collin thought about sending Kathy another telegram. But why should he? She hadn't the courtesy to acknowledge his earlier one. And what would he say, anyway? He had no news about Claire, and Kathy could read all about what he was finding out regarding the Rising in his *Tely* reports.

I've got to get back to Queenstown and Cork City to interview Jack and this fellow Boyle.

But he couldn't leave Dublin and his obligation to his paper, his Irish host Healy and *The Irish Times*. Not yet. The fate of ICA leader and Dublin Commandant James Connolly still hung in the balance, especially since he had been shot during the Rising and was hospitalized at Kilmainham Gaol.

Fortunately, Maureen had left him alone since Monday. She had some other assignment.

Something was bothering him about his recent experiences in Dublin, and he couldn't figure out what it was. It was on the tip of his proverbial tongue.

♣ ♣ ♣ ♣

In the interests of saving time, Tadgh had skipped the day of touring that he planned for Morgan to see Derry's ringed wall fortifications with its ancient tribal history. Instead, they had navigated the northwest coast through a sizeable ocean chop with storm clouds brewing. Tadgh admired Morgan's seafaring fortitude. She was becoming a true sailor after his own heart. In fact, she had imprisoned his heart, and he had no desire to be set free.

Wednesday night they laid by in a shoreline cove and secured the tent on the deck to prevent a howling wind from blowing it overboard into a storm-tossed sea. By the morning, the weather finally cleared, and they passed by a relatively large island on their starboard side some three miles off the Donegal coast.

"Do you see that island, Morgan? It's Arranmore."

"Isn't that where Peader plans to teach school?"

"That's right. Good memory, lass. The strange thing is that it's mostly Gaeltacht and Peader isn't completely fluent in Gaelic, but he said he was working on learning the Gaelic language at St. Patrick's. He's a clever one, he'll manage well enough." Tadgh turned his attention to the landscape. "Do you see that promontory fort on the south shore? It goes back to pre-Celtic times.

"Was that before St. Patrick brought Christianity to Ireland?"

"Yes. In fact, you'll remember that Peader already told us how St. Patrick used his crozier to strike the sign of the cross on Cenél Conaill's shield, back in about 480 A.D, as did St. Columba, who followed him sixty years later. They instructed the founders of the O'Donnell Clan to carry this Constantine Cross symbol into battle and they would be victorious. So, yes, St. Patrick ministered in this area of Ireland and Peader's earliest ancestors became Christians."

"So this part of the country was pivotal to Ireland's development as a nation following Papal doctrine then."

"Not exactly, Morgan. Celtic Christians didn't always obey the Pope, although they were mindful of God's will."

"Are we back to the discussion of Divine intervention? I believe in it, you know. And now that we're here, I feel something magical."

"Do you now, lass? It must be my magnetic personality." Tadgh put his arm around her, right there at the tiller and squeezed.

Morgan laughed and kissed him on the cheek. "Are we close to where Peader's family lives?"

Tadgh consulted the map that Murphy had thoughtfully tucked in with their provisions. "Yes, I think so. I've never set foot in this part of Ireland before, but Dungloe, where he's from, should be that town you can see at the end of the bay on our port side."

"It looks like a fishing village. I see a boat like Maurice's coming out from the docks."

"We agreed to visit Peader here when he completes his studies at St. Patrick's. He said that he would return home near the end of June, but he has to go to the school on Arranmore right away to prepare his lessons for the fall. Should we stop in and meet his family since we are here, Morgan?"

"I say yes. What if we need to reach him after we return home and they don't have a telephone up here? It looks pretty remote."

"Oh, all right, let's try to find them. But then we need to be on our way to reach Aidan, lass."

Tadgh hailed the outbound fishing trawler and confirmed in Gaelic that this was indeed Dungloe, near a secondary port called Burtonport to the north at the mouth of the bay. More importantly, he learned of a tailor, Brigid O'Donnell, who owned and ran a clothing shop on the main street of the town. The captain didn't know if she had a son named Peader.

Half an hour later they were tied up at the dock in Dungloe, and after a twenty-minute walk, they had found themselves at Main Street off the Quay Road. Being two thirty in the afternoon, Morgan blurted out, "Can we eat first, please?"

"We might miss her if we wait. Let's find her shop first, and then we eat."

The Dungloe Weaving and Tailor Shop was a tidy clothing store on Lower Main Street. Morgan loved the tweed outfits in the window, and one in particular with a turquoise check on a cream color background captured her attention.

Glancing through the window, Tadgh could see three women working weaving looms, their shuttles flying. Near the back an older woman waited on a customer. At about five foot two, the shopkeeper looked stooped and shrunken, like someone who had endured a very hard life.

Tadgh went in, pulling Morgan along with him. He waited for the shopkeeper and customer to finish their transaction. It would never do to get in the way of bargaining.

The customer was not impressed with this large man's patience and sniffed at him as she took up her purchase and left the shop. The little shopkeeper turned her watery blue eyes to him. "Yes, young man. How may I help you?"

"I didn't want to take you away from your customer, but I've come to ask if you have a son named Peader, ma'am." The whole conversation was in Gaelic. Tadgh noticed that Morgan wandered off to examine the clothing neatly arranged on hangers.

"Why, yes. Do you know him? He's away in Dublin at school right now, and I'm worried sick because of the terrible Rising. I have no telephone here in Dungloe, and I haven't been able to reach him."

"Yes, ma'am. I am a friend of his and was with him just a week ago. I believe that he survived the Rising and is back in school."

"Oh, thank God. Thank you!"

Tadgh extended his hand, "Sorry for my rough manners, Mrs. O'Donnell. I'm Tadgh McCarthy, ma'am."

"Thank you so much for bringing me this good news."

Tadgh realized that he was still providing a useful communications function, even though the Rising was defeated.

"Are you a Larkinist like me and my boy, Tadgh?"

"In a manner of speaking, yes. Peader and I are fighting for the same outcome." Tadgh knew that he was stretching the truth, but Peader did seem to be taking a more militant line of thinking. *Or maybe it was just wishful thinking on my part.*

"I'd like to introduce my partner," Tadgh continued. He grabbed Morgan from amongst the clothes racks and brought her to the lady. "Mrs. O'Donnell, this is Morgan." He spoke in English.

"My name is Brigid, but you can call me Biddy, lad. Everybody does."

Tadgh thought Morgan looked chilled as she wrapped her arms around her middle.

He saw the elder woman staring at Morgan's smoky green eyes, a natural reaction, he guessed.

"Hello, Morgan. Pleased to meet you. What's your last name, girl?"

Tadgh could see that Morgan didn't want to go through all the explanation. "Just Morgan, Biddy."

He started to open his mouth, and she shook her head at him.

Biddy noticed that they weren't wearing rings. "You're quite a couple, don't ye know."

"We're birds of a feather, that's for sure," Morgan said, holding tight to Tadgh's hand.

"A lucky man ya be, Tadgh McCarthy."

"Don't I know it, Biddy, to be sure."

"Can I get you a wrap, lass?"

"No thank you, Biddy." *There is something familiar about this woman.* Morgan couldn't put her finger on it. *Is it her voice?*

"Where do you live, the both of you?"

It was Tadgh's turn to cut Morgan off with the evil eye. "Down south, ma'am."

"I need to tend to Mrs. MacIntosh who is waiting over there by the window, but why don't you come up for supper later. I live just up the street in Meenmore, just north of town. You could stay the night and tell me more about what happened in Dublin. We get such little news out here in the wild."

"That's kind of you, ma'am, but we'd best be off since we need to meet up with my brother as soon as possible."

"Tadgh, can I talk to you please, while Mrs. O'Donnell takes care of her customer?" Morgan drew Tadgh behind a rack of clothes.

"I'm really enjoying our Irish adventure and history lesson, and the tent on the *Survivor* is cozy to a point, but a girl eventually needs to freshen up, if you know what I mean." Morgan tilted her head and threw back her curls, a clear sign she would not be dissuaded from the request she was about to make. "I would love a bath. Can't we stay one night? Biddy seems to be a grand person and she wants more information about Peader."

"You said it yourself, aroon. We need to get to Aidan."

"But you assured me that he's in good hands."

"I don't want to have to lie outright to the woman, Morgan."

"Then don't. You're good at that."

"At what?"

"At controlling what you say. Please?"

"One night?"

"Just until tomorrow."

"All right, but I'll have to go and batten down the hooker first."

Morgan waited until Biddy had finished serving her customer and then approached her.

"Can I help you, lass? Is there some fashion you fancy before you go?"

"You have beautiful clothes, Biddy, and someday I'll buy some. But not today. Tadgh and I have discussed your kind offer, and we would love to take you up on your hospitality this evening. We'd like to give you more information about your son."

"Would you, lass? Thank you. You go on up the Main Street, north, past the Dungloe River bridge. The street becomes Mill and then Meenmore Road. We live at Number Two Hundred Ten Meenmore about a mile from here, on the way to Burtonport

279

Harbour. It's a white two-story farm house. Only one around."

"Thank you, ma'am. We haven't had the comforts of home for a long time now, what with the Rising and all."

"I'm happy to oblige, Morgan. You tell the children that I sent you. I'll be along presently."

Morgan was happy, more so than the circumstances might have warranted. Sure, the prospects of a home-cooked meal, a bath, and a soft bed were enticing, but there was a warmth about this woman, a strange familiarity.

Three hours later, bathed and refreshed by a good meal, Morgan sat in a rocking chair by the parlor fire. The children were gone to who knows where, and Tadgh was sipping a Jameson.

"You have a lovely home here in the Rosses," Tadgh offered, taking another bite of his ginger snap.

"We get by. My husband James has left for Scotland in preparation for the summer potato harvest, like so many of our men. And the shop helps, although times are tough for all."

"If you don't mind my asking, you don't seem to have been affected by the Rising up here."

"It's true, lad. Thirty-three men mobilized in Creeslough. They ordered the RIC back into their barracks at gunpoint. But with the MacNeill countermand, they didn't know what to do, so they stood down. Some tried to get to Dublin to fight, but there were no trains running beyond Dundalk."

"You mentioned being a Larkinist. Are you active for independence, then?"

"Civil unrest, yes. Armed insurrection, no. What are your politics, Tadgh?"

"The English must leave our country, ma'am. That's all there is to it."

"Then you're a Republican. And what of my son?"

"He's a devout Larkinist like yourself and focused on his studies, I believe."

"I tried to bring him up right."

"That you did, Biddy. I can assure you."

"So how do you know my son?"

"We met him in a Dublin pub having a pint with Sean O'Casey and friends."

"The playwright?"

"Aye. The same."

"That makes sense. Peader has always told me that he wants to be a playwright and a novelist someday."

Morgan, who had been sitting quietly, trying to understand the strange déjà vu feelings that had grown stronger since they had entered the O'Donnell home, joined the conversation. "He told us about that."

"More tea, lass?"

"No, thanks. Tadgh is a playwright himself, you know." The fire crackled in the grate and Morgan shifted closer to it.

"Are you? What plays have you written?"

"Just one, I'm afraid. O'Casey helped me back in 1914. It played briefly at the Abbey Theatre, though."

"What was it called, lad? Maybe I've heard of it."

Tadgh was surprised that Mrs. O'Donnell, way out here in the rural outskirts, would take such an interest in the arts. "Its title is *A Call to Arms.*"

"No wonder it had a short run, then."

"Very short. One week. The police shut it down, and let's just say that I had to leave Dublin."

"On the run, are you now?" Biddy sat on the edge of her chair, eyes twinkling in what seemed to be anticipation of a good story.

Morgan got up and came over to sit with Tadgh on the chesterfield. "You could say that, yes. We both are."

"But Peader's not involved, is he?"

Tadgh shot a glance at Morgan who said, "No, Biddy. Not in any playwrighting, as far as we know."

"I mean, he's not wanted by the government, is he?"

"We don't think so. No." Both guests shook their heads in unison.

"So, tell me about the Rising and the rough handling of it by the scoundrel English."

Tadgh, with some help from Morgan, gave their host a rundown of the events of the Rising, the heroics of the rebels, and the dastardly overkill of the English retaliation, leaving out personal details of their own participation in the fight and its aftermath.

"We're not as militant, but we side with you, Tadgh. Donegal wants a united and free Ireland."

"I would expect that position, given your Gaelic roots and ongoing culture. You have been able to keep the English at bay up here."

"In the tradition of Red Hugh, our namesake. How could it be any other way? We'll be here for you when the time comes."

"I'm glad to see that you view this Rising not as an end, but as our beginning."

"Yes, lad, I do. It seems obvious that this was Padraig Pearse's call to arms for the country."

"I feel that Peader sees it that way too," Morgan said.

"I'm sure he does, lass. Now, how about another drop of Jameson, Tadgh?"

Tadgh was glad that he had acquiesced to Morgan's wishes to stay at the O'Donnells. And now there might be lovemaking in the offing in a soft, warm bed. "I'd love another wee dram before tucking in for the night, Biddy. Thank you."

Morgan was in a very good mood when they snuggled into bed. The eider cover on clean cotton sheets was a decided improvement to the rough blankets and hard decking of the *Survivor* with no more than the thickness of the canvas tent flooring for protection. Especially when it rained and the wind whistled through.

"Now you'll say I'm being silly, Tadgh, but I feel a strange comfort here with Biddy," whispered Morgan, as she curled her body up around her man.

"How so, aroon?" Tadgh began stroking the lustrous black locks out of her beautiful green eyes. He ran the back of his hand along the sweet fragrant curve of her dimpled cheek into the creamy dip of her chin.

"It's so frustrating. I feel like I have met her, or heard her voice before, but I can't remember. Her face doesn't look familiar, and her name doesn't ring a bell."

"I think it would be a coincidence if you had known her before, lass. What are the chances that we would come all this way and run into someone who you had met before your amnesia?"

"Pretty slim, I would have to agree. And she clearly doesn't recognize or remember me. So it must be my imagination."

"Or your hidden wish, my love. Her home is a sight more comfortable than the deck of *Survivor* in a rainstorm, that's certain." Tadgh's hands were under the nightshirt that Biddy had given her. "She seems to be such a warm person."

"You seem to be warming up yourself, mister."

"You know how I get after I've had my Jameson." One of his hands returned to touching her cheek as Tadgh covered her mouth with kisses.

"Yes, I do, mavourneen. And I love it." Morgan ran her tongue along the fullness of Tadgh's mouth, and her hands found his awakening manhood. Her full-throated sigh told Tadgh everything he needed to know.

"You are taking hold of me, my love. Please, don't let me go." Tadgh's body rippled, coiling against her. Morgan raked his nipples with her teeth, teasing him, nibbling. She knew from experience that this would release any inhibitions he might be feeling.

"My God, Morgan. You bewitch me." Tadgh found her wetness with his hand and began pressing inward. Tadgh took his turn at fondling Morgan's breasts, first with his encircling tongue and next with pinches by his fingers. She started to moan softly.

He heard, "Don't stop," when he let go of her right breast. He ripped his own nightshirt off and pushed hers up over her

283

head. He touched her so gently, she rose up to meet him, her body coming to full arousal.

"I need you now, lass." Tadgh moved between her legs to enter her. At her words of sweet breathless entreaty, his rising waves flooded and filled her with rhythmic passion, pushing and thrusting to the point of their surrender. Tadgh put his arms around her waist and pulled himself even farther inward, touching his soul to hers.

Chapter Nineteen
Homeward Bound

Friday, May 12, 1916
Kilmainham Gaol, Dublin

*C*ollin and Maureen stood in the rain under open umbrellas at the entrance to the gaol at six in the morning. Maxwell had announced that more rebels would be executed. The fate of James Connolly was at stake, and this brought out more onlookers and journalists. Collin had learned from one of the jailors that ninety prisoners had been sentenced to death. The general had subsequently made a heavy-handed self-serving announcement about it.

"It looks like we may be coming here quite often then, Collin." Maureen fidgeted with her shawl since the wind at that hour was bitter.

"They're just digging a bigger hole to crawl out of."

"What do you mean?"

"Can't you see that the tide is turning? The people are angry."

"Of course they are angry. Our city is in ruins."

"I'm afraid that you are still looking at this through the eyes of *The Irish Times*. The people are angry with the English. The more rebels that they execute, and without a fair public trial, the more upset the citizens will get."

"Do you really believe that?"

"Absolutely. You have a police state now with all the arrests, and barbarian behavior by the military. Take a hard look around. Put yourself in the shoes of the average factory worker. I've gone out to see them at work and at home while you have been on other assignments. It's pitiful what they earn and how they are treated. They live in slums like the Ward back home, not on Mountjoy

Square. The English factory managers don't care for their well-being, only for the profit they can generate for the owners. That's why they treat them like slaves. Hell, they *are* slaves, for all that."

"I see."

But Collin could see that she didn't, not really. Maureen might agree in principle with the concept of freedom, but she didn't comprehend the gritty conditions of the average citizen. "This is going to be the subject of my articles back to the *Tely* from now on. The common man and his plight. And what his reaction is going to be because of the English behavior. I hope to change your mind along the way, lass."

"Fair enough, then. But I may not be able to co-author such articles, Collin, and Mr. Healy may get mad."

"I understand. That's why I am telling you about my plans. I don't report to Mr. Healy, and I can operate out of a much less lavish hotel, if necessary."

"I'm not his lackey you know, Collin."

"I beg to differ. Although unwittingly, I think you are. One other subject I plan on writing about is the split personality here of Irish soldiers fighting for the British in the trenches of the Western Front while others are fighting the English government to liberate Ireland. I think my Canadian readers will want to be much more informed on that subject. After all, Canadian soldiers are fighting and dying by the thousands in Belgium and France, and their loved ones live in fear and apprehension."

"I certainly know the plight of those left behind. My Duncan is on the Front right now."

This was the first Collin had heard of Maureen's private life. "Your brother?"

She swallowed before replying, "No, just a good friend I was sharing my apartment with before the war."

A volley of shots rang out from inside the Gaol. Women in the crowd screamed. Five minutes later, a second staccato volley jarred the crowd. Then silence from within.

A soldier of the Black Watch marched out of the prison's front door and posted a sheet on it. Women rushed to see if the list contained the name of a loved one, while others cowered under umbrellas, sobbing. The reporters noted that this was a terrible repeat of what had happened the day Mallin had died.

"He's gone!" one woman screamed. "James is gone." Her cry caused the crowd to erupt. Some started throwing refuse against the wall, and one woman raised a revolver and shot it into the air. Collin heard shouts of "Kill the English bastards."

It only took a minute for the military to act. A dozen Black Watch soldiers streamed out of the prison and formed a line of defense. Their leader fired a shot into the air to silence the throng. "Go home now. The show is over for today."

When the crowd hesitated, he yelled louder, "Do it now, before anyone gets hurt."

The soldiers aimed their rifles, waiting for the order to fire, which never came. The crowd backed up and dispersed, many mumbling as they went. One muttered, "Connolly was wounded and seriously ill. They shot him anyway, the goons."

"See what I mean, Maureen?"

"Yes, Collin. That's quite a different reaction from the beginning of the week, isn't it?"

"It's no wonder. Connolly led the common man in the Dublin lockout strike of 1913. Twenty thousand honest workers against 300 greedy employers. He followed Larkin who had formed the Irish Transport and General Workers' Union."

"You've learned a lot in the short time that you've been in Dublin, Mr. O'Donnell."

"I have to while away my time in some fashion, now don't I?"

"I can think of something better to do." Maureen flicked her skirt momentarily above her knees.

"I guess out of sight is out of mind."

"It's war time. Anything goes, my boy."

Collin didn't want to comment on that last remark for fear

that whatever he said would be misconstrued as an encouraging solicitation.

Instead, he went forward and read the note on the door. "It confirms that Connolly has been executed along with Sean MacDiarmada. All the seven signatories of the Republic declaration have now been killed."

Maureen had taken out her note pad and flipped to the page that contained the complete list. "There are still seventy-five left on the list, by my calculation."

A Black Watch soldier came to stand duty at the door. Maureen approached him. "Excuse me, Sergeant, I'm Maureen O'Sullivan with *The Irish Times*. Can you tell me how Mr. Connolly was shot, with his serious injury and all?"

"He couldn't stand, so we tied him to a chair. Bloody humane of us, in my opinion. I'd a strung him up by his thumbs first if I was the general, I would."

As Collin and Maureen turned to walk away, the Canadian journalist said in a hushed voice to his colleague, "Do you see what I mean? Mark my words. They just started a time bomb ticking that will blow up in their face. I think that will be the lead for our story today."

"Your story, you mean, not mine."

Clearly, she was still under Healy's thumb. He would fire her if she wrote something he didn't like.

Meanwhile, over breakfast that morning, Biddy O'Donnell had said to her guests, "Why don't you come back after Peader gets home? I expect him on July fourth."

"That's the Americans' Independence Day."

"Yes, Tadgh. I just wish that the Rising had been successful so we could have our own Independence Day."

"Amen to that, Biddy. We will, to be sure. We had actually

planned to do so with Peader when we last saw him in Dublin. Can we send you a telegram when we will be coming to visit?"

"The telegraph office in town has been unreliable ever since the terrible storm last November. Just come when you want. You have an open invitation."

Tadgh said, "We have important business with your son. We will come back on July sixth, so that would give him a couple of days to settle in at home."

"That's grand, lad. I'll tell him when he gets here."

"Goodbye, Biddy. Thank you." When Morgan wrapped her arms around the woman in a big hug, the hair on her neck tingled again at its roots.

"You're a fair lass, Morgan. Godspeed to you both."

Tadgh and Morgan left the O'Donnells and walked into bright sunshine, the kind of morning that could fool the heather into blooming prematurely.

It took five hours to travel the forty-five miles south to Donegal Town. When they sailed into Donegal Bay, Tadgh pointed out the ruins of the Franciscan monastery. "This is where the four Masters wrote their Annals, which is a chronicle of ancient Irish history from the Deluge, roughly two thousand years after Creation, to the year 1616, when the British finally defeated Peader's ancestors and destroyed the monastery."

"I thought you said that you had never been to this part of Ireland."

"Peader told me about this history, lass. Terrible tragedy, don't ya think?"

Morgan got a puzzled look on her face, so Tadgh asked, "Does this place ring a bell for you, my love?"

"I can't put my finger on it, but it's like I've been here before. That statue. In my dreams, maybe. But I can't really remember."

"Let's go and look." Tadgh came about to kill the wind and glided up to the stone wall flanking the monastery quay.

"There you go, lass." He looked at the plaque. "That's a statue of Red Hugh himself, standing proud, grounding his sword in his right hand with a learned scroll in his left."

"Quite a fearsome-looking but handsome man," Morgan said, straining to see the inscription at the base. "Kind of like you."

"Maybe in some former life you were a nun following in the footsteps of St. Clare and St. Francis of Assisi, aroon."

"Given what we've been doing in the evenings in our tent and last night in Biddy's bed, I certainly don't feel like a nun," she murmured, and blushed. "And it's only a matter of time until—"

"You've always been careful, you know—right?"

"Ever since Ostend, when I talked to the other nurses."

Their visit to Donegal Town and its medieval castle did not invoke any more déjà vu feelings in Morgan, at least none that she shared with Tadgh. He didn't ask. They spent the rest of the day sailing to Westport in Clew Bay, County Mayo.

"What's that pointy mountain to the southwest?" Morgan asked as they berthed at the end of the bay for the night.

"I know this country from experience. That would be Croagh Patrick, known locally as *The Reek*. It is said that on that mountain St. Patrick fasted and prayed for forty days and nights in the year 441. As a result, it has been a place of pilgrimage from early medieval times, or perhaps earlier. The last Sunday in July is Reek Sunday, when pilgrims climb the mountain barefoot as an act of penance, carrying out rounding rituals where they pray while walking clockwise around features of the mountain."

"The Irish soil is soaked with the mystical traditions of St. Patrick and the Christian church, isn't it, Tadgh."

"There is much of the history of this land that either lies forever buried or which has evolved mythologically through verbal and physical rituals, Morgan. Back to the time of the Druids, to the time of the Duatha de Dannon. Only the faeries know the truth, and they are as elusive as the history itself, lass."

"I can feel the faerie people all around us, Tadgh. I felt their presence the first time I touched the house wall in our garden back in Creagh. We had better take care not to give offence to either the pagan or the sacred."

"I've heard that there is another location like *The Reek* where pilgrims have come to do penance since the time of St. Patrick. That place is on Lough Derg in Donegal, not that far from Donegal Town. It, too, is associated with St. Patrick, where the seanachai tell that he found the entrance to hell."

"There's a place I never want to go to, Tadgh."

"No place for me, either, I must admit. But this Roman-inspired town must have a cozy pub that is inviting. It's a bit of a walk, just a good stretch of the legs. Let's go find it."

Saturday dawned cloudy with a cold fresh wind out of the northwest. "Great sailing weather, lass. With luck we might make Barrow Bay by nightfall if we catch the morning tide."

"Can you get underway while I rest here in the tent for a bit? You kept me up late with your shenanigans."

"Is that what you call it, aroon?"

"Yes, and my ending up ripe with child as a consequence of all this tomfoolery."

"Oh g'wan. You're only codding me."

"Surely a good Catholic lad such as yourself knows about consequences, mavourneen."

"But you're joking, right?"

"Yes, love. But if we keep this up, I can't be held responsible. Your passion knows no bounds, mavourneen." Morgan leaned over the tiller and kissed him square on the mouth.

"Our passion you mean, Morgan." Tadgh lifted her over the tiller and crushed her breasts against his barrel chest. "God will see to it that we can complete our mission for him and my ancestors, before little McCarthys grace our home, so he will. Don't worry."

"I'm not worried, my love." The twinkle in her green eyes gave away her desire for a family. *Maybe that will stop his obsession with revolution.* Yet she knew she was kidding herself. The martyrs of the Rising had families. She had better be more careful.

Morgan worked the sails to take advantage of the brisk winds that skimmed them across the waves of Clew Bay heading southwest. Both were preoccupied with thoughts about their future together. August fifteenth couldn't come soon enough.

All morning they sailed past the area known as Connemara on their port side, where Tadgh shared that the ancient Tuatha de Dannon tribe had settled according to the Annals of the Four Masters. At noon, when they lost sight of the homeland, they spied the large island of Inishmore to the east. Just as Tadgh was explaining that beyond that island lay Galway Bay, a hooker quite similar to their own rounded the southern tip of the island, heading out to sea.

"Hail the *Galway Girl*," Tadgh yelled to the other vessel as it approached on the port beam.

"Hail the *Survivor*. Where be ye headed?" The captain of the other hooker pulled his boat alongside, pacing Tadgh's.

"Home to Queenstown," Tadgh lied.

"You've a long way to go, then. Where'd you come from?"

"Belfast, Captain."

"Have you heard if true Irishmen rose there?"

"Are you sympathetic to the Volunteers?" Tadgh asked, veering to port to close within fifteen feet.

The two captains sized each other up.

Apparently satisfied, the other captain answered, "Aye, you?"

"Aye. A few good men rose but quickly dispersed near Belfast because of MacNeill's countermand."

"Liam Mellows marshaled five hundred at Athenry here, but without the rifles, we were outgunned. I wouldn't recommend landing at Galway City. The HMS *Gloucester* is still in the bay. She shelled the fields around Athenry on the twenty-seventh and forced Mellows to retreat to Moyode Castle. He's on the run now, along with Kenny and Lardner. It's a sad day for Ireland."

"From the recent reaction of Irishmen, I believe that it will turn out to be a glorious day for Ireland, Captain—"

"Brennan, Captain Brennan."

"McCarthy here. We thank you for your advice, and we wish you Godspeed, Captain Brennan. Keep the faith."

"And you also, Captain McCarthy."

Both men saluted and the *Galway Girl* headed north, up the coast.

Tadgh gave Morgan a sly grin. "I guess we'll skip the tour of the boatyards where my hooker was built."

As the sun dipped toward the western horizon, they cruised by Banna Strand with the Samphire light beacon ahead to guide them. Inching into Barrow Bay, Morgan used Tadgh's plumb bob to check the draft.

"I wish we had been able to contact Maurice ahead of time," Tadgh said as he tied up at the Barrow House pier.

"Yes, it's impolite for a chaste young woman such as myself to show up unannounced."

Tadgh knew that this banter was a weak attempt to cover up her anxiety. "Then you have no need to worry, lass."

Morgan stood up, stretched, and stepped gingerly over the gunnels onto the stone stairs. They had been eleven hours on the water and needed to set foot on dry land.

Their reservations evaporated when they saw Aidan emerge from the manor front door, hopping down the stairs and across the lawn.

"What kept you away so long, brother?" He hugged them in turn. "Damn, it's good to see you both alive!"

"We're bruised and battered, but glad to be here," Morgan replied. "Looks like Maurice and Martha have been taking good care of you, brother."

"Maurice is in Fenit, I expect, offloading the afternoon catch. He'll be glad to see you both."

"So that we can take your freeloading carcass off his hands, to be sure, brother," Tadgh's rough words belied his relief to find Aidan safe.

"Let's go into the house where it's warm and brightly lit," Morgan suggested, leading Aidan back up the stairs. "Is Martha home?"

"Yes, Sis. She'll be happy to see you, to be sure."

Once settled in the parlor with tea and scones provided by their welcoming hostess, Aidan said, "We've had some excitement here since you left, Tadgh. They came back to search the house again."

"Not Boyle, surely."

"There's no word about him, I'm afraid. If I'd heard, he'd be dead by now."

"Obviously, they didn't find you," Morgan replied, giving him a loving glance.

"I think those RIC goons have given up on us. But they've been rounding up Irishmen for questioning, according to Maurice. Put a lot of them in jail, I understand. Austin Stack is one, I think. You know him?"

"He's the head of IRB here in Tralee, Aidan. Or, at least he was. The bastards are witch hunting. We've had our own excitement, don't ya know. Morgan has a leg wound that rivals yours."

"Really, Sis?" Aidan put his left leg up against hers to compare wounds.

"Careful with Morgan, there, brother." The two maimed warriors eased back down on the chesterfield, arm in arm, with Tadgh shaking his head.

Later that evening, after they had devoured Martha's chicken dinner in the elegant dining room, they shared some of their recent adventures, leaving out any reference to the Clans Pact information.

"Bollocks, I should have been there with you two."

"You had already saved our lives, Aidan. You did your part magnificently," Morgan said, carefully putting the bone china teacup back on its saucer while nibbling on a wafer. "So did you, Maurice."

"The bastards have executed fourteen brave Irishmen, so far," Maurice informed them. "The last one to be shot was Connolly, who had such a bad ankle wound that he couldn't stand. They tied him to a chair."

"I saw James get that wound, so I did," Tadgh remarked. "He was the best soldier of them all. It looks to me that Padraig's plan will succeed."

"What do you mean?" Maurice asked, putting down his own cup and leaning in closer. "The Rising was a military fiasco. Central Dublin is in ruins, and the British are killing or imprisoning all the conspirators. Maxwell and his thug Charles Blackader sentenced ninety to death, but Asquith thankfully put a stop to it. Most of the rest are going to Frongoch in Wales."

"They are martyrs, you mean. What's the mood in Tralee, do ya think, Maurice?"

"People are damn mad at how the British bastards are handling this."

"I rest my case. The fight for freedom has just begun!"

"Did the paper say what has happened to Countess Markiewicz?"

"She has been spared so far and likely will go to prison, Morgan."

"Thank God."

"Did you meet her?"

"We fought together at St. Stephens Green, brother."

"I'd love to have been beside you." Aidan drew his pistol and pretended to shoot the imaginary enemy.

"Put that away, Aidan. You know my rule about guns in the house," Martha said, as she started picking up the dishes, carrying them to the kitchen.

Tadgh could see that Aidan had already become a valued member of the Collis Clan.

"Maurice, have you heard anything more about that Head Constable, Boyle? I was hoping he died from his wounds."

"I asked some questions, privately, you understand. He's still alive in the Tralee workhouse, but he's in bad shape and won't be going anywhere soon."

Aidan pulled out his gun again. "Why didn't you tell me, Maurice."

"Because you're a hothead and you needed to rest, lad."

Aidan looked at his brother. "Can we go and finish him off, Tadgh?"

Tadgh saw the look in Morgan's eyes. "All in good time, Aidan, all in good time. We'll get you home first so you can mend. Then we'll come back with a plan."

"But he might be gone then." Aidan didn't seem happy, but he holstered his weapon before anyone could reprimand him again.

That night, before they went up to bed, Tadgh casually said, "Aidan, I have a task for you if you'll accept it."

"Of course I'll accept. What is it?"

"It's an arduous task, lad. I'm not sure you're up to it."

"Sure I am. Does it have to do with the revolution? The hooker?"

Morgan smiled.

"You'll have to make a speech, Aidan."

"A speech?"

"Morgan and I are getting married and we need you to be the best man."

Morgan leaned forward and embraced Aidan. "Will you, brother?"

Aidan's face lit up with a delighted smile, "Of course, if we follow Gaelic tradition. When did you propose, Tadgh?"

"When we were being shot at, lad, crossing No Man's Land to get to a glass house."

The trio set off in the *Survivor* for Creagh early the next morning, after thanking the Collises profusely for their support and inviting them to the wedding. The Sunday church bells were ringing off in the distance in Fenit as they started for home. Morgan looked forward to sleeping in her own bed at last. They were ready for a breather.

When they approached the Berehaven Royal Navy Harbor, Tadgh advised them to be on the lookout. The U-boats and British defenders were still on the prowl despite the Kaiser's restraining order as the war to end all wars intensified. The sailors manning the loop magnetometer didn't even notice the blip as they sailed by, and they met no warships all the way to the Fastnet Light. It was after dark when they glided to the dock on the Ilen River at Creagh.

"It seems like a year since we left home," Morgan told Tadgh, reaching over from her seat at the tiller to cleat the stern line. "But it's only been twenty-four days." She'd been counting.

"In that time, the world has changed, lass," Tadgh commented, dragging his tired body up onto the dock. "Help me cleat off the bow, Aidan. We'll store her tomorrow."

Morgan spoke for the three of them as she wearily trudged up the steps to the front door. "It's good to be home. We surely need a rest."

Chapter Twenty
Ultimatum

Healy's Office, *The Irish Times*, Dublin
Wednesday, May 17, 1916

"Collin, you obviously heard from your boss, John Ross," John Healy addressed him, as the *Tely* journalist and his own reporter Maureen O'Sullivan were seated in his plush leather chairs and fed tea and scones.

"Yes, sir. I received a message at the Shelbourne this morning to come and meet with you."

"We shared telegrams yesterday. He wanted to get my opinion on the wind-down of the Rising stories. He had good words to say, lad, about your journalism."

"What did you tell him, sir?"

"I told him Prime Minister Asquith had stopped the executions and that the roundup of the rebels and their supporters has been completed with three thousand five hundred detained. I also reported that General Maxwell is being recalled to the war in Europe, and martial law has been lifted."

"What did he say to that?"

"He told me you should clean up your reports, and he asked me to send you home as soon as possible. But I wanted to meet with you before I answered."

Healy and Maureen exchanged glances.

"Where do you stand in your search for your sister, lad?"

"I've checked all the police offices and jails as well as the hospitals here in Dublin, with no success. She isn't among the detainees. I tried to meet with Sir Neville Chamberlain, but the Inspector General wouldn't see me. I have heard that the RIC is also searching for her and her Irish companion. They call them German spies and murderers."

"Do you believe that?"

"I don't know what to believe yet, sir. I haven't seen her in ten years."

"The story of your family fascinates me, Collin. And it would captivate our readers. Maureen will make sure of that." Healy and Maureen nodded in agreement. "I'd like to find a way to keep you on and aid you in your search. What do you suggest I say to John Ross?"

"I'd like nothing better as well. I don't think that the complete Rising story has been told. I realize that you want to wrap up the stories now that it has come to a successful conclusion from your point of view, and the sooner the better, I expect."

"Yes, so that we can focus on rebuilding Dublin's burned-out core."

Collin got up and paced the room before responding to the publishing giant. "I see something different. Miss O'Sullivan, here, has undoubtedly informed you of the anti-government sentiment that we found when we visited Kilmainham Gaol for the executions."

Collin looked over, and Maureen shook her head.

"Well, perhaps not. These past two weeks, I have been visiting people in their homes and where they work. Unrest is building below the surface, sir. This is the story that must be told while the city undergoes its transformation. Your government must address your citizens' issues if you hope to defuse the negative reaction to the English brutality in crushing the Rising."

"I don't see it that way, Collin, but if you can convince John Ross that your views are meritorious, and as long as Maureen here doesn't write reports of this nature for our paper, I can support you."

"Thank you, sir. I can try to persuade him."

"You do that. The fact that *The Times* is supporting your reporting must never come to light, son. Understood?"

"Yes, sir."

"So I will let you deal with John Ross, then. Get back to me, lad."

"I will. Thank you, sir."

"I've also looked into what happened to your father, Collin. It was a long time ago. I regret to tell you what I found out. The records of the *Donegal Democrat* are sparse, I must say. Mr. Finian O'Donnell, cobbler at Eighty-One Bridge Street, Donegal Town, age thirty-five, was found shot in the head up on the Road to Nowhere just north of Castle Lough Eske on the night of May twelfth, back in 1905. The police attempted to find his wife Shaina, son and daughter, but they had disappeared."

"What about the culprit, sir?"

"He was never apprehended, Collin, but the church wardens provided the funds to bury him in the cemetery in Donegal Town, and his business was sold, with the proceeds going to the church fund."

Maureen's eyes looked teary at the sad news. "That's awful, Collin. I am so sorry."

"Thank you, sir. It's all right, Maureen. It is as I expected. Of course, the paper didn't have the benefit of my personal experience."

"What is that, son?"

"I was there and tried to stop the man who questioned my Da about some hidden equipment, I'm not sure what. It was night, and our family was returning from a day at the Castle and the street was deserted. He threatened to kill my Ma if he didn't get what he wanted. I tried to attack the man, and my Da stepped in between. That's when my Da got shot the first time. Ma broke free, and Da yelled at her to run with us kids. The bastard said he would kill us all if we didn't stop, but we kept running. I heard more shots being fired. We stayed that night with an aunt and left for America two days later. We never heard what happened to Da."

"Well, at least you know now that he was given a proper burial, Collin. He sounds like a brave man who did his best to protect his family. You should be proud of him."

"I am, sir. And there's one other thing."

"Yes?"

"The man who killed my Da was wearing an RIC uniform."

"Was he, now. That wasn't reported in the paper."

"I don't suppose it would be, sir, now would it. They look after their own."

Healy frowned and pushed away his empty scone plate. "Yes, well—there is one more aspect of the rebellion that I want both of you to cover—a leak from high government sources that a Royal Commission is being chartered tomorrow under Lord Hardinge of Penhurst to investigate the causes of the insurrection. I expect that Chamberlain, Birrell, Nathan and others will be questioned. This will be conducted in London, and I want you to follow and report on this story, Miss O'Sullivan. You will need to travel to London and keep Collin informed here in Ireland for his paper. This may add weight to your argument to stay here for a time, lad."

"Yes, sir. I will include this story in my request to Mr. Robertson, to be sure." This time, when Collin looked over at Maureen, she had looked crestfallen.

Healy took a sip of his tea and continued. "Now then, Collin. Assuming you are successful with your boss, how can I help you with your private investigation?"

Collin leaned forward in his chair with his elbows on Healy's massive desk. "I want to return to Cork and Queenstown to interview the Cunard manager and local RIC constabulary. They are the ones that have had contact with my sister."

"If indeed it is your sister, Collin."

"I am convinced of it, sir."

"But is that conviction, or just wishful thinking?"

"Time will tell, won't it, sir?"

"I can arrange for you to meet with Chamberlain if that would help."

"Yes, sir, that would. Thank you."

"All right, then. You two have your marching orders. Collin, let me know what John Ross says. In the meantime I will notify you of what I can set up with the RIC Inspector General."

Sam realized that the benefit for Kathy to be reunited with her students was helpful, but not sufficient to keep her occupied until Collin's return. He understood the deep psychological forces driving his protégé's obsession in finding his sister, but there was a real danger that this could permanently fracture his marriage.

Lil had been staying up late most nights counseling her best friend to help keep her on an even keel. This was taking its toll on her ability to keep the household, now with four small children, functioning smoothly.

Kathy's parents Ryan and Fiona were applying pressure to get their daughter to move back in with them in Rosedale. This would ease the load on the Finlays, but without Lil's support, Kathy would crumble. So the O'Sullivans frequently came to see their grandson and check on their daughter. Their visits were pleasant enough but added to Lil's workload.

"Have you seen Collin's latest report in the afternoon's *Tely*, Sam?" Kathy asked on Saturday the twentieth, while they were all resting in the parlor after putting the children down for a nap.

"You mean the one about the history of the Larkinist movement and how it led to James Connolly being the military commandant of the whole Dublin Brigade?"

"Yes. that's the one. It gave me shivers to read about the sad fate of the mothers and wives. He wrote so eloquently, but I wonder if this Maureen O'Sullivan who shares the byline was more than helpful."

"Come on now, Kathy. You don't know anything about her. She could be a great-grandmother."

"Not likely." Kathy handed him the Friday newspaper. "You see how their parts of the stories intertwine. There's a familiarity there, an easiness, that's for certain."

"I think that you are reading too much into the words, lass."

"Am I? I don't think so. Why is it that he hasn't sent me a telegram in almost three weeks?"

"As I said the last time you asked me, probably because you have not responded to the first telegram he sent you when he first arrived in Ireland."

Sam was tired of going over and over the same ground with no progress.

Lil had been listening to the conversation from the kitchen. "I think that it's high time you sent him a telegram, dear." She walked in, dishtowel in hand, and sat down in her favorite spindled rocker. "Why agonize in isolation from him?"

"I saw a barrister yesterday on Kingston Road during my lunch break."

"Did you now, girl? And what is your intent?"

"He told me I have grounds for divorce. It's called abandonment."

"Oh, Kathy, it's not come to that, surely," her friend said. "He'll be returning to you soon. You saw in the telegram that he cares. And what about our churchgoers? They don't take lightly to divorce, even for infidelity, especially during these dire times with the men off at war."

"I don't care what other people think, Lil."

"Then what will your parents say, girl?" Sam added.

"They split up already."

"Yes, but they reconciled, didn't they? They're happy now." Kathy leaned forward in the rocker.

"Well, they stayed in the same city."

"Honestly, Kathleen, if you weren't my best friend . . ."

"You'd what? Disown me? What would you do if Sam treated *you* this way, with a babe in arms and all?"

"Why, I'd choke the living daylights out of him if I could get my hands around his throat."

"You make my point."

Exasperated, Sam broke in, "Lil, you're not helping."

"Well, Sam, you wouldn't do that to me, would you?"

"Of course not, astore." Sam realized that he wasn't helping either, at this point. "All we ask is for you to try to communicate with Collin before taking any drastic steps, lass. Can you do that?"

"I'll think about it. I do still love him, down deep, inside. But the overwhelming evidence is that Claire died on the *Lusitania*. Collin will never believe it and he will never give up looking for her in Ireland. You two weren't with us in New York. He's obsessed and Liam and I are certainly having to play second fiddle. You wouldn't accept that, Lil, nor can I. And one more thing. Since I've been back teaching the children, I've realized just how important proper parenting is for the very young. You can never get those years back after you've squandered them."

Sam tried a last-ditch suggestion. "Remember your vows, lass. I want you to go and meet with Reverend Dixon at St. Aidan's. He's always given me good advice."

"I guess I can do that much, Sam."

The girls came bounding down the stairs. "Liam and Ernie are babbling to each other in your room. Can we get them up, Mommy?"

"Norah, let me go with you to see if they need changing. Dot, you can come, too."

Sam left Kathy to consider his request and escaped to his studio where at least his paints wouldn't argue with him. He loved the smell of the oils and the purity of the colors that opened the kaleidoscope of his creative imagination. Here he could be free once again, with the window open on the world, and his completed and unfinished works lining the walls. This time, though, he couldn't get Kathy and Collin's problem out of his mind. The canvas in front of him was a blank white sheet. He reached for his Prince Albert and lit a pipeful of the fragrant tobacco. Then, as the smoke curled up and into his nostrils, a possible solution began to materialize.

On Monday morning, Sam dropped Kathy off at school early so he could visit his former boss, Jim Fletcher, the *Tely's* news director before work.

"Jim, where do you stand with supporting Collin in his war correspondence assignment in Ireland? It seems like the Rising is over, and the authorities have retaken control of the country. What is the news for him to report?"

"It's costing us a pretty penny to have him over there, Sam, even though *The Irish Times* is footing most of the bill. Mr. Robertson is happy with his reporting though, but he's suggested that it may be time to bring him back."

Sam was torn between his allegiance to Collin who needed to find his sister and the needs of his marriage. He doubted that the lad had found Claire, he probably never would. But he would be miserable if he was dragged back to Canada empty-handed. *Family comes first.*

"I think that it's time to call him home, Jim. His wife and child need him here. It's serious."

"I'll talk to John Ross and let you know."

"That's all I ask. Thank you, sir."

Two hours later, Jim was in his boss's office.

Robertson pushed a telegram across his desk to his news editor, "I got this from O'Donnell. He says the real story is the long term impact on the populace, and he wants to stay to pursue it at least until the next troop transport is coming west on June fifteenth."

"But that's three weeks from now."

"I know. I then exchanged telegrams with Healy at *The Irish Times.* Although he's not as sure of the merits of this follow-up story, he will provide the finances for us to keep Collin there to follow the story on the Royal Commission that is tasked with investigating the Rising."

"That should be an internal matter, surely, of little interest to our readers, boss. When is this body supposed to release its findings?"

"June twenty-sixth."

"Well, I say we bring him back on the fifteenth, no matter what, John Ross. The other journalists on our staff think it's wasteful. They're jealous."

"That's my decision, not theirs, Jim. Let's see how Collin's story on the aftermath of the Rising and the commission's work pans out. I will notify Healy and O'Donnell."

"Do you remember Sam Finlay, boss?"

"The illustrator?"

"That's the one. He came to see me this morning. He recommended we hire O'Donnell in the first place. I trust his judgment. He says it's important to get him home right away for the peace of his family."

"We have three hundred and thirty thousand men in the field in Europe, all of whom are in hell's fury. I'm sure their loved ones desperately want them home, too. O'Donnell's safe and sound, so that argument doesn't cut the mustard with me."

"All right, sir. You're the boss."

Healy was true to his word, and he had some clout. The RIC headquarters in Dublin was located on the main floor of the Castle, south wing close to the liaison office for the Dublin Metropolitan Police. Collin was ushered into the Inspector General's office five minutes early for his appointment at nine on Wednesday morning, the twenty-fourth.

The Inspector General rose from behind his paper-strewn desk to shake Collin's hand. "I like a man who's prompt. Have a seat."

"Thank you, sir. Here is my card."

"What can I do for you Mr. O'Donnell? I assume that this is official business."

"Not exactly, I'm afraid." Collin explained the situation regarding his search for Claire.

"But John Edward said this was important."

"It is to me, sir, and to Mr. Healy who thinks it makes a terrific human interest story tied to the sinking of the *Lusitania*."

"I see. Then how can I help you?"

"Your detachment in Cork City reports that a person who could be my sister is in the company of a rebel Irishman and both of them are now wanted for murder and possible treason as spies related to the failed gun-running on Banna Strand."

"Who informed you?"

"It came from District Inspector Maloney who was passing on information from his Head Constable Darcy Boyle, I believe, is his name."

"Boyle, is it? I wouldn't trust him farther than I could throw him." The Inspector General explained he felt that way because of the head constable's attitude after causing a traffic accident subsequent to Rossa's funeral, supposedly chasing the rebel and his colleen. Chamberlain called in his adjutant and gave him instructions. "It'll just take a minute. May I offer you tea, Mr. O'Donnell?"

Collin had never been offered so much tea in his life. "Love some, sir."

They spent several minutes discussing the run-up to the Rising. Apparently, Sir Neville had warned both Chief Secretary Birrell and Under-Secretary Nathan that an insurrection was imminent, but they had continued to believe in a passive course of action. Unfortunately, he hadn't believed the report that a gun-running attempt would be made on the southwest coast and had therefore taken no pre-emptive action himself.

The adjutant returned and handed a written report to Chamberlain.

"I am sorry to tell you that a rebel fugitive named Tadgh McCarthy is wanted for four separate crimes. First, he is a fugitive in connection with an illegal play he wrote in 1914, that incited riots at the Abbey Theatre. Next, he and a woman killed two constables in Cork City last June as he was being pursued for the first offense. Then he assaulted a DMP officer during the Rossa funeral events and finally, according to Head Constable Boyle, he or his brother killed Boyle's subordinate, Constable James, a Tralee constable, and severely wounded Boyle himself. On the last three of these occasions, the woman abetted him."

Tadgh McCarthy. Where have I heard that name before? He couldn't remember. "Has there been an identification of the woman?"

"No positive identification. But she is known to be about twenty-five, five and a half feet tall, with ringleted black hair. Boyle reports that she is a real looker, his words. Since the Cork City murders were in late June of last year, it is possible that the woman was on the *Lusitania* when it sank in early May."

Collin's heart plummeted. Claire was the captive of a very bad man. "Does that report say where this fugitive lives or can be found, sir?"

"No, but from information provided by the Cunard Operations manager and Boyle, this McCarthy fugitive uses a motorcycle and a Galway hooker with an unique gray lug sail for transportation. We think he must come from somewhere in West Cork, and we are actively searching for him."

"Is there a physical description?"

"He is taller than six feet and has a heavy moustache. We consider him armed, dangerous and elusive. I am sorry. This is clearly not what you wanted to hear, is it?"

"I appreciate your information. It helps me with my search. I cannot, nor can the Cunard Manager, believe that my sister would support illegal activities."

"But you haven't seen her since she was a mere child ten years ago. Much may have changed."

"I'd like to talk to Head Constable Boyle, sir. I am told that he is incapacitated, and I can't see him."

Chamberlain summoned his man again. "What's Boyle's status?"

The adjutant popped his head in the doorway with a sheet of paper and checked its information. "He's under constant care at the Rathass Union Workhouse Fever Hospital near Tralee, sir. This report says that a bullet nicked his heart artery and passed through his left lung, collapsing it. Surgeons operated on him to seal the artery but don't know if the closure will hold. This is a new procedure. He is still very weak. No visitors this week due to the potential for infection."

"Keep checking with the hospital. I want to authorize them to allow Mr. O'Donnell to interview him as soon as he's able." He dismissed the adjutant and turned his attention back to Collin. "Now, how can I contact you? Where are you staying?"

"I am at the Shelbourne Hotel, sir."

Chamberlain whistled under his breath. "Pretty ritzy for a newspaper man."

"I agree, sir. My paper and Mr. Healy of *The Irish Times* are taking care of expenses."

"I must apply to work at *The Times* when my job as RIC Chief Inspector is finished, which I expect to be any day now. You seem like a resourceful journalist, Mr. O'Donnell. Keep us informed of any progress in your search, and we will do likewise."

Chamberlain pushed a button under his desk, and his secretary appeared to show the reporter the exit.

At least Collin had heard about what the RIC knew from the horse's mouth.

As he drove through a downpour to pick up Kathy that Friday afternoon the twenty-sixth, Sam dreaded the task of passing on what he had heard from Jim at the *Tely*. Kathy met him at her classroom door, keyed up about what Mr. Fletcher might have said regarding ordering Collin home from Ireland. She had procrastinated about sending a telegram until she heard what Collin's boss had to say.

"Well, Sam? What's the word from the *Tely*?" she asked, before Sam could even open the passenger door for her.

"Get into *Lillie* for heaven's sake, Kathy. You'll catch your death of cold." He slammed the door after she climbed in and walked around to the driver's door. She wanted to immediately hear what Fletcher had said, there was no denying her.

"Well?"

"You know that the paper must do what's best for circulation, lass."

"What does that mean?"

"They've decided to have Collin stay and follow up on the mood of the citizens over there after the Rising, at least until he can catch a ride home on the next westbound troop ship."

"No. They can't do that. He was only supposed to go for the insurrection."

"Well, he can't come home until there's a ship to bring him, can he now? Be reasonable, lass."

"When is that ship leaving?"

"Fletcher says June fifteenth."

"That's over two weeks from now. He wouldn't be home for over three weeks then."

"That's the earliest, I'm afraid."

"Well, I won't have it. He'll never come back if he doesn't find Claire, and he won't find her because she's dead at the bottom of the Celtic Sea."

Sam had to admit that he shared that view. But he didn't say so and he couldn't accept that outcome, at least not yet. "Did you meet with Reverend Dixon?"

"Yes, this morning before school."

"And?"

"He told me that God marries people for life, except for cases of physical abuse. But he understood the agony of abandonment."

Sam could see that the wrath of God had not swayed Kathy. "Now, now, lass. I remember you being a person who looked at life with optimism. What happened to that girl?"

"She died when Collin unexpectedly left her." Kathy went silent for the rest of the way home to Number Ten Balsam. This helped since Sam needed to have his wits about him to navigate the waterlogged Toronto streets. The newfangled windshield wipers that they had just installed didn't work worth a damn.

The Finlays noted that the only time Kathy was ever happy was when she was caring for her baby, Liam. When she and Sam arrived home, Kathy made a beeline for her son. Without him, the situation in the Finlay home would have been intolerable. As it was, the weekend was shaping up to be a tense one.

On Sunday morning, Kathy came down with Liam asleep in her arms. "I've made a decision. Since the paper will not recall him now, I am going to have divorce papers written up. If he doesn't come home on the June fifteenth troop ship, I am going to have them served to him in Ireland. My mind is made up. Liam needs a decent father. If that doesn't bring Collin home, then I'll have to start looking for a new one."

"Are you sure that you're not being unreasonable because of how your father treated you, Kathy?"

"That's nonsense, Sam."

"Is it, girl?"

Tired of hearing Kathy's threats, Lil tried a different tack. "What about all the Canadian soldiers fighting in the war. Don't their loved ones need their fathers, too?"

"It's not the same. They have to fight in the war and want to come home to their families as soon as possible. Collin can choose to come home and doesn't want to."

Sam picked up on his wife's train of thought. "But you know well that he is fighting the war within himself. He's as compelled to fight that war as the soldiers on the front are to fight theirs."

"I don't agree with what you say, Sam. It's not the same at all. As I said, my mind is definitely made up."

"What about sending him a telegram now?"

"I think I'll do that with this ultimatum."

"Why not just send a message of love and encouragement, dear, and not try to force his hand? It'll be a shock to his system. and may just drive him to stay longer."

Kathy put her hands over her ears. "No, Lil. An ultimatum." Kathy burst into tears and ran from the room.

Chapter Twenty-One
Boyle

Tuesday, May 30, 1916
Shelbourne Hotel, Dublin

Kathy's telegram to Collin was pushed under his door at the Shelbourne at five in the morning. He was already getting dressed in anticipation of retrieving the impounded Cunard car so he could drive back down to Queenstown.

Opening the seal, he first saw Kathy's name. *Finally she is responding to my telegram. I hope she has calmed down. Based on our time together in New York and Rhode Island, she knows how important this quest is to me.*

Then he read the note,

> 'Husband Collin. Stop. Not heard from you. Stop. Presume you are preoccupied. Stop. You will not find Claire alive in Ireland. Stop. Liam and I need you home now. Stop. Next return ship leaves June fifteenth. Stop. Be on it or I file for divorce! Stop.'

Collin couldn't believe it. It had been only a month, for heaven's sake. *Bloody bollocks! My telegram expressed my love.* He folded the document and shoved it in his coat pocket. *I've got to contact Sam.*

At the telegraph office on Grafton Street, Collin composed his message for Sam—

> 'Received Kathy's telegram demanding my return on June fifteenth ship or face divorce. Stop.

Unreasonable. Stop. Making progress finding Claire. Stop. Tell Kathy I love her but must find Claire. Stop.'

With that transmitted, Collin headed for Portobello Barracks. At two in the afternoon, he parked at the Cunard docks and walked to the Seafarer's Bar where he and Jack had arranged to meet.

Collin saw Jack sitting in a regular chair, a crutch leaning against the wall. "Jack, am I glad to see you, my friend. Where's the wheelchair?"

"I've been practicing. Each step closer to Claire. The hospital sends a nurse to help. I can make it just as far as the bar as you can see. Two pints of stout and then I can make it back to the office again."

"That's grand, Jack, really grand."

"What have you learned about Claire in Dublin?"

The waitress came and they each ordered a sausage roll and a B&C Stout.

"Precious little, I'm afraid." Collin proceeded to tell him what Sir Neville Chamberlain had said, which corroborated what Jack had told him already.

"They seem to have a strong case against the German spies, Collin. Maybe we should wish that the woman isn't Claire."

"Don't say that, Jack. I'm hanging my hat on your belief that you saw her."

"I believe I did, but I don't wish her ill, you know."

"Do you remember anything else about seeing her that might help me, Jack? Anything."

Jack thought for a minute. "The Galway hooker had a dark gray lug sail. Most are dirt red. Apart from that, no, not offhand."

"I need to talk to Boyle."

"Boyle's not a nice man, Collin."

"I've known some not so nice men in my time, I can tell you. I am waiting for approval from the Inspector General to see the officer in charge. He doesn't like Boyle, either."

"Do you have any idea when you might be talking to him?"

"No, but it has to be before your next ship sails west."

"I was going to mention that I had a telegram from your friend, Sam Finlay, wanting to know that information."

Collin debated how much to share with Jack, but decided to go all in. "My wife is very upset that I'm here, especially since we just had a baby boy. She's demanding that I return on the first ship out of Liverpool, or else."

"Or else what?"

"Maybe divorce."

"We can't have that now, can we? The *Aquitania* should weigh anchor on June fifteenth after being repaired."

"I heard that date."

What happens if you don't find Claire by then, Collin?

"I'll cross that bridge when I come to it."

"I can book your passage, but I will need your decision by the thirteenth to get you to Liverpool."

"Thank you, Jack. You'll have it before then."

"Meanwhile, why don't you go and talk to District Inspector Maloney, Boyle's commander at the Cork City RIC barracks? He was not very helpful to me a while back, but you may be better at extracting information, being a journalist and all. I'll set up a meeting for you."

Collin grabbed Jack's wrist. "Please do. Time is short."

"That it is, my friend. Now help me back to the office. You can stay with me for the time being."

Dean Maloney's office at the RIC Headquarter Barracks was located on South Terrace at Rutland Street, just south of the Lee River. It was an austere space on the first floor of what was in fact a stone jail, complete with bars on all the windows. Collin showed up on Monday, June fifth at noon, the earliest date that Jack could get an appointment.

Collin was surprised at the first words out of the inspector's mouth after he gave him his press card. "Can we speak off the record, Mr. O'Donnell?"

Here was a man trying to hide something or very concerned about protecting his job. "Of course, Inspector." Collin reached out to initiate a handshake. "I would like any information that you can share about your head constable's search for the rebel who shot him in Tralee."

"Yes. Nasty business, that. Head Constable Boyle is being treated for his wounds in Tralee and won't be back on duty for quite some time, I understand."

Collin wasn't going to tell Maloney that he had already gone above him in the chain of command. "I see. What can you tell me of the matter, sir?"

"Boyle was handling the case. His reports are incomplete, I'm afraid, due to his serious injuries. I do know that his pursuit started just after this rebel that Boyle calls a German spy shot and killed two of my constables down by the Beamish & Crawford brewery in June of last year. One constable was found floating in the Lee River, and the other has never been found."

"I understand that there was a woman with this spy."

"Yes, that's what Boyle said. He thinks that she is an accomplice, especially now that both of them were apprehended with Roger Casement when the German gun-running plot was foiled in Tralee just prior to the Rising. That seems to corroborate Boyle's assertion that they are German spies, doesn't it?"

"Unless, of course, your head constable is mistaken."

"That is unlikely, especially since Constable Coltrain from our Tralee barracks led the arrest of Casement and the two spies."

"Did Constable Coltrain have independent confirmation that these two rebels were German spies?"

"I spoke with him. It's what Boyle told him."

"If they were caught, as you say, then how did they escape, killing and wounding your men?"

"That's not clear. Coltrain said that Boyle's vehicle wouldn't start and he and the spies got separated from the rest of the constables and Casement on the way back to the barracks."

Collin smelled a rat. He had already heard both Jack and Chamberlain's opinion of the head constable's character. "So there is no witness to corroborate Boyle's story about the gun battle after Coltrain left. His deputy is dead. Is that correct?"

"Yes. Are you questioning the integrity of my officer?"

Collin could see Maloney shifting in his seat. He was clearly uncomfortable with this line of questioning. "Of course not. I'm just asking questions. You know, reporter and all. It's my job."

"Yes. I see. Boyle is demanding and pushy, but that comes with the job, especially in such uncertain times."

"Speaking of that, did the Rising spread down here to Cork City?"

"Thank heavens, we had but little bloodshed. Twelve hundred Volunteers mustered under Tomas Mac Curtain in Cork County on Easter Sunday. But then came the MacNeill countermand in the papers. Head Constable Rowe and his men held them to a standoff down at the Volunteers headquarters on Sheares Street without a shot being fired. They had very few arms, the German supply ship having been sunk at the entrance to our harbor."

"I read that the Germans scuttled their ship."

"That's right, lad. I believe that Mac Curtain received quite a few conflicting orders from Dublin early in the Rising. Eventually, we and the Catholic clergy convinced him to surrender, much to the consternation of his men. That happened on Wednesday."

Collin could see that the inspector thought himself a hero for avoiding bloodshed and putting down the local revolt. Clearly, he would have been cowering in his office during the conflict.

"There was one incident after the Rising was over. Rowe was rounding up the dissidents for questioning down at Bawnard House on May second. The Kents engaged in a three-hour gun battle from inside their home, and Head Constable Rowe was shot dead. One of the Kent brothers died after being shot while trying to escape. The military convicted Thomas Kent of killing our man, and he was executed on May ninth in Victoria Barracks. So that's the end of that."

"What happened to Mac Curtain?"

"He was detained and is in Wakefield Prison."

Returning to his previous line of questioning, Collin asked, "Do you have any idea where these so-called German spies are located?"

"None, whatsoever. Based on the suspect sightings by Jack Jordan, it is likely in West Cork somewhere, likely at the coast. But that's just a guess."

"Have you searched the homes in that direction?"

"Too much territory to cover. And it may be east and not west."

"I appreciate your time, Inspector. Will you let me know when I can visit Head Constable Boyle?"

"I'm afraid that is out of my hands."

Collin realized that this coward was not going to be a conduit to Boyle.

After they had arrived on May fifteenth, Tadgh, Morgan, and Aidan had settled in at home in Creagh. With the Rising crushed and its leaders exterminated, there was no military urgency. That time would come. Now it was time to focus on the Clans Pact mystery and Boyle.

"I don't think it's wise for you to go back to your flat in Cork City just yet, Aidan," Tadgh warned his brother. We won't be needing the safe house any time soon, so we can make it up as your living quarters."

Aidan's leg wound still ached. "I'm after acceptin' your hospitality with thanks, brother, if I can use the hooker for fishing."

"Then it's settled!" Morgan exclaimed, opening the linen cupboard to bring bedding down to the boathouse. "Get him to start writing his speech."

"What speech?"

"For the wedding, silly."

On May sixteenth, after working all afternoon to resurrect the vegetable garden, Morgan came into the kitchen with some early wild strawberries.

"Morgan, is that you? Come up here right away." Tadgh sounded agitated.

Morgan dropped the fruit in the sink for washing and bounded up the stairs as quickly as her healing leg would allow. "What's wrong, my love?" Morgan asked, looking anxiously through the small door to Tadgh's secret office.

"Come in, come in."

"Any revelations, dear?" she asked, when she saw him poring over the family Bible.

"Look here, lass," he pointed excitedly with his fingers holding open two locations.

Morgan saw hand-drawn circles around the headings for Psalm 30, Verse 10 and Psalm 105, Verse 13, with no other markings on those pages.

"That ink is faint. It looks old. You were right, mavourneen. Florence and Red Hugh altered the content of *an Cathach* to leave us one or more clues. Alpha and Omega. But what do they mean?"

"I couldn't say but look at this." He leafed through the pages, and Morgan saw that the only other verse with a circled heading was Psalm 68, Verse 26.

"That verse is buried in the welded folios of *an Cathach,* isn't it? What does it say?"

Tadgh read, "'Praise God in the great congregation; praise the Lord in the Assembly of Israel.' This reference has to be significant."

"Psalm 68 is halfway between Psalms 30 and 105. What does the Clans Pact say after 'Blessed be the Alpha and the Omega'?"

Tadgh dug the sacred document out of a drawer in the roll top desk. ". . .'and the Balance of Justice'," he read.

"The balance could be the center point Psalm and the 'Assembly of Israel' could be 'justice'."

"Good thinking, Morgan, but it's still a mystery to me. I think that we have to consult with Peader."

"Doesn't sound like we can do that until he returns from school on America's Independence Day."

"Well, we aren't going back to Dublin to talk to him just now, make no mistake about that."

May gave way to June. They had passed many a sleepless night perplexed about the meaning of those confounding passages.

Tadgh awoke on Wednesday, June seventh with a plan. "I've wasted too much time. I'm going to take care of Boyle."

Morgan paused while pulling on her jumper and eyed him closely, "Kill him, you mean."

Tadgh didn't answer but swung himself out of bed to wrap his arms around her and nuzzle his mouth against her neck. Morgan twisted out of his grasp and warned him, "You can't talk about wicked murder and then distract me with your abundant charms."

"Killing Boyle isn't wicked. It would be a boon to all mankind."

"Why can't we just be content to live our life here now that the Rising is over? You are always talking about killing someone. Why don't we talk about our marriage day? Or maybe you are having cold feet, mavourneen."

"No, lass, no cold feet. But I am concerned that Boyle could still cause us harm if he's not eliminated."

"And I am concerned that any attempt to do that could get you arrested or killed."

"Nonsense. It would be best to deal with him while he is still in hospital. Besides, I have several of my cat lives left." Tadgh had to accept the truth. He was a killer when it came to self-defense, family, and liberation of his country. But that distinguished him from Boyle and his kind who murdered for profit and power. And now was certainly a time of risk to the family.

That morning at breakfast, Tadgh explained his plan to Aidan. "Can I go with you, Tadgh? Together we can finally dispatch the bastard who killed our parents."

Tadgh looked across the table at Morgan. "That should give you a measure of comfort, lass. Aidan can make sure we don't get killed, like what almost happened at Rahoneen Castle. And you can rest your leg at home."

Inwardly he had reservations. Didn't the Lord's prayer say, 'forgive us our trespasses, as we forgive those who trespass against us'? Hadn't he killed as many men as Boyle had? Who knew, but he couldn't go back to innocence. He remembered other biblical sayings. What were they? 'Vengeance is mine sayeth the Lord', and in the same breath, 'Blessed are the meek for they shall inherit the earth'. But, dammit. Boyle was evil, he had killed Tadgh's parents in cold blood, and he threatened Morgan. The man had to be stopped before he tried to kill them again.

Morgan had to admit that these brothers were finally taking action together against the devil who killed their parents. Such a difference from a year ago. She said to them, "All right, but you promise not to take chances and to come back to me, the both of you."

While he was waiting for news, Collin went to talk to the Tralee RIC personnel. Maureen had notified him from London that she was returning and wanted to meet with him to exchange notes. He suspected that she had more in mind than that.

On checking into the Tralee Grand Hotel in Denny Street on Thursday the eighth, Collin had two messages, one good news, the other bad. Sir Neville wrote that Boyle could meet with him at the hospital on June fifteenth. He would be out of danger of infection by then. Mr. Healy cautioned that Robertson might insist that Collin be on the next ship bound for Canada. Collin sent responses thanking the inspector general and the publisher and letting them know of his whereabouts and progress or lack of it.

Tralee District Inspector Kearney agreed to meet with Collin on the following Saturday at the Ardfert RIC Barracks for a tour of the area where Roger Casement had been arrested. Collin spent the next two days completing his report on the mood of the populace subsequent to the Rising. His report emphasized that Cork's citizens appeared to be unaffected by the conflict. That city, had after all, been a bastion of English Protestantism in the midst of the Catholic South.

Collin's meeting with Kearney confirmed what Maloney and Chamberlain had told him. Their visit to McKenna's Fort proved to be a waste of time, a trivial hole in the woods.

"You know where the gun battle took place with Head Constable Boyle?"

"Yes, we do. Boyle babbled something about the Rahoneen Castle ruins when we found him slumped over the wheel, bleeding heavily. I think he wanted us to apprehend the spies. The poor fellow had rolled his car into a tree just outside the New Street RIC barracks. I'll take you to the ancient ruins."

"Aren't we going in the opposite direction from where your constable would have gone to return to your barracks?" Collin asked, as the district inspector headed northwest from McKenna's Fort.

"Yes, that's right."

"So why was Boyle leading the so-called spies, in the opposite direction?"

" I don't know . . . unless the rebels had them at gunpoint before they left the fort."

"Didn't Boyle and his deputy James, with your man Jamison have the prisoners under control at gunpoint when Constable Coltrain left them at the fort?"

"Yes, that's right."

"Then I think it highly unlikely that the prisoners could have taken immediate control of the situation."

Collin took his time examining the ruins. He kicked at something in the dirt at the base of the altar. "Did you see the frayed piece of rope attached to this metal ring?"

"No, when we got here after the gun battle, our attention was focused on the men. We found Constable Gordon James with his guts torn out and poor Constable Jamison with a bullet in his brain. We dug a nine-millimeter Luger bullet from the lad's skull, I might add."

Collin picked up the ring and searched until he found what he was looking for. "I'll bet that the ring came from here." He pushed the retention pin deep into the matching hole in the altar, lodging it in place.

Kearney inspected the penetration. "Could be, but what does that prove?"

"That at least one person was tied up without his or her consent." Collin shivered at the thought that it could have been Claire. "It would have taken a great deal of effort to break this free. Did Boyle, James, or Jamison have rope burns on their wrists when they arrived at the hospital or morgue?"

"I don't know. I'll have to check."

"If they didn't, then someone else was tied up, sir."

"I see your point. If our men were not tied up, why would the Head Constable take his prisoners in a direction away from our barracks and then bind them to this altar? Perhaps it was to force them to talk about all the gun-running culprits."

"Would that be standard procedure?"

"Not at all. Such inquisitions are supposed to take place at our headquarters with our personnel as witness."

"So you see. This is why I must speak to Head Constable Boyle as soon as possible. I was told that he won't be available until Thursday unless you can gain access for me sooner."

"Being a reporter from Canada, why do you take such an interest in this matter, Mr. O'Donnell?"

Collin had not shared his true motive with the district inspector earlier for fear of being branded a traitor by association. He lied to the man. "The girl in this matter might be an undercover journalist from our newspaper back home and a member of the Canadian Expeditionary Force."

"You don't say. What's her name?"

"Claire, ah, O'Sullivan." Collin knew he was getting into hot water if Kearney checked with his paper.

"I'll see what I can do for you lad, and I'll let you know," he offered on their ride back to the Ardfert barracks. "I'll also check the condition of the wrists of the three men when they were recovered."

On Sunday morning, Kearney summoned Collin to his office.

"Tomorrow, at one in the afternoon, you can talk with Head Constable Boyle for a few minutes. He is at the Tralee Union Workhouse Fever Hospital in Rathass on the north side of Quill Street. Be there twenty minutes early for processing."

"Thank you, sir. I appreciate your assistance in this matter."

"One more thing. In response to your question, none of the RIC men had any sign of rope burn on their wrists."

When Collin returned to his hotel, he was surprised to find Maureen waiting for him in the lobby. She rushed up to him and grasped his hands warmly. Startled, Collin stepped back and blurted, "What are you doing here?"

"Mr. Healy told me where you were and asked me to find out how your search was progressing. The deadline is only four days away." She stopped, her mouth turned down. "You don't seem happy to see me," she pouted, touching his arm delicately with the tips of her fingers.

Collin knew she was lying. Healy could have called him personally. This Grand Hotel had a telephone. Despite his misgivings, he agreed. "Well, since you are here, I'll fill you in and you can tell me how the Royal Commission is going in London."

"I prefer to discuss this away from the public lobby. It's private newspaper business. I got a room for the night."

"All right, but it's just business, lass."

326

"Of course."

Maureen's room must have been the honeymoon suite. It looked in many ways like a smaller version of the rooms he and Kathy had shared at the Knickerbocker back in Times Square. At least there was a parlor area away from the bedroom. They sat at the table while Collin brought her up to speed on what he had found about with Kearney, and that he was to visit Boyle the next day.

"I'd bet that Boyle tied up someone, maybe your sister, if she was there."

"For what purpose?" Collin didn't like to think what that might have been. But then, Claire had dealt with oppression in the past, if it was that. The hair on the back of Collin's neck rose in alarm.

"We don't know that yet. This meeting with Boyle is crucial, I would say." Maureen shook off her jacket and loosened her collar. "Is it hot in here?"

"Not really. So what have you learned in London?"

"They've interviewed Birrell, Nathan, and Chamberlain so far. None of those men looked very happy going into sessions that the press has been kept out of. Lord Hardinge looked very austere going in and out of the nine-day proceedings. They are deliberating now, and I don't think the principals will get off lightly, Collin. We all expect the commission to finish its report on the twenty-sixth. Can I come with you to see Boyle tomorrow?"

"I need to see him alone, but you can come to the hospital with me if you wish."

"Good. Why don't we get comfortable, Collin? Have a seat on the chesterfield and I'll get us some ale."

Collin chose to stand while Maureen crossed to the sideboard and brought out glasses, bottles, and an opener. She crossed to face him, offering the beverage.

Collin moved away and sat down empty-handed. "I am not comfortable being alone with you in your room."

"Then why did you agree to come here? Don't you find me attractive?"

Of course, Collin had noticed and appreciated her figure at several angles. He would have been blind or dead, or both, to miss her feminine charms. He missed Kathy terribly, but she seemed hell-bent on proceeding towards divorce. So why had he agreed to come up into the spider's lair?

"You are a beautiful, intelligent, and independent young woman, Maureen, quite refreshing in this day and age. But I'm married, although my wife is upset with me at the moment, and I have a young son."

"Your wife seems to be abandoning you."

"What? How did you find that out?"

"I didn't. You just told me. Why don't you share with me? I listen well."

Damn. Oldest trick in the reporter's handbook. And I fell for it. Or did I just want to tell her? "My wife, whom I love, does not want me to be here. She feels that my sister probably died when the *Lusitania* sank, and I am on a fool's errand. She is pretty upset about it. Our son was born only four months ago."

Maureen crossed the room and pushed the glass of ale into his hand. She sat down next to him and casually put her hand on his knee. "You should relax. A virile, handsome young man such as yourself has needs just as I do, which should not be denied for very long, surely. It is war time and we should live for today since we don't know what might befall us tomorrow."

"We're not at the Western Front, Maureen, and the Rising is over."

"But you don't know what these German spies might do if you actually found them, do you?"

"I am going to find them, damn it."

"It is hot in here." A warm flush spread up her neck as she slowly unbuttoned her blouse. She kept her eyes down in a demure manner, but they both knew she was in no way a shrinking violet. "Drink up. There's more where that came from." Her silk chemise came open to reveal dark nipples tipping breasts that begged for him to taste.

Why am I not stopping her? Collin's manhood started to rise, and he could not look away.

When he didn't move, Maureen slid over so their thighs touched and took his right hand, lifting it to her breast. "There now, isn't that better?" She slid her hand to his thigh and pretended to gasp in surprise when she closed her fingers over his pulsing member. "Come closer, dear," she breathed, "I won't bite, much." When her lips found his mouth, he knew he was sliding away from promise and honor and fidelity.

Then he remembered that first time with Kathy at the Knickerbocker, and that first laugh from Liam. He remembered home. "No, Maureen. I can't do this. You are a very tempting woman, and I am far from home. But home is in my heart and there it will stay, no matter what comes. So we cannot do this, I will not do this."

He shook himself as if waking from a nightmare and got unsteadily to his feet. When Maureen made to rise, he put his hands up as if to push her away.

"A girl has to try, doesn't she?" She shrugged her shoulders and pulled her blouse back on. "I'm disappointed, but I'll get over it." She took a swig of her ale and let her hand rest between her legs. "And I'll be glad to accompany you tomorrow."

"Good, we'll leave at noon."

"You won't tell Mr. Healy about this, will you?"

"No. It's a private matter between us, Maureen."

"Good. Can we meet for dinner later?"

"Of course. I understand this hotel has an excellent chef."

Collin promised himself he would keep her at a distance for the remainder of their time together.

Collin and Maureen arrived at the Fever Hospital at twelve-thirty the next afternoon and signed in. The process came with a rigorous set of questions that took ten minutes to complete.

Collin noticed that a security officer watched them most of the time.

"There's a waiting room at the end of the hall on your right," the receptionist said, when he handed them their badges. "George will show you the way." They were to be escorted.

After leaving Maureen in the waiting area, Collin accompanied the security officer to the third floor where Boyle's private room was located.

"You keep a tight security on this facility, I see."

"Yes sir, this wing is for special patients, usually police or detainees."

"I see. That's wise, I'm sure." Collin saw armed guards outside a couple of the rooms.

"There's Head Constable Boyle's room, sir, number 312. The nurse at the station down the hall will give you his status before you go in." He indicated a glassed-in desk farther on. "I'll be back at reception if you need me."

"Thanks, Officer."

A pretty blond nurse rushed toward him. "Hello, I'm Sister Emma. I understand that you are a newspaperman, sir."

"Yes, ma'am. "What can you tell me about Mr. Boyle's condition?" Collin handed her his press card.

"Well sir, he's a cantankerous cuss, that's for sure. He was in a critical state when he first got here with a punctured lung and nicked cardiac artery. He had lost a lot of blood. But we patched him up with a new grafting procedure. He's stable now, so we are just watching him to make sure the graft holds and that he doesn't get an infection. Such germs could prove deadly, so we must take every precaution." The nurse handed him a mask and directed him to put it on.

"I see. I'll try not to agitate him."

"Of course. You can go in now, but don't be long. You are his first visitor."

Collin approached the room and looked through its corridor window to see a man lying in bed and covered with a sheet pulled up to his chin. He appeared to be sleeping fitfully.

Stepping cautiously into the room, Collin saw the man turn towards him.

"What do you want?"

"I'm a reporter, sir. I need to ask you some questions if you're up to it."

"Go away."

"I can't do that. Inspector General Chamberlain sent me." Collin thought that might carry some weight.

"Dammit! Not that fucking imbecile. Get out."

"It won't take a minute."

Boyle tried to sit up, and Collin came forward to help him up and adjust his pillows.

"Leave me be. I can manage."

Collin heard an inflection in the voice that triggered his memory, then saw the skull and crossbones tattooed on the man's left temple. He had to resist the impulse to jump back. *It could be a coincidence. Check the finger.*

As if reading Collin's thoughts, Boyle pulled his hands from under the covers to reveal that his right was missing its little finger. "What do you want of me?"

My God. Eleven years ago, this man murdered my Da. Although older, there was something familiar about that sinister face, those beady black eyes and arched eyebrows. And those two unique features couldn't be mistaken.

Collin balled his fists. His anger rose as he remembered that night so long ago, his mother cowering, the man threatening. *How am I going to kill him?*

"Well, boy?"

Collin needed time to think. "I am writing a piece on German infiltration of our country during the war and I would like to know more about the two spies that you have been chasing."

"That I caught, you mean."

"Yes, that's right. That you caught."

Boyle began a diatribe about he how he tracked them down and arrested them. Collin wasn't listening. He looked around the room for an implement of death to use. His insides churned. *Why would he be chasing Claire?* Then he remembered a snippet of conversation when Boyle interrogated his father. "Where is the treasure?" Boyle had kept repeating those words "Where is the treasure?" as he pounded on his father. Collin had wondered about that at the time. *My God in heaven, Boyle is not a bona fide RIC head constable at all but a treasure hunter and knows the girl is my sister. This proves that the girl is Claire.*

"Are you listening to me, boy? I was saying that after the McCarthys and their girl killed Gordo and poor Constable Jamison, I fought them off single-handed until they shot me twice."

"Yes, yes. I heard every word, Head Constable. An admirable defense, I must say." *What was that name he said? I've heard it before.*

"Yes, well. What did you say your name was? You look familiar to me, boy."

Collin had to think fast. He couldn't tell him his real name. If he killed Boyle, then he couldn't lead him to Claire. He hated to use Claire as a decoy, but it couldn't be helped.

"Well, out with it, boy."

"Collin, with the *Toronto Evening Telegram*." He wasn't about to give his family name. He quickly changed the subject. "When do you think you will be up and back to work, sir?"

"Any day now. I feel fine."

Collin could see that wasn't the case.

He hated to leave the murderer there, alive, but it couldn't be helped. "Thank you again, Head Constable Boyle. I'll leave you now to your convalescence."

♣ ♣ ♣ ♣

Tadgh and Aidan had driven the Kerry up to Tralee on Sunday and stayed overnight with Maurice and Martha at Barrow House. From his hospitaller medical colleagues, Maurice knew that Boyle was still recuperating at the hospital in Ratass just east of downtown Tralee.

Alone in their room they planned their attack.

"Tomorrow we will execute Boyle to avenge our parents, whatever happens. We won't know how until we check out the hospital in disguise."

After they bid farewell to their hosts the next morning, the brothers headed into Tralee in the rain. Tadgh parked the Kerry behind the hospital in the St. Catherine's churchyard. They circled the Fever hospital looking for the tradesman's entrance. At 12:40 they entered through the deliveries bay at the back of the building, lifting a couple of crates that were sitting on the loading dock to cover their faces. The security guard on duty didn't even notice their entry.

Having dropped the crates at the entrance to the kitchen area, Tadgh told Aidan, "Wait here. I'll be right back." A few minutes later, Tadgh reappeared, wearing a white lab coat and face mask over his mouth and moustache. "This way, brother."

He led Aidan along the basement corridor to a laundry area where the doctors' white lab coats were stored. They waited until several doctors had cleared the area before selecting a lab coat for Aidan. On the way back into the corridor, Tadgh grabbed a stethoscope from the rack and slung it around his neck.

Tadgh went up the stairs to the first-floor nursing station and checked the patient roster. Aidan waited in the shadows. No patient named Boyle on that floor or the second floor. On the third floor, Tadgh found Boyle's name registered in Room 312. He walked to the room and through the glass saw the patient in animated conversation with a visitor. Tadgh couldn't hear through the glass or the closed door.

A security guard had lingered and was chatting with a pretty nurse near the end of the corridor. They needed an alternate escape route if things went awry. He checked. The connecting room to 312 was 311, with its corridor door around the corner. He went in and checked the patient's chart at the foot of the bed. She was coughing up a storm and appeared delirious. Then he went to the nursing station.

"Can I help you, Doctor—?"

"Swanson, nurse, Jack Swanson. Yes, I'm looking for Rebecca Schultz." He had noticed that name on Room 311.

"You're new here, aren't you?"

"Yes, from St. Stephens Hospital, Cork City, you know Blue Coat. I specialize in pulmonary illnesses." Tadgh read on her chart that Mrs. Schultz had consumption.

"Yes, of course. Becca is in very bad condition. You can look in on her if you like."

Tadgh was impatient for the visitor to leave Boyle and did his best to appear as if he belonged on the corridor so he wouldn't attract any attention. When the visitor finally came out, he bumped into Tadgh. "Excuse me, doctor." The young man hurried off and passed Aidan at the top of the stairs before descending.

Tadgh motioned to Aidan to join him. They saw through the room's interior window that the patient appeared to have dropped off to sleep, so they quietly entered the room, confident that Boyle would not be alarmed if he awoke and saw two white coats. Tadgh crossed the room to try the door and opened it to 311.

As he walked down the stairs to where Maureen was waiting, Collin's thoughts were racing. The pieces of the puzzle were beginning to emerge, but they were all jumbled up. Had he done the right thing to let that bastard live? It would have been so easy to wring his neck. But there would be time for that later, after Boyle had led him to Claire. How was he going to track Boyle after he was released from the hospital? So much to think about. He realized that he would have gone berserk in years gone by. But Sam and Kathy had taught him restraint, and that was a good thing.

Maureen wanted to know what Collin found out, but he was not prepared to tell her. Instead, he put on a stern expression and escorted her to the hospital entrance. He shook open his umbrella when he saw that it was raining hard.

"Damn, Maureen, we walked a half mile over here under cloudy skies. Why don't you wait here, and I will bring the car."

She accepted gratefully and Collin trudged westward past St. Catherine's Church. When he saw the Ablinger Kerry with its Watsonian wicker sidecar, he stopped in his tracks. The puzzle pieces started to fit together. *I've seen that motorcycle before, but where? Can it be a coincidence? There can't be many of these machines around. Yes, I saw it in the backyard of Sean O'Casey's house. He said it was his. Wait a minute. McCarthy. That's the name the constable used at O'Casey's home, and Boyle just used it. He's the man who shot Boyle at Rahoneen, not that I blame him. He's the one that Claire is connected with. My God, it was her I saw enter O'Casey's house! She must have been somewhere in the house all the time. How could I be so blind. Now this must be McCarthy's motorcycle. It's no coincidence. He must be here, and I'll bet he's going after Boyle again.*

Collin dropped the umbrella, turned, and ran for the hospital entrance. A minute later he was bounding up the stairs. Maureen saw him flash by and ran after him. The security guard on the third floor saw the commotion and rushed down the corridor leaving the nurse to trail behind.

Collin reached the viewing window of Room 312 ahead of his pursuers. The curtain was closed. He rushed to the corridor door and opened it. Inside, he saw two doctors holding down a struggling Boyle. The smaller man held the head constable's legs while the larger one with his back to the door firmly clamped a pillow over the man's face. *God, it's the same doctor I bumped into a few minutes ago. Now I've got the Irishman to chase.* Collin rushed into the room and yelled, "McCarthy, they're coming. Kill the bastard!"

Aidan was startled and turned to see a visitor standing in the doorway, with a woman. He could see a security guard and a nurse rushing towards the room and the open door. The guard released the safety on his revolver and was pointing it in their direction..

Tadgh was intent on his mission of finishing Boyle off.

"Tadgh, we've got to go now!" Aidan screamed, letting go of Boyle's legs which had stopped flailing. "The guard has his gun drawn."

For a split second, Tadgh toyed with the thought of unholstering his Luger to shoot Boyle in case he wasn't already dead, and his hand twitched. Then he remembered his promise to Morgan not to get caught. He wasn't going to risk a shootout in the hospital room with innocent bystanders. And Aidan had already paid the price with a bullet in the leg during their earlier run-in with Boyle.

"Now!" Aidan repeated, grabbing Tadgh's shoulder and pulling him towards the connecting door to Room 311.

Collin tried to get a look at their faces, but they had streaked through the interconnecting room door before he could identify them.

The security guard burst into Boyle's room. The nurse rushed past Collin to her comatose patient, and Maureen waited in the corridor.

After the guard tried the interconnecting door and couldn't open it, he bolted for Boyle's corridor door.

Collin needed to chase McCarthy but didn't want the security guard to shoot his quarry before he could extract the information he needed about Claire's whereabouts. He did the only thing he could do. He blocked the corridor doorway, pretending to be confused.

"They're coming out of Room 311, heading for the stairs!" Maureen yelled, pulling at Collin's sleeve.

Then Collin took off in hot pursuit down the stairwell with

the security guard following a floor above him. Someone pulled the corridor alarm. Bells started ringing somewhere in the hospital. By the time Collin reached the stairwell exit to the building, the McCarthy brothers were halfway to their motorcycle and hard to see in the rain.

Collin closed the gap to seventy-five yards by the time the McCarthys reached their vehicle. The larger fellow was having trouble starting the machine. Bullets whizzed by Collin as the running guard shot through the downpour to stop the motorcyclists. Their Kerry coughed and sputtered, just as a bullet found its mark, ricocheting off the rear wheel frame, barely missing the petrol tank. Collin heard Tadgh gun the throttle, and the beast roared to life.

Still thirty yards back, he yelled out through the pouring rain, "Stop, McCarthy. I'm Claire's brother!" He saw the fellow in the sidecar look back, pointing as the deafening machine started to roll in the deluge. *Damn, if Boyle's dead and they get away, I may never find Claire. No!*

Collin lunged forward.

THE END of Book Three

Book Four titled ***McCarthy Gold*** is coming soon!

Cast of Characters

North America – Historical

John Devoy	Leader of Clan na Gael in America, New York
Dorothy Finlay	Sam and Lil's Youngest Daughter
Elizabeth Finlay (Lil)	Sam's Wife
Ernest Finlay	Sam and Lil's Newborn Son
Norah Finlay	Sam and Lil's Eldest Daughter
Samuel Stevenson Finlay	Artist & Director of Art at Riverdale High School, Toronto
Joseph McGarrity	Leader of Clan na Gael in America, Philadephia
John Ross Robertson	Publisher and Editor-in-Chief, *Toronto Evening Telegram* (*Tely*)

North America – Fictional

Jim Fletcher	*Toronto Evening Telegram*, News Director, Collin's Boss
Collin O'Donnell	Young Irishman in Toronto
Fiona O'Sullivan	Kathleen's Mother
Kathleen O'Donnell (Kathy)	Young Irish Woman in Toronto, Collin's Wife. (née O'Sullivan)
Liam O'Donnell	Kathy and Collin's Son
Ryan O'Sullivan	Kathleen's Father
Rita	School Superintendent for Kathy's School

Cast of Characters

Europe – Historical

Thomas Ashe	Led Volunteers at Asbourne, North of Dublin
Herbert Henry Asquith	British Prime Minister during WWI
Augustine Birrell	British Secretary for Ireland
Richard Boyle	Lord Cork, Lismore Castle, British Leader Confederate War, 1640s
Lord Broghill	Roger Boyle, Richard's Son, Laid Siege to Blarney Castle in 1643
Edward Carson	Ulster Unionist Political Leader, Organizer Ulster Volunteers Fought Against Home Rule
Sir George Carew	British Lord Totnes, President of Munster in 1601
Sir Roger Casement	Irish Volunteer, Ambassador to Germany, Recruiter of Irish Brigade
Eamonn Ceannt	Commandant of Battalion #4, South Dublin Union Hospital, Military Council, Proclamation Signatory, Co-Founder of the Irish Volunteers
Sir Neville Chamberlain	Chief Inspector, Royal Irish Constabulary (RIC) Ireland
Thomas Clarke	Lead Member of Irish Republican Brotherhood (IRB), Military Council, Lead Proclamation Signatory
Con Colbert	Commander of Marrowbone Lane Distillery Rebel Position

Cast of Characters

Walter Leonard Cole	Republican, Founder Sinn Fein Organization & Publishing Company House at Three Mountjoy Square Used for IRB Meetings
Michael Collins	Member, Irish Volunteers, Joseph Plunkett's Aide in Easter Rising
James Connolly	Head of the Irish Citizens Army (ICA), Dublin Commandant, Military Council, Proclamation Signatory
Sean Connolly	James' Brother, First Fatality Capturing City Hall
Oliver Cromwell	English Military and Political Leader, Lord Protector of the British Commonwealth, Conqueror of Irish in 1640s
Edward "Ned" Daly	Commandant Battalion #1, the Four Courts, Easter Rising
Queen Elisabeth	Queen Elisabeth Gabrielle, Valérie, Maria, Wife of Albert I of Belgium, called Queen Nurse
James FitzThomas FitzGerald	Earl of Desmond, Maurice's Ancestor, Captured and Jailed mid 1601 before the Battle of Kinsale
Lovick Friend	British Major General, Commander-in Chief, Ireland in WWI
Maud Gonne (MacBride)	Irish Revolutionary and Suffragette, Married to John MacBride, Yeats Muse

Cast of Characters

Sir Arthur Guinness	Lord Arlibaun, Owner of Guinness Brewery
William Hall (Blinker)	British Captain, Director of British Intelligence, Broke German Code
Lord Hardinge	Lord of Penhurst, Viceroy of India, Head of British Royal Commission of Inquiry into the Easter Rising, 1916
John Edward Healy	Publisher, *The Irish Times*
Sean Heuston	Rebel Commander of Mendicity Institute, near Four Courts
John Kearney	Tralee Head District Inspector, RIC
Thomas Kent	Irish Nationalist, Killed RIC Defending Home North of Cork City
Reverend J.H. Lawlor	Professor of Ecclesiastical Studies, Dublin University Researcher of Ancient Gaelic Documents Including *an Cathach* of St. Columba
Lewis Lord of Kinalmeaky	British Commander, Destroyed Kilbrittain Castle in 1642 Richard Boyle's Son, Delivered *Book of Lismore* to his father
Brigadier General Lowe	Commander, British Forces, Easter Rising
Dr. Kathleen Lynn	Senior Rebel Doctor
Captain John MacBride	"Foxy Jack," 2nd in Command, Battalion #4 during Easter Rising

Cast of Characters

Florence MacCarthaigh	Clan Chieftain until 1601, Arrested by George Carew before Battle of Kinsale in January 1602
MacCarthaigh Raibhaigh	Lord Finghin, Recipient of the *Book of MacCarthaigh Reagh*
Tomas Mac Curtain	Head of IRB for Cork, Tadgh's Commanding Officer
Sean MacDermott	IRB Leader, Member of Military Council, 2nd in Influence in IRB, Proclamation Signatory
Thomas MacDonagh	IRB Leader, Assistant Principal St. Edna's School, Commandant, Jacob's Biscuit Factory, Military Council, Proclamation Signatory
Colla MacDonnell	Built Kinbane Castle in Ulster in 1550 (aka Collin O'Donnell)
Eoin MacNeill	Chief of Staff, Irish Volunteers
Brigadier Maconchy	Head of British Military Court, Tried the Easter Rising Leaders
Agnes Mallin	Wife of Michael Mallin
Michael Mallin	IRB Commandant of St. Stephen's Green. Battalion #2, Chief of Staff of ICA
Lieutenant Mike Malone	IRB Leader of Northumberland Road Ambush/Resistance
Constance Markiewicz	Countess, Deputy Commandant Battalion #2, St. Stephen's Green
General Sir Grenfell Maxwell	Commander-in-Chief, British Affairs During and After Rising

Cast of Characters

McCarthy Mor	Muscry Chieftain, Blarney, Leader Confederate War Rebellion, 1640s
Dennis McCullough	"President" of the IRB, Belfast, Minor Rising in Coalisland, County Tyrone
Liam Mellows	Republican Leader, Galway, Easter Rising at Athenry
Jacques de Molay	Last Head of the Knights Templar, Burned at the Stake in 1314
Sir Matthew Nathan	British Undersecretary for Ireland
Sean O'Casey	Irish Playwright, Tadgh's Literary Mentor
Brigid O'Donnell	"Biddy," Peader's Mother in Dungloe, Tailor
James O'Donnell	Peader's Father, Seasonal Worker in Scotland
Peader O'Donnell	College Student, Later to be a Revolutionary Leader, "Peadar"
Red Hugh O'Donnell	Last Free Chieftain until 1602, O'Donnell Clan, Battle of Kinsale
Elizabeth O'Farrell	Member Cuman na mBan, Nurse at GPO, Surrendered for Pearse
Michael O'Hanrahan	Co-Commandant, Joseph's Biscuit Factory
Michael The O'Rahilly	Director of Arms, Irish Volunteers, Allegiance to Eoin MacNeill

Cast of Characters

Padraig Pearse	Lead Member of the IRB and School Master St. Edna's, Military Council, Commandant-General in Easter Rising, Proclamation, Signatory, "President" of the Proclaimed Republic of Ireland
William "Willie" Pearse	Padraig Pearse's Brother, Captain in the Volunteers, Sculptor
Joseph Mary Plunkett	Member IRB, Foreign Minister, Military Council, Proclamation Signatory
John Redmond	Irish Nationalist Politician, Organized National Volunteers to Fight for the Allied Cause in WWI, Believed Britain Would Pass Irish Home Rule
Head Constable Rowe	RIC Officer Killed by Thomas Kent in Cork
Austin Stack	Head of IRB for Tralee
Colonel Taylor	Shot and Killed 15 Civilians on North Street in Easter Rising
Wolfe Tone	Father of Irish Republicanism and Leader of 1798 Rebellion
Eamon de Valera	Commandant Battalion #3, Boland's Bakery and Mill
Captain Raimund Weisbach	Watch Officer on *U-20* then Kapitanleutnant of *U-19*
Colonel de Courcy Wheeler	British Officer, Accepted Surrender of most Commandants, Staff Captain to General Lowe

Lord Wimborne	Ivor Churchill Guest, British Lord Lieutenant for Ireland
William Butler Yeats	Famous Irish Poet and Pillar of both Irish and British Literary Societies, Co-founder of the Abbey Theatre in Dublin

Europe – Fictional

Benandonner	Scottish King, Enemy of Finn MacCool, Irish Mythology
Captain Brennan	Galway Fishing Captain
Darcy Boyle	Head Constable, Royal Irish Constabulatory (RIC), Cork City
Captain Maurice Collis	Fishing Captain, Fenit, Ireland, Descendant of the FitzMaurice Clan, Supporter of Tadgh
Martha Collis	Wife of Maurice Collis
Frank Coltrain	RIC Constable, Tralee, Captured Sir Roger Casement
Deirdre	Owner and Barkeeper of the Temple Bar Pub, Dublin, Ireland
Ernie	Assistant Security Officer, Poolbeg Power Station
Captain Haig	Captain of the Troop Ship *Aquitania*
Henderson	Head Gardner, St. Stephens Green
Henri and Marg	Neighbors of Sean O'Casey
Henry Hollingsworth	Graduate Student, Working for Professor Lawlor at RIA

Cast of Characters

Constable Jamison	Tralee Constable Killed by Darcy Boyle
Corporal Robert Johnson	Troop Ship Battle Readiness Coordinator
Jack Jordan	Third Boson's Mate, HMS *Lusitania*, Manager Cunard Operations, Queenstown, Ireland, Looking for Claire
Officer Lewis	Security Officer, Poolbeg Power Station
Finn MacCool	Leader of the Fianna, Irish Mythology
Dean Maloney	District Inspector, RIC Cork
Marshall	Canadian Soldier on Train and Troop Ship *Aquitania* with Collin
Aidan McCarthy	Tadgh's Younger Brother, Irish Volunteer
Tadgh McCarthy	Young Irish Revolutionary. Member of Cork IRB, Communications and Transportation Specialist
Morgan	Irish Woman Rescued by Tadgh McCarthy, Tadgh's Lover & Partner
Martin Murphy	Captain of Supply Ships for Beamish & Crawford (B&C) Brewery
Doctor O'Callihan	Hospitaller Doctor at Fenit
Finian O'Donnell	Collin's Father, Murdered in Donegal

Cast of Characters

Shaina O'Donnell	Collin's Mother, Murdered in Toronto
Paddy O'Shea	Waiter at the Wicklow Hotel, Friend of Tadgh's from Kerry
Maureen O'Sullivan	Journalist for *The Irish Times* Newspaper, Dublin, Ireland
Sergeant Saunders	Leader of British Raider Squad during Mountjoy Square Witch hunt
Rebecca Schultz	Patient in Next Room to Darcy Boyle in Tralee
Gus Tanner	Irish Sea Captain, Friend of Martin Murphy
Captain Thompson	Captain of the HMY *Helga*
Jeffrey Wiggins	Transportation Leader, Beamish & Crawford (B&C) Brewery, Cork City, Ireland, and Tadgh's Colleague at B&C

The purpose of this historical background is to illuminate the historical facts imbedded in Book Three, particularly those associated with the Clans Pact adventure.

In Book Two, *Entente*, I included significant background on the history of World War I and its horrific trench warfare. I did so since this terrible war killed over seventeen million people. Although connected with the Irish fight for freedom, it was not central to the Irish storyline and could therefore not be addressed in overall terms within the novel storyline itself.

I could also have included a thorough account on the Irish Easter Rising of 1916 in this background material but chose not to do so. The treatment of the Rising in ten chapters of this novel, as well as in three chapters regarding the lead-up to the rebellion at the end of Book Two, *Entente*, taken together, provide an accurate description of this pivotal event in Irish history. Instead, some historical details about the leaders of the Rising and references for further reading are included. I hope this background is useful and informative.

Ref.	Subject	Location
1.	Easter Rising Rebel Leaders and Statistics	Ch 1, 24, 30
2.	Mountjoy Square's Notable Inhabitants	Ch 3, 61
3.	*Cumdach* and *an Cathach* History	Ch 6, 103, 201
4.	U-boat - Kapitan Schwieger	Ch 12, 174, 175
5.	W.B. Yeats' "1916" Poem	Ch 16, 229
6.	Poems	
	6.1 "Ireland's Vow"	
	- Denis MacCarthy	Inspiration
	6.2 "Rhyme of the Restless One"	
	- Robert Service	Ch 17, 252
7.	Photographs	
	7.1 Dublin Bay	Ch 9, 144
	7.2 Howth Harbour	Ch 16, 234
	7.3 Howth Harbour Lighthouse	Ch 16, 238

1. Easter Rising Rebel Leaders and Statistics

The seven members of the Irish Republican Brotherhood (IRB) military council signed the Easter Proclamation in 1916, which was read and then posted by Commander-in-Chief Padraig Pearse at the General Post Office headquarters at noon on Easter Monday, April 24, 1916, just after the Republicans took over that facility at the start of the Rising.

On Easter Sunday, the military council met, and its members decided to proceed with the Rising, despite both the loss of German arms, intercepted by the British earlier that week, and the head of the Irish Volunteers, MacNeil's countermand to his men. This essentially committed the rebels to martyrdom.

Planning the Rising
Military Council Meeting, Sunday, April 23, 1916
Painting by Norman Teeling (B&W rendition)
Seated at the table left to right;
James Connolly, Thomas Clarke, Eamonn Ceannt, Padraig Pearse.

POBLACHT NA H EIREANN.

THE PROVISIONAL GOVERNMENT

OF THE

IRISH REPUBLIC

TO THE PEOPLE OF IRELAND.

IRISHMEN AND IRISHWOMEN : In the name of God and of the dead generations from which she receives her old tradition of nationhood, Ireland, through us, summons her children to her flag and strikes for her freedom.

Having organised and trained her manhood through her secret revolutionary organisation, the Irish Republican Brotherhood, and through her open military organisations, the Irish Volunteers and the Irish Citizen Army, having patiently perfected her discipline, having resolutely waited for the right moment to reveal itself, she now seizes that moment, and, supported by her exiled children in America and by gallant allies in Europe, but relying in the first on her own strength, she strikes in full confidence of victory.

We declare the right of the people of Ireland to the ownership of Ireland, and to the unfettered control of Irish destinies, to be sovereign and indefeasible. The long usurpation of that right by a foreign people and government has not extinguished the right, nor can it ever be extinguished except by the destruction of the Irish people. In every generation the Irish people have asserted their right to national freedom and sovereignty : six times during the past three hundred years they have asserted it in arms. Standing on that fundamental right and again asserting it in arms in the face of the world, we hereby proclaim the Irish Republic as a Sovereign Independent State, and we pledge our lives and the lives of our comrades-in-arms to the cause of its freedom, of its welfare, and of its exaltation among the nations.

The Irish Republic is entitled to, and hereby claims, the allegiance of every Irishman and Irishwoman. The Republic guarantees religious and civil liberty, equal rights and equal opportunities to all its citizens, and declares its resolve to pursue the happiness and prosperity of the whole nation and of all its parts, cherishing all the children of the nation equally, and oblivious of the differences carefully fostered by an alien government, which have divided a minority from the majority in the past.

Until our arms have brought the opportune moment for the establishment of a permanent National Government, representative of the whole people of Ireland and elected by the suffrages of all her men and women, the Provisional Government, hereby constituted, will administer the civil and military affairs of the Republic in trust for the people.

We place the cause of the Irish Republic under the protection of the Most High God, Whose blessing we invoke upon our arms, and we pray that no one who serves that cause will dishonour it by cowardice, inhumanity, or rapine. In this supreme hour the Irish nation must, by its valour and discipline and by the readiness of its children to sacrifice themselves for the common good, prove itself worthy of the august destiny to which it is called.

Signed on Behalf of the Provisional Government,

THOMAS J. CLARKE.

SEAN Mac DIARMADA.   THOMAS MacDONAGH.
P. H. PEARSE.   EAMONN CEANNT,
JAMES CONNOLLY.   JOSEPH PLUNKETT.

The Easter Proclamation, 1916

The following is a display of Mr. Teeling's portraits of the Military Council members, at the Oriel Gallery, Dublin, during his commemorative Easter Rising Paintings Collection opening on March 11, 2016, just prior to the centennial celebrations held at Easter in Dublin that year.

The heroes, in clockwise order starting at the left, are Thomas Clarke, Sean McDermott, Thomas MacDonagh, John Connolly, Padraig Pearse, Eamonn Ceannt, and Joseph Mary Plunkett.

The portrait of Sir Roger Casement, IRB member, is featured on the back cover of Book Two, *Entente*.

General Sir John Maxwell wanted to immediately execute the leaders of the Rising but could only do so if he had evidence that at least one of the Republicans was legally found to be aiding the enemy. In this case, the enemy was the Germans since Britain was immersed in World War I. Maxwell found a letter Padraig Pearse wrote to his mother regarding communications with the Germans. As a result, Maxwell stated he was legally obliged to order the death penalty.

His hurried trial process ended with the sentencing of ninety Republicans to death, but British Prime Minister Asquith stopped the proceedings after all the leaders (see Table 2), except Casement, had been executed. Asquith understood that the impact of these brutal executions without a public trial would inflame the Irish

Table 2. Easter Rising, 1916 - Republican Leaders and their Fates

Name	Rank	Location
Eamonn Ceannt	Director Communications Commandant #4 Battalion	South Dublin Union Hospital
Thomas Clarke	Senior Leader of IRB	GPO
James Connolly	Head of ICA Dublin Commandant	GPO
Thomas MacDonagh	Commandant # 2 Battalion	Jacobs Biscuit Factory
Sean MacDermott	Second-in-Command IRB	GPO
Padraig Pearse	President and Commander-in-Chief	GPO
Joseph Plunkett	Foreign Secretary	GPO
Sir Roger Casement	Attempt to Form Irish Brigade IRB Lead to Get German Arms	Germany
Con Colbert	Leader	Marrowbone Lane Distillery
Edward 'Ned' Daly	Brother-in-Law Tom Clarke Commandant # 1 Battalion	The Four Courts
Sean Heuston	Commander 5th Company	Mendicity Institute
Thomas Kent	Member of Irish Volunteers	At Home in Cork
John MacBride	Vice-Commandant # 2 Battalion	Jacobs Biscuit Factory
Michael Mallin	Chief of Staff ICA Commandant	St. Stephens Green
Constance Markiewicz	Vice-Commandant	St. Stephens Green
Michael O'Hanrahan	Quartermaster General Vice-Commandant # 2 Battalion	Jacobs Biscuit Factory
Willie Pearse	Irish Volunteer Padraig Pearse's Brother	GPO
Eamon de Valera	Commandant # 3 Battalion	Boland's Bakery
Total		

Table 2. Easter Rising, 1916 - Republican Leaders and their Fates

Force Size	Background	Execution 1916
100	Co-Founder Irish Volunteers	8-May Shot
300	Fenian Leader 15 Years Incarcerated	3-May Shot
300	Followed Syndicalist James Larkin Founder, Irish Socialist Federation	12-May Shot
100	Asst. Headmaster St. Edna's Poet and Playright	3-May Shot
300	Original Member, Irish Volunteers Striken with Polio, Used a Cane	12-May Shot
300	Headmaster, St. Edna's School Teacher, Barrister, Poet, Writer	3-May Shot
300	Went to Germany to Secure Arms Sick with Tuberculosis	4-May Shot
3	British Colonial Service, Congo & Peru Wrote Irish Volunteer's Manifesto	3-Aug Hanged
100	Drill Instructor, St. Ednas Member Youth Fianna Eireann	8-May Shot
250	Howth Gun-Running Supporter Captain in the Irish Volunteers	4-May Shot
26	Member Youth Fianna Eireann Vice-Commandant Dublin Brigade	8-May Shot
1	Nationalist Family County Cork Shot RIC Howe	9-May Shot
100	Irish Soldier in the Boer War Married to Maud Gonne	5-May Shot
100	Scots Army, Fought in India Silk Workers 1913 Lockout Strike	8-May Shot
100	Revolutionary Suffragette & Socialist Founder Cumann na mBan & ICA	Spared Woman
100	Member Sinn Fein Administrator, Irish Volunteers	4-May Shot
300	Supported St. Edna's School Noted Sculptor	4-May Shot
120	Born in USA, Came to Ireland at 2 Years Took Part in Howth Gun-Running	Spared US Born
~1200		16

citizens. He was right, but it was too late. The British had reaffirmed their oppressive regime. The citizens would remember. Martyrdom would prove to have a strong impact on future events.

The atrocities of killing fifteen unarmed civilians after the surrender on North King Street near the Four Courts, and an additional six civilians, including Francis-Sheehy Skeffington at the Portobello Barracks by British soldiers, further fueled the citizenry to rise again in the Irish Revolution, starting in 1919.

In all, eighty-two rebels, one hundred twenty-six British forces, and two hundred sixty civilians were killed in the Rising. At the Mount Street Bridge from the Northumberland Road, twelve Republicans had killed or wounded two hundred forty British soldiers, in a gun-battle often referred to as the 'Irish Thermopylae' (see Author's Note).

Four hundred fifty citizens were arrested for looting. In total, thirty-five hundred people were arrested in connection with the witchhunt that followed this pivotal rebellion.

British artillery and machine gun fire devastated those portions of Dublin near the rebel strongholds and disrupted the infrastructure of the city for weeks. James Connolly had been wrong in his belief that the British would not destroy their own city. The worst of the damage was centered in the areas around the General Post Office on Sackville (O'Connell) Street, immediately north of the River Liffey, and the Four Courts area, and included the torching of the Lindenhall Barracks.

Afterwards, the Dublin Chamber of Commerce accused the Castle of "unpardonable laxity" in not averting the Rising and for shelling the city. Businessmen and property owners formed the Dublin Fire and Property Losses Association to force the British Treasury to pay restitution for the destruction of the establishments. Claims of damages totaled at least £2,500,000, or $82,000,000 (2017 dollars U.S.).

Most reconstruction efforts were delayed until after World War I ended in 1918 when labor became available. The General Post Office remained derelict until it was finally restored in 1929.

Siege on the GPO, Friday April 28, 1916
Painting by Norman Teeling (B&W Rendition)

The Aftermath I - General Post Office Shell After the Rising
May 1916
Painting by Norman Teeling (B&W Rendition)

2.   Mountjoy Square's Notable Inhabitants

Mountjoy Square has had many famous inhabitants throughout its history. One of the earliest was Arthur Guinness, of Guinness Brewery fame, who died there in January 1803. Subsequently, his descendant Desmond Guinness and first wife, Mariga, attempted to save and restore the gracious character of the square from 1966 through 1975, and, along with members of the Irish Georgian Society, bought Number Fifty and several demolished lots.

Seán O'Casey, the Irish playwright and founding member of the Irish Citizen Army, lived at Number Thirty-Five Mountjoy Square during the Irish War of Independence. During his time there, it is said that the house was raided by the Black and Tans. The Royal Irish Constabulary Special Reserve (Black and Tans) was a temporary force recruited starting in 1919 after the Great War ended, mostly of British soldiers to assist the RIC who wered being attacked by rebels during the Irish War of Independence. Winston Churchill, then British Secretary of State for War conceived of this plan. They continued the barbaric ways of the occupying forces. The name comes from the wearing of mixed khaki British army and rifle green RIC uniform parts.

John O'Leary, a leading Fenian, poet, editor of The Irish People, and mentioned in W.B. Yeats' poem "September 1913," lived at Number Fifty-Three Mountjoy Square West in the late 19th century and early 20th century. Yeats, as a friend of O'Leary, was known to have stayed there, having sent letters from that address.

Patrick Pearse, a leader of the 1916 Easter Rising, attended meetings for planning the Rising in Mountjoy Square.

Dáil Éireann, the Parliament of Ireland, suppressed by the British authorities as a dangerous organization in September 1919, met before the foundation of the Irish Free State at the home of the Republican Walter L. Cole at Number Three Mountjoy Square. When the volunteers met on Easter Monday in 1916, the 1st battalion met at Blackhall Street in the Liberties with the intention of capturing the Four Courts. The exception was the twelve men of D company under the command of Captain Seán Heuston who met at Mountjoy Square with the mission of taking the Mendicity Institution across the river from the Four Courts.

T. M. Healy resided at Number One Mountjoy Square, having lived previously on the adjacent Great Charles Street in number Fifty.

Seán O'Casey set all three plays of his *Dublin Trilogy* (*The Shadow of a Gunman, Juno and the Paycock* and *The Plough and the Stars*) in tenement houses in Georgian Dublin. In particular, *The Shadow of a Gunman* opens in a return-room in a tenement house in Hilljoy Square, which is raided by the Auxiliaries during the play. This room is thought to have been based on O'Casey's former tenement home. Although the original house was demolished in the 1960s, it was later replaced by a building with a Georgian façade that now stands on the site. O'Casey subsequently lived in another Georgian house very close to Mountjoy Square at 422 North Circular Road; in that house which still stands today, he wrote the trilogy, before later moving to London during the 1920s.

* References: *Wikipedia* Sources and *mountjoysq.com*

3.   *Cumdach* and *an Cathach* History *

St. Columba, an O'Donnell noble, was born in 521 CE (AD), the great-grandson of Niall of the Nine Hostages. He chose to follow God and lead his ministry instead of becoming clan chieftain. I could relate more information than what is mentioned here about St. Columba's self-sacrifice and his church leadership, but the material is readily available to readers. One excellent source is a book titled *Vita Columbae*, written by St. Adamnan who became abbott of Hy (Iona) approximately a hundred years after St. Columba founded the abbey.

In about 561 CE, long after studying at the famous Clonard Abbey, he scribed and kept a copy of a unique Roman vulgate manuscript of the *Psalms*, owned by St. Finnian while they were at Movilla Abbey. St. Finnian found out about it and demanded that the copy be turned over to him. The High King sided with St. Finnian in the first known copyright trial in recorded history.

St. Columba refused to return the precious document, claiming that the words of the Bible are open for all people. A pitched battle of Cúl Dreimhne in Sligo ensued over the ownership of this Psalter, as it was called, and 3,000 men died. St. Columba was victorious and retained the document. This is the first known battle over copyright infringement. Pope John III nearly excommunicated St. Columba over this issue.

To avoid this terrible consequence, St. Columba exiled himself from Ireland to live and work miracles among the Picts for the rest of his life. With his disciples, he built a monastery on the island of Hy, later called Iona, in the Inner Hebrides of what would ultimately be called Scotland.

Before he left his beloved Ireland, he met with his relative, the King of Tir Conaill, and gave him the Psalter, calling it *an Cathach*. He claimed that if a soldier without sin, carrying the Psalter encircled the king's army three times in a clockwise manner before battle, that the Tir Conaill Clan would always be victorious. The Clan followed his direction and until 1602, always came out the victors. The O'Donnell Clan continued to rule Northwest Ireland for eleven hundred years.

Near the end of the eleventh century, monks at Kells created an ornate jeweled box called a *cumdach* to contain *an Cathach*. An attached chain allowed it to be worn around the neck of the soldier without sin beforee going into battle, a member of the McGroarty Clan. The chieftain ordered that the *cumdach* was never to be opened.

Today, *an Cathach* only contains 58 folios of damaged, incomplete vellum. The original manuscript would have consisted of 110 folios of the complete *Book of Psalms*. The first folio of the existing manuscript contains the text of Psalm 30:10 and the last folio is Psalm 105:13. The maximum folio size is 7.5 by 10.5 inches.

The only illumination in the Psalter is simply the first letter of each Psalm. An image of folio 48R is shown on the back cover of this novel, courtesy of the Royal Irish Academy.

It is believed that this *cumdach* was carried, as was normal practice, into battle at Kinsale in January 1602, where the Clans were roundly defeated by the English. Could it be, as I have postulated, that Red Hugh O'Donnell and Florence MacCarthaigh Reagh, back in 1600, truncated *an Cathach* to provide clues for future descendants, which perhaps could have negated the power of this talisman to ensure victory for the O'Donnells? We will never know, will we.

Presumably, Red Hugh's brother Rory carried this *Cumdach* containing *an Cathach* back to Donegal immediately after the Battle of Kinsale. Red Hugh traveled to Spain in a vain attempt to convince King Philip II to send Ireland more troops to help fight the English. Then in 1607, when Rory, his family, and other Clans members fled to Catholic France, in what was called the Flight of the Earls, he likely took the talisman with him.

The unopened *cumdach* containing *an Cathach*, was brought back to Ireland from France by Sir Capel Molyneux, the brother-in-law of Sir Neal O'Donel, in 1802. This rediscovery of the Psalter had a dynastic importance to the clan. Sir William Betham wrote that "it was a tacit acknowledgement of the O'Donnells of Newport being now the chief of this illustrious family" [G.O. Ms. 169]. It was also de facto evidence that the O'Donnell family could trace its direct lineage back to 561 CE. The O'Donels gave this precious ancient Psalter to the Royal Irish Academy for safekeeping in 1843. Sir William Betham, an important antiquarian who pursued the rediscovery of early medieval manuscripts, obtained permission to open the *cumdach* in the presence of Capel and Sir Richard O'Donel, son of Neal, and cousin of Charlotte Stoker, Bram Stoker's mother.**

They found a very damaged, unbound manuscript inside. Betham noted, "It was so much injured by damp as to appear a solid mass."

Reverend Hugh Jackson Lawlor did try to improve the legibility of *an Cathach* in the early 1900s using unorthodox methods, but failed. Lawlor noted, "At the last moment, however, an unexpected difficulty has arisen: I have been unable to apply chemicals to the manuscript—as I had hoped to do—and have been obliged to content myself with what my eyesight could reveal to me, assisted only by good light and some little patience."

Today, *an Cathach* resides in the secure library of the Royal Irish Academy. Its ornate *cumdach* is located in the National Museum in Dublin. I took the photograph of this magnificent box, which appears on the back cover of Book One, *Searchers*, when I visited the museum. This image is repeated here, in black and white.

The *cumdach* is a marvelous relic of Celtic Irish antiquity. I can only imagine the sun glinting off its surface as McGroarty urges his steed to gallop thrice around the O'Donnell army on the hill outside Kinsale in the crisp January air of 1602.

* References: *Wikipedia* Sources and The Royal Irish Academy

** Bram Stoker's mother knew that her own grandmother was Eliza O'Donnell of the O'Donnell family of Newport. Undoubtedly, Stoker, author of *Dracula*, would have been told the tale of St. Columba and the famous *an Cathach*.

4.   U-boats and Kapitänleutnant Schwieger *

Kapitänleutnant Walther Schwieger was a U-boat commander in the Imperial German Navy during WWI. He became notorious for sinking the passenger liner *Lusitania* on May 7, 1915, only eight miles off the south Irish coast at Kinsale with the loss of 1,198 lives as described in Book One, *Searchers*. Thus, he was nicknamed "Baby Killer" by the British.

He also torpedoed SS *Hesperian* in September 1915, and SS *Cymric* on May 8, 1916.

Schwieger captained three different U-boats during this war and sank a total of 49 ships weighing 184,000 gross register tons, becoming the sixth most successful submarine commander of World War I. This was the primary naval tactic of the German General Staff, to strangle Britain by preventing its forces from getting necessary supplies to successfully fight the war.

You will recall that at the outset of this protracted war, the only weapon that the Allied navies and commercial vessels had available to fight the U-boat menace was their own ships, used as battering rams for submarines on the surface. This was seldom successful. As a result, the U-boats essentially roamed at will with very low casualties. But war is a driver of technology. By 1916, the Allies had invented depth charges, which were jettisoned off the stern of surface ships; also, they used buoyed mines tethered just below the sea surface in critical harbor locations. Immediately thereafter, they invented a crude sonar system to find and track their submerged enemy.

Transport convoys with support destroyers and aircraft spotting near shore further thwarted the U-boat peril. After those military advancements, submariners had the highest casualty rate of any branch of the German navy.

In total, the U-boats sank nearly five thousand merchant ships, with fifteen thousand Allied sailors dead in WWI. This resulted in the loss of nearly fourteen million tons of supplies over that period. The Germans employed three hundred fifty-one operational

U-boats, of which one hundred seventy-eight, or fifty percent, were sunk in combat. Another thirty-nine, or eleven percent, were lost for other reasons (chlorine contamination being one major cause). As a result, five thousand German submariners lost their lives.

On September 5, 1917, Walther Schwieger's skill or luck ran out. His U-boat, *U-88*, hit a British mine while being chased by *HMS Stonecrop*. It sank north of Terschelling, an island in Northern Netherlands, with the loss of all hands.

* References: *Wikipedia* and
https://uboat.net/wwi/men/commanders/322.html

5.   William Butler Yeats * Poem "1916"

In Chapter Sixteen, upon the execution of John MacBride on May 5th, 1916, I introduced the subject of MacBride's feud with W.B. Yeats, the famous Irish poet and playwright who had, among other achievements, co-founded Dublin's Abbey Theatre in 1904. Yeats had been the ardent suitor of English-born Irish revolutionary, suffragette, and actress Maud Gonne, and he had unsuccessfully proposed marriage to her on several occasions. In his mind, she was his muse, but John MacBride won her hand. They married and had a child before they divorced, Maud claiming domestic violence. The potential claim against MacBride of child molestation was never proven in court.

I wanted to show that Yeats had a turn of heart as a result of MacBride's honorable participation and death in the Rising, and to give a glimpse of how he viewed the impact of this rebellion. So I have introduced his famous poem "1916."

I learned that Yeats did not publish this important poem until 1920 and may not have written it until then. I therefore invoked author's privilege in a fiction novel, to presume that he wrote a draft immediately after the Rising and shared it with his colleague, Sean O'Casey, well before the time when he felt it opportune to publish it. For this presumption, I apologize to Mr. Yeats.

* References: *Wikipedia* W. B. Yeats and Maude Gonne

6. Poems

6.1 **Denis Florence MacCarthy** *, a prolific Irish poet, translator and biographer, was born in Lower O'Connell Street in 1817, and died in Dublin in 1882. During his life, he lived in Dublin, continental Europe, and London. In 1846 he was called to the Irish bar, but never practiced law.

He was a prolific translator, notably of Pedro Calderón de la Barca, the Spanish Shakespeare, and he edited notable poetic compendia such as *The Poets* and *Dramatists of Ireland* and *The Book of Irish Ballads*. He greatly admired Percy Bysshe Shelley and published Shelley's Early Life while living in London.

Denis's own *Ballads, Poems, and Lyrics* was published in 1850. Three of his poems with excerpts quoted in the novel are included below in their entirety.

"Ireland's Vow" by Denis Florence MacCarthy

Come! Liberty, come! we are ripe for thy coming—
Come freshen the hearts where thy rival has trod—
Come, richest and rarest! —come, purest and fairest! —
Come, daughter of Science! —come, gift of the God!

Long, long have we sighed for thee, coyest of maidens—
Long, long have we worshipped thee, queen of the brave!
Steadily sought for thee, readily fought for thee,
Purpled the scaffold and glutted the grave!

On went the fight through the cycle of ages,
Never our battle-cry ceasing the while;
Forward, ye valiant ones! onward, battalioned ones!
Strike for your Erin, your own darling isle!

Still in the ranks are we, struggling with eagerness,
Still in the battle for Freedom are we!
Words may avail in it--swords if they fail in it,
What matters the weapon, if only we're free?

Oh! we are pledged in the face of the universe,
  Never to falter and never to swerve;
Toil for it!—bleed for it!—if there be need for it,
  Stretch every sinew and strain every nerve!

Traitors and cowards our names shall be ever,
  If for a moment we turn from the chase;
For ages exhibited, scoffed at, and gibbeted,
  As emblems of all that was servile and base!

Irishmen! Irishmen! think what is Liberty,
  Fountain of all that is valued and dear,
Peace and security, knowledge and purity,
  Hope for hereafter and happiness here.

Nourish it, treasure it deep in your inner heart—
  Think of it ever by night and by day;
Pray for it! —sigh for it! —work for it! —die for it! —
  What is this life and dear freedom away?

List! scarce a sound can be heard in our thoroughfares—
  Look! scarce a ship can be seen on our streams;
Heart-crushed and desolate, spell-bound, irresolute,
  Ireland but lives in the bygone of dreams!

Irishmen! if we be true to our promises,
  Nerving our souls for more fortunate hours,
Life's choicest blessings, love's fond caressings,
  Peace, home, and happiness, all shall be ours!

* (Reference: *Wikipedia* Sources and
http://www.gutenberg.org/ebooks/author/4460)

6.2   Robert Service * was an English adventurer born in 1874, who is often called the Bard of the Yukon, because he spent much of his life in the western United States and Canada, including a time in Whitehorse and then the Klondike, arriving there ten years after the Klondike gold rush was over. By that time, his poetc reputation had been made with poems like "The Cremation of Sam McGee"and "The Shooting of Dan McGrew." One of his best-loved poems is,

"Rhyme of the Restless One" by Robert Service

We couldn't sit and study for the law;
The stagnation of a bank we couldn't stand;
For our riot blood was surging, and we didn't need much urging
To excitements and excesses that are banned.
So we took to wine and drink and other things,
And the devil in us struggled to be free;
Till our friends rose up in wrath, and they pointed out the path,
And they paid our debts and packed us o'er the sea.

Oh, they shook us off and shipped us o'er the foam,
To the larger lands that lure a man to roam;
And we took the chance they gave
Of a far and foreign grave,
And we bade good-by for evermore to home.

And some of us are climbing on the peak,
And some of us are camping on the plain;
By pine and palm you'll find us, with never claim to bind us,
By track and trail you'll meet us once again.

We are the fated serfs to freedom—sky and sea;
We have failed where slummy cities overflow;
But the stranger ways of earth know our pride and know our worth,
And we go into the dark as fighters go.

Yes, we go into the night as brave men go,
Though our faces they be often streaked with woe;
Yet we're hard as cats to kill,
And our hearts are reckless still,
And we've danced with death a dozen times or so.

And you'll find us in Alaska after gold,
And you'll find us herding cattle in the South.
We like strong drink and fun, and, when the race is run,
We often die with curses in our mouth.
We are wild as colts unbroke, but never mean.
Of our sins we've shoulders broad to bear the blame;
But we'll never stay in town and we'll never settle down,
And we'll never have an object or an aim.

No, there's that in us that time can never tame;
And life will always seem a careless game;
And they'd better far forget—
Those who say they love us yet —
Forget, blot out with bitterness our name.

   * References: *Wikipedia* Sources and
https://www.poemhunter.com/poem/the-rhyme-of-the-restless-ones/

7. Photographs
7.1 Dublin Bay

Photograph of River Liffey Exit into Dublin Bay,
Showing the Poolbeg Power Station
and the Great South Wall with its Eastern End Lighthouse
Photograph looking south by S. F. Archer
when landing in Dublin, 2016

7.2 Howth Harbour

Photograph of Howth with Howth Harbour,
Showing Location of the Lighthouse,
The HMV *Helga* and Tadgh's Hooker, Survivor
Photograph looking south by S. F. Archer
when landing in Dublin, 2016

7.3 Howth Harbour Lighthouse

Photograph of the Howth Harbour Lighthouse
from the West Pier Edge
by Kathy Archer, March 2016

Stephen in Front of the Temple Bar in Dublin, Ireland,
March 8, 2016
On the Occasion of his First Book Launch There,
The Irish Clans Book One *Searchers*
Two Weeks Before the Centennial Celebration of the Easter Rising

Stephen Finlay Archer

was brought up in Toronto, Canada. His mother is Dot in the novels
and his Irish grandfather is Samuel Stevenson Finlay, an artist of some
reknown.

Following acquisition of a Masters of Science degree from the
University of Toronto, Stephen spent thirty-five years as an aerospace
engineering manager, working initially in Canada and mainly in the
United States. He directed satellite systems design, implementation,
launch, and mission programs with the U.S. Navy and with NASA/
NOAA, among others.

Upon retirement, Stephen completed courses in short story and
novel writing with the Long Ridge Writers Group in Connecticut. He is
a member of Writers Unlimited in California Gold Country.
Stephen can be reached at

stephenarcher@earthlink.net or *www.stephenfinlayarcher.com*

27017388R00206

Made in the USA
San Bernardino, CA
25 February 2019